OTHER BOOKS BY KATE L. MARY

The Broken World Series:

Broken World
Shattered World
Mad World
Lost World
New World
Forgotten World
Silent World
Broken Stories

The Twisted Series:

Twisted World
Twisted Mind
Twisted Memories
Twisted Fate

The Blood Will Dry

Collision

When We Were Human

Alone: A Zombie Novel

The Moonchild Series:

Moonchild
Liberation

The College of Charleston Series:

The List

No Regrets

Moving On

Letting Go

Zombie Apocalypse Love Story Novellas:

More than Survival

Fighting to Forget

Playing the Odds

The Key to Survival

Anthologies:

Prep For Doom

Gone with the Dead

FORGOTTEN WORLD

Book Six in the *Broken World* Series

KATE L. MARY

Twisted Press

Published by Twisted Press, LLC, an independently owned company.

ISBN-13: 978-1519417152
ISBN-10: 1519417152
Edited by Emily Teng
Cover art by Kate L. Mary

CHAPTER ONE

The man turns and his eyes meet mine, and everything in Hope Springs freezes. The people standing around me disappear, and suddenly I'm thrust back in time. Back to Vegas and the Monte Carlo and a broken man desperate to save his sister from a fate worse than death. Back to feelings of terror as we tried to escape. To the days following Vegas, our group hiding in our underground shelter while Hadley and I licked our wounds. Then the attack, and all the uncertainty surrounding us as we spent weeks on the road, struggling and fighting to survive. The devastating loss when this same man disappeared, taking Hadley with him.

All the memories hit me at once, bringing with them a million different emotions. The feelings are so strong that at first I can't move. Can't breathe or think or react. Not even when the man steps forward. His mouth dropping open as his eyes move from me to Axl to Joshua. Now that he's finally standing in front of me, it hits me that I never really expected to see him again.

I've been fooling myself. I just didn't know it until now.

Sobs force their way out of me, shaking my body, and before I even know what's happening, I'm running. Tears stream down my cheeks but I can't control the sobs. I'm not even sure I want to. This is the moment I've been praying for.

"Jon," I whisper, still not totally able to believe what I'm seeing. Then I'm running faster, and his name breaks out of me again, only this time it sounds more like a victory cheer. "Jon!"

Like me, Jon seems to be in shock. He hasn't moved other than that one step, and his mouth is still hanging open when I slam into him, throwing my arms around him. Crying. I'm crying so hard I can't talk.

"Vivian," Jon finally says, pulling back. His hands go to my face, and he grins back at me, looking like he thinks he just might be having the best dream of his life.

"We thought you were dead," I manage to say, the words somehow able to make it out despite almost getting tangled in my sobs. "I never thought we'd see you again."

Jon shakes his head, then looks over my shoulder and smiles. I turn as Axl and Joshua walk up, and behind them, the man from Hope Springs—Richard—looks like he can't figure out what just happened.

"Friends of yours?" he asks, shaking his head but smiling too.

"Old friends," Jon answers.

That's when I think of Hadley. Of the baby and how I discovered after she and Jon had already disappeared that she was pregnant.

"Hadley," I say turning back to Jon, grabbing his hand. "She's with you, right? She has to be!"

Jon's smile wavers, and his eyes go back to Richard, who looks even more lost than he did a second ago.

"Hadley?" the older man asks. He narrows his eyes on Jon like he doesn't understand English.

My heart drops, taking my stomach with it. It had never occurred to me that the two weren't together. I always thought if I found one, the other would be with them too. But judging by the look on Jon's face, that isn't true, and it fills me with the sudden urge to hurl. Surely after everything she's been through, Hadley deserves to find some peace and happiness. Doesn't she?

"Hadley's not with you?" I ask, the words coming out so soft that they can barely be heard over the chatter of the surrounding community.

"Shit." Jon swipes his hand through his hair and glances around before saying, "She's here." He looks at Richard and frowns. "She doesn't want anyone to know who she is. Do you understand? She wanted to put the past behind her. That's why she changed her name. I don't want you to think she's been lying to everyone. She just needed a fresh start."

I don't have a clue what's going on, but I can actually see it when a light bulb goes off in Richard's head. His mouth drops open and he blinks a few times, and then he smiles. He even lets out a little chuckle. "Hadley… So Ginny is Hadley Lucas?"

Jon steps closer to the older man, lowering his head as his eyes dart around. He's acting weird. Like he's afraid the paparazzi are going to show up and start hounding Hadley.

"You will keep her secret," he says in a low voice. "Won't you?"

Richard chuckles as he nods. "You don't have to worry about me, but I got to say I feel kind of dumb at the moment. I'm not sure how I didn't see it before, to be honest. She always looked familiar, but I thought she just reminded me of somebody I used to know or something. I never dreamed…" He shakes his head again. "It sure is crazy."

"Thanks," Jon says, slapping Richard on the arm. "Ginny thanks you too."

Richard waves him off. "We all deserve a new start, but I reckon it would have been a lot harder for her than the rest of us, all things considered. It makes sense. You can tell her that her secret is safe with me."

"Thank you, Richard."

"No need for that." The old man is still shaking his head when he takes a step back. "I have stuff to do, so I'll leave you to catch up and help these folks out." He turns away, waving over his shoulder as he heads off. "Nice to meet you all."

Jon watches him walk away for a few seconds before turning to face us. He doesn't say anything, though, and when his eyes move over us, it sends a shiver shooting through my body. He acts like he can't believe we're really here. Like if he looks away we'll disappear again. I can't blame him, though. This all feels so unreal. Almost like a dream.

"I can't believe you're here," he finally says. "Ginny is going to be so…thrilled." Jon laughs, and I find myself smiling. "I really never thought this day would come. I guess I kind of thought you might be dead, even if I wouldn't let myself acknowledge it."

"What's all this Ginny business?" Axl asks.

"It's her name," I say, remembering the conversation she and I had in the Monte Carlo. Back when we were trapped and had no idea if we'd ever make it out of that casino alive. Back when we did anything and everything to distract ourselves from what was happening around us. "She told me she changed it when she moved to Hollywood. Makes sense that she'd change it back now."

"She's changed a lot," Jon says, waving as he heads down the road. "I'll take you to our house."

Axl grabs my hand as we take off after Jon.

"Richard called you Ginny's husband," Joshua says from Axl's other side.

"Yes," Jon says, smiling in a way that makes me think he isn't even aware of the gesture. "We consider ourselves married. It's not really official, but to us it is." He pauses, smiling even more before saying, "And we're having a baby."

It isn't news to Axl and me, but Joshua almost stops walking. "A baby?"

Jon just nods.

The conversation we had with Dax at the clinic comes back to me, and I suddenly feel stupid for not suspecting Jon and Hadley were here to begin with. Back when we were still waiting for word about Sophia—before she lost her baby—Dax told us they had someone here who had gotten pregnant after the virus.

"Hadley's the one Dax was talking about!" I say, squeezing Axl's hand. "She's the one who got pregnant after the virus!"

"Yes," Jon says. "*Ginny* is pregnant."

"Sorry." I shake my head. "That may take some getting used to."

We pass a couple men who nod at Jon while looking the rest of us over. They don't seem threatening, though, just curious. In fact, nothing since we've been here has seemed overly threatening, and now that we know Hadley—Ginny—and Jon are here, I'm beginning to wish we'd decided to risk it and come earlier. We put it off for so long, suffered through the whole winter, and all this time we could have been here. Where they have electricity and doctors and supplies. And our friends.

"So this place is as good as it seems?" Joshua asks when the men are out of earshot. Like he's been thinking the same thing that I have.

"Better," Jon says. "It's safe and secure and organized, and we're in contact with two other groups. One in Atlanta and another down in the Keys, although the distance makes it harder to talk to them."

Joshua shakes his head, but he's grinning, and the excitement in his expression is something I've never seen before. It's something bigger than hope, and I can't blame him. "That's amazing."

"Sure sounds good," Axl says even though his eyes are still moving. Still studying the area around us like he's waiting for a punch line—or an attack.

I squeeze his hand again, but Axl doesn't look my way when he returns the gesture. He's too busy studying Jon. I can't blame him. Everything about Jon looks so different from the last time I saw him. Back then he was weak and unsure of himself, practically starving. Little more than a broken shell of a person. After losing his sister, Jon spent weeks following Hadley around like something even more insignificant than a shadow. Now he looks healthy and in control, happy and strong. Like someone you could lean on. Exactly the kind of man Hadley would have needed to move forward.

Jon points things out as we walk. The library—which is open and in high demand now that there's no Google to look things up on—and a pharmacy, as well as a building that holds the town's supplies. They have a couple greenhouses built and started growing food over the winter, and they even have a large selection of animals that makes our little garage back home seem insignificant. No wonder we couldn't find any more farm animals than we did—Hope Springs took them all.

By the time Jon turns off the main road, my head is spinning. There's so much here, and they're so prepared. It's everything we've wanted to do but haven't been able to, and it gives me such a strong sense of hope that I can't help imagining myself here. Living and raising a family. Having the home I've wanted for Axl and myself since I first realized I was in love with him. It could all come true now.

"This is our neighborhood," Jon says, not even looking over his shoulder.

He's too focused on the houses we pass. Like he still can't believe they're real. The street reminds me of something out of a TV show. The houses aren't new and they're a bit on the small side and many are in need of repair, but they're real homes. Something I was sure had gone extinct.

The further we walk the more excited I get, thinking about seeing Hadley—Ginny—again. Even though I've searched for her every time I left home, and even though I've thought about what I'd do when I saw her again a million times, part of me never really believed I would. It was all part of the charade, like playing house when I was a kid. Something that made me happy and made me feel like the future held some real promise, but also something I didn't really think could happen. Especially not for me.

"This is it," Jon says, heading up the walk of a little brick house. "Our home."

He smiles like saying it gives him more joy than he could have imagined possible, and I can't blame him. After everything that happened back in Vegas and afterward, I'm sure he never thought he could feel happy again. I know for sure Hadley didn't.

Jon opens the door, and we follow him inside, stepping into a living room that's small and cozy. The scent of cinnamon clings to the air, and flames flicker inside the small, red candles set up in a perfect line on the mantle. From the kitchen comes the quiet hum of someone who sounds a million times happier than Hadley Lucas could ever be. Whoever this Ginny is, she's content and settled in. Ready for the future.

"Ginny!" Jon calls as he pulls his weapons off.

He drops them into a basket that sits next to the door before heading through the living room. I'm right behind him, so anxious to see Ginny that I feel like a kid on Christmas morning.

"In the kitchen!" a voice I'd recognize anywhere calls. "I'm making a pie."

Her back is to me when I first lay eyes on her, and from this angle, I never would have guessed it was her. Not in a million years. She's round now and probably close to twenty pounds heavier—not including her belly. On top of that, her hair has been cut short—it's only around four inches long—

and it isn't strawberry blonde. It's brown. Even in all the movies she did before the virus hit, I never once saw it this color. No wonder no one here has recognized her.

"Hadley," I say, stopping halfway to her. My heart is beating too fast to go another step, and my legs are wobbling. I'm also on the verge of bursting into tears, but I know that's something I won't be able to control.

Hadley freezes in the middle of rolling out a piecrust, and her breath catches in her throat. Like her, I'm holding my breath, only I don't know why, because all I really want to do is run to her. Then she finally turns and our eyes meet, and I can't hold back. I burst into tears as I rush forward, throwing my arms around her shaking body. She hugs me back, crying just as much as I am as we sink to the floor, still hugging. Our tears mixing together.

"You're here," she says, pulling back after a few seconds so she can get a better look at me. "You're alive."

"I'm here," I say, looking her over. Marveling at how different and healthy she looks. "Look at you! You look amazing. So healthy and happy. I never thought I'd see you like this again. I didn't think it was possible."

Hadley looks past me, and I follow her gaze to where Jon and Axl and Joshua stand on the other side of the room, watching us. None of them unaffected by our emotional reunion. I swear all three of them have tears in their eyes, although I doubt any of them will admit it later.

"You're all here?" Hadley asks, looking back at me.

"Not all of us," I say, pulling myself to my feet while also helping her up.

"Tell me everything," Hadley says.

"Sit down," Jon says, waving toward the table. "I'll make coffee and we can talk."

Hadley starts to lead me to the table but stops and starts laughing. "Look what I did to you." She wipes something off my shoulder, and I look down to find my jacket covered in flour.

"It's no big deal," I say, taking her hand. "I don't care, I'm just glad you're here."

"Me too," Hadley says, squeezing my hand. Her eyes fill with tears once gain, but she blinks them away. "Let's sit down."

We settle in around the table, Joshua on the other side of Ginny and Axl next to me. He sits so close that his body heat warms me. His hand finds mine, and he gives it a squeeze. When our eyes meet, he smiles. For the first time in months, I give him what can be called a *real* smile.

"I can't believe this," I whisper.

He nods in agreement. "Never thought it would happen."

Me neither is what I want to say, but my throat is too clogged with emotion to get it out, so I just squeeze his hand.

When the coffee is brewing, Jon slides into the seat across from me. "It will be a few minutes."

"Tell us everything," Hadley says again. "Where are you living? How did you get away from the hot springs? Is everyone okay?"

The hot springs. It's been so long since that happened, I had totally forgotten Jon and Ginny didn't know about the people we lost there. And since. Everything that's happened since the last time I saw her last flips through my mind, along with dozens of questions, but it's all overshadowed by the most recent tragedy. Sophia.

"There's a lot to tell you." I exhale and shake my head. "Almost too much to comprehend. But first, you should know that we brought Sophia here."

Hadley squeezes her eyes shut and nods. "The baby. Is it done?"

I nod even though she still isn't looking at me. "It is. We should have come sooner, but we weren't sure about this place. Sophia went into labor and there were complications. It was an emergency that made us finally take the plunge." I reach across the table and grab Hadley's hand so I can give it another squeeze. Just to reassure myself this is real. "I can't believe you've been here this whole time. If only we'd come months ago!"

Hadley opens her eyes, and even though they shimmer with tears, she smiles. "You're here now, and that's the important part. I'd almost given up hope."

"I think I had," I say, laughing a little.

Hadley nods. "Maybe I had, too."

We hold each other's gazes, all the things we've been through together hanging over us like a cloud of emotions and pain and fear clogging the room. But it's better than the uncertainty I've lived with for the past few months. So much better.

"Now, tell me about the hot spring," she says.

"We got overrun," I tell her, letting out a deep sigh as I relive that horrible day. "Zombies came in the middle of the night, a whole horde of them. There were so many and we were caught off guard. Trapped. It was close, but just when things started to look bad, Darla, Angus, and Parvarti made it back." I wince at the mention of my mom. Yet another loss. "Thanks to them, most of us made it."

"Most?" Hadley whispers.

"Moira and Liz, Dylan and Jessica." I shake my head and suck in a deep breath. "Jake died a couple days later."

"We didn't get the meds in time," Joshua says, the pain of the loss just as raw today as it was the day Jake died.

"What about you?" I ask Hadley. "What happened to you guys?"

"We got separated in that town when someone opened fire. Jon and I hid for hours. Waiting until the coast was clear. By then Parv, Darla, and Angus had left. It's a good thing, since they saved your asses. Jon and I headed out, too. We made it back to the hot springs, but it was too late. After that we tried to follow your trail, only the snow made it impossible and we had to give up."

Hadley looks us all over, her gaze lingering on Axl for a second longer than the rest of us. Pink spreads across her cheeks, and she glances away, squirming as she reaches across the table to take Jon's hand. When I turn toward Axl, he too seems to be uncomfortable. It takes me back to the day Hadley and Jon disappeared. She and Axl had been fighting that morning. I'd forgotten all about it.

"We met a teenage girl named Gretchen who told us about this place and decided to come here," Hadley continues, keeping her gaze away from Axl. "I knew I was pregnant, and somewhere along the way I told Jon."

"I had to get her somewhere safe."

"Course you did," Axl says, his voice lower than usual.

"So you've been here ever since?" Joshua asks.

"Yes. Jon has helped clear the streets and I created a new identity." Hadley looks up but keeps her eyes on me. "It's very important to me that no one knows I'm Hadley Lucas."

"Your secret is safe with us," I say.

"You look good." Hadley's eyes move over me. "Healthy. I'm assuming you found a place."

"Got us a gated community 'bout twenty miles from here. It's a good deal," Axl says. "Thanks to you folks gettin' the water goin', we're sittin' pretty good. Electricity would be nice, but we got us some kerosene heaters and stuff. Kept us warm durin' the winter."

"We can get you electricity now that we know where you are," Jon says.

"But they won't need it." Hadley shakes her head and focuses on me. "You'll be coming here now, right?"

"Some of us will." I glance toward Axl, unsure if he's still determined to stay out there or if he's willing to make the move now that he knows Jon and Hadley—Ginny—are here and this place is absolutely safe.

"What do you mean some of you?" Jon asks. "Ginny makes a good point. Why stay out there when we have a real working town?"

Axl sits up straighter, but he still doesn't look at Hadley. "We got things set up real nice, and we ain't that far."

"Twenty miles during a zombie apocalypse is a big distance," Jon says. "Especially now. Now that the snow is gone and those bastards have thawed out. They're all over the woods. Not to mention the fact that there are some nasty groups out there. We don't have to tell you that."

"No," Axl says stiffly. "You don't. We had a run-in with a few assholes durin' winter. Took care of it, though."

"But there are bound to be more," Jon says. "We're working with Atlanta to establish a government. It's nothing like the old one, unfortunately, but for the time being it will have to do. We've established a group of guards that will do the double task of dealing with zoms and marauders. We've also elected a judicial officer—kind of like a sheriff. They want one central person in charge of dealing out punishments."

"Justice has to be swift and harsh these days," Hadley says.

"Sounds great," Axl replies, "but I don't know what the group is gonna decide. Sophia and her girl are comin' out here, but other than that I got no idea."

"Did you lose anyone over the winter?" Hadley asks, focusing her green eyes on me.

I look away, but not before she sees the pain in my eyes. "Darla. Back when those assholes attacked. She was shot trying to save me. Angus has taken it really hard."

"And Winston," Joshua says. "He—he never really recovered from losing Jess. Took a handful of pills just a couple weeks ago."

"Dear God," Hadley gasps. "I can't believe it."

She shakes her head, and Jon grabs her hand, giving it a little squeeze. I slip my own hand into Axl's.

"Everyone else is okay, then?" Jon says. "Parv and Anne? Angus?"

"Everyone is okay," I say, nodding. "Although Angus is another story altogether."

Hadley snorts despite the sorrow in her eyes. "He's always been a pain in the ass, though."

"It isn't just that," I tell her. "The craziest thing happened back in November, not too long after we lost you guys. We went out to gather some supplies and we were overrun, and in the middle of it all Angus was bitten. We thought it was the end, but…I don't know. Nothing happened."

"What do you mean nothing happened?" Jon asks, dropping Hadley's hand and sitting up straighter.

"Just what she said." Axl shrugs. "He's immune. Or somethin' like that."

Hadley and Jon stare at us like they think we're crazy, and I can't say I really blame them. It feels crazy, telling someone outside the group about what happened with Angus. After all the people we've seen die, it's incredible to think he's survived all this. And it hasn't changed him at all. No infection. No adverse effects. You'd think after the damn virus killed most of the world something would have happened to Angus, but he's the same as he was before he was bitten.

"Immune," Hadley says, only it doesn't sound like a question. "And you're sure he was bitten?"

"Ain't easy to miss it when a zombie sinks his teeth into somebody's shoulder," Axl snaps, and I shoot him a look. Why's he being such an asshole all of the sudden?

Jon and Hadley look at each other.

"We have to tell someone," Hadley says.

Something about the expression on her face tells me we are missing something. Something big.

"What's going on?" I ask, sitting up straighter. Squeezing Axl's hand until the bones in our fingers grind together and he's forced to wiggle his hand free.

Hadley tears her gaze away from Jon and turns my way. "When we first got in touch with Atlanta, they told us someone down in the Keys had claimed to have been bitten and didn't turn," she says, and suddenly all the air is sucked out of the room and replaced with something that makes my head feel lighter. "They were going down to extract the girl, but before they could get to her she was killed. It seemed crazy, but when we got in touch with the Florida group, they confirmed it."

Holy shit. Angus isn't the only one who's immune. It makes sense, but I didn't think we'd ever hear about someone who had the same gift. The world is too spread out. It seemed impossible. Nothing is impossible anymore, though.

"Since then we've been looking for someone else who might be immune," Jon says.

"Why you lookin' for somebody immune?" Axl asks, eyeing Jon like he's sure the other man is about to jump him.

"The CDC is still working in Atlanta," Ginny says. "If they're able to find someone who is immune, they think they'll be able to create a vaccine."

"Oh my God." I can't believe it, because it doesn't make sense. How can we have discovered so much hope after so many months?

"Holy shit," Joshua says.

Ginny and Jon nod, and the five of us just sit there, staring at each other. All of us thinking about what this might mean. If we can get Angus to Atlanta and they can create a vaccine, then none of this other stuff will matter. Any baby born will have a chance of survival. If we inoculate everyone, getting bitten won't be a death sentence. We'll be able to go out and kill these dead bastards off and rebuild even faster. The future will be more certain.

And Angus James could be the key to it all. The savior of the human race.

CHAPTER TWO

Everyone is talking at once, and not only is it impossible to focus on what they're saying but impossible to think. The hall stretches at least twenty feet in both directions, but everyone is crammed into a ball as they fight to be near the office door. It's so loud their voices feel like they're bouncing off the inside of my head. Plus, none of this really makes sense. Angus was bitten and he lived, that we've come to accept. But other people are out there, not just starting over but working to create a vaccine? At the CDC in Atlanta? I just can't wrap my brain around it, not after all the time we've spent thinking society has come to an end.

"We got them!" someone yells over the crowd, and I look up just as a pudgy, bald man sticks his head out of the office.

The leader of Hope Springs, Corinne, pushes her way through the crowd toward the door. She's tall enough that she towers over every woman around and most of the men, so it's easy to follow her progress. Everyone watches as she disappears into the room, but the talking doesn't stop. If anything, it seems to grow louder, and I have to fight the urge to scream at everyone to shut up. I don't know who's on the other end of the radio—someone important down in Atlanta, I'm sure—but if these people don't shut up, Corinne won't be able to hear them.

"Who did they get?" Joshua asks, raising himself up on the tips of his toes so he can see over the crowd. With his tall frame, I don't know why he needs to do it. Maybe it's just an automatic reaction.

"The CDC," Hadley—Ginny—says.

She's right at my side, standing so close her arm is pressed up against mine. In front of us, Axl and Jon and Joshua stand. Even though everyone around us has been talking a million miles a minute, the five of us have barely spoken. I'm not sure what's going on in Jon's and Hadley's heads, but I'm pretty sure Axl, Joshua, and I are in shock. It's been a while since we saw this many people together or were surrounded by this much noise and chaos. It's a lot to take in.

"They're going to want to take him there," Jon says.

Axl draws his lips into a purse, but he doesn't say anything right away. I meet his gaze, trying to focus while also resisting the urge to cover my ears. Around us, the voices seem to grow louder, but there's a good possibility the noise has more to do with the questions circling through my head than the people in the hall. There are a million of them—questions, I mean—so it takes me a few seconds to sort through. Something about Jon's statement has my stomach buzzing uncomfortably.

"Who's *they*?" I ask, still not totally sure what part of all this is bugging me.

"Us. Hope Springs. Atlanta. We'll put a group together so Angus has plenty of protection out there, so I'm not sure who will go or how many men there will be, but I know they're going to want to get Angus to Atlanta as soon as possible," Jon replies.

"That's gonna be up to Angus," Axl says, breaking his silence. "He's gonna have a say in this. It's his life."

"What the hell does that mean?" Ginny asks, looking directly at Axl for the first time in a while. Only the expression on her face isn't friendly.

Axl's gray eyes hold hers, and they're stormier than I've seen them since our first few days together. "Angus don't gotta go if he don't want to."

"We're talking about helping the human race." Hadley shakes her head. "You can't leave it up to a selfish prick like Angus. You need to *tell* him to go."

Axl doesn't blink. "Selfish prick or not, he's gonna have a say in it."

Hadley glares at Axl and Jon shakes his head, but before either one of them can say anything, Joshua lifts his hand. "I agree with Axl. You're talking about asking someone to become a science experiment. To sacrifice his freedom. It's only fair that he should have a say."

My stomach flips, and that's when it hits me: if Angus goes to the CDC, he isn't going to have a say in anything that happens to him. They're going to use him as a way to produce a vaccine, which means he'll be giving up everything. It wouldn't surprise me if they locked him in a cell and had armed guards watching him at all times. His life would be over, and just when he'd reached a point where it actually had some meaning.

"So you'd just let humanity disappear rather than sacrifice one person?" Ginny spits as a little bit of the Hadley I knew sneaks her way to the surface. Even though she was a tortured person, I can't help being glad to see her.

"And you'd force him to give up his life?" Joshua asks, holding her gaze. "Is that what we've come to? This is still America, even if it looks different than it did a year ago. Angus deserves to know the facts."

Hadley scowls, but Jon stays silent. His eyes move across us, seeming to stop on Axl and Hadley longer than Joshua or me, and I can't help wondering what's going on. There's so much intensity in his gaze and so much tension between Hadley and Axl.

What the hell is going on with everyone?

Corinne comes back out of the room, followed by Dax, who keeps right at her side. His chest is puffed out like someone who's trying to make himself look bigger. Maybe even more important. He looks the group over, and when his eyes stop on me, he smiles. Something about it sends a shiver shooting through my body, and even though I think it's stupid and I might be overreacting, I find myself moving closer to Axl.

Corinne stops, and around us, the talking eases to a quiet hush. "We managed to get in touch with the CDC in Atlanta, and they're quite eager to have your brother arrive. Would you like an escort to go with you and retrieve him?"

Dax steps forward—almost in front of her—like he's ready to volunteer.

Before he can say anything, Axl shakes his head. "We'll head on back to our place, but we'd like for you all to keep your distance. Give us a chance to talk all this over and decide what we're gonna do."

Corinne blinks. "Excuse me?"

"There are things to take into consideration," Joshua says, stepping forward to stand on the other side of Axl. "Angus is the one who is going to be poked and prodded, and it's only fair that he knows what he's in for. It's his life."

Corinne presses her lips together as she glances around, and Dax takes another step toward our group like he thinks he's going to strong-arm us into doing what he wants. Axl meets his gaze, not the least bit intimidated by the larger man, and Dax frowns.

"He has to say yes." Corinne shakes her head. "We have so much riding on this."

"We'll talk it over," Axl says firmly.

The people standing around us start murmuring again, and the mood changes from excited and hopeful to slightly hostile. For a second, I worry a fight's going to break out. Maybe we shouldn't have told these people where we live. What if they follow us? What if there's a fight or they kidnap

Angus in the middle of the night and drag him to Atlanta? We can't fight all these people off. There's no way.

"We just need some time to prepare," I say, flashing Dax a smile. I don't know him, but I don't want to risk him running off and doing something we're all going to regret. "This has all been such a big shock, but I'm sure Angus will understand how serious the situation is."

Axl shoots me a look, but I force the smile to stay on my face.

"Yeah," he says, slowly. "We gotta get movin' so we can talk this through. Our people are gonna be wonderin' where we're at. We'll be back tomorrow."

Corinne nods, but with the way her eyes narrow on Axl, I don't think she totally buys it. I'm starting to get really concerned that these people will resort to force if they have to.

AXL IS PRACTICALLY RUNNING WHEN WE STEP OUT of the building, and even though I have to jog to catch up, I don't blame him. I can't wait to get back home. So much has happened. Sophia's baby, Hadley and Jon, Atlanta and the CDC, and now a possible vaccine. We need to talk about it all, but I also want some time to absorb it with people I know and trust. Away from all the chaos.

I only hope no one tries to follow us.

"What are you thinking?" Joshua asks, keeping pace with Axl and me.

Axl doesn't slow. "They ain't gonna let Angus say no."

"I agree," Joshua says.

"Will he say yes?" I ask.

Saying no would be selfish, which has been one of his defining characteristics since he first picked me up on Route 66. Only, for some crazy reason, I think Angus will be okay with doing this. That giving up his life won't matter as much now as it would have. Which is crazy, because I'm pretty sure he hated everything about himself before all this. Now, though, he has a purpose and a reason for living.

Which is exactly why I think he just might be okay with making such a huge sacrifice.

But it *should* be up to him. It's his life, and if he wants to say no, it's his right.

"Not sure," Axl says.

"Vivian!" Hadley yells from behind me.

Axl swears and doesn't slow, but I do. He's not going to leave without me.

Hadley and Jon hurry our way, and I let out a deep breath. They're part of our group, but they're also part of Hope Springs, and I'm not sure if bringing them back with us is a good idea. Then again, it's not like they have the ability to force Angus to do something he doesn't want to do. None of us have succeeded in that, except maybe my mom.

"We want to come," Hadley says when she catches up with me. "I want to see everyone, but I also want to be there to talk some sense into Angus if he needs it."

"You can't force him," I say. "You know that, right? This is his life."

Hadley narrows her eyes, and I brace myself for some sort of verbal attack, but instead she says, "They've already started planning. They're going to want to head out as soon as possible. This is important."

"I understand, but so is Angus's life."

I end the discussion by turning to head after Axl and Joshua. Hadley and I can go back and forth about this for hours, but it's obvious neither one of us is going to back down. The best thing we can do right now is head home and let Angus make the decision.

Hadley and Jon follow me, but neither one talks. I can only hope they're thinking this through and that they'll decide to stand by us if Angus says no. After all this time praying and hoping we'd find them, I hate the thought of this coming between us.

We make it back to where our SUV is parked and pile inside, missing Sophia but feeling snug thanks to the two extra people we're bringing back with us. Even though I'm still reeling from what just happened and wondering who's side Jon and Hadley will take, I can't deny that I'm thrilled to have them back. To know that they made it after all, and that Hadley—Ginny—is healing. The determination that I admired in Hadley Lucas has returned, but the woman next to me is softer, too. Like someone who finally understands the beauty of life.

"When are you due?" I ask as Axl drives through the streets of Hope Springs. "So much happened that I didn't get a chance to ask before."

"June sixth," Ginny says, running her hand over her growing stomach.

"Boy or girl?" I ask.

"We didn't find out. We still don't know what's going to happen and I felt like finding out the sex would make it all too hard if…" She shrugs and looks away, but her hands don't stop moving across her stomach. "You know."

"Yeah," I whisper. "I understand."

"We gonna talk 'bout this Atlanta thing or not?" Axl snaps.

"What else can we say?" Jon replies. "We've told you how important this is. The thing is, we shouldn't have to. You know how big it would be if they created a vaccine for this thing."

Axl nods. "I do."

"Then you understand why everyone is concerned. Angus *has* to say yes." Hadley lifts her head stubbornly.

Axl's hands tighten on the steering wheel even more with every word out of her mouth. Something big happened between the two of them, but now isn't the time to ask about it. There are too many other things going on, and whatever it was can wait.

"Is that why you're here?" I ask, turning my body so I'm facing Hadley. "Did they send you to make sure Angus does what he's told? You of all people know that's not how he works. Sure, he's changed and grown. Matured even.

But you're still talking about asking him to sacrifice himself. He could be giving up everything for this, and I think it's only fair that he gets at least a couple hours to consider what that means."

Hadley shakes her head, but Jon nods and says, "They're right. We'll give him the details, but ultimately it's up to him."

Axl nods, looking slightly satisfied, but he doesn't ease his grip on the steering wheel.

We lapse into silence as Axl drives. The landscape we passed just a short time ago now seems different, less depressing somehow. Maybe it's the realization that Ginny and Jon made it or the fact that the hope we've been searching for is real. I'm not sure which one, but whatever it is, I can't help smiling when I look Hadley's way.

"You look happy," I say after a few minutes of silence.

"I am."

She takes Jon's hand, giving it a squeeze, and he smiles too. They seem so different from the last time we saw them, and it's hard to believe that so much could have changed in such a short time. Then again, Axl and I went from being strangers to something more profound than husband and wife in the matter of weeks. The end of the world will do that to you.

When our little community comes into view, Hadley sits forward, straining her neck to get a look out the window as Axl slows to a stop in front of the gate.

"Wow," she says. "You guys were this close all these months and we had no idea. I can't believe it, but I'm glad you found somewhere safe. I worried about you over the winter."

"We had our rough moments," I say as Joshua hops out to unlock the gate. "But we worked together and made it through. Most of us, anyway."

I sigh, thinking about Winston once again. If he had held on just a little bit longer, this might have made the difference for him. He might have heard about the CDC and the possible vaccine and seen a light at the end of the tunnel. Maybe.

Hadley shakes her head, wiping her eyes when they fill with tears. "I can't believe Jess and Winston are gone."

"I think Winston was the hardest one," I murmur, causing Axl to glance back at me. Our eyes meet, and it feels almost like he's trying to give me a hug. I wish he were sitting next to me so I could lean on him.

He drives through, and Joshua locks the gate behind us, then hops back into the passenger seat. Axl starts driving again, passing Al and Lila, who wave and head after us, probably anxious to find out what happened with Sophia. Boy are they going to be in for a couple big surprises.

I throw the door open the second the car comes to a stop, hopping out. Al and Lila are still a good distance away when Hadley steps out behind me, followed by Jon, and the second the teens see our long-lost friends they start to cheer.

"Hadley! Jon!" Lila screams, jumping up and down before running faster.

"Holy shit!" Al says, shaking his head. Laughing.

We're all going to have a tough time getting used to calling her Ginny.

Brady's front door opens, and people come pouring out. Anne and the kids, Parvarti. Everyone is talking at once, asking Jon and Hadley questions while they hug and cry. Brady is the only one who doesn't come over to greet the two, but even he smiles.

Angus is the last one out of the house, spitting as he heads down the steps. "What's all the racket out here?" he shouts.

"Angus!" Hadley calls, smiling.

"Holy shit. Didn't think I'd ever see you again, Hollywood," Angus says, shaking his head as he heads over to meet her. His eyes move over her, and he swears. "I was pretty sure you two had turned into popsicles by now, but it looks like you found a way to keep warm out there."

Hadley rolls her eyes as she throws her arms around Angus. "I'm stronger than that, and you know it!"

"Sure do." Angus pulls back and grins, but there's a softness in his eyes. Even though it's made an appearance more and more lately, it's still hard to get used to. "Even the strong fall these days."

"Not all of them," Hadley says. "I hear you've proven it's possible to be stronger than even this damn virus."

"Don't wanna brag," Angus says, pulling the collar of his shirt aside to reveal the healed bite. "But them zombies shoulda known they couldn't take Angus James down."

Hadley stares at the bite, shaking her head, and when she looks up to meet Angus's grin with one of her own, she says, "Do you even know how important you are to the world?"

CHAPTER THREE

Angus's eyes are focused on the floor, and he doesn't move, but he isn't alone. No one has made a sound since Hadley—Ginny—told them about Atlanta and Key West and how they're looking for a way to create a vaccine. I can't really blame everyone, but I also can't take my eyes off Angus, so I have no clue what they're all thinking.

"Angus?" Hadley says after a few seconds of silence.

He pulls his gaze away from the floor and looks up, meeting Hadley's green eyes with his gray ones. "They're makin' a cure."

"Well, a vaccine," Jon says. "I don't think there's any hope of a cure for what those poor bastards out there have, but a vaccine could mean there's hope for us."

"They want you to go to Atlanta," I say. "The people of Hope Springs are already getting a group together so you have plenty of protection. It's like an armed escort."

Angus nods slowly as his gaze moves across the room, stopping for a few seconds on each one of us before finally coming to rest on his brother. Something flashes in Axl's eyes, and without thinking, I reach out and slip my hand into his.

"Guess that means I'm pretty important," Angus finally says, flashing a half-grin that reminds me of a lost little boy trying to make a joke despite how terrified he is. "Never thought I'd be nobody important."

"You don't gotta go," Axl says. "You don't gotta do nothin' you don't wanna do."

"What do you mean he doesn't have to go?" Lila says, getting to her feet. "Of course he has to go! He could be the only person left who's immune. His blood could save the human race!"

"It could also make him a prisoner," Joshua points out. He swipes his hand through his hair as he lets out a deep breath. "Axl's right. Angus should have a say in this, because once we get there, I have a good feeling he'll be under lock and key. Probably for the rest of his life, but at the very least until they create a working vaccine."

"He'll be little more than a science experiment," Brady mutters.

"It ain't like they're gonna do experiments on me or nothin'," Angus snaps.

"We don't know what they have in store for you." Joshua's voice is firm. "One thing is for certain, though, you need to be damn sure you understand what you're getting yourself into."

Hadley exhales and gets to her feet. She walks to the other side of the kitchen, then huffs again before coming back and throwing her hands into the air. "Fine!"

"Fine what?" I ask, eyeing her.

"We find out what they have planned and make sure he stays safe. We make a deal with Atlanta before we go out there. Hope Springs has resources and men who will be willing to sacrifice themselves to get you there safely."

"That don't guarantee he's gonna be okay once we're there!" Axl voice booms through the kitchen.

Hadley winces, and I don't miss that she refuses to look

his way. Once again, that last day at the hot springs comes to mind. What kind of disagreement or argument did they have that they can't let go of even after all these months?

"We'll make sure he's okay," she says, quieter this time.

"He has the final say," Brady says from the corner.

"And if he says no?" Al asks. "What then? Will the men from Hope Springs knock our gates down and drag him to Atlanta?"

"We'll duck outta here before they know we're gone," Axl says, glancing toward Hadley like he's afraid she might be a spy. "You all can stay, but Angus and me'll high tail it outta here. Find a new place where nobody wants to cut him up."

My heart stutters like it's threatening to stop. He can't seriously think I wouldn't go with him.

"You're not leaving me," I say firmly.

Axl slips his arm around my shoulder, and I move closer to him.

"If it comes to that," Joshua says, "I think it would best if all of us head out. We're a family."

Al and Lila nod, along with Parvarti. Anne, however, remains quiet. She'd want to go with Joshua, though. Right? After all the time they've spent together, I can't believe something romantic hasn't developed there. Still, I have a sneaking suspicion we'd be saying goodbye to Sophia. Probably Brady, too. This is his home. Where his wife is buried. I don't really see him ever leaving this place.

Angus snorts and gets to his feet, and the legs of his chair scrape against the ground so loud that my heart starts pounding faster. "No need to worry 'bout all that. I'll go to Atlanta."

"You don't have to," I say.

Angus lifts his head, and his mouth scrunches up when his eyes meet mine. "It's the right thing to do, ain't it?" I shrug, unable to answer, but no one else does, either. "'Sides, I'll be savin' the world. That'll pretty much make me a hero."

"It will make you a superhero," I whisper.

Angus a hero. Who would have thought?

"When will he go?" Anne says, her voice even quieter than mine was a second ago.

Joshua's eyes are on her, but Anne's head is down. Almost like she doesn't want to look his way. For the first time since Jake died, she seems to be shying away from Joshua. They've gotten so close over the last few months that I didn't expect this, and judging by the expression on the doctor's face, neither did he.

"We'll head on back to Hope Springs in the mornin'," Axl says. "Sophia's anxious to get Ava back anyway." He frowns and shakes his head. "She's decided they're gonna live there from here on out."

Lila lets out a disappointed noise that reminds me of a hurt kitten, and Al puts his arm around her.

"I guess it would make sense that she wouldn't want to go to Atlanta," she says. "Not with a kid."

"They will let us all go, right?" Al says.

"They don't gotta choice." Angus gets to his feet.

"How soon do you think they'll be ready to head out?" I ask Jon and Hadley. They know more about the way Hope Springs works than any of us do.

"As soon as possible," Jon says. "But I'm assuming it will be a week at least. We need time to get people together and figure out what supplies to take and how many trucks. So the sooner we get back and let everyone know they're going to have nine extra people to plan for, the better."

"Not nine," Anne says, speaking up but keeping her head down. "I'll be staying in Hope Springs with Sophia and Ava and Max."

"No," Lila says, stepping toward her.

Joshua frowns, but he doesn't argue, and I can't help wondering what that means. Even though they never show any signs of affection, I thought they were a couple. I just figured they preferred to keep it private.

"I'm sorry," Anne says, shaking her head. "I'm going to miss all of you, but I just can't do it anymore. Weeks on the road with no end in sight. I just don't have it in me. Not now."

"It wouldn't be weeks," Jon says. "A couple days max, depending on how clear the roads are."

"We don't know that for sure," Anne says, looking up finally. "Anything can happen, and we all know that from firsthand experience."

Jon nods, and so does Hadley, and I have to admit Anne has a point. We've been surprised more than once.

"I'm afraid that I, too, will be staying behind," Brady says, clearing his throat.

"You don't have to be alone anymore," I say even though I know any argument I could throw his way would be wasted. He won't leave this house.

"I'm afraid I just can't stomach the idea of leaving Kristine behind." Brady gives me a tight smile that doesn't reach his eyes, and I think back to the time I saw him talking to his wife's grave. It's possible her death left him a little unhinged. Maybe staying here is just about comfort, but maybe not.

"You'll be missed," Joshua says, and I get the feeling his words are meant more for Anne.

Brady nods but doesn't respond, seeming to think the same thing. Anne still doesn't look Joshua's way.

"Guess we oughta get packed up," Angus says, stretching. "We gotta get movin' in the mornin'. Don't want them folks comin' out here after us 'cause they think we're tryin' to skip town."

"They wouldn't do that," Hadley says, shaking her head.

I arch my eyebrows, and she sighs. That's what I thought.

MORNING COMES, AND WE'RE ALL UP EARLY, squeezing into Brady's kitchen for what will probably be the last time. He splurged, preparing the last muffin mix we have and making extra coffee. The air is thick with the scent of blueberries, and the mood is a mixture of excitement and sadness. Brady especially seems to not be himself. Even if he's careful to keep the smile plastered on his face. It also doesn't escape my notice that Joshua and Anne are keeping their distance from each other. Whatever they talked about last night, it must have been serious.

Before I know it, breakfast is done and everyone is heading out. Ready to load the cars and get a move on. Instead of following, though, I head to the sink with a stack of dirty dishes. I know that the longer it takes for us to make it back to Hope Springs, the jumpier Dax and his men will become—something about the big man makes me uneasy, and the last thing I want is for him to show up at our gate—but I'm reluctant to leave.

"You don't need to do that," Brady says, carrying a second stack of dishes over to me.

"It's fine," I say, smiling even though a part of me wants to cry. "It's the least I can do after running out on you."

"You don't need to feel bad about leaving," Brady replies, giving me a sad smile. "We both know I could go if I really want to. I just…" He shrugs as he hands me a plate.

I get to work rinsing the leftover scraps of food off, too choked up to say anything to him. I keep my focus on the crumbs as they swirl around the porcelain sink and disappear down the drain. I may have only known Brady for a few months, but we've been through a lot together. We saved his life when we found him in the woods, and he in turn saved ours when he let us inside this fence. I can't help thinking that leaving him alone like this is a death sentence. True, Hope Springs isn't too far away, but that doesn't mean they'll be around to save him if he gets in trouble. Who knows what the future will bring his way?

"I wish you'd reconsider and come with us," I say, still not looking at Brady.

Out of the corner of my eye, I see him smile, but even without looking right at him, the sadness in his expression is obvious. It goes so deep that it physically hurts me.

"I don't think I'm meant to leave this place, to be honest. I feel a bit like I'm tethered to it, and a part of me thinks that if I tried to leave it would pull me back. It's good to know that

Hope Springs is out there and that they're friendly. Sophia and Anne won't be too far off, and if I get lonely it will be just a short drive down the street and I can sit and talk with old friends."

"Very true," I say, but the words come out as little more than a whisper. My throat is too clogged with tears for anything more.

Brady nods, and we finish the dishes in silence. When they're done, we head outside together. The others are just finishing loading the cars. Meaning soon we'll be driving away, saying goodbye to the home that kept us safe through the longest winter of our lives.

It's warmer this morning than it has been in months, and the sun is so bright that I'm forced to squint. For some reason, despite the pain clouding my brain, the day makes me hopeful. Like the first ray of sunshine after a storm or a rainbow after the rain. My eyes meet Hadley's, and I smile.

When she returns it, I say, "We aren't through the worst of things, but I can't help feeling like we're nearing the finish line for good this time."

"I know. It's strange, don't you think? After all the people we saw die and all the times we worried that we would be next, there's now a chance to erase all that."

"I really didn't think it was possible."

Hadley smiles. "Me neither."

"You ready?" Axl asks, not even looking my way as he tosses the last bag into the back of the SUV.

"I am," I say. It isn't a lie, even if saying goodbye is tough.

I stand back while everyone takes turns telling the man who took us in goodbye. For Anne it's easier because she knows she'll see him again. For the rest of us, this could be the last time we ever see Brady.

"You will be missed," I say, when it's my turn, kneeling down to give him a hug.

Brady hugs me back, and when I pull away, there are tears in his eyes. My own eyes are oddly dry, though. Maybe I'm finally cried out.

"You will be missed as well. Even though I can't make myself leave this place, I think you all saved my life when you came here. Even if it was only temporary, you gave something to live for and helped me get everything in order." Brady nods once. "I think I can hang on now."

I'd thought he was hanging on before we came—he did clear this neighborhood out on his own—but maybe he wasn't. Maybe he was at the end when we found him, and us being here kept him afloat.

"Try. Don't do what Winston did," I say, giving his hand one last squeeze before standing.

Brady nods, and I turn away. The rest of us pile into the cars, and less than a minute after the last door is shut, Axl drives off. Behind us, Brady stands in his yard, watching us but not waving. Just standing in front of his house, once again alone.

CHAPTER FOUR

Dax is waiting at the gate to Hope Springs when we drive up. Axl pulls to a stop and rolls his window down as the other man jogs over, smiling. His gaze moves behind us when the van holding the rest of our group also pulls to a stop, and when he turns back, his smile has grown wider. There's something about it that sends a shiver down my spine, though.

"We were going to head out to see you this afternoon if you didn't come back," he says, the smile frozen on his face. "Glad we didn't have to."

We were right. If necessary, they would have used force.

"Told you we'd be back," Axl snaps, wringing the steering wheel like he's wishing it were Dax's neck. "We had to make plans and pack our things."

"Glad to know you're a man of your word." Dax doesn't look away, and I get the feeling he's waiting for Axl to return his smile. It doesn't happen, though, and finally the other man steps back and waves us ahead. "Head on up to the dorm and

I'll be right behind you. We'll have a word with Corinne, and then we'll get you a place to live for the time being. We're not totally sure when we're going to leave just yet, but I promise we won't keep you waiting too long!"

Axl nods once before rolling his window up, and when he pulls through the gate, he's frowning. This time, I can't help sharing his discomfort. Something about Dax just feels off.

"Pretty nice setup they got here," Angus says from the backseat where he's squeezed in between Joshua and Parvarti.

"Hadley told me she and Jon have a little house," Parv says, staring out the window at the buildings we pass.

"They do," I say. "We were there yesterday."

Parv nods, and so does Angus, both of them looking out at the street as we drive through town. I glance behind us to make sure the van is still on its way. It is, and not too far behind it, Dax follows in his little golf cart. Looks like he's in a hurry.

We stop in front of the dorms and pile out, but we don't hurry inside. I'm not sure what's going to happen from here on out, but I have a feeling every second is going to be a fight. Dax likes to be in control, but that's something we just aren't ready to give up. Axl is already on edge thanks to the looks the other guy's been giving me.

Dax pulls into a spot on the other side of our SUV, flashing me a smile when my gaze meets his. His eyes move down, and every hair on my head stands up. We need to ask Jon and Hadley about this guy. There is something very off about him.

"Head on in!" Dax calls as he climbs out. "We'll fill you in on the plans we've made before we get you in a house."

"You have a house for us?" Lila asks, her eyes lighting up.

Dax nods, still grinning. "Need to give you some place to sleep. It will be at least a week before we head out. Probably close to May first."

"I'd like to see Sophia," Anne says. She has one child on each side, their hands gripped in hers. "And I know she'd want me to bring Ava to her."

Dax nods, but before he can say anything, Joshua steps forward. "I can take them to the clinic."

"Perfect," Dax says, smiling wider.

That's when it hits me: he smiles too much. That's what bothers me about Dax. No one smiles that much, especially not these days. It can't be real, and thinking about what he's trying to hide behind that smile makes me nervous.

"Thanks," Joshua says as he heads off with Anne and the kids.

Even though they're side by side, she still shies away from him. Something she hasn't done since Jake died. Joshua cares about Anne, but maybe she doesn't feel the same way. Or maybe she's just scared. Fear can make a person do some crazy things.

No one talks as we move toward the dorm in a group. People stop to stare, probably trying to figure out which one of us is the future of the human race. I step closer to Angus like I can somehow shield him from everyone but right away feel stupid. This is Angus. He doesn't need me or anyone else protecting him. Angus has always been capable of taking care of himself, and a couple bites hasn't changed that.

"That the same guy we saw back at Sam's Club?" Angus asks, nodding toward Dax, who's at the head of the pack.

"Yup," Axl says.

Angus presses his lips together, his eyes boring into the back of Dax's head. "He's still checkin' Blondie out."

"Yup," Axl says again. Not glancing my way.

"Stop," I say, my gaze moving toward Dax. "Right now that isn't important. What is important is being sure these people know how serious we are about our demands. We can't let them get the upper hand."

"You think they're gonna argue?" Angus asks.

"I'd bet my life on it," I say firmly.

The lobby is empty when we step inside, and I'm glad. After all the chaos that surrounded the little office holding the ham radio, I wasn't looking forward to more noise. I want to be able to hear myself think.

Dax hurries toward a door, but it opens before he's even had a chance to knock, and Corinne steps out. He must have radioed ahead.

"You're back," Corinne says, her smooth British voice filling the empty room. She looks us over, her eyes stopping on every one of us before finally coming to rest on Angus. "You're the one who is immune?"

"Sure am," Angus says, pursing his lips as he looks her over.

When we first met, I would have been nervous—you never knew what was going to come out of Angus's mouth when we were in the midst of diversity—but not anymore. Now I know he's just trying to get a handle on the situation before it gets a handle on him.

"This is Angus," Jon says, stepping up.

"Nice to meet you." Corinne gives him a slight nod. "And you've decided to go to Atlanta?"

Angus hasn't stopped eyeing her. "That I did."

Corinne steps aside and motions toward the open doorway. "Very good. Please come in and we'll go over a few details."

Dax leads the way, and I don't miss when Corinne frowns. She doesn't say anything, but I get the feeling she isn't thrilled to have him here. Which is just great. If the people in this town have doubts about this guy, I don't want to be anywhere near him. Let alone out *there* with him.

We follow the big man in, spreading out once we're in the small apartment. Hadley lowers herself into an oversized chair, and Jon balances himself on the arm. I take the couch with Axl and Angus while Parv takes the other chair. There aren't enough places to sit, so Lila and Al settle onto the floor. Dax stays standing, his hands resting on his hips as he looks us all over. Like he's passing judgment or trying to size us up. Maybe both. Whatever he's thinking, the creepy smile has at least faded a little.

Corinne frowns his way, but she doesn't say anything. She too stays standing, but I think it has more to do with the lack of chairs than trying to assert her authority the way Dax is.

"Thank you for doing this," she says, focusing her gaze on Angus. "I know what a sacrifice you're making. Believe me, I want to make sure you are safe. Both on the way to Atlanta and once you get there."

"Sacrifice?" Dax snorts.

Corinne doesn't glance his way. "Yes. Sacrifice."

"I ain't real worried 'bout myself," Angus says. "Way I figure it, this is 'bout the only real good thing I've ever done in my life, and it's a helluva lot more than I ever expected to do. I guess what I'm sayin' is, when do we leave?"

"That's not up to me." Corinne grabs a chair from the small table on the other side of the room and drags it over, lowering herself onto it with a sigh. "We have a group getting supplies together, and they'll head out whenever they think they're ready. Dax is in charge of that side of things."

Dax puffs his chest out—again—and smiles. Again. "That's right. Atlanta is anxious for us to get there, but we want to make sure we do this right, so we're getting a group together. If we get overrun when we're out there, we need to be sure we have enough men to protect you. Keeping Angus alive will be our number one priority."

"Well, you'll have more than enough hands to back you up," Al says, grinning at his own joke.

"Excuse me?" Dax's blue eyes move over us, stopping on Al's stump, and a frown that looks a lot more natural replaces his constant smile. "I never intended for any of your people to go. We've got a good group put together already. We'll keep him safe, I can promise you that."

"We don't doubt you on that," Axl says calmly. "Angus makin' it to Atlanta will be just as good for you as it will for us, but we're still goin'. We're a family, and splittin' up ain't an option for us."

Dax shakes his head, but Corinne stands before he can argue. "They go."

She turns to face Dax, whose frown deepens when their eyes meet. A silent confrontation follows that makes all of us squirm—Jon especially.

"We don't need them," Dax finally says.

Corinne doesn't blink. "It's not up to you. The committee voted. I'm in charge."

"But you put me in charge of this." The words have to push their way through Dax's clenched teeth.

"Yes, and you know why I did that."

"What the hell have we gotten ourselves into?" I mutter.

Corinne blinks and steps away from Dax, turning toward us. "It's just a small issue. Nothing to worry about, really. Dax is our best man, and I know he would never do anything to risk the mission."

Dax presses his lips together, his eyes on Corinne for just a second longer before he turns to face the group. The smile that finally spreads across his face looks faker than ever.

"Corinne's right, and I'm sorry. Of course you can all join us. I would never dream of splitting up a group that is obviously as close as all of you are." His eyes move between Axl and me. "Just be sure you pitch in out there and we won't have any problems."

"Hard work is something we're used to," Axl says, scooting closer to me.

"Good. Then it's all settled." Dax slaps his hands together, and the clap echoes through the small room. "I'll let you know when we pick an exact date, but in the meantime we'll get you all into a house."

We stand, and when I turn to face Hadley, my gaze goes right to her hand, slowly making circles across her stomach, and I freeze. It didn't occur to me until now, but it should have. She and Jon won't be coming with us. They can't. It wouldn't be safe for her on the road. Not this close to her due date. Which means going to Atlanta will require us leaving Hadley and Jon behind. Again.

"We have houses for them, yes?" Corinne says, staring at Hadley.

"We do." Hadley shrugs and shoots us an apologetic look. "We had two houses free on our street, but I already gave one to Sophia, Anne, and the kids. The other is only three bedrooms, so it will be a tight fit for the rest of you."

"We have the dorms," Corinne says. "There's plenty of space here."

"We'd rather squeeze into a small house than be separated," I say before I've even checked with the others. None of them argue, though, and Lila even nods.

"It ain't for long," Axl says.

"We have space." Jon turns to Hadley. "We have two spare rooms. The one has a crib, but the other has a full-size bed in it. There's no reason Axl and Vivian can't stay with us."

Hadley cringes even as she nods. "Yeah," she says, focusing on me. "Of course."

Axl doesn't say anything, and even though he doesn't look insanely uncomfortable the way Hadley does, it's obvious he's avoiding looking her way.

Her eyes dart toward him, so briefly most people probably wouldn't notice it, and then she turns and heads for the door. "Let's go. We can have dinner together."

The group follows, and I go with them, walking at Axl's side. I shoot him a questioning look, but he just shrugs. What the hell am I missing? It's obvious something is still bugging Hadley, but now isn't the time to get into it. We have a million other things to worry about, and whatever it is, it's probably stupid and none of my business. Let those two work it out.

AXL HANDS ME A PILE OF DIRTY DISHES, AND I TAKE them. The normalcy of the act isn't lost on me, and the hope that sprouted in me the second I found out Jon and Hadley were here grows. It isn't he first time I've fantasized that Axl and I could have a real life, but now that dream has grown so big it physically hurts. If Atlanta is anything like this place, we could be starting a real future very soon.

"What?" Axl asks, tilting his head as he looks me over.

"I'm just thinking about the future," I say.

"Atlanta will give you a real chance," Hadley says, sighing.

"I know you can't go with us," I say as I hand the dirty dishes off to Hadley, "but I wish you could."

She presses her lips together as she runs a plate under the water. "Atlanta would be a better place to give birth."

I turn to face her, unsure of what she's getting at, but she isn't looking up.

"You're not thinking about going. Are you?"

"I don't know." She shrugs as she continues rinsing plates. "The doctors here are clueless and they don't have the technology to study this virus, let alone the knowledge. But the CDC has been studying it for months. Pretty much since this whole mess started. They've even managed to keep a baby alive. Maybe it's just a coincidence, but I'm not sure if I'm willing to take that risk. I don't think Jon will be either. Losing this baby will be as devastating for him as it would be for me."

It seems too risky to me. There's so much unknown between here and there.

I shake my head, but before I can respond, Jon walks into the kitchen behind us. "I have something for you, Axl."

"What you got?" Axl asks.

His back is to me, so I can't see his expression when Jon holds a knife up, but I do hear the little chuckle he lets out.

"Shit," Axl says, taking the knife. "Thought I'd lost this back at the hot springs."

I get a closer look at the knife, and right away I recognize the thing. It has a wood handle and a blade so long it could probably go all the way through a zombie's skull. I've seen Axl slam that knife into a zombie's head more times than I could count, and I know he's missed it.

"You've had that this whole time?" I ask.

Jon nods. "I borrowed it the last day we were at the hot springs, and I've held onto it."

"I'm glad," Axl says, slapping Jon on the arm. "Angus gave it to me for my birthday. Back when we was kids. I'm pretty sure he stole it, but I didn't give a shit. I love this knife."

"I'm glad I hung onto it, then."

"Me too," Axl says, smiling.

He stares at the knife like he's suddenly gotten back the only good part of his childhood. It's cute.

Someone knocks on the door, and Hadley starts to dry her hands, but Jon puts his hand up to stop her. "I'll get it."

She shoots him a smile. "Thanks."

"You two sure are different," I say, turning to face her when Axl follows Jon out.

Hadley nods as she goes back to washing the dishes. "I reached a point where I knew I had to make a decision. Either give up or put everything I had into living this life. I knew Jon loved me, but I wasn't sure if I could love anyone. It wasn't him, it was me. I hated everything about myself."

"Which is why you got rid of Hadley Lucas."

"I would really like for you to start calling me Ginny," she says, her eyes focused on the water. "I realize I'm not going to be able to get the rest of the group to understand, but I know you will. You know, better than anyone, what it was like in there, and you have to know why I can't be that person anymore. Why I need to be Ginny Lewis now."

"I do," I say, putting my hand on her arm. "From here on out, you are Ginny to me. And I'll talk to Axl too. I'll make him understand."

She swallows and shoots me a look that seems slightly terrified. "Let me talk to him. Okay?"

"Sure." Maybe that's a good idea. Things are definitely awkward between them, and it won't hurt to have them get whatever this thing is out in the open. I want them to get along.

"Thanks," she says, going back to washing.

"Ginny!" a feminine voice calls from the other room.

I turn just as a teenager walks into the kitchen. She's cute, even if she does look totally out of place in this world. She has her red hair piled on top of her head and her make-up applied perfectly, and she's so dressed up she looks like she's on her way to a club. It doesn't make any sense.

"You haven't introduced me to your friends." The girl smiles when our eyes meet, and her gaze moves over me in a way only a teenager's can. Like she's trying to size up the competition.

"This is Gretchen," Ginny says, smiling at me. "Jon and I found her after we got separated from you. She'd been by herself for months."

"Wow," I say, turning to face the girl. "Tough kid. I'm Vivian."

I hold my hand out, but Gretchen frowns. "Kid? I'm seventeen. I can't be much younger than you."

She crosses her arms, and her blue eyes narrow on my face, making my scalp prickle. It takes me back to high school. To girls who sneered at my holey gym shoes. Who whispered about trailer parks behind their hands. Who spread rumors about the slutty blonde named Vivian whose mom ran out on her and whose dad was always too drunk to care what the hell she did.

Shit. I thought I'd escaped that kind of stuff.

"Nice to meet you," I say even though I have the sudden urge be as bitchy as she's being. "Ginny and I have been through a lot, but I'm glad to find out she had someone else to lean on after we got split up."

Gretchen crosses her arms and sniffs, and I do everything in my power not to roll my eyes.

"How's Mark?" Ginny asks, the corner of her mouth twitching in amusement. I'm glad she thinks it's funny.

"Better," the girl says. "I'll be happy when he can go back to work, though. He's driving me crazy. Expecting me to wait on him hand and foot. Like I'm a maid."

Is this girl for real?

"He did get shot, Gretchen." Ginny shakes her head.

"I'm going to go see what the guys are up to," I say, inching my way toward the living room.

When Ginny doesn't ask me to stay, I practically run from the room.

I find Axl and Jon on the couch, talking about everything we've seen since splitting up.

"It's crazy that we found you after all this," I say, sitting on the arm of the couch at Axl's side.

Axl nods and pats my leg. "Not gonna lie. I didn't think we would."

"I had my doubts too," Jon says.

"You gonna tell me what this place is really like?" Axl asks. "It ain't perfect. There's no way. Corinne is alright, but there's something 'bout Dax that gets under my skin."

Jon exhales. He glances toward the kitchen, then leans closer to Axl. Probably doesn't want the teen gossip queen to hear what he's about to say. "We had a problem with Dax a couple months back. He challenged Corinne, but she stood up to him. The council backed her, but Dax hasn't been happy about things since then. I don't think he'll do anything to risk the mission, but I'd keep my eye on him if I were you anyway. Just in case."

"Great," I say. "There's nothing like being in the middle of zombie-infested country with a guy no one can count on."

"We don't need to count on him," Axl says. "We got each other."

"You're right," Jon says. "You don't need Dax to be anything but a chauffer. You took care of each other before you found Hope Springs, and you can do it again."

Jon's right. That's what we do. Take care of each other.

CHAPTER FIVE

Ginny won't sit still, and it's making my head spin. We're all crowded into her living room, and she acts like she's trying to clean around us. Which is weird, because back in the shelter when we shared a condo, her room was a disaster.

"Are you cleaning?" Parv asks, watching as Ginny runs her hand across the mantel. She acts like someone is going to do a white glove inspection on the living room.

"I'm just checking things over," she says. "I want to make sure the house is nice when the baby comes."

"It's fine. Sit down," I tell her, waving toward an open chair.

"I can't seem to relax lately," Ginny says, shaking her head.

"You're nesting," I say.

"You mean like a bird?" Lila asks, her nose scrunching up.

"No. Like a woman who's about to give birth." I stand up and grab Ginny's arm, forcing her over to the chair. "Now sit."

Ginny relents, letting out a sigh when she's finally off her feet. "I guess that's what it is. I feel like nothing is ready and nothing is good enough. It's driving me batty."

"You're a woman," Angus says, grinning. "Don't got too far to go for that."

Ginny just rolls her eyes.

I go back to my space on the floor in front of Axl. My back is up against the couch, and he sits behind me. It reminds me of when I was a teenager. Back when I was dating my only nice ex-boyfriend and I used to go over to his house in the evenings to watch TV. We'd snuggle together on his living room floor, and he'd rub my back—trying to cop a feel whenever we were alone. Until his mom found out I was from the trailer park and decided I wasn't good enough for her perfect son, that is.

"So what are we supposed to do all day?" Lila asks from where she and Al are lounging on Ginny's couch. "Everyone here has jobs, but we're getting ready to leave, so there doesn't seem to be much of a point in us getting one. So we just hang out?"

"It's kind of nice for a change," Al says, grinning down at her.

"Borin' as hell is what it is." Angus grunts and shakes his head. "Should go out huntin' or somethin'."

"No way they'd let you do that," Ginny says with a laugh. "You should see the way they treat me. Just because I'm pregnant with what might possibly be the first immune baby born here, they act like I can't do anything."

Angus snorts and grins her way. "Can you? With that belly of yours, I'd be afraid you'd fall over."

Ginny sticks her tongue out.

"What does Jon do?" I ask, ignoring their little exchange. They can pick at each other better than anyone, and even though it's nice to be around it again, I'm more interested in figuring this place out right now.

"Jon's working on the crew that's making the walls stronger," Ginny says. "We got some details about what Atlanta did, so we're following their lead. It's going to take some heavy labor, but it should pay off."

Angus hauls himself up off the couch. "We can help with that. No reason to just sit on our asses when there's work to be done."

"Speak for yourself," Al says. "I plan on taking a nap, then maybe checking out the library. There's a zombie book I read a few years back I was hoping they'd have." Lila rolls her eyes, but the teen just grins. "It's helped us out before. Plus, I'd love to find some kind of prepper or survival book. Just in case we get into trouble on the road."

"Shit," Axl says, getting to his feet and knocking me in the head in the process. "We been on the road before. Don't need a book to tell us how to live." I glare at him as I rub the sore spot on my scalp, but he isn't looking my way. He probably didn't even notice.

"There are all kinds of neat tricks you can learn from a book," Al says.

Angus shakes his head. "Can't learn nothin' from a book that life ain't gonna teach you."

"How about performing surgery?" Joshua says, grinning up at Angus.

He just frowns.

"Where they workin'?" Axl asks Ginny.

"On the other side of town." She focuses on Angus. Of course. "The west end of the fence."

"Let's head on out. See what they're up to," he says, nodding to his brother. "No reason we can't get our hands dirty."

Axl nods but turns to me. "You comin'?"

"Sure," I say, taking his hand when he offers it to me. "Might as well get a look at the fence and see what they're doing."

Ginny hauls herself up too, grunting. "I'll show you where they are. It's going to earn me a few dirty looks, but I get tired of just sitting on my ass for hours."

"Walkin' 'cross town ain't gonna hurt you, Hollywood," Angus says, throwing his arm over her shoulder as we head out.

Ginny looks up at him out of the corner of her eye. "Ease up on the nickname, okay? People around here know me as Ginny Lewis from Ohio. Not that other person. As far as I'm concerned, that's how it should stay."

"I ain't gonna give away your secret," Angus says, smiling down at her.

"Anyone else?" I ask, looking around the room.

"I'll come," Parv says.

"No," Joshua says even though he gets to his feet. "I'm going to head over and check on Sophia. I may not be her doctor anymore, but that doesn't mean I can't make sure she's doing okay."

I don't say what I'm really thinking: that he's going so he can check on Anne more than Sophia. I can't help wondering if Joshua hasn't given up hope that Anne may change her mind and decide to come with us. She has time, and it's not like I can't understand her hesitation. Being out there isn't fun, and the thought of doing it all over again does fill me with terror. But it isn't like before. We have a plan. We have a destination, and we have protection. We won't be on the road for weeks with no end in sight.

"Tell her we'll stop by later to say hello," I say, smiling as I turn to face the teens, who haven't moved from the couch. "What about you two?"

"I was thinking of taking a nap." Al grins and shoots Lila a wink.

"Real subtle," she says, shoving him.

Al just laughs.

"Please," Ginny says, rolling her eyes. "Not on my couch."

"What's wrong with napping on your couch?" Al flashes

her a smile that doesn't look the least bit innocent, and I swear Lila turns pink.

"Whatever," Ginny says, turning toward the door. Al is still laughing when we head out, and Ginny is still shaking her head. "They aren't going to listen."

"Doubtful." I slip my hand into Axl's as we follow Ginny and Angus down the street.

We aren't the only ones out, and if it weren't for the fact that everyone we pass is armed, it might be possible to mistake this town for a normal city during normal times. People smile and wave, and we even pass two women pushing strollers and another walking a dog. I haven't seen a dog since this whole thing started—unless you count the dead ones those assholes used to lure the zombies into our shelter. It's crazy to think people still have pets.

It's going to be tough saying goodbye to all this. Even after one day, I've gotten oddly attached to the normalcy surrounding this place, and we have no guarantees about Atlanta. They paint a pretty picture over the radio, but there's no telling what things are really like out there.

"Is Dax on this crew with Jon?" I ask Ginny, suddenly thinking about heading out and how the trip will go. And wondering if we can trust this guy.

Angus glances back, grinning. "You like the attention, blondie?"

I roll my eyes. "No. I'm curious about the guy. He's going to be leading the group that takes us across the country, and I want to know what we might be getting into. What do you think about him?"

Ginny frowns but doesn't look back. "Dax has been trouble, but most people like him."

"Not Corinne," Axl points out.

"No. He challenged her for leadership, but a lot of people didn't see it as a big deal since his main argument was that she isn't an American."

"But that's not why he challenged her," Parv says. "Is it?"

Ginny shakes her head. "No. He wants to be in charge. Jon isn't crazy about Dax either, and Jim, Jon's partner from clearing the streets, can't stand the guy. There was also an incident when they went out to Duncan to find survivors. It was right after we learned people could be immune, and we were looking for someone who might be the key to all this. It must have occurred to Dax that we wouldn't know whether or not people were immune unless they were bitten, because he let one of the men they picked up get attacked."

I stop walking. "What?"

Ginny stops too, and she turns to face me. "Jon and Jim were there, not me. They don't know anything for sure, but that's how it seemed."

"So you're tellin' me this asshole let a guy get bit on the off chance he might be immune?" Angus narrows his eyes on Ginny. "And this is the guy who's supposed to get us 'cross the country?"

"It's not like he's going to endanger your life," Ginny points out. "He is really dedicated to getting an immune person to Atlanta."

Axl shakes his head. "Don't mean he's gonna be watchin' the rest of our backs. If anything, it puts us at risk. I bet you my right nut he'd be willin' to push any one of us in front of a horde if it meant savin' Angus."

"And his own ass," Ginny says. "He also ran out on a few of his guys when someone opened fire."

"Shit," Angus mutters. "Sounds like a real winner."

"Jon didn't say anything 'bout this the other night," Axl says, shaking his head.

"Maybe it was because Gretchen was in the house?" I want to give Jon the benefit of the doubt, but I have to admit I'm not thrilled that Jon didn't tell us.

"He wouldn't want to bring it up in front of her," Ginny says. "Her boyfriend, Mark, was shot that day. Even if he swears that isn't how it went down, Mark is one of the guys Dax ran out on."

"This keeps getting better and better," Parv says, trading

looks with Angus.

"Shit," Angus says.

He pulls out a pack out cigarettes and passes one to Parv, who takes it despite the dirty look Ginny shoots her way. The two light up, and she takes a step back, still scowling.

"Why did Corinne put this guy in charge?" I ask, unconcerned about the cigarettes even if Ginny is pregnant. We've got way more important things to worry about right now. "Is she trying to get rid of him just so she can make her own life easier?"

Ginny shrugs but says, "It wouldn't surprise me. She's been more and more tense with him around, and I know she's worried he's going to stage some kind of coup or something."

"Fuckin' great." Angus takes a long drag off his cigarette, then turns and heads down the street. Parv walks by his side, and the two exhale at the same time, twin streams of smoke floating into the air above them.

Ginny, Axl, and I start walking, and she shoots me a look. "When did she start smoking?"

"After we left the hot springs. I don't even notice it anymore."

"She's trying to kill herself," Ginny mutters.

"No," I say. "I'm pretty sure if she wanted to do that, she would have done it by now."

Axl glances at Ginny, then jogs to catch up with his brother while I stay at my friend's side. They haven't talked yet, but I hope they manage it soon. I'm tired of this awkwardness. So much so that I have the urge to ask her what happened between them. Only there's a part of me that doesn't want to know. Not really.

"You think this is a good idea?" I ask instead. "Putting our lives in this guy's hands?"

Ginny swallows, and I have a feeling she was sure I was about to ask and that she's relieved I didn't. "He won't be the only one out there, and it isn't like you can't take care of yourselves."

"We can take care of ourselves," I say, not feeling the least bit confident about Dax but knowing we will be able to handle whatever comes along. Assuming he doesn't get in our way.

We walk in silence, and after five minutes, the fence comes into view. It isn't very high right now—ten feet at the most—but they're in the process of using a crane to pile old cars up around it. Making it stronger and higher. Thicker, even. It's a good plan, but something about it sends a shiver shooting straight through me.

I stop walking when it hits me.

"What's wrong?" Ginny asks, stopping too.

"Don't you see it?" I whisper, staring at the wall of cars. "Doesn't this remind you of the hospital?"

She shakes her head twice, then freezes. All the color drains from her face, and I know, like me, that she remembers that day. The day we spent looking for medical supplies in Vegas. We went to the hospital and got separated from the same two men with us right now. Ginny—no, Hadley—and I found our way to the ER, only it was cleaned out and a barrier had been built around the fence. Cars were stacked on top of each other. They'd made it a trap. How they did it and why has never really been something I could wrap my brain around, but it doesn't matter. Not when just thinking about it makes the world around me spin.

"Sometimes I wonder if I'll ever be able to escape that day," Ginny says.

I nod, but I can't find words. That makes two of us.

"What you doin'?" Angus calls, waving us forward. "You in labor or somethin'?"

Ginny shakes her head and starts walking, and I follow. My throat is too tight to talk, and my head is still spinning with the craziness of this situation. What are the odds that two different groups would come up with the same plan? It has to be a coincidence, though. The group in Vegas did this first, and there's no way anyone from the Monte Carlo made it all the way to Atlanta and gave them this idea. Not if they've had the wall built as long as Ginny says they have. It's just two people who had a similar train of thought: how to use the resources available to meet their end goal. Thank God that end goal is different.

"I'm going to have to ask you to stop here," a man says, blocking our progress a good ten feet from the fence.

I get it—the giant crane moving a car to the top of the pile is dangerous, even if we aren't with both Angus and Ginny—but I still wish we could get a closer look at the wall.

"Need help?" Axl asks, nodding toward the fence at the man's back.

"You're not on the crew." The guy looks us over like he suspects we're carrying a bomb and want nothing more than to blow up the wall they're busy trying to build.

"We ain't on the crew, but that don't mean we can't help out," Angus growls.

The Hope Springs guy, who is more than a head shorter than Angus and probably thirty pounds lighter, takes a step back. "I'm just following orders. Dax doesn't want anyone around who doesn't know what they're doing."

Angus and Axl exchange looks. Parv just smokes, eyeing the guy like she is afraid to let him out of her sight.

"Jon around?" Ginny asks, trying to look past the man in front of us.

"Yeah. I'll get him as long as you promise to keep your friends back and out of the way."

Ginny rolls her eyes. "We aren't going to sabotage your project."

The guy gives us one more look before turning and heading back toward the other workers. He jogs like he thinks he has to hurry.

"What the hell was that 'bout?" Axl asks. "You'd think they'd be happy to have some help. Get the work done faster."

Ginny shakes her head. "Dax is a control freak."

"This guy sounds better and better the more I hear about him," I mutter.

Ginny just shrugs, which makes me feel a little better. If she isn't worried about Dax being out there with us, we shouldn't either. Right?

Less than a minute after the Hope Springs guy has disappeared, I catch sight of Jon heading our way. He's decked out in leather, which is apparently the uniform for anyone working even remotely near the zombies. I get it, though. Zombies can rip through clothes—we know that from experience—but leather has to be a little bit tougher for them to sink their teeth into.

Another guy who is also decked out in leather walks at Jon's side. The second man looks more at home in the stuff, though. He's younger than Jon, and smaller, but everything about the way he carries himself gives off how confident he is. The cigarette hanging out of his mouth, looking like it's about to drop to the ground at any second. The way he flicks his blond hair out of his eyes and even the way his gaze moves over the people he passes. Like he can barely be bothered to notice them. There's something very tough about him.

"Who's that?" I ask Hadley when the two men are still too far away to hear.

"Jim," she says, "Jon's partner. They worked on the cleaning crew together, clearing out the city over the winter. Now they're doing this." She turns her green eyes my way, giving me a serious look. "You can trust him. Out of everyone here, Jim is someone I would trust my life with."

"What about Corinne?" I ask, glancing back toward Jim and Jon. "She's the leader and you seem friendly with her."

Ginny purses her lips for a second. "Yes and no. I think she's doing her best, but there are going to be times when she will put herself first. Like with this Dax thing. She has to know he's going to be a huge pain in the ass out there on the road, but she chose him to lead the group because it will get him off her back."

"But Jim won't put himself first?"

Ginny shakes her head. "Not like that. He'd never run away from a fight, and if he makes a promise, he'll keep it."

Jon and Jim stop in front of us, and the new guy looks us all over for a few seconds before his gaze settles on Angus. "So you're the guy?"

"The very one," Angus says, narrowing his eyes on the blond man in front of him.

"This is Jim," Jon says, nodding toward his partner.

Jim pulls the cigarette out of his mouth and grins. "Nice to meet you folks. I've heard lots of stuff about the group Jon used to be with. Asshole never shuts up."

Jon chuckles and introduces the rest of us and gives Jim some backstory, keeping the details about how we all actually met so brief anyone would be stupid not to realize he's leaving things out. Jim barely bats an eye though, and I get the sense he already has a good idea of what went down. It seems odd that Jon would tell anyone—I know how bad he feels about what happened at the Monte Carlo—but if these two really have been working together for months, it makes sense that they'd know a little bit about each other.

We're in the middle of talking when a voice booms through the air, cutting our conversation short. "Hey there!"

We all look up, but none of us even crack a smile when we catch sight of Dax jogging our way. Like Jim and Jon, he's dressed in leather, but unlike the other two men, he doesn't seem to be dirty. Guess he's been barking off orders instead of pitching in. It goes in line with what Jim and Jon have told us, so it shouldn't be surprising.

"You out exploring our town?" Dax asks when he stops in front of us, his eyes focused on me.

"We came by to pitch in," Axl says.

Dax barely glances his way. "No need. As you can see, we have it covered." He finally tears his eyes off me when he turns to face the fence being constructed. "She's a beauty, isn't she?"

"Sure does look strong," Angus says.

Dax nods a couple times before turning back to face us, this time his eyes on Angus. "She is. Atlanta had the idea, but we're adding some extra reinforcement just to be sure.

I like everything secure. Like with the bus and truck we'll be taking when we head out. Steel plates welded to the side windows to keep us safe. No zombies will be able to reach in grab you that way."

He glances my way again and winks, his grin growing wider. It sends a shiver through me because it looks so unnatural. Like a clown who's had his smile painted on. No one acts this way for real. There has to be something very off about a person to make them feel like they need to always be smiling.

"The steel plates won't stop bullets," Axl points out, drawing Dax's attention his way.

"Bullets?" Dax snorts. "Good thing zombies can't fire guns. With the way we're going to be decked out, zoms are the only things out there dumb enough to try and take us down. Any men we come across will be too intimidated. Trust me."

"You can't be serious," I say before I have a chance to think better of it.

Something flashes in Dax's eyes, but it's gone in a second, replaced once again by a smile. "Sure I am. I know there are dangerous people out there, but they are going to be looking for small, vulnerable groups to attack. Not a group like ours. We're going to be armed and tucked inside our vehicles. We'll be too secure. They'd be fools to try anything."

"Don't know 'bout that," Angus says. "I think we'd be the fools to believe nothin' could touch us."

Dax chuckles. "You guys have been out there too long. Trust me. Anyone we cross paths with will be running to hide."

Parv snorts, while Axl and Angus trade a look that I can read from a mile away: Dax is a moron. Jim, Jon and Ginny stand off to the side, saying nothing but obviously thinking the same thing as the rest of us. If we weren't such a prepared group, I'd be concerned. But we are and we've been here before, and we'll come together. As for Dax and his men... We've warned them. It's going to be up to them to listen to us, because there isn't a doubt in my mind that we're going to run into trouble of some kind.

"Okay..." Dax looks back over his shoulder toward the fence. "Have to get back to work. As for your earlier question, it looks like we'll be heading out early next week. We're planning on getting together tomorrow morning to take care of a few last-minute details. And we're going to give Atlanta a call. Let them in on the plan as well."

"Sounds good," Axl says. "Keep us in the loop."

Dax looks back long enough to flash us yet another smile, but this one is so tight that it looks more like he's in pain. "Of course."

CHAPTER SIX

"Asshole," Angus growls as we head down the street. Away from the fence. "Once we leave, that guy's gonna learn pretty fast who's in charge."

Damn. I can just picture our two day trip across the country: Angus and Dax at each other's throats the whole time. The rest of us choosing sides. It's going to put us all in danger and they have to know it, but anyone can see that's how it's going to be. Angus doesn't take orders, and Dax just loves to dish them out.

"I don't know," I say, shaking my head. "I think with a guy like that it's better to fly under the radar. Do what he says until we absolutely need to rock the boat. If every step of the way is a fight, it's going to make it that much harder when something serious comes up."

"She's got a point," Axl says. "No reason we can't let him think he's in charge. Long as it ain't gonna put nobody at risk."

Angus stops walking and purses his lips, staring at his brother. "So you want me to just sit back and do what that asshole tells me to?"

"At the most, all he's going to tell you to do is sit back and stay out of the way," Ginny points out. "He wants to keep you safe, and for some reason he thinks he's the only thing standing between you and a horde of the undead. It's not going to hurt you to just stay out of the way."

She has a good point, but I know there's no way in hell Angus will be able to sit back if Dax is doing something idiotic that might get the rest of us killed.

"As long as Dax doesn't do anything to endanger the rest of us," I point out.

"Right," Ginny says, nodding.

"Shit." Angus spits, and even though it doesn't come anywhere near her, Hadley glares at him. "I hate doin' it, but you got a point. I'll let that prick think he's in charge long as I can. But I can't promise we're gonna make it all the way to Atlanta without me kickin' his ass."

Ginny pats him on the arm and smiles, the spit obviously forgotten. "I don't think anyone would expect that much self control out of you."

Angus chuckles.

We're still several houses away from Jon and Ginny's place when I spot Sophia sitting on her front porch. In front of her, Max and Ava play with a set of blocks that are probably way too young for the older boy. Of course, after everything we've been through and all the people we've lost, the poor kid might not care what he has to play with as long as he's safe.

"I want to check in on Sophia," I say, jogging toward the porch.

She looks up when I'm still a good distance off, but the expression in her eyes almost makes me freeze. It reminds me so much of the first day we met. Back in San Francisco when the death of her husband was still new and the grief still raw. She looks older now—months of stress will do that to a person—and her dark hair is longer. Back then it was cut short, almost like a boy's, but now it's so long it hangs almost to her chin. Other than that, though, she looks exactly like the woman who walked into our suite with Winston and his group.

"What?" Sophia asks when I don't say anything.

I shake my head and force my legs to keep moving. "Nothing. I was just remembering the day we met. At the hotel in San Francisco. We were all so scared and unsure."

Sophia gives me a sad smile. "There are so few of us left now."

She's right. We lost Mike first, before we even made it to the Mojave Desert, then Trey in Vegas. Arthur was killed in the shelter when those assholes from the Monte Carlo had us cornered. He sacrificed himself to save us, and even though he was sick and didn't have much time left, it was still a big loss. Then Jess and Winston and so many other people we picked up along the way.

"We've been through so much together," Sophia says, her eyes on the two children playing in front of her. "It's hard thinking about saying goodbye, but I know it's the right thing to do. The world is too uncertain. Even if Atlanta is safe, there's so much open road between here and there, and we have no idea what to expect."

"No one blames you for deciding to stay, Sophia. You have to do what's best for you and Ava."

She smiles. "No, but Joshua is having a hard time accepting it. It's more about Anne, I know, but the whole idea of walking away is hard on him."

I nod, and behind me, footsteps come up the porch stairs. Sophia looks up and smiles when Ginny moves over to sit next to her. I stay where I am on the stairs, watching the kids play. Angus and Parv keep walking—most likely because they're still smoking and the kids are on the porch—but Axl stops at my side. I lean into him, feeling the warmth of his body spread through me even though it isn't cold anymore. Just chilly. But it won't be for long. Soon we'll be in

Atlanta and summer will settle in, bringing with it the suffocating humidity. But also joy, because it will mean we made it through the worst of it. Through the chaos and confusion.

Too bad Sophia and Anne and the kids will still be here.

"Where are Anne and Joshua?" I ask after a few seconds of silence.

"Inside." Sophia shakes her head. "He thinks he can change her mind, but he's wasting his time. She doesn't have it in her. There's no more fight left. Here we can at least pretend life is normal—assuming nothing changes."

"On the road it would be too uncertain," I say, trying to reassure her that we get where she's coming from even if Joshua is having a tough time. "We understand."

"He doesn't."

"I'm sure it's hard to say goodbye," Ginny says, patting Sophia's leg. "But he will be okay."

"You think he's gonna decide not to go?" Axl asks.

Sophia looks up, but shakes her head. "No. He said you guys need him. Here they have doctors already, and he doesn't want to send you out there without him."

I stand up straight, realization slamming into me. "Wait? Are you saying he doesn't want to go?"

Joshua never mentioned it before, but we didn't exactly ask him either. We just assumed he would be coming with us. Is it unfair of us to drag him across the country when he might have ties here?

"He wants to keep the group together," Sophia says firmly.

"But it isn't..." My words hang in the air, but no one responds to them. No one tries to reassure me that we're doing the right thing by Joshua.

We obviously have to talk to him about the whole thing.

As if on cue, Joshua comes out of the house, practically running. He slams the door behind him, and all of us jump. No one moves, not even when Joshua turns to face us. His face is bright red, but not as red as his eyes.

"I didn't know you were out here," he says, moving his gaze to the ground.

"Everything okay?" Ginny asks.

Joshua doesn't look up. "Perfect."

"We were just talking about you," I say. "I wanted to make sure you were up for this trip. You don't have to go to Atlanta with us, you know. There's no reason you can't stay."

Joshua shakes his head as he steps over the kids, heading for the porch stairs. Not glancing my way. "There's nothing for me here."

He jogs down the stairs and takes off, but not toward our house. I don't know where he's going, but I guess he needs to be alone. Whatever he and Anne talked about, it must not have been good.

"Poor Joshua," Sophia whispers as we all watch him head off.

"There you all are!" Al yells from behind me.

I pull away from Axl as the teens head our way.

"Thought you two would be rollin' 'round in the nude," Angus calls from down the street.

He drops his cigarette to the ground before heading over. I get the feeling that he suffers from fear of missing out these days. Parv follows Angus, but at a much slower pace. And she doesn't put out her cigarette.

"Shut up," Lila says to Angus, but there's no venom in it.

"We had a productive day," Al says, grinning as always. "On all accounts."

Lila rolls her eyes. "Don't listen to him. We went to a bookstore that was covered in dust and dug through books about zombies. It was a huge waste of time."

"You call this a waste of time!" Al scoffs and holds up a couple books.

I take the top one and study it. There are a couple creatures on the front that I'm assuming are supposed to be zombies but look nothing like the real thing, and behind them stands a group of people decked out in army gear and loaded down with weapons. I guess they're supposed to be the survivors, but I can tell the author from experience they wouldn't be quite as excited as these models seem.

I roll my eyes and hand the book back to Al. "I hate to say it, but I'm with Lila on this one."

"Not that book," Al says, letting out an exasperated sigh. He flips through the books for a second before finding the one he was looking for and shoving it in my face. "This one."

I jerk my head back so I can get a good look at it. "*Surviving the Zombie Apocalypse*." My gaze moves past it to Al, and I have to try really hard not to roll my eyes. "Seriously?"

I know he's had a few good ideas from books in the past, but in case he hasn't noticed, we've already survived the zombie apocalypse. We're more qualified to write that book than the author was. By a long shot.

"I know it sounds crazy, but there are actually a few really cool survival tricks in here," Al says, flipping through the books. "Like common plants that are edible, first aid tips when you're on the run, and even simple ways to start a fire. They're little things, but they're also things that would be useful if we lost all of our supplies or somehow got separated from the rest of the group."

He has a point. Again.

"Lemme see that," Angus says, ripping the book out of Al's hand.

He turns it over and reads the back, snorting every few seconds. When he's done, he flips through it a little, but it's obvious he thinks the whole thing is stupid.

"There's useful stuff inside," Al says defensively.

"Sure there is." Angus tosses the book back. "Too much readin' for me. I'll stick to what I know."

Since I've caught him reading, I'm guessing Angus thinks the book is a waste of time and just doesn't want to hurt Al's feelings. Or show that he has some of his own.

"I'll read it," Al mutters.

"When you find useful things, mark the page," I say. "I believe you."

Angus snort, and no one else seems to be the least big interested. Even though I don't know if it's going to help, it won't hurt us, and it will give Al something to do. We're seriously short on things to keep us occupied these days.

I ROLL OVER TO AN EMPTY BED, AS USUAL. AXL'S always up before me, but there's something about this that feels wrong. We've gotten too used to the safety of fences and walls. Too complacent about our relationship. It's like we've been floating through life lately, and we can't keep going on like this. Especially not when we're about to head out to Atlanta.

I roll out of bed, yawning even though I feel rested. That's one good thing about doing nothing the past few days. I feel like I've finally caught up on all the sleep I've lost since this whole thing started.

The aroma of coffee hits me when I open the bedroom door, and I head straight for the kitchen. I've only made it a few steps when Axl's voice causes my ears to perk up. A few seconds later, it's followed by Ginny's, which makes me freeze altogether. I don't want to interrupt them when they're finally talking this whole thing out. It's too tense, and I'm over it, especially when we're going to be saying goodbye to Ginny in a couple days. I want to be able to enjoy the few days we have left.

"I just—I thought we should talk about it," Ginny says. "I wanted to explain."

"I didn't tell her," Axl says. "You don't gotta worry 'bout that."

Tell who *what*? Me? What does this whole thing have to do with *me*?

"Why?" Ginny's voice shakes, and I have the urge to hug her. But I know they're talking, and I know they need to. Need to get all this out in the open so they can move on. Plus, I'm even more curious than before.

"'Cause it didn't mean nothin'," Axl says, "and there's no point in upsettin' anybody over nothin'."

"It didn't. That's what I wanted you to know. It didn't mean anything." Ginny pauses, and I hear her take a deep breath. "I was scared. That's all it was."

"I know," Axl says firmly. "Never thought it was anythin' else."

Ginny clears her throat. "I'm going to tell her. I just have to figure out a good time. Do you think she'll forgive me?"

"'Course she will. Vivian ain't petty, and she's gonna understand." Now Axl's voice is soft like he's trying to comfort Ginny. I'm glad. They used to get along. Used to like each other, and I want it to be that way again.

"Good," Ginny says. "Because I couldn't live with myself if I didn't tell her the truth."

I wait for them to say more. To explain what happened and what all this tension has been about. To give me a heads up on what I can expect. Nothing happens, though. There are footsteps, and cabinets open. There's a clink of metal against ceramic like someone is stirring a cup of coffee. That's it, though. No conversation. Nothing to tell me what all this has been about.

After a few seconds, I give up and head for the kitchen. So Ginny has something she wants to tell me. So what? I don't know what it is, but I do know I will give her the chance to explain. It's only fair. We don't have much time left together, after all.

"Morning," I say, forcing out a yawn as I head into the kitchen. Acting like I didn't hear a thing.

Ginny's eyes get huge. "Hi!" she says, her voice high. Like she's going through puberty, not about to have a baby.

I freeze. "Are you okay?"

"Fine," she says, shaking her head. "Coffee?"

She turns away, and when I glance at Axl, he isn't looking at me either. It's a little weird, considering they were just talking about *me*, but maybe Ginny isn't ready to talk about it. She did just work things out with Axl. She may need more time before she talks to me about whatever happened.

"Here you go," Ginny says, flashing me a huge—and forced—smile when she turns back around with a cup of coffee in her hand.

"Thanks," I say, returning her fake smile.

I take a sip, savoring the hot liquid like it might be my last cup of coffee ever. Which it could. There are a lot of things we may not be able to start making again any time soon. Even if Atlanta and a few other places are back on their feet, we don't have coffee beans. It's all going to take time.

"We excited about this meeting?" I ask, smiling over my coffee.

Axl shakes his head. "Excited ain't the word I was gonna use." He glances toward the clock. "We got an hour before it starts, but I'm gonna head out now. Talk to Angus and figure out what we're gonna do 'bout this whole thing. I want all of us there, too, so I better give everybody a heads up."

"Okay," I whisper. "I'll get dressed and head your way in a little bit."

Axl nods. He downs the rest of his coffee as he crosses the room, setting the mug in the sink when it's empty. On his way back out, he pauses long enough to kiss me on the side of the head, but it's half-hearted. An afterthought rather than a necessity.

He heads out of the kitchen, his footsteps pounding across the floor on the way to the front door.

"What's going on?" Ginny says the second the door has shut.

"What do you mean?" I ask even though the nagging thought that met me when I first woke up this morning hasn't gone away.

"Something's bugging you."

There's fear in her eyes, but I don't know why she's scared, and I don't have it in me to figure it out right now. Not when I'm thinking about what I want to say to Axl.

I put my cup down and let out a deep sigh. "We've gotten too comfortable, which would be fine if we were a normal couple and these were normal times. But they're not, and we're getting ready to go back out there. We need to remember how dangerous it is."

"You need to talk to him. To clear things up so you aren't stressed when you head out there. You want to be confident. Right?"

"Right."

"Then you need to talk to him," Ginny says. "Today. Don't wait. Get it all out in the open so you can figure out what's going on. Tell him how you feel."

She's right. I can't wait any longer. Life isn't going to get less stressful any time soon.

CHAPTER SEVEN

The office is even more crowded than the first time we were here, but this time Axl doesn't settle for hanging out in the hall. He pushes his way through the group of men shoved into the small space, his hand wrapped firmly around mine as he goes. Angus is behind us, but he's the only one who follows.

Elbows and arms knock into me, but I keep pace with Axl. We're going out there, so we want to be in on the planning. It isn't just about not trusting Dax, either. We're used to calling the shots for our group, and there's no way in hell we're going to cross a zombie-infested country without knowing what we can expect from these men. Men who are definitely not interested in having us along and will most likely sacrifice our lives if it comes down to it.

"Watch it," a big man growls when Axl pushes him aside.

He doesn't bat an eye, and he doesn't slow.

We finally make it through the crowd, and the desk comes into view. On it sits the ham radio, and in the chair,

Corinne is leaning forward. Adjusting the dials with her eyes focused straight ahead. Behind her, Dax looms like he's ready to shove her aside so he can take over. When he looks up, his gaze meets mine. At the moment, his usual smile is gone, and with the way he's standing, I can't help thinking of a statue of some evil dictator who slaughtered half his country during a takeover. Someone who doesn't have an ounce of sympathy for others or value human life outside his own. It sends a shiver shooting through me, and every hair on my body tingles as it stands on end. This guy is even more trouble than we originally thought.

"We're just getting through to Atlanta," he says, his tone strong and cool.

I nod and step closer to Axl.

"You don't have to be here." Dax's gaze moves from me to Axl, then over to Angus. "You don't need to be concerned. You are our number one priority."

"If you think I'm gonna let you folks drag me out there without knowin' what the hell to expect, you're outta your damn mind." Angus shakes his head and crosses his arms, glaring Dax's way. "I don't doubt that you wanna get me to Atlanta in one piece, but I'm gonna make sure I know what I'm in for."

Dax frowns, but before he can say anything, a voice crackles through the air. All around us, a hush falls over the crowd, and in the chair, Corinne sits up straighter.

"This is Major Hendrix, over."

"Major Hendrix," Corinne says into the receiver. "This is Hope Springs. We're calling to let you know we have a group together, and they'll be heading your way at the beginning of next week. Over."

"Why next week?" the man on the other end says. "Why not earlier? Over."

Corinne lifts her head and looks around, her eyes landing on Angus. "We need time to prepare. Over."

Dax shifts behind Corinne, and her shoulders slump forward. Almost like she's trying to keep her distance. I study them as Corinne continues her conversation with the man out in Atlanta. The way she shies away from the big man behind her, how her eyes cloud over whenever Dax makes a sound. We were right. Corinne is trying to get rid of him. He's threatened her position in the past, and he won't stop. She knows it, so she's sending him away. He may know it too, which doesn't bode well for our trip. It concerns me that this man would be in charge of getting us across the country. Sure, he'll keep Angus alive, but he doesn't give a shit about the rest of us.

The big man's eyes narrow on the back of Corinne's head, and Axl swears, shaking his head.

"You okay?" I whisper.

"This dude is dangerous."

Axl's voice is low, but we're packed in so tight that I'm worried someone will hear us, so I take his hand and pull him with me as I push my way back through the crowd. Angus glances our way, but he doesn't move. Good. I want him to stay so he can find out what the plan is, but I want to be able to discuss this whole thing with Axl now. Before things get out of hand or we lose control of this situation.

We make it into the hall, and the crowd thins out. It's cooler, and the air is fresher. I hadn't realized how stuffy it was in the packed office until now.

Across the hall, Jon, Ginny, Parvarti, Lila, and Al stand, talking.

"I hadn't thought of it before," Lila says, shaking her head. "But Jon could be right."

"Right about what?" I ask when we stop in front of the group.

Al holds up his stump. "The bite. Jon brought something up I hadn't thought of before. What if I'm immune to this thing? What if cutting my arm off didn't do a thing to stop the virus?"

All thoughts of Dax and Atlanta disappear, and suddenly all I can think about is the day Al was bitten. About holding his good hand while Joshua tortured the poor kid by cutting his arm off. Lila crying. All the blood. How weak he was for weeks after that. There were times when I was sure he was going to die, and Jon is absolutely right. It all could have been for nothing.

"It can't be..." I shake my head, and I want to look around at everyone else so I can figure out what they're thinking, but at the moment, all I can do is stare at Al's stump.

"Don't bring it up to Joshua," Al says, and I finally pull my gaze away from what's left of his arm. "We didn't know it was even possible, so we did what we had to do. The doc is going through enough shit right now, he doesn't need this thrown on top of it all." Al grins and glances toward Lila. "Plus, chicks dig scars."

The other teen rolls her eyes. "Please."

Al just chuckles and wraps his good arm around her.

"What's going on in there?" Jon asks, nodding toward the crowded office at our backs.

"Just talkin' to Atlanta 'bout us comin'," Axl says, but shoves his hand through his hair. "I gotta tell you though, that asshole has got me worried."

"Dax?" Ginny whispers, her eyes darting to the door behind us.

I glance back, but no one is paying attention to us. They're all still focused on whatever Corinne is talking to the guy in Atlanta about.

"Yeah," Axl says. "He's got an ego bigger than I've ever seen. I'm worried he's gonna put us all in danger."

"Do you think Corinne would put someone else in charge?" I ask, focusing on Ginny. She seems to know the leader of this group pretty well, and it's possible she might have some pull when it comes to Corinne. "If we asked her, that is."

Ginny exhales. "I don't think so."

"Because she wants to get him off her back," I say flatly.

Ginny nods, and around me, everyone else shuffles. When I glance toward Lila and Al, I can tell the reality of what we are about to face hits them. We aren't afraid to go out there. We've been on the road before. Spent weeks just wandering, looking for somewhere safe that might not even exist. We survived. But we did it together. We worked as more than a team. We were a family—still are—and if we have to do it all again, we can. But the idea of being out there with someone who isn't on our team…that's the scary part. That's the part that will get one or more of us killed.

Before anyone has had a chance to say something else, the crowd begins to break up. Men pass, glancing our way, their eyes narrowed and suspicious. It's like they think we're plotting to run off and take Angus with us, when all we really want to do is be with him and be part of the group that will keep him safe. We are definitely the outsiders, and it's obvious by the hostility radiating off everyone in this group.

Axl heads for the door when the room has mostly cleared. I'm right behind him, and at my back, the others follow as well. Inside, Corinne, Dax, Angus, and another man I don't know are crowded around the desk. In the corner, Jim stands with his arms crossed over his chest. So still and silent I'm not even sure if the others know he's there. But he's watching. Waiting to find out what's going on.

The new guy is as dark as Corinne and almost as big as Dax but even more muscular.

"This is Donovan," Dax says when we stop in front of them. "He's kind of my second in command. Unofficially, of course." Dax shoots a look at Corinne that is cloaked in hostility, but she doesn't even blink.

"Atlanta is all ready for you," she says instead of responding to Dax's comment. She has the best poker face I've ever seen.

"So we leave Monday?" I ask.

It's Wednesday, which gives us less than a week. I'm torn over the news. On one hand, I'm ready to be on the road and get this over with. On the other hand, I don't feel prepared. It doesn't seem like enough time to plan such a long trip.

"Monday," Dax says firmly. "It will probably take us two

days, which means in just a week we'll be safe and sound in Atlanta."

"Two days?" Al says doubtfully.

"It took us weeks to get from Vegas to Colorado." Parvarti shakes her head. "Two days seems optimistic."

"Weeks?" Dax snorts. "You guys sure know how to drag your feet."

None of us moves as the tension that already surrounded our group mounts and expands, filling the empty space around us.

"We didn't drag our feet," Axl says through clenched teeth. "We worked our asses off, but the world has gone to shit."

Dax shakes his head. "Well, we're prepared. It will be fine. Even if we run into a horde, all we'll have to do is run them down."

"You can run a small horde down," I say, "but when there are hundreds, it's a little harder."

"Hundreds?" Corinne's eyes are huge as she looks us over. "You've seen hundreds?"

"Of course they haven't," Dax says, waving her worries off. "These things are dead. They don't have the ability to think, and they don't travel in packs like dogs. They walk in circles. I've seen it. I've been out there just as much as they have."

"I think you're underestimating the risks," I say, trying again. Hoping he'll listen to reason.

"I think you all have been out there for too long." Dax shoves himself off the desk. "I have things to do if we want to leave on Monday."

He doesn't give us a second look as he heads for the door, and none of us speak. Not even after he's disappeared. We just stand there in silence, each of us no doubt going through a list of things that could go wrong. It's a long list, too.

"Have you seen hundreds?" Corinne asks, finally breaking the silence.

I turn to face her, holding her gaze. "I wouldn't have said

it if we hadn't."

Corinne exhales.

"We gotta talk 'bout this guy," Axl says. "He's dangerous."

"I know." She doesn't even try to cushion the blow. "But he's more dangerous here. Out there you'll be safe in the bus, and then you'll be in Atlanta and they can worry about controlling Dax. I don't want him here. Not anymore. He's risking everything we've worked to build." Corinne gets to her feet like the matter has been settled.

Before she can get anywhere, Axl steps in front of her. "You can't send him out there with us. We gotta get Angus to Atlanta in one piece, and that asshole is gonna put us all at risk."

"It's already been decided," Corinne says firmly. She straightens up even more, emphasizing her height. She's almost as tall as Axl and very imposing for such a soft-spoken woman. "Dax will get you there. It's his mission, and he takes it very seriously."

Axl swears and shakes his head, and Al and Lila glare at Corinne. I'm not thrilled with her either, but I don't bother with the dirty looks. We aren't going to get rid of Dax, which means we need to be sure we're covered out there. And that we know what to expect once we get to Atlanta.

"What's the word from Atlanta?" I ask.

Corinne turns my way, her eyes moving over me like she's looking at me for the first time. "They're ready, as I said."

"That's not what I mean and you know it. What can Angus expect when he gets there? We've been assured that all of this is up to him, and I want to make sure they understand that."

"They know Angus is doing this of his own free will, and they've promised that he won't be a prisoner." She glances toward the man in question. "However, he will have to live at the CDC. They want to make sure he's safe. The city is secure, but things are still precarious. As you know. They feel it will be safer for him to live close to the lab."

"You okay with that?" Axl asks his brother.

"Long as they don't try an' stop me from smokin', I don't give a shit."

"That's something you'll have to take up with them," Corinne says.

"What else is going on out there?" Ginny asks. "It's been a while since I was in on the calls."

Corinne exhales and leans against the desk. "They've made more progress on the new antibiotics. It seems that when this virus was released, it didn't just start the zombie apocalypse. Something about it has mutated even simple infections, making them stronger. Resistant to a lot of the drugs we had before all this. The CDC has been working to fix that."

"Wow," I say, shaking my head. Thinking of Jake and how fast his illness took him. Maybe it wouldn't have mattered if we'd gotten the antibiotics sooner. He might have died anyway.

"Yes." Corinne nods once, then glances at Ginny. "They've also managed to keep a second baby alive. Just like the first, it got sick shortly after birth but responded well to the antibiotics."

Ginny stands up straight, dropping Jon's hand. "So there's a chance?"

"We don't have the same antibiotics," Corinne says slowly.

Ginny nods and glances my way. I can see the wheels turning in her head. She's still thinking about going. Jon is going to flip out. I don't know how Corinne will react, but Dax will definitely be pissed. Not that I think he'd have the final say in whether or not Ginny goes with us, but it sure as hell will put him in a pissy mood.

"Now," Corinne says, standing again, "if you don't mind, I'm going to head out. I have a few things to discuss with the council before I head to dinner."

We murmur our goodbyes as Corinne leaves, silence once again falling over us. It isn't until she's gone that Jim uncrosses his arms and heads our way. I'd forgotten he was here.

"What do you think?" Jon asks, turning to face his partner.

"Dax is on a power trip and all Corinne wants at this point is to get him off her back. She doesn't give a shit whether or not your friend makes it to Atlanta. Not as long as he takes Dax with him when he goes."

Axl purses his lips as he stares at the floor, not saying a word.

"What are you thinking?" Jon asks.

"Maybe we should back out," Axl mutters. "This thing is too messed up."

"You do that and Dax could do something even more dangerous," Jim says. "No. I think you need to stick with this. You'll be fine because you've got two things going for you. One, you're aware of the problem."

Axl looks up. "What's the second thing?"

"You know how to defend yourself."

Axl nods slowly, then glances toward his brother. "What'd you think?"

"I think we gotta go. We owe this to the world and we got no other option." He grins. "Plus, I was really lookin' forward to bein' a hero."

"Fine," Axl says, but he shakes his head. He obviously doesn't share his brother's positive attitude. "We gotta watch each other's backs, though."

"You'll be fine," Jim replies. "Don't need to worry about that."

He slaps Axl on the back and gives Jon a nod before heading for the door.

I exhale, taking a look around the office for the first time. My gaze lands on the framed picture of a blonde woman, and before I've even thought about it, I'm crossing the room.

"What's wrong?" Ginny asks.

"This is Kristine," I say, picking the picture up.

"Who?" Axl asks.

I'm not looking at him or the picture in my hand. I'm looking around, at the other pictures and the diplomas hanging on the wall. At the name printed on them. *Brady Sanford.* It's strange that of all the offices on campus, this would be the one we'd find ourselves in.

"This was Brady's office," I say, putting the picture back down. "This is his wife. Was his wife."

"Weird," Ginny says. "I've spent hours in here, staring at the pictures and diplomas. Imagining what he was like. I never thought I'd actually meet the man who used to work here. I figured he was dead."

"I think a part of him is," I say, turning away from Kristine when a shiver moves through me. "He lost his wife and his unborn baby. I think a part of him is buried with her. That's why he couldn't leave."

"How sad," Ginny says, rubbing her hand across her round stomach.

Jon slips his arm around her, and Lila curls into Al's side. My eyes meet Axl's, and I know I need to talk to him now. We've been floating lately, and it has to stop. It isn't that we love each other less, but just that we've gotten too comfortable.

CHAPTER EIGHT

"Axl," I say, grabbing his arm. "We need to talk."

Ginny glances back, but she seems to be the only one who notices when we don't follow them out of the office. Her gaze moves from Axl then back to me, looking oddly terrified. Only I'm not sure what she'd be scared of. Maybe she's just worried for me? But things with Axl and I aren't that bad. We've just gotten too comfortable. Right?

When we're alone, I turn to face Axl, taking a deep breath. "This thing has been between us for months, but we haven't dealt with it. You know what I'm talking about, right?"

He nods, but doesn't meet my gaze. "I do."

It's odd, but for some reason, I can feel him shutting down, and it reminds me of the way he was back in the basement after Angus was bitten. Something about it scares me more than facing a horde of the undead ever has. This is the Axl I don't know how to deal with. He's too much the old Axl. The one who pointed a gun at me the day we met on Route 66. The one who did his brother's bidding, who took

Angus's side even when he knew it was wrong. This is someone I thought had disappeared but who obviously hasn't. Not totally.

"Axl," I say, stepping forward. Taking his hand. "Look at me. Tell me what you're thinking."

"You tell me," he says, his voice gruff.

I do the only thing I know to do. I swallow the lump in my throat and take a deep breath, then dive in. "We've been floating for the past few months. I don't know why, but I know I should have talked to you sooner. I think we've gotten too comfortable. We found a safe place and were trying to start over, and even though I could feel this distance growing between us, I didn't want to bring it up. I didn't want to face it because for once I wanted to believe we had all the time in the world to deal with it. That we were finally safe and things were finally good and we could deal with it down the road when life was easier. Only now I know that isn't true."

"I ain't sure it's ever gonna be true," he says, and the pain in his eyes makes me ache for him. He takes on too much. Always blames himself for too much, and I hate that he does that.

"I'm sorry," I say, taking his hand. "We should have talked about this all before, but you have to know that nothing has changed when it comes to how I feel about you. We've just been going through the motions, but we can't do that now. Not when we're about to go out there again." I step closer to Axl, taking his face between my hands. "I'm sorry for how things have been for the past few months. I let a wall build up between us, and I don't want to do that anymore. Whether we're behind a fence or on the road, I want us to live every day like it's the last moment we're going to have together. Which means making love every chance we get."

Axl's hands move up my back, and he pulls me closer, his lips pressing against mine. When he pulls back, he says, "I'm sorry too. I shoulda remembered to fight for you."

"Always fight for me," I say against his lips, kissing him harder.

Axl's mouth moves faster over mine, and his hands slide up my back. Under my shirt. Seconds later, he has my bra undone. Then his hands move around to cup my breasts, and our kissing becomes more frantic. Like the way it used to be. Back when we only had minutes alone.

I've missed this feeling. Knowing I had someone who would always be there for me.

"I love you," I say again. I want to say it every day. I don't want a day to go by when those words don't cross my lips.

"I love you," Axl replies.

I work on his zipper while his hands move to mine, and then we're both shoving our clothes off. We end up on the floor, and our lips never stop moving. With each tangle of our tongues, my body heat increases. It seems to only take seconds before all our clothes are off, and then Axl's hands are moving over my body. It reminds me of when we were first together, how he couldn't get enough of me. How he took his time, exploring every inch of my body in the safety of that shelter. Like he needed me to live.

"I missed you," I say, wrapping my legs around him. Pulling him closer to me. Feeling his warmth on every inch of my skin.

"I shoulda talked to you sooner." His lips move down my neck to my chest. "Shoulda done this."

We move together, unconcerned about the hard floor or the fact that someone could walk in at any moment. Only concerned with *now*. With being together and savoring this moment, because it could be our last. Anything could happen, and I refuse to let a distance like this build up between us again.

When Axl finally collapses on top of me, we're both sweating and panting. Our hearts beating together like we're one person.

"Shoulda done that months ago," Axl says, rolling off me.

He pulls me against him, and I lay my head on his chest. We're both naked and in the middle of the office floor, but I don't care if the whole town comes in right now. I just want to stay here where I'm warm and safe and comfortable. With Axl. Just the two of us.

"You okay?" Axl says when I don't respond.

"I'm scared," I say, squeezing my eyes shut. Feeling like a coward or a child. I'm not sure which one. "I know we can do this. I know we can make it to Atlanta. I just don't know if we can *all* make it, and I'm scared of losing more people. Especially you. I've seen what that kind of loss has done to people. Parvarti is practically a robot, and Winston let it destroy him. Anne is a shell. I'm not sure I'd do much better."

Axl's hand moves across my forehead, pushing the sweaty hair out of my face. "You would. You're stronger than them. You been through more."

"I don't know if that's true."

"It is," he says, his lips brushing my cheek. "Plus, I'm gonna make you promise."

I open my eyes and twist to face him. "Promise what?"

Axl's gray eyes hold mine, and he takes a deep breath. Blowing it out as he brushes the hair off my forehead and out of my eyes. "Promise me that you won't give up. That if somethin' happens to me out there, you'll keep movin' forward. I hate thinkin' you'd end up like Parv or Winston. That ain't you."

"What about you?" I ask. "Would you be able to keep going?"

"I would." He exhales. "I'd do it even if I didn't want to. 'Cause givin' up ain't in me."

He's right. I can't see Axl giving up on anything. Even if it kills him to keep putting one foot in front of the other, he'd do it. It hurts a little, thinking that he'd fare better than I would, but I'm also glad. I don't want to think about him giving up.

Just like he wouldn't want me to throw my life away.

"Okay." My eyes fill with tears, but I wipe them away. "I'll keep going. For you."

I lay my head on Axl's chest, and his arms tighten around me. It helps hold off the sobs that are trying to force their way out of me, but just barely.

"Good," Axl says. "I ain't plannin' on goin' nowhere, but I wanna know you'll be okay if somethin' does happen."

I nod, but I don't bother pointing out the fact that I never promised to be okay. Not giving up and being okay are two very different things, and I know for sure that I definitely would not be okay if something happened to Axl.

IT'S AFTERNOON BY THE TIME AXL AND I MAKE IT home. Ginny must have been waiting for us, because the second we open the door she jumps to her feet.

"You're back." Her eyes move to Axl then back to me. "Is everything okay?"

"It's fine." I give Axl's hand a squeeze. "We worked it all out."

She nods a few times, but I get the impression that she isn't really thinking about my relationship problems. Especially when her hand moves across her stomach.

"Are you okay?" I ask hesitantly.

"I am. But I need to talk to Jon and I want you to back me up. It's about the baby, and Atlanta. We have to go."

"What?" Axl looks back and forth between us.

"I don't know if that's a good idea," I say, shaking my head.

"You heard Corinne. They have the drugs and everything else they need to keep this baby alive. I'm going. I've already made up my mind. Either it's with your group or on my own. It would just be a lot safer with the group."

I glance toward Axl, and he frowns. I understand how he feels, but I also understand Ginny's worries. And I think I'd be feeling the same thing. Thinking the same thing. With all the babies that have died here, it doesn't seem like hers stands a chance unless she's in Atlanta. It might be the only way.

"We're already going," I say, holding Axl's gaze. Trying to make him understand. "It makes sense."

He shakes his head. "Seems irresponsible."

I ignore him and turn to Ginny. "Where's Jon?"

"Kitchen," she says, jerking her head behind her.

"I don't know if my opinion will matter, but I'll be here to support you at least."

Ginny lets out a shaky breath. "Thank you."

We head into the kitchen, but Axl hangs back like he doesn't want to be a part of it. He'd be against the trip if the situation was reversed, or at least he thinks he would. He always puts me first, and that's all he can think about right now, but if we had a baby on the way… I think he'd see things differently.

"Hey," Jon says when we walk into the kitchen. "Everything okay? You and Axl were gone a long time."

"They were having sex," Ginny says.

Jon's eyebrows shoot up. "Okay. You know you can do that here, right? We're okay with it."

"That wasn't what it was about," I say, shooting Ginny a look.

"Sorry," she says. "I don't get nervous often, but when I do I babble."

Jon frowns. "What are you nervous about?"

Ginny swallows and wrings her hands over her stomach. Still, she doesn't talk right away, and she has to keep swallowing. It's like the words are trying to come out on their own and she's having a hard time keeping them in. Only I didn't think she wanted to keep them in. I thought she wanted to tell Jon they were going to Atlanta so it was all settled.

I meet her gaze and tilt my head toward Jon, trying to urge her to just say it. Ginny only shrugs.

Great.

I exhale, then suck in a deep breath before saying, "She wanted to talk to you about something."

"Okay," Jon says, smiling as he turns toward the counter. He grabs a mug, watching his wife out of the corner of his eye as he picks up the coffee carafe. "Shoot."

Ginny swallows, and this time she manages to get some words out. "I want us to go to Atlanta."

Jon freezes in the middle of pouring his coffee, the hot liquid running into the mug and his eyes on Ginny. He blinks, and the coffee gets closer to the rim, threatening to spill over, but he doesn't seem to notice. Ginny takes the carafe from his hand and sets it down.

"What the hell are you talking about?" Jon asks, shaking his head.

"Just what I said. I know you're going to think I'm nuts, but they have real doctors who have a better understanding of this thing. You heard what Corinne said today, this isn't just about the babies. This is about everything. This virus has changed everything, and after everything that's happened..." Her voice cracks, and she inhales slowly. "I have to go. *We* have to go."

"Don't be crazy, Ginny." Jon shoves his hand through his hair, looking slightly panicked. "It's too dangerous. You're too far along and we don't know what could happen. You wouldn't just be putting your life at risk. It's dangerous."

"No more than being here is," Ginny argues. "We could get attacked, a huge horde could get in. Then we'd be trapped. At least this way, I'd be on my way to real doctors and a real city that's fortified and ready for an attack. If anything happens along the way, Joshua will be there to help me. This isn't any less risky than anything else in this world."

Jon shakes his head again. "No. I just can't let you do this."

"I love you," Ginny says, grabbing his hand. "But I need this and I'm not asking your permission. I'm only asking for you to come with me."

"I think it's a bad idea."

"Listen," Ginny says, putting his hand on her stomach. Holding it there while her gaze traps his. "This baby means something to me. Something I never knew it could." She pauses and takes a deep breath, swallowing when tears fill her eyes. "Because of you, I can see a real future for us. But we've lost so much already, and I'm not sure if we'd survive losing this. I'm afraid it would destroy us."

The last few words are said so quietly that she sounds like a child, but Jon nods, and I know he didn't just hear her. He understands her. He understands where Ginny is coming from and what she needs, and he's going to be there for her no matter what. They're so different than they were the morning they left the hot springs, and it's so strange to see them like this. But so wonderful, too.

"Okay," Jon says, his voice strained and his eyes full of tears as he wraps Ginny in his arms. "Okay. I'm sure no one is going to like it, but I will make this happen. We'll go to Atlanta to have this baby."

Ginny rubs her face against his chest and whispers, "Thank you."

Jon kisses the top of her head, nodding despite the tears.

I turn and tiptoe out of the kitchen, heading out to join Axl on the couch. As excited as I am to learn that I will not be saying goodbye to Ginny in a few days, the idea of her coming causes a sinking feeling to form in my stomach. What she's saying makes sense, but I can't help worrying that she might be risking too much. We don't know the condition of the rest of the world or what we might run into.

I sink onto the couch at Axl's side, and he wraps his arms around me the way Jon did just a few seconds ago with Ginny. "You okay?"

"Yeah," I whisper. "It's just hard getting used to the fact that every decision you make could result in your death. That's how it is now, you know? Everything we do has risks."

Axl nods. "Yeah. It ain't easy to live with."

CHAPTER NINE

"You all packed and ready to go?" I ask Ginny as I hold the door open for her and Lila.

Ginny waves a piece of paper in front of my face. "I don't have much other than the supplies on this list. I'm a lot less high maintenance than I used to be."

Lila snorts. "No kidding. I used to *live* in Neiman Marcus. I got a fifty thousand dollar car for my sixteenth birthday and I had a personal masseuse that came to my house weekly."

I stop walking and turn to face the teen. "Are you serious?"

Lila's eyes get huge. "Yeah. Why?"

"Nothing." I blink, then shake my head. There's no sense in making the girl feel bad even if I didn't even own a computer. None of that matters now anyway. "It just sounds crazy after everything we've been through."

"Yeah, it does," Lila says as she walks past me.

Ginny's eyes meet mine, and she shrugs. She was rich too, so even though she may think a personal masseuse for a seventeen-year-old is excessive, she doesn't know where I'm coming from. Even before she became Ms. Hollywood, Ginny had a nice upbringing. A good family. Middle class, but I doubt she ever wanted for anything. I learned to do without the things I wanted, and most of the things I needed.

When we reach the hall, Lila stops, looking both ways before saying, "Which way?"

"The supplies we're going to need are this way." Ginny nods to the right. "Last room, if I remember correctly."

She turns down the hall with me and Lila trailing behind her. I'm so busy going through my mental checklist that I don't notice Dax until he's grinning my way. Not that it matters. It isn't like I can run off and hide, especially not when we need the things on our list.

He's in the middle of talking to one of his men, so all he can do is wave. "Tomorrow morning! You ready?"

I nod and shove Ginny forward. "Faster. Let's get out of here while he's occupied."

"But he's always so happy to see you," Lila says, nudging me with her elbow.

I roll my eyes. "Not funny."

Dax finishes whatever conversation he's having less than a second later, and as soon as the other guy turns away, Dax is jogging toward me. Figures. I never could catch a break.

"Hey! What's the hurry?" He smiles even wider when he stops in front of us. A guarded smile that hides something frightening behind it.

"Just busy getting things done," I say, ignoring the way my skin prickles under his gaze.

He gives me the creeps. The more I'm around him, the more he makes me feel like I'm back in the Monte Carlo, which is bad news, considering we will be on the road tomorrow.

"That boyfriend of yours send you here?" Dax asks, his eyes on me. Only on me. "Seems like he could have carried this stuff on his own."

"Husband," I snap. "And there's no reason I can't carry

all this stuff. You think that just because I'm a woman I'm not capable of pulling my weight?"

Dax's eyes flash, and I realize I hit the nail on the head. That's exactly what he thinks. This guy is a caveman, and I was dead on when I compared him to the men at the Monte Carlo. He'd be right at home with them.

"Husband?" Dax says like that's the only part of what I just said he can concentrate on.

"You think we'll be heading out on time?" Ginny asks, jumping in to save me.

Dax shakes his head and finally tears his eyes off me so he can give Ginny a strange look. "We?"

"You weren't told?" Ginny asks. "Jon and I are coming with you."

"No," Dax says firmly, his voice booming through the hall. "This can't happen. You hear me? We can't take you out there. It's too dangerous."

"I thought you weren't worried about running into trouble," Lila shoots at him.

"We can always run into trouble," Dax says, glaring at the teen. "And if we do, she's going to slow us down."

"I'm the hope for the future," Ginny says, not backing down. "You've said it yourself a dozen times, and it's safer for me to deliver this baby in Atlanta where they have drugs and real facilities and they know more about what we're dealing with. Hope Springs is a death sentence for this baby and we all know it." Even though her expression remains hard and unwavering, there's a tremor in her words that gives away just how scared she is.

"You *were* the hope for the future," Dax says, stepping closer like he can intimidate her with his size. He's wrong. Ginny has faced much more terrifying opponents than this asshole, and none of them won. She didn't let them. "Now, things are different. We have Angus, and he's my priority. We get him to Atlanta. That's all that matters."

"That doesn't have anything to do with me," Ginny spits at him.

Dax steps closer. "You aren't going."

"What the hell is going on here?" Jim stops behind Ginny, frowning as he looks us over. His eyes are colder than ice when they turn on Dax.

"He says I'm not going," Ginny says.

"Corinne already agreed. I was with Jon when he talked to her, and even though she wasn't thrilled, she agreed. And the council backed her up. This is our best chance at keeping this baby alive. She's going. So is her husband, and so am I."

This is the first I've heard about Jim joining us, and after my revelation about Dax, I'm more than happy to have another friendly face on this trip. The more the merrier, as long as they think Dax is an asshole who can't be trusted.

Dax shakes his head, and his mouths scrunches up so much he looks like he's going to spit. "Shit. This is a bad idea, but it looks like I don't have a say in it." He steps back but keeps his eyes on Ginny. "If trouble comes and you slow us down, you're on your own. Angus is my priority."

Jim stiffens at Ginny's side, looking like he's ready to pounce on Dax. Luckily, he doesn't need to, because the big man turns and walks away. Looking more pissed than ever before.

Jim watches the other man, frowning. Looking like he wants nothing more than to hit something. "You sure this is what you want to do?" he says, not looking at Ginny.

"Yeah," she whispers.

"Fine." Jim lets out a deep breath, still not looking Ginny's way. "I already let Dax know I was coming, but you can tell Jon when you get home. I have a few things to do before morning."

He's shaking his head when he turns and heads off, not looking back.

Lila exhales when the blond man has disappeared down the hall. "He sure does have that sexy, brooding thing down."

I turn to face the teen, eyebrows raised and a smile on my face despite the confrontation we just had. "Sexy? How do you think Al would feel if he heard you say Jim was sexy?"

Lila's cheek turn pink, and she shoves her dark hair out of her face. "He doesn't need to know. It's not like I'm interested, I'm just stating the obvious. I love Al. I don't want anyone else. I—"

I laugh and give her a playful shove. "Relax, Lila, I'm joking."

She rolls her eyes.

"Let's get our things and get home," Ginny mutters as she takes off down the hall. "We have a lot to do before tomorrow morning, and I'm not interested in hanging out where we can run into more of Dax's men."

"I THINK THAT'S EVERYTHING," I SAY, STANDING UP straight and twisting my back until it pops.

Ginny nods, rubbing her belly as she looks the nine bags we have over. It isn't much, just one book bag for each of us, but we won't risk bringing more. Even if we're going to be on a bus and there's plenty of space—something Dax has brought up more than once—the essentials are all we need. That's something we learned from being on the road for weeks at a time. Only bring what you can carry. That way, if you run into trouble, you don't have to worry about what you're leaving behind. Most things can be picked up along the way, and luxuries are something we can't afford these days.

"I feel like we're forgetting something," Ginny says after a few minutes of silence. "But I think that's just because we don't have weapons yet."

"Jon, Axl, and Angus will take care of that."

I don't bring up the fact that they have to get through Dax. That goes without saying, though. We've insisted our group be armed, but like everything else, the leader of this little expedition has been fighting us every step of the way. He doesn't understand why we all want weapons. In his mind, we'll be on the bus and safe—at least that's what he says. I'm concerned he's just trying to hold on to his power, and he knows giving us weapons will put some of that in our court.

"Good," Ginny says, nodding once.

The door opens, and Al comes in with Lila right behind him. Parv follows a second later, and then Sophia, Anne, and the kids. I wait for Joshua to come, but he doesn't. I haven't seen him other than in passing since he stormed out of Anne and Sophia's house, and I'm worried. He still says he's going, but he won't talk about what happened with Anne or what's going through his head. After Winston, I'm afraid to let anything go for too long.

"Everyone packed?" Sophia asks, her eyes moving to the pile of bags on the floor.

"We are," I say, nodding.

Her gaze meets mine, and she smiles, but it doesn't mask the pain in her expression. "I can't believe we're saying goodbye."

I'm on the verge of telling her it doesn't have to be this way but stop at the expression on Anne's face. She doesn't looks sad. She doesn't look torn. She doesn't look like she gives a shit about any of this. And Sophia, when she looks at her daughter, is confident. Like she knows she's making the right choice, even if it is hard on her. She knows she's doing what's right for Ava. These women will not be changing their minds, and I won't waste my breath trying to convince them.

"We came to say goodbye," Sophia says, taking a deep breath. "You're leaving early and we didn't want to get the kids up and drag them over there…" She shrugs. "Plus, it's just too hard. You know?"

"I get it," I say.

Sophia's bottom lip trembles, and I cross the room so I can pull her in for a hug. Her arms go around me, and her shoulders shake, but the tears are silent. We've been together for months, but I still never thought it would be this hard to say goodbye. I thought it had become too common to bother me. It seems like every time I turn around we've lost another person. Of course, we usually don't have a choice when it comes to those goodbyes. This is different.

"We will miss you," I say when I pull back.

Sophia nods as she wipes the tears from her eyes. "Us too."

"Don't forget to check on Brady. He's alone out there, and it isn't going to be easy. Maybe, if you give him a little more time, he'll decide to come here. Try to convince him."

"I will," Sophia says. "I promise."

I nod once, then turn away before her tears infect me.

Ava and Max stand next to the door, looking sad. I give them each a kiss on the top of the head. "Be good and take care of your mom and Anne..." It's an odd thing to say. I'm not sure who Max considers his mom. Maybe it's neither one of these women.

The kids nod, and the little boy doesn't even blink.

Behind me, the others say their goodbyes to Sophia, but I focus on Anne. She keeps close to the door, her arms crossed over her chest. Acting like she doesn't want to be here. I'm starting to think that's the real truth: Anne doesn't want to be here or back in our gated community or in Atlanta, or anywhere else for that matter. She just doesn't have the guts to end it the way Winston did.

"Take care of Sophia," I say when I stop in front of her, unsure of what else to say.

Unlike the other woman, I didn't get really close to Anne. She was a tough woman when we met—a former cop who saved the little boy she found wandering the streets—but she gave all of herself to Jake. From the moment they met, she was his mother. There wasn't enough of her to go around when he was alive, and when he died, he took most of Anne with him. After that she pitched in where she could, but she didn't talk much. Except to Joshua.

That didn't turn out the way I thought it would, that's for sure.

"We'll be fine," Anne says, not meeting my gaze. "You—" She swallows, and a tortured expression crosses her face. "Watch out for Joshua."

"We will," I say, reaching out for her.

Anne shakes her head and jerks away. She glances up just long enough to meet my gaze, and the look in them makes me take a step back. She looks guilty.

Her eyes go back to studying the floor. "Good."

Anne spins around and rushes from the house. Running down the steps to the sidewalk then down the street. Away from her house, even. Where she's going I don't know, but I have a strong suspicion she won't be with Sophia for much longer. There's no fight left in her.

Sophia is sobbing behind me, and I tear my gaze away from the now empty street just as Lila wipes her own tears from her cheeks. Everyone seems to have said goodbye, and based on the expression on Sophia's face, I'd guess she's ready to escape this emotional torture.

"I need to go," she says, inching her way toward the door. "Get dinner for the kids so they can get to bed. They have school tomorrow. It's not perfect, but..." She shrugs but doesn't look at any of us again. "I'll be praying you make it safely."

Sophia hurries from the house, dragging the kids with her. I stay by the door, watching her rush away. Knowing this will be the last time I ever see her or Max or little Ava. We face this possibility every time someone leaves these days, but it never gets any easier. Probably never will.

"That sucked," Al says from behind me.

I turn, nodding.

Ginny wipes her eyes, and Lila pulls Al in for a hug. Parv doesn't look torn up or ready to cry, but she has pulled away from the group and she doesn't look happy. Not that she ever does, but right now it's easy to pretend it's because we just had to say goodbye to our friends. Not because this life sucks.

"At least it was a happy goodbye this time," I say. "We'll all be in relatively safe places. We all have a shot at starting over. It may be in two different cities, but we can at least have lives."

"That's true." Lila pulls away from Al and gives him a

little nudge. "You okay?"

"Yeah." The teen clears his throat like he's trying to push the tears back inside. When he looks up, he's smiling. "I'll be fine, and so will everyone else. Thanks to me."

He holds that book up again. The one he said he was going to read through. This time there are tabs sticking out of it in multiple places, and in his hand he holds a couple bags.

"You find something good?" I ask, anxious to change the subject.

"Sure did." Al holds a gallon Ziploc bag out to me. Inside is the book and a few other things. "I marked anything useful and gathered some supplies that might help us out. Then I went back to the bookstore so I could get more copies. I wanted all of us to have one in case we got separated, but I only managed to find three."

"Good work," I say, staring at the plastic bag in my hand. It has an odd assortment of things in it, but I trust Al knows what he's doing. "I'll put one in my backpack."

"Awesome." Al says, grabbing his own backpack off the floor. "I'll take the second one. Who should I give the third one to?"

"Let me have it," Ginny says. "I'll stick it in my bag."

Al grins and hands it over, looking proud of himself, and Ginny returns the smile.

I'm not sure if the book will help us or not, but it's better than nothing. That's for sure. If we do run into problems, that is.

By the time Axl, Angus, and Jon come back, it's almost time for dinner. Ginny and I are in the kitchen making spaghetti when the men come in, and we rush out into the living room so we can check out what they got.

I freeze when I see the small stash laid out on the table. "That's it?"

"All that asshole'd let us have," Angus mutters.

Jon sets one box of bullets down, and I do a quick count in my head. We all have knives, of course, but we've been low on ammo for a while now. We were hoping to stock up before heading out—Hope Springs has more than enough. I'm just not sure why they didn't let us have more than one measly box. And it isn't like those bullets will work for all the guns we have.

"Why?" I ask, tearing my gaze away from the table so I can look at Axl.

"The group heading out already took their share from the armory," Jon explains, "which means they wouldn't give us any more of the inventory. They told us to ask Dax for weapons since we were going out, but—"

"The prick told us no," Axl says. "Told us we'd be fine with knives since we was just ridin' in the bus."

Jon glances toward Ginny. "He was pretty pissed off by the time we got to him. Ripped me a new one for deciding to take you to Atlanta."

"We saw him when we went to get supplies and he was furious."

"He threatened to leave Ginny behind if she slowed the group down," Lila spits out.

Jon's face gets red, and he clenches his hands at his sides. "He threatened you? I'll kill that asshole."

"Just to leave me behind if things got bad," Ginny says. "It's not like he threatened to slit my throat while I was sleeping."

"Doesn't matter." Jon shakes his head. "A threat is a threat. He's crossed a line."

"He's crossed a lot of lines," I point out. "But didn't we decide we were better off going and laying low?" I look around, and everyone nods. "Is that still how everyone feels? We have knives and one box of bullets. How many of our guns will these work for?"

"They're 9mm, so that's good." Axl looks at his brother. "We got three?"

"Yup," Angus says.

"Three guns. How many rounds in the box?" I ask.

Axl's gaze holds mine. "Fifty."

That sucks, there's no way around it. But we've been in

worse places. There have been times when we had nothing but knives and we made it. Made it through horrible situations. This we can do. We'll be on a bus, and the odds of something happening are slim. Well, not slim, but not high. Most of the population has been wiped out, so we could make it Atlanta without running into anyone. It's possible.

"Okay, then," I say, nodding. Trying to sound confident. "We have fifty rounds of ammo. No big deal. We'll be okay."

Axl nods slowly, and around him, everyone else nods as well. The room is tense, but we all know this is something we have to do. If we don't go, Dax will just drag Angus there himself. Then none of us will be around to keep an eye on him. That's not how we want this thing to happen, so we all go. And we will be okay.

"Two days on the road," I say. "Then we'll be in Atlanta."

This time, no one nods.

CHAPTER TEN

"You ready?" Axl asks, easing onto the bed at my side. When I nod, I keep my eyes on my boots. There's no way I want him to know how uncertain I am, and if I look up, he'll know it. It has to be written all over my face.

"All I have to do is finish tying my boots, then grab my bag." My voice comes out amazingly calm, but the tremor in my body doesn't go away.

Axl puts his hand on my knee, and I find myself looking up.

"Not what I meant," he whispers.

"I know. I just don't know how to answer. Am I ready to leave a city that's been cleared out so we can be on the road yet again? No. Am I ready to put my life in Dax's hands? No way. But I'm ready to be there for Angus. That I can do."

"Thought you didn't know how to answer," Axl says, the corner of his lips twitching.

I laugh, but it does little to ease the tension in me. "I thought I didn't, but I guess I was wrong about that." I go back to tying my boot. Focusing on the task at hand instead of all the things that can go wrong. There are so many of them. "Tell me we are going to make it out of this alive," I say after a few seconds.

"We're gonna do what we gotta."

"That's not what I asked you."

My fingers tremble so much I have to stop and take a deep breath. When the shaking in my hands has lessened, I try again, looping the laces through each other until there's a bow. It looks like a five-year-old did it.

When I finally look up, Axl is staring at me.

"You want me to lie?" he asks.

"No." I let out a deep sigh as I stand. My legs only wobble a little. "I just want it to be true."

Axl stands too, and he forces me to turn to face him. His gray eyes hold mine as he runs his hands up my arms to my shoulders, never once taking his eyes off me. "It'll be true," Axl says firmly.

There's so much confidence in his words that I find myself believing them. We are going to be okay. I have to believe it otherwise I'm not sure I'll be able to force myself to leave this house.

Axl takes my hand, and together we head out of the bedroom.

Voices float down the hall from the kitchen. One is Jon, and the second is another man. Jim, I'm assuming.

"I didn't mean you had to do something like this," Jon is saying. "I only asked you to get her out if Dax did something stupid and I wasn't around. I'm here. You don't have to come if you don't want to."

"Made a promise," Jim replies. "And I'm gonna keep it. Besides, what makes you think Dax isn't going to do something moronic just because he leaves Hope Springs? The asshole is dangerous, and every decision he makes is dangerous."

"I know," Jon says, his words almost getting lost in the sigh he lets out.

So much for the confidence I felt a few seconds ago.

Both men look up when Axl and I step into the kitchen.

"Morning," I say, heading for the coffee. "Figured we should get our caffeine fix before we head out."

"Us too," Jim says, holding a mug up.

I grab two mugs and fill them to the brim.

"Where's Ginny?" I ask, handing a cup of coffee to Axl.

"She should be out in a minute," Jon says. "Then we'll get our shit and head out. Dax is going to be pissed if we're late."

"We're not supposed to leave for another hour," I say.

"Doesn't matter." Jim grins my way. "He's going to be pissed off no matter what you do. Because he doesn't want you around."

"Too bad he don't got a choice," Axl says, leaning against the counter at my side.

Jim lifts his mug, still grinning. "You and I know that, but Dax is a little on the slow side."

I snort, but instead of getting into a debate about how dumb Dax really is, I focus on my coffee. It helps keep my mind off what we're about to do. Kind of. The worries are never gone completely.

By the time Ginny comes out of the room, the coffee is gone and the mugs have been washed, and before I know it, we're heading out. Each of us with our backpacks slung over our shoulders and our knives strapped to our waists. Before heading to our meeting spot, we stop by the other house to pick up Angus, Parv, Lila, Al, and Joshua. Like us, they are all ready to go. Or as ready as they can be.

Then we're walking. None of us saying a word as we head through town. The streets are still empty since it's so early, and a silence has fallen over the town that sends a shiver shooting through my body. It feels deserted, forgotten even, and it reminds me of all the towns we passed through before we found Brady. How hollow they all felt.

"I'm scared about what could happen," I say, holding Axl's hand tighter as we walk. "But I'm also not looking forward to seeing more of the country. We saw enough. I don't want to witness any more death or find any more bodies."

Axl gives my hand a squeeze before letting me go. Before I've had a chance to feel abandoned, he has his arm around me. I press my body into his, allowing his strength to seep inside me.

"It's there whether we see it or not," Axl says.

"I know. With some things, though, I'd rather just live in ignorance."

He kisses the side of my head as we round the corner and Dax's group comes into view. There's a big truck and a bus, both of which are decked out in steel plates. Just like Dax said they would be. The sight of them doesn't make me feel all warm and fuzzy, though. Not after how reckless Dax has proven himself to be.

Around the vehicles, the men and women who are going on this trip have already gathered. They're loading last-minute supplies into the back of the truck, drinking coffee, and smoking. Laughing and talking like we aren't about to go on the most terrifying journey they will ever take. Near the front of the truck, Dax is busy barking orders. He already looks like he's in a pissy mood, so I steer the group toward the bus and away from him. If I can avoid him this entire trip, I will be happy.

"Let's just get on the bus and wait," I say.

No one argues.

We head toward the bus as a group, ignoring the many suspicious looks people shoot our way. Even Angus—who is supposed to be the priority on this mission—doesn't get more than a nod. These people really aren't happy to have us on this trip.

"It's going to be a fun couple of days on this bus," Lila says, rolling her eyes.

"No kidding," I say under my breath. "You'd think we were the ones who started the apocalypse."

"Assholes," Angus mutters.

I trade worried looks with Ginny, who is pressed up

against Jon's side. She seems to be getting most of the dirty looks, which doesn't make sense, considering what she told us when we first got here. Before we arrived, she was the town's prize possession. Now they act like they're ready to throw her in front of the bus if it will get them to Atlanta faster.

A guy I've never seen before steps in front of us when we're still five feet from the bus's open door. He's tall and covered in tattoos that he probably believes makes him look tough, but there isn't anything really scary about him. I was at the Monte Carlo with Tat. This prick has nothing on that psycho.

"You folks sure you don't want to stay behind and let us do our jobs? We signed up to get this guy—" he jerks his head toward Angus, "—to Atlanta in one piece. Not to babysit."

"Good thing you don't need to worry about babysitting us," Al says, holding up his stump. "We've been through things that would make you cry yourself to sleep at night."

The guy's eyes narrow on Al's arm, then go to the kid's face. "You lost that out there?"

"After I was bitten," Al says.

"Shit." The tattooed guy steps back, shaking his head. "Shit," he mutters one more time before turning away.

"These guys are morons," Al grumbles.

"They're ignorant," I say. "They don't know what they're up against."

"Don't matter." Axl pulls me toward the bus once again. "We keep our heads down and we make it to Atlanta. That's all we gotta do."

I nod even though I don't know if that's true.

"There you are!" Dax calls from behind us.

None of us are thrilled about the idea of talking to Dax, but we stop anyway.

We turn as Dax jogs up, his usual smile gone. He looks us over, shaking his head like we're the sorriest group he's ever seen. "We've been waiting for you."

"We aren't late," Ginny points out.

"Right." Dax frowns even more. "Anyway, I just wanted to take a moment before we left to lay down some rules. I'm in charge out there. Questioning me isn't an option. This is my mission, and as long as everyone does what they're supposed to, we will make it there okay. Anyone holding us up will be left behind. Getting Angus to Atlanta is our only priority. Understand?"

A couple men come up behind Dax, joining their leader in glaring our way. Like they're letting us know they agree with Dax. I look around and notice they aren't the only ones. Everyone seems to have stopped what they're doing.

I knew people weren't happy about this situation, but this is taking it too far.

"You can't just toss people aside like they don't mean anything," I say, pulling away from Axl so I can get in Dax's face. "We're *all* here for Angus."

Dax's eyes flicker over me, and for a second, he doesn't say anything. All around us, tension builds. Behind Dax, his men look ready to pounce, and at my back, things aren't much better. We agreed to lay low, but only if this guy didn't put us in danger. Threatening to leave us on the side of the road is the exact opposite of that.

"You're risking everything by coming on this trip. It's just more baggage that we have to worry about."

"We aren't baggage," I say. "Which you would know if you'd bothered to get to know us. We survived out there for weeks while you were hiding behind this fence. Yes, you may have gone out on runs and looked for supplies, but you did it armed and using trucks to keep you safe. We camped in the woods with almost no food or supplies and very few weapons. All of the people standing behind me right now are survivors."

"Fine," Dax says, shaking his head. "You may be able to take care of yourself, but she's a liability. Letting her come is stupid and I'm not going to let her drag us down. I have a mission, and I mean what I say. I'll leave her ass behind if she does anything to mess with my end goal."

My face gets warm, and I clench my hands into fists. I really want to hit this guy. Punch him right in his stupid, arrogant face.

"You ass—"

"Fuck that," Angus says, stepping between Dax and me. "Don't know what you folks do 'roud here, but we don't leave our people behind. Hollywood and me'll be walkin' through the gates of Atlanta together, so you better just get used to the idea of havin' her 'round. I told you folks when I first got here, they don't go, I don't go. I meant it."

Dax glances around, but the look in his eyes tells me he knows he isn't going to win this fight. Without Angus he has no mission, and it isn't like he can knock him over the head and drag him onto the bus right in front of us.

After a couple seconds, Dax steps away from Ginny and lets out a deep breath. Then he smiles, which looks even more out of place than ever before.

"Sure. No hard feelings, okay? I'm just doing my job and sometimes I get carried away. Take things too seriously. I know it. That's why I need people to keep me in check. I'm just an intense guy." He chuckles as he glances around like he's waiting for us to join in. We don't, of course.

Axl slips his arm around my shoulders again and steps past Dax so he can lead me toward the bus, and the others follow. We may have settled that issue—for now—but the tension isn't any less intense. Dax's men look even more pissed, and our group is even less enthusiastic about him as a leader. This is going to be a miserable trip.

I head down the aisle. More than anything right now, I want to get moving and get this trip over with. We have a long day ahead of us, and I have a feeling I'm going to be biting my tongue every step of the way.

ROLLING THROUGH THE GATES OF HOPE SPRINGS fills me with even more dread than I thought it would. The uncertainty of what we're going to find between here and Atlanta has me on edge, and the hostility surrounding us is suffocating.

A part of me wishes we were driving at night. Maybe then I'd be able to sleep. At the moment, no matter how hard I try to relax, I find it impossible to get my mind to shut off. All I can do is go through everything that could go wrong, listing the things that could happen and how we'll respond. Replaying all the comments Dax has made and trying to figure out what to do about him. There's nothing I can do, but that doesn't stop me from worrying.

"You okay?" Axl asks, pulling me against him.

"I am. Just thinking."

He nods but doesn't say anything. I scan the bus, counting. Fifteen men and women in Dax's group, plus three in the truck. We could take them if it came to a fight, but it would be tough. We have ten, including Jim. But that's also counting Ginny and Angus, neither of whom need to be involved in a confrontation that could get them killed.

But they aren't our only weaknesses, and Dax knows. Lila and Al, for example. He's missing an arm, and she's small. She tries, but any of these guys could take her down in a second. Ginny would distract Jon, and Axl would do anything to save me. And vice versa. Parv, though good with the bow, is just as small as Lila. She's tougher, but she wouldn't stand a chance against most of these men. Then there's Joshua. He's never killed a person, not to mention the fact that right now he looks like someone just ran over his dog.

"You think Joshua is going to be okay?" I ask, trying to distract myself. Even if all I'm doing is replacing one worry with another.

"The doc'll be good. He was down in the beginnin', but he pulled through. He'll get through this, too."

I nod, remembering how hard Joshua took all of this when we first picked him up. I thought he'd be a liability, but he came around. This is different, though. I'm not sure if he'll make it through this.

"I'm going to talk to him," I say, getting to my feet.

Axl moves his legs so I can get by, and I head down the aisle to where Joshua is sitting. He's alone and staring at the wall like the window isn't covered in metal and he can actually see the passing landscape. He doesn't look good.

"How are you doing?" I ask, sliding into the seat at his side.

He tears his gaze away from the window and turns his whole body my way. The smile he shoots me looks painful. "Okay."

"You're lying."

He doesn't blink as the smile fades away. "Yes, I am."

I pause, holding his gaze and waiting for him to say something. To tell me what he's thinking or what happened with Anne. Anything, really. I want to make sure he's okay.

"Do you want to talk?" I ask when he doesn't say a word.

Joshua sighs and shakes his head, and I'm pretty sure he's going to tell me to get lost. Then he says, "What would you like me to talk about, Vivian? About how I lost a patient I had grown close to or how it almost destroyed me? How about how Anne saved me and how I thought she was the person I'd be able to lean on for the rest of my life? Or how I fell in love with her? How I thought she felt the same way? How we slept together—yes, we had sex—every night, but when the end came she didn't choose me. Turns out, she never wanted me to begin with. She just wanted *someone*. Anyone. She even said she would have slept with Angus if he hadn't been with Darla. I was nothing more than a warm body to her. Is that what you wanted to hear?" Joshua's eyes are red, and his shoulders heave like he's trying to catch his breath, but he doesn't cry. He just stares at me. His eyes flashing with all the anger and hurt that's piled up over the last few months.

"I'm sorry," I say. "Maybe I shouldn't have asked. I just wanted to make sure you were okay."

"I'm not," he says, turning away form me. "But like Angus, I have a job to do. I'm a doctor, and the world needs me. I refuse to let everyone down, and I refuse to let these dead bastards get the better of me."

I don't know if Joshua is on the verge of crying, but I know I am. My eyes are so full of tears that I have inhale a few times before I try to blink them away. I don't want him to see me cry, because he will know I'm crying for him, and he doesn't need that kind of pressure or pain added to everything else he's going through.

"I am sorry, Joshua," I say, getting up. "And I'm also here if you need to talk to someone. You have friends."

He nods but doesn't look my way. I wait a few seconds, hoping he'll decide to open up. When he doesn't, I go back to my own seat.

CHAPTER ELEVEN

Somehow I get my mind to shut off long enough to take a nap. I wake a couple hours later to discover that Jon and Axl have moved closer to the front, which also means closer to Dax. I'm sure not being able to control what's happening is driving Axl nuts—he usually likes to be the one in the driver's seat—but I don't have any real desire to join him up there. Not with Dax glaring at everyone associated with our group.

"You get a good nap?" Jim asks, drawing my attention to the row behind me.

He sits by himself, leaning against the side of the bus and totally alert. Like he's on watch and he can't rest if anyone else is sleeping.

"It was better than I expected it to be," I say, twisting to face him. Out of the corner of my eye, I find Ginny watching me. "I didn't sleep well last night."

"I hear you," Jim says, pulling a pack of cigarettes out.

"Don't light that," Ginny snaps.

Jim shrugs and shoves himself off the seat. "No worries."

He heads to the back of the bus, and even though Ginny has to know he's going to smoke the thing back there, she doesn't say anything. I don't either. In this world, everyone deserves a vice or two to get them through the day.

"I kept dreaming about getting stuck or being surrounded by zombies," Ginny says when Jim has wandered off. "It's a long way to go, and we'd be stupid to believe we won't run into trouble."

"Tell me about it." I roll my eyes, thinking of Dax and how insanely arrogant he was when we talked about this mission. Like he's God and can somehow control the future. He wishes.

"Would you two stop yappin'," Angus mutters from one row in front of me. I turn as he pushes himself up, his hair smashed down on one side. "It's like a damn henhouse in here."

Ginny rolls her eyes as she climbs to her feet. "I need to stretch my legs."

"Hold onto the seats," Angus mutters. "Last thing we need is for you to take a nosedive, *Hollywood.*"

He chuckles, and Ginny returns his smile. Ever since the Monte Carlo, those two have had a strange bond. Like siblings. Just like everyone else, Angus gets on her nerves, but Ginny has a soft spot for him. And vice versa. Angus can be a softy when really wants to be.

"Sure is strange to have her back," he says, shaking his head as Ginny heads to the front of the bus where Axl and Jon sit. "Never really thought it would happen."

"It does seem like a miracle. With everyone we've lost, it's about time we had some good luck."

Angus nods, his lips pursed as he thinks. Probably about Darla.

I feel a little bit like an ass, because we've never talked about it. It's been weeks since she was killed, and I haven't brought it up since the day she died. Part of it is that I have a lot of guilt surrounding my mother, but it's also about Angus.

I don't want him to hurt more than he already does. I don't want to pour salt into an open wound.

Still, maybe he needs someone to talk to…

"I'm sorry," I say, then look down at my hands. Hoping to give him so privacy. "About my mom, I mean."

"Yeah, well, it was bound to happen. Life never was all sunshine and roses for me. Shoulda known this wouldn't be no different." Out of the corner of my eye, I see him shake his head. "Stupid thing was, it took me by surprise. I thought life had finally dealt me a good hand. You know, between this immunity thing and her."

"Even a little time with someone you love is better than nothing. Right?" I say, finally looking up to hold Angus's gaze. "And you still have Axl. I know it's not the same, but he's more important to you than anyone else, and he's here."

"I kept him alive," Angus says, his eyes moving to the front of the bus where Axl sits. "Truth is, I'd still die for him if it came down to it. Don't matter what Dax says or what anybody in Atlanta wants me for. Axl is better than me, and he deserves to make it outta this."

I stare at Angus, unsure of how to respond. His statement has me torn. Of course I want to see Axl make it out of this alive. He's the love of my life, and I know that if he left me, there wouldn't be much in this world worth living for. Not with the way things are now. But Angus has an important role to play in all this, and it's bigger than Axl and me. It's about the whole world and whether or not the people fighting to move on have a future.

I should tell him he *can't* do something like that. That it would be stupid to sacrifice himself for Axl. That the world needs him to live.

Only, I can't.

Angus nods when I don't say anything, the expression on his face one of total approval. I look away when guilt swirls through me, and my eyes meet Jim's. He must have finished his cigarette and was heading back up to his seat. He heard. Heard it all.

Jim's eyes move from Angus to me and back again. I don't know the guy, so I can't tell what he's thinking, but he is part of Hope Springs, and to them, Angus isn't a person. He's a symbol, and they don't give a shit what happens to the rest of us as long as he makes it to Atlanta. If Jim is anything like Dax, we could be in for some trouble down the road.

But Jon trusts this guy. Which should mean we can trust him too. Right?

"WE'RE ALL ON!" DAX CALLS AS GINNY—THE LAST person outside—climbs on board.

We stop every two hours for a bathroom break. Not a minute later and not a minute earlier—Dax has us on a tight schedule. The power trip he started on back in Hope Springs has apparently taken the scenic route.

The bus lurches forward, and Ginny grabs the seat to steady herself, grinding her teeth together. She glances back at Dax, but the guy isn't paying attention, so he doesn't get to see the killer look she shoots his way.

Ginny keeps walking, shaking her head. She stops next to me, and I scoot closer to the wall, making room so she can slide into the seat.

"Where's Jon?" I ask as the bus bumps down the road.

He got off the bus with her, but he didn't get back on. I know we didn't leave him behind, though.

"He rode in the truck." She says, shaking her head. "It's his turn to keep watch. Parv is there too."

She doesn't look happy about it, and I can't blame her. I only hope Dax is too threatened by Axl to ask him to take a turn in the lead truck. Despite how safe Dax thinks we are in these vehicles, I have serious doubt about that. I want Axl as far away from any danger as possible.

"Of course Parvarti would volunteer to take watch," I say. "Maybe I should too even though I don't want to. Dax did insist that if we came on this trip we would need to pitch in. It could be a peace offering between our groups."

Ginny arches an eyebrow, looking up toward the front where Dax stands in the aisle like he's propelling the bus forward with his presence. "I have a feeling he'd rather you stay on the bus with him."

"All the more reason to volunteer," I mutter.

Of course, there's always the chance that if I volunteered, he would suddenly feel the need to be in the truck as well. His interest in me is past annoying at this point, and not just because of Axl's aggression. Because I haven't encouraged him *at all*.

Ginny shrugs, and we ride in silence for a while, the tires thumping over the road and the bus bumping up and down under us. It's dark, but with the steel plates over the windows, we can't see anything anyway. Which means I'm constantly studying the people on the bus. One row up, Angus is curled up like he's asleep, while a couple rows back, Al and Lila are curled up together. Joshua leans against the wall, his lanky figure looking out of place in the school bus and his expression just as dark as it has been since his fight with Anne. At the front, Axl sits in the first row while Dax stands at his side. He probably won't sit down the entire ride. I know he feels threatened because Axl was the one in charge of our group—if we had a leader, that is. It's a stupid pissing contest that I have no desire to get involved in, though.

In the back, Jim is once again smoking, and everyone else on board is nothing more than nameless bodies to me. Dax's men, who still haven't warmed to us and don't give a shit what happens to us between here and Atlanta. They're all here with the intention of doing anything to keep Angus alive, but there's nothing comforting about it. Probably because I know they'd do it at the expense of the rest of us or because they aren't really prepared for what's out here. Or maybe it's a little of both.

Ginny winces, and I turn to face her, pulling my attention away from the men who would most likely shove me in front of a horde to save Angus's life. "You okay?"

She nods and rubs her stomach. "Yeah. This baby has a powerful kick."

I laugh and shake my head, and this time when I think back to my own pregnancy, I don't feel sad. Emily died, but maybe she's better off. The world is harsh now, and scary. It doesn't really seem like a place for a child…

Not that I would say that to Ginny.

"You don't have much time left," I whisper, trying to push away the thought that Ginny is going to have her work cut out for her. Being a mom in normal times is hard enough, but she's going to have to protect this baby from so many things that were never a concern before.

"A few weeks," she says, staring down at her stomach. "I can't believe it."

"How are you feeling?"

"Big and uncomfortable," Ginny says, laughing.

"But happy?" The words almost stick in my throat because right now, in this moment, as we barrel down a dark road toward an uncertain future, it seems impossible that someone would say yes to that.

"So happy." Ginny's smile grows wider as her hands make a trek over her round stomach. "You know what I've been through, so I don't have to pretend with you. There were moments, especially back at the hot springs, when I was sure I wanted it all to end. It didn't seem like we could have any kind of happiness. But Jon changed all that for me, and this baby is the start of something new and big, and now that we're heading to Atlanta, I feel like it has a chance."

I nod when my throat tightens. I hope she's right. Not just for her sake, but for all of our sakes.

The bus slows, and I look up just as the truck in front of us has stopped. The entire bus shudders when we roll to a halt, and my body is thrown forward, slamming into the seat in front of me with a force so violent part of me wonders if we've hit a wall. We haven't and I know it, but I can't help sitting up straighter so I can see out the windshield. In front of us, smoke puffs out of the other truck's exhaust pipe, but as far as I can tell, no one is getting out.

"What's going on?" Lila calls, clinging to Al.

At my side, Ginny stands, worry etched in every line of her face as she stares at the truck in front of us. The one Jon is riding in.

"Not sure," Dax calls. "I can't see anything."

He pulls out his walkie-talkie and holds it to his mouth. "Donovan, what the hell are you doing? Over."

When he releases the button, static fills the silence surrounding us. We wait, but no one answers.

The static cuts out when Dax puts the walkie back up to his mouth. "Donovan! Where—"

His words are cut off when a boom cuts through the silent night.

The bus shudders, and a fireball bursts from the truck in front of us, lighting up the dark sky. Around me, people cry out and duck or jump up. Lila screams, and I pull myself up, my legs so shaky that they barely hold me. Axl turns my way, his wide eyes reflecting the fire blazing in front of us as they hold mine from across the bus.

The crack of gunfire cuts through the shouting, and all around me, people go crazy. Yelling, pushing, shoving their way toward the exits while they pull out weapons. Cursing and growling.

"Vivian!" Axl calls, trying to push his way through the crowd to get to me.

The aisle is too full, though. He'll never make it.

"Vivian!" Lila shouts from behind me.

I spin around, still standing in front of my seat, and through the crowd of men rushing to the exit, my eyes meet hers. Then Ginny grabs my hand, pulling my attention her way. Her cheeks are streaked with tears, but like everyone around me, she's pulled out her knife. As if she's ready to fight. Only fighting isn't what she needs to be doing right now.

Behind us, Lila, Al, and Joshua are frozen in place while Angus, surprisingly, is still standing in front of his seat. I can tell he's itching to run out, but for once, he follows instructions and stays put. His hands grip the seat in front of him, and even through the crowd and darkness, I can see how white his knuckles are.

At the back, people jump from the emergency exit, pouring out into the chilly night as more gunfire erupts with every passing second. In front, they do the same, charging down the stairs. Dax and Axl stand in their original spots, one desperate to get back to me, and the other determined to protect the last hope for humanity.

But all I can think about right now is Jon. How is Ginny going to deal with this if something has happened to him? It's too dark to be able to see how much of the truck in front of us was damaged, but the fire is still going.

"We don't know what happened," I tell Ginny, my gaze still on the fire raging in front of us. "We can't see anything back here. They could be okay."

"I know. I know. I know," Ginny says.

The trembling in her voice goes straight to my heart, but I do my best not to focus on it. We need to plan. To figure out what's happening and get Angus to safety. To get all of us out of this alive.

The bus finally clears of everyone but our group and Dax, but outside, the world has turned to chaos. Light flickers through the darkness as men fire at each other, illuminating figures here and there. It's impossible to tell who's firing from inside the bus, whether it's just our group or someone else is out there with them. I do know that it won't be long before the noise draws zombies our way, though. Then we'll really be in trouble.

"We have to get out of here!" Dax calls as he and Axl charge down the aisle to our group. "They've got us surrounded!"

"Who?" Lila screams just as Ginny says, "I'm not leaving without Jon!"

"There's no time," Dax shouts as he grabs Angus's arm.

"We ain't leavin'." Angus grunts and shoves the other

man off. "Not 'til we know what's happenin'."

"That is *not* the goal of this mission and you know it!" Dax growls. "Our objective is to get you to safety. If everyone else dies along the way, so be it, but I'll be damned if I fail at keeping you safe."

Angus takes a step toward Dax, putting his face so close to the younger man's that there's less than an inch of space between them. "You're gonna hafta carry me."

"Shut up!" Axl calls, forcing the two men to tear their eyes away from each other. "We go, but not 'til we know what's happenin'. It'd be dumb as shit to run out there right now when we got no idea where the shootin' is comin' from."

"What the hell do you suggest?" Dax spits at him.

"We need to look around," I say, pulling my hand from Ginny's. "If one of us climbs out and keeps low to the ground, no one will notice us. We'll be able to get a better idea of where to go from here."

Dax lets out a deep breath as he glances back and forth between the two exits: the one at the back and the one at the front. Then he nods. "Fine. But I stay with him." He jerks his thumb toward Angus.

"Wouldn't have it any other way," Axl says.

He shoves his way past Dax and Angus, heading for the emergency exit, and I run after him.

"There is no way in hell you're going alone," I say, grabbing his shoulder. "We do this together. Do you understand me?"

Axl purses his lips, but he nods before turning to head back down the aisle. "Fine," he says, pulling one of our only loaded guns out of his belt and shoving it my way. "Take this. I got the other." He pauses at the open door, studying the road behind us through the window before turning back to me. "Just remember. We got fifty rounds. That's it."

Perfect. "Okay," I say instead of throwing my sarcasm his way.

Axl slips out the door and crouches at the back of the bus, and I'm right behind him. The air chills my exposed arms, but the goose bumps covering my skin have nothing to do with the cold. The gunfire has let up, and all around us, people scream and yell, but it's the moans that have my heart beating faster.

"Low," Axl whispers as he moves around the side of the bus.

I follow, practically on my hands and knees as I make my way past the bus at Axl's side. All around us, the night explodes with violence. A woman screams, taking me back to the Monte Carlo, and I search the darkness for the source. With as crazy as it is, though, it's impossible to see anything other than a few shapes darting through the black night.

The truck in front of us is still burning, but when we get closer, I'm able to relax just a little. It's only the engine, and the rest of the cab seems to be intact.

My eyes adjust to the dimness of the night and the constant bursts of gunfire a little better, making it easier for me to distinguish some of Dax's men. All their firepower seems to be directed toward the road in front of us, meaning if we have to make a run for it, we might be able to head back the way we came.

"There," Axl says, pointing toward the forest in the distance.

I stop and squint, trying to see through the darkness. A couple seconds later, a burst of light breaks through the branches.

"They're in the trees."

"They ain't firin' much. Most of this is our guys. I got a feelin' they're waitin' us out. Hopin' we run outta ammo so they can swoop in. At this rate, it won't be long neither." His eyes hold mine. "We gotta move."

Axl starts moving again, and I follow, forcing the lump that's formed in my throat back down.

When we reach the front of the bus, Axl only pauses for a second before charging forward. A couple people look our way, but they ignore us. Whoever has attacked us is too focused on the men with guns to pay any attention to Axl and me. Lucky for us.

Someone jumps from the cab of the truck before we've even made it all the way there, but the sudden brightness of the fire makes it impossible for me to see who it is. My right hand automatically tightens on my gun as I lift my left hand, shielding my eyes so I can get a good look at the person. It still takes a second for Jim's face to come into focus against the fire blazing behind him.

"You're here," he says, nodding once before turning back to the truck. "Good. I need your help." Jim doesn't even bother trying to stay low or out of sight, and he doesn't have a weapon drawn. Instead, he's focused on the truck, which doesn't do anything to ease the pounding of my heart. Jon must be in trouble.

"Is Jon okay?" I ask, getting to my feet at the same time that Axl does.

"He's been hit." Jim pulls himself back up into the cab. "Help me get him down."

Axl tucks his gun away, his eyes searching the area. "Keep close to the truck," he says to me. "Stay outta sight, but be ready."

I press my back up against the side of the truck. "I will."

Axl climbs up after Jim, blocking my view of the cab completely. With him out of the way, I'm able to get a good look at the road in front of us, and I can see now why Donovan had to stop. A roadblock of some kind has been set up, making it impossible for anyone to drive across the bridge. It's a trap. I'm not surprised, since we tried to warn everyone, but I'm also not happy about being able to say *I told you* so to Dax. I'm sure he won't be happy to hear it, either.

I look up where Axl and Jim are crowded into the cab, straining to get a glimpse of what they're doing inside. I'm too low and the cab is too high, though, and all I'm able to see is Axl's back. What they're doing up there I don't know, but I do know the gunfire around us seems to have slowed down even more, and in the intervals between the shots, I'm able to make out the moans of the dead. Only I have no idea which way they're coming from.

I look back toward the bus, searching the darkness for movement or some other indication that our only way of escape is blocked. It's pitch black, so it takes a few seconds for my eyes to focus after looking into the brilliant flames raging from the truck's engine. When they do, I'm able to make out some movement, but it's impossible to know what it is for sure. It could just be my eyes playing tricks on me, or it could be zombies heading our way.

When Axl hops down next to me, I nearly jump out of my skin. I tear my eyes away from the darkness as Jim and Axl help Jon out. He's bleeding, but I'm not sure where it's coming from or how serious it is. With the expression of pain on his face and the amount of blood on his shirt, it can't be good though.

"What happened?" I ask, hurrying to their side.

"Shot," Axl says. "No sign of Parv."

"She left you?" I ask Jon.

"Went to get help. She must not have made it." His voice is strained and can barely be heard over the moans and grunts surrounding us.

"We need to get moving," Jim says.

He pulls Jon's arm around his shoulder, bearing most of the injured man's weight as he takes off. Axl and I turn to follow just as a bullet pings against the truck above my head. He grabs my arm and pulls me forward so hard I stumble, but I don't have a chance to fall. Not with Axl's arm around me or the way he's holding me up. Not with how he propels me forward.

"We gotta get off this bridge," I say as we follow Jim toward the bus.

Behind us, the gunfire has eased off even more, but the moans of both injured men and zombies are louder now.

"I got a pretty good look when I was in the truck. The way in front of us is blocked. I ain't sure if it's men or zombies, but I ain't waitin' 'round to find out."

"Me neither," I say, moving faster.

Jim has just made it to the front of the bus when the first zombie comes into view, stumbling down the road we just drove in on. Five more figures are visible behind him. Instead of heading to the back of the bus, Jim pulls Jon in through the open front door.

Axl shoves me in after the other two men, and I stumble up the steps behind them, my heart pounding and my breath coming out in gasps.

"Shut the back door!" I call as I scurry up the stairs.

Axl rushes in, slamming the door behind him, and Dax hurries toward the emergency exit at the back. I don't look at him long enough to see when it's shut, because I'm already focused on Ginny. Her eyes are on Jon, who is being eased onto a seat, and her skin has lost all its color.

"What happened?" Ginny asks, dropping to her knees in the aisle. Right next to her husband.

Axl and Dax and Angus are at the back of the bus, looking through the window. Trying to figure out how we're going to get out of here. The gunshots have stopped, and in their absence, men are yelling and screaming. I'm not even sure if it's from the zombies that have crowded onto this bridge or if it has to do with the men who ambushed us. I only know that those of us on this bus are on our own.

"Shot," Jim says, looking up. His eyes searching the bus for Joshua, who is already on his way.

"I need space," the doctor says, dropping his bag into the seat behind Jon.

"Ginny." I push through the men, past Jon and Jim and Joshua, grabbing Ginny's arm and forcing her back. "We need to give Joshua space."

She nods, but she doesn't take her eyes off Jon. "He's going to be okay. Tell me he's going to be okay."

"Joshua is going to do everything he can."

"How bad is it?" Jon asks, but the seats are too high to be able to get a good look at his face.

"It's not good," the doctor says.

Ginny's body trembles next to mine, and I wrap my arm around her tighter. If I can help hold her together, I will. I just don't know if it's possible.

"We have to leave!" Dax growls from somewhere in the back of the bus.

"Shut the fuck up," Angus replies, not looking at Dax.

"This isn't part of the plan," Dax says, and then he turns on us. His eyes on Ginny. "I knew you would slow us down."

I'm shaking now. Anger and hurt swirl through me, making it hard to stay still. In my arms, Ginny is trembling, and in front of us her husband may be bleeding to death, and right now all I want is for Dax to shut the hell up. This is his fault. We tried to warn him, and if he and his men had taken us seriously, this wouldn't have happened. Donovan shouldn't have driven down this bridge. The second he saw it was blocked, he should have stopped and radioed to Dax, and we should have found another way.

I'm ready to tell Dax exactly what I think of him when Jon lets out a scream. Ginny's body jerks and all my anger melts away, and in its absence, all that's left is hurt and worry and fear.

"I'm sorry," Joshua says. "The bullet's still in there and if we don't get it out—"

He doesn't get to finish explaining, because his words are cut off once again by Jon's scream of pain. Ginny's sobs increase, and outside, zombies start banging on the doors. Lila and Al stand across from me, clinging to each other. All I can do is hold Ginny and hold my breath and pray. Pray that we make it out of this. Pray that this isn't the end, no matter how horrible it looks. There has to be a way out of this shitty situation.

My eyes meet Axl's, and the fear in them chills me to the bone. He's at the back again, looking out. We must be surrounded, because I've only seen that look a few times. Once in Vegas, when we were trapped in a car. So sure it was the end that we were ready to end it. To use the last bullets we had to put ourselves out of our misery before the dead bastards could get us. The second time was in that basement, when we thought Angus was going to die. Only the really close calls make Axl look at me like that.

"Stop." Jon's shaky voice draws my attention his way. "Stop."

He gasps for breath, but Joshua sits back. His hands are covered in blood and his face is white, and his eyes are telling the truth even though his mouth hasn't said the words yet. There's nothing he can do to save Jon.

"We both know this isn't going to work," Jon says, his words strong even though his voice trembles. "I'm going to end up bleeding to death no matter what you do, and the more time you spend trying to save me, the more likely the rest of you are to die."

"We're all going to die! Don't you get it?" Dax's voice booms through the bus. "We are surrounded by the dead!"

"Not if I have anything to say about it," Jon says, sitting up. His gaze focused on his wife. "I won't put you at risk."

"This can't be happening," Ginny says.

She pulls out of my arms and pushes her way past the men. I step forward too, and for the first time, get a really good look at the gunshot wound. It's in Jon's chest, and it's oozing blood. So much that I don't know how he isn't gone yet. He's right. There's nothing Joshua can do about this. Not on a bus, not with little to no equipment and no operating room. Not when we don't have the time or resources to do a blood transfusion. Jon is going to die.

Axl's arm slips around my shoulders before I even know he's there, but I don't look away from the scene in front of me. Ginny is on her knees at Jon's side, sobbing into his chest. His hands moves down her head, smoothing her hair back over and over again as she cries.

"You can't leave me," Ginny says, the words distorted by her sobs and the fact that her face is pressed against Jon's chest.

He stops rubbing her head and forces her to look up.

"You'll be fine. You have family to take care of you, and this baby to love."

"But I *need* you." She rubs her hand across her face, wiping away the tears, but they're replaced a second later by more. "I don't know if I can do this without you. If it wasn't for you, I wouldn't be here. I would have given up. *You* are my reason for living."

"No," Jon says firmly. "All I did was help you find yourself. You are stronger than you think, and you're strong enough to go on. You don't need me."

His face scrunches up and he lets out a deep exhale, and just like that, Ginny is sobbing again. Axl's arm tightens around me as tears fill my eyes, and even though I don't want to look away, I force myself to. I turn and wrap my arms around him and bury my face in his chest. Willing myself to hold it together. To be strong so Ginny has someone to lean on, because she is going to need it.

"Don't…" Ginny's voice fades, but a second later she says, "Jon."

Tears shake my body, mixing with Ginny's sobs. I hold my breath, but Jon doesn't answer, and when I look back, I expect to find him gone. His skin pale and his face slack. But that isn't what's happening. Instead he's on his feet, and he has Ginny in his arms. He's hugging her, and his blood has covered her stomach, so round and full of the reminder of exactly what Jon is leaving behind.

He pulls back and takes Ginny's face between his hands. "I love you. I love our baby and I love the time we had together. I love that we created something out of scraps, and I love that you are strong enough to pull through anything. Even this. Don't forget that. Don't forget what you overcame or who you are, because you are the strongest woman I have ever known, and you deserve to make it to the end of this thing. To see the world rebuilt and to watch our child grow."

He kisses her on the forehead, leaving his lips pressed against her skin so long that time seems to pause. When he pulls away, it's so sudden Ginny doesn't have time to react.

Her face is streaked with tears when Jon steps back, giving her one last look before shoving his way past us.

"You won't have a lot of time," he says, heading for the back door. His hand is on his wound even though it isn't helping. More blood seeps out with every step he takes. He's so weak that he looks like he's dragging himself. Like he can barely lift his legs. But he doesn't stop until he reaches the door. "I'll draw them away, but we all know it isn't going to last long."

"No!" Ginny says, moving toward Jon.

Jim is the one who grabs her. "You sure about this?" he asks, his eyes on her husband.

Jon's hand is on the latch that opens the back door. "Yes." His face contorts in pain, and he stumbles back. He squeezes his eyes shut and exhales a couple times before opening them again. "I don't have much time left. Don't forget your promise."

"I won't," Jim says, holding Ginny tighter as her eyes grow to twice their size.

"You can't do this," she screams, thrashing in Jim's arms. "I can't let you!"

She's still struggling when her husband pushes the door open. A chorus of moans fills the bus, along with the putrid stench of decay. Then Jon throws himself into the horde and is swallowed up by a sea of decaying arms.

"No!" Ginny screams.

Angus takes her from Jim, who runs for the front of the bus, and just like that, we're all on the move. Axl pushes me forward, and I sweep my backpack up as I run by, looking back just long enough to see that the other door has been swarmed. The zombies aren't just interested in Jon now. They want us.

"The front!" Dax screams.

Al and Lila reach the door first, but Jim and Joshua are right behind them. Axl has his arm around me, and behind us, Angus pulls a still-sobbing Ginny with him. He has to drag her to get her to move, but he manages it, mostly because Dax is at his back pushing as well. Then we're all crowded around the door, and Jim pushes his way past the teens. He takes a few deep breaths through his mouth before blowing them out through his nose. His eyes are focused on Ginny.

"We're going to have to jump," he says. "When you get out, head for the water. Get as close to the middle of the river as you can get. Too close to the edge and the water might be too shallow."

"We don't even know how deep the middle is!" Lila screeches.

Jim turns and holds her gaze. "It's this, the zombies, or the men in the woods. You choose."

With that, he shoves the door open and runs down the steps. The second he's down, he's yelling for us to move. Then we're all climbing out, one after the other after the other until it's my turn. I grab Ginny from behind me and shove her toward the stairs, and I don't even have to force her to go. A split second after she's out, I follow.

My feet hit the pavement, and the overwhelming stench of rot fills my lungs. I scurry forward, shoving Ginny toward the side of the bridge. Over the moans and screams and occasional burst of gunfire, the roar of the rushing water below us fills my ears, and I say a silent prayer, asking God to protect us from the fall and from the roaring current.

"Go!" I hear Jim shout as he waves us toward the edge of the bridge.

Axl pushes me forward, but we're cut off when Dax rushes in front of us. Pulling Angus with him. Angus climbs up the side with our leader right behind him, and beside me, Axl fires into the advancing zombies. In the distance, men groan and scream. Ginny reaches the railing and leans against it like she can't find the energy to move, and Angus stands on the rail, looking back. Probably trying to find his brother.

"We have to go!" Dax screams, urging him to jump.

"Go, Angus," I say, waving toward the river.

Angus squeezes his hands into fists before letting them

relax. He gives Axl one final look before throwing himself from the side. Dax is gone a second later, looking like nothing more than a shadow as he jumps into the river below. Once they're gone, Al pulls Lila to the edge, urging her up. They jump together only seconds later.

I pull Ginny forward, looking over my shoulder as Axl struggles with a zombie. "Axl!"

He pushes the zombie back, and Jim fires at the thing, taking it out as Axl runs toward me.

In front of us, Joshua climbs up the railing. "Come on!" he calls, holding his hand out to Ginny, who still hasn't moved.

She reaches for the doctor just as a zombie comes out of nowhere, tackling him. Joshua and Ginny and the zombie all hit the pavement, and I find myself screaming in frustration as I charge forward. More of the dead come from nowhere, seeming to materialize out of the darkness. Axl and I reach the one on Joshua. We manage to pull him off before anyone is seriously injured while Jim helps Ginny to her feet. But more zombies move in.

"Go!" Jim calls, firing at the dead as more and more stagger our way.

Axl shakes his head and joins him, and I do the same despite the curses Axl throws at me. We fire together while Joshua and Ginny climb the railing. They jump, and Axl nudges me to move, but I refuse to go alone. I pull him with me, still firing with one hand while urging him to move toward the side. Like us, Jim doesn't let up, but still more zombies come, and the horde around us grows so thick I'm not sure how we're going to make it.

Just as that thought enters my mind, the pop of an automatic weapon fills the air, and the dead around us fall.

Like a dream, Parvarti runs from the darkness, still firing as the zombies head our way. "Jump!" she screams as she bolts over the bodies at our feet.

Axl and I climb, and the others are right behind us. We reach the top of the railing, and the wind blows my hair so violently I can't even see the river when Axl pushes me forward.

Then I'm falling. Through the dark night with the cold air whipping around me, and the sounds of the river and screams and gunfire pulsing through my brain. In what seems like the blink of an eye, my body slams into the river. Cold water engulfs me, and the current reaches up with its icy fingers, pulling me into its darkness. I flail my arms and legs, trying to push myself up, but it only takes a second to realize I'm not totally sure which way up is. All around me, the river swirls, pulling me down as it rushes to its destination. My eyes are shut and my lungs are so full of stale air that they feel in danger of bursting, but still I can't figure out how to get away. The river has become a string of icy rope, twisting around me until I'm sure I'll never be able to break free.

My backpack is weighing me down. I twist, trying to break free of the straps, but it's impossible. *It's going to drag me to the bottom.* That's the only clear thought going through my head.

Then all at once I'm thrown to the surface, giving me a chance to suck in a mouthful of fresh air before I'm pulled down again. This time, I know which way is up, and I'm only down for a few seconds before I manage to kick and claw my way back to the surface. My head pops out, and I inhale, kicking harder to keep myself above water. Wet hair is plastered to my face, making it hard to see much, but from somewhere in the distance I hear the sound of people yelling over the rushing of the water. I search the dark river, barley illuminated by the moon, and spot a couple objects bobbing up and down not too far in front of me that just might be my friends. Or Axl.

"Axl!" I scream just as I'm sucked under once again.

The mouthful of water I take in doesn't make it to my lungs, and when I manage to resurface, I spit it out. Oxygen so cold and harsh it burns its way through my body gets sucked in, and when I exhale, my teeth chatter together from the effort.

My skin has turned to ice, and what's worse is that I can feel the frigidness of the water seeping inside me. Freezing my joints and muscles. Making it nearly impossible to kick.

Kick. Kick! Don't stop!

The water seems to thicken until every move I make is labored and slow. I find it more and more difficult to keep my head up, and the numbness in my limbs is too pronounced to ignore. But still the current moves me forward with a speed that makes me dizzy, and I can't fight it. I don't have the energy.

"Vivian!"

Ginny's voice breaks through the water rushing in my ears, and I dig deep, searching for strength so I can kick harder. I comb the darkness, and thanks to the light of the moon, I'm finally able to spot some movement in the distance. On the riverbank, someone is climbing out of the water, joining a few other people.

"Here!" I scream, waving. Kicking my feet. Trying to move to the edge as the river pushes me faster and harder in the other direction. I feel like we're in the middle of a game of tug-of-war, only it's me against a team of linebackers.

My boots weigh a thousand pounds and my arms are as limp as cooked noodles, but somehow I manage to pull myself closer to the edge, where six people stand waiting. Someone wades out into the water, and I kick harder, trying to propel myself to the side as the river rushes to meet the bank.

"Grab my hand!" Axl calls.

Just hearing his voice gives me enough energy to push myself. I scream as I kick and claw and pull myself through the water. My legs hit the bottom of the river, but the current is moving too fast for me to find my footing. I kick again, pushing myself against the river floor until I'm closer to the edge. Less than six feet to go.

"Axl!" I gasp, pushing harder.

He rushes forward, the water up to his waist, and Angus is right behind him. Like a good shadow, Dax follows, and then my feet find solid ground once again and I push against it with all my might, throwing myself toward the waiting men.

Hands pull me forward, so many I can't figure out what belongs to who or which one of these men I have to thank for saving my life. They pull me to land, and I collapse on top of Axl, coughing out water. Ginny is at my side in seconds, patting my back the way a mother does when a child chokes. It isn't helping, but I'm panting and coughing too hard to tell her to stop.

"You're okay," Ginny says, patting me harder. "You're okay."

I nod, trying to embrace her words even though even inch of my body aches. The coughing subsides, but shivers instantly take their place, and I know they have no intention of stopping. At least not as long as I'm soaking wet.

"F-fire," I manage to get out, turning to look around. Praying a lighter or matches magically materialize.

"We're still missin' some people," Axl says.

My gaze moves from Axl to Ginny, then over to Angus and Dax and Jim, finally stopping on Joshua. No Lila. No Al. No Parvarti.

"No," I moan, hating how beaten and pathetic I sound.

CHAPTER TWELVE

"They could still be alive," Ginny says as she helps me to my feet. "Maybe they got out of the river sooner, or maybe they were washed farther down."

"Parvarti was with you when I jumped," I say, turning my attention to Jim. "Did you see what happened to her?"

"All I saw was water," Jim says. "I'm not even positive she jumped."

I shove wet hair out of my eyes and turn to face the river like she'll show up at any second. "There's a chance she didn't even make it off the bridge, then."

"The bastards had us surrounded," Axl says.

"But Al and Lila jumped well before us, and there's no reason to assume they drowned!" Ginny throws her hands up in frustration.

"Nice to see your boyfriend dyin' didn't destroy your optimism," Angus says, his voice low. "Face it: they're dead."

Ginny's green eyes snap his way, and she takes a step toward him, her hands balled into fists at her sides. "My husband," she hisses. "My husband died. Can't you stop being a bastard for one day at least?"

"Lookie here, Hollywood," Angus says, staggering toward her. "I ain't bein' a bastard just 'cause I'm willin' to accept the truth while the rest of you walk 'round with your heads up your asses. We lost most of our shit and most of the people we had with us, and the last thing that's gonna help get us to Atlanta is holdin' onto hope that don't exist. Al's dead and so is the little piece of ass that's been followin' him 'round last few months. Does it suck? Fuck yeah. But it's the truth, and there's no point in focusin' on that when we got a whole lotta other shit to keep us occupied."

"Fuck you, Angus!" Ginny snaps, stepping closer. Her lips quivering. She grabs his shirt and uses it to pull herself closer, closing the distance between them as tears stream down her cheeks. "Just because you've never loved anyone but yourself doesn't mean the rest of us are weak or stupid for caring!"

"See, that's where you're wrong *Holl-y-wood,*" Angus says, narrowing his eyes on her face as he drags the nickname out. It's like he's using it as a weapon, and by the way Ginny winces, I can tell it worked. "I ain't never loved myself. Never thought I was worth much. But now I know that ain't true, and I'm gonna do what I gotta do to get my ass to Atlanta."

Ginny's fist tightens on the fabric of Angus's shirt. "So what? Just because you're immune the rest of us are disposable. You going to throw us in front of a horde if it comes down to it?"

Angus doesn't blink. "I'm gonna do what it takes."

Ginny's face scrunches up, and without warning, her hand lashes out. The crack of her palm making contact with Angus's cheek echoes through the silence, sounding even louder than the water rushing by us.

"You're a selfish prick!" Ginny says. "Even when you're trying to do the right thing, you're wrong."

"Ginny," I say, trying to pull her back.

Angus waves me off, still staring at Ginny. "No, Blondie,

you let her have her say."

"Jon was worth a million of you. All he thought about was others. Of making up for the mistakes he'd made that were totally out of his control. Compared to him, you're nothing but a speck of dirt on the sole of my shoe."

Tears stream down Ginny's face, and her shoulders shake with silent sobs. Her fist tightens until it looks like she's trying to tear Angus's shirt from his body. They stare at each of other for a few seconds, and then all at once, Ginny's expression changes from anger to anguish. Right in front of our faces Ginny crumbles, and without a word, Angus wraps his arms around her. He pulls her against him, hugging her while the rest of us stand there in total silence, surrounded by nothing but the rush of the river and the rustling of the trees, and the utter devastation of Ginny's sobs.

"What's the plan?" Angus asks, not letting Ginny go. His hand moves up and down her back so slowly that it reminds me of a mother trying to soothe a child. Of my mother and what Angus lost.

I sink into Axl when my stomach tightens.

Jim shakes his head as he scans the surrounding trees. "We need to follow the river, figure out where we are."

"We gotta get dry," Axl says, putting his arm around me.

"In case you hadn't noticed," Dax snaps, turning his blue eyes on Axl. "We're a little short on supplies. Unless you can figure out a way to start a fire in the middle of the woods, we're shit out of luck."

That's when I remember the book Al found. How he went back and got extra copies. How he gave me one for my pack, along with a bag full of stuff that also could help.

"Al," I mutter, pulling away from Axl so I can take off my backpack. "Damn kid was a zombie freak. It saved his ass, and ours more than once. Looks like it's going to help us again."

"What you got?" Angus asks, and even Ginny's sobs stop long enough for her to look my way.

"That book," I say, pulling the Ziploc bag from my pack. I rip the book out and hold it up for everyone to see. It may be dark, but the moon is just bright enough that they'll be able to make it out at this close range. Not that they haven't seen it before.

"*Surviving the Zombie Apocalypse*," Dax mutters, then shakes his head. "It's fiction. Written back when all this shit was fiction. Doesn't mean a thing."

"That's what you think." I flip it open, thumbing through the pages Al marked. He took his time. Sorted through all the bullshit to find the important stuff. The stuff that would keep us alive. "Chapter three: making fire."

"So?" Dax asks, sounding even more impatient than before.

"Shut up and let her read it," Jim says.

"Thanks." I scan the list of supplies until I find what I'm looking for. "All we need to get a fire going is a battery and a foil gum wrapper."

"Perfect," Dax mutters. "Let's just run on down to the local drugstore and we can pick that stuff up. Along with a bag of Doritos and some Mountain Dew."

Jim snorts and rolls his eyes like he thinks Dax is the biggest asshole in the world, and Joshua sucks in a deep breath.

Before anyone else can say a word, though, Ginny pushes away from Angus and wipes her nose on her sleeve. "Shut up."

"We have those things already, you asshole," I say, reaching into my pack and pulling the baggie out. If Al were here, I'd kiss him. "Al planned ahead."

"Balls of steel," Angus mutters.

Joshua nods and lowers his head. Even though I've never seen him do it, I can't help wondering if he's saying a silent prayer for the two missing teens.

"We can't make a fire out here," Jim says, looking around.

Axl grabs my hand. "Yeah. It'd give us away and draw any zombies that are hangin' out in the area. Let's walk a bit, and maybe we'll find us a good place to set up for the night. I don't wanna travel in the dark like this, and we'll be able to figure out where we are better once the sun is up."

"Sounds like we got us a plan," Jim says from behind us.

The others start moving, and not even Dax argues as Axl leads us through the woods and away from the river.

The bank going up to the road is steep, forcing us to climb. I look over my shoulder as I heave myself up the hill and find Angus helping Ginny. Damn. That guy never ceases to amaze me.

The top of the hill is literally within my grasp when I lose my footing. My feet slip through the loose earth, and I slide a foot or so down the hill. Back toward the riverbank. Axl reaches back to grab me, but before he has a chance, Dax is at my side. His hands on my hips as he hauls me the rest of the way up. I'm panting by the time I finally make it to the road.

Dax doesn't remove his hands.

"Thanks," I say, stepping out of his grasp.

His eyes go to my face and Axl takes a step closer, but I move between the two men.

Angus lets out a chuckle and slaps his brother on the back. "Let it go. You can kick his ass after we've found us a place to hunker down for the night."

Axl nods, but his jaw is clenched tight.

I turn away from Dax—who is still staring at me—so I can get a better look at the area. Just like almost every other street in the world, the road is empty and silent and dark. Trees line both sides, making me feel more boxed in than I like, but there isn't a sound other than the distant river and the rustle of branches knocking together above us. And the air is clear of death.

"Upstream," Jim says, heading down the street. "We keep moving that way."

Axl grabs my hand and follows the other man. Angus goes too, his arm around Ginny, and Joshua trails after us. A few seconds later, the sound of Dax's feet scraping against the pavement fills the remaining silence, and I know he's coming too.

"There's nothing to worry about," I say, slipping my hand into Axl's.

"I know."

"Then why do you get bent out of shape every time he looks at me like that?"

"'Cause it makes me think of the Monte Carlo. Don't like men lookin' at you like that. Like they want to have their way with you."

Jim looks over his shoulder, his eyes narrowing on us like he's trying to figure out what we're talking about. I look away when the hair on the back of my neck stands up.

"You can't stop it, you know," I say, lowering my voice even more.

Axl's hand tightens on mine. "I can try."

"You'll fail," I say, trying to bite back a smile.

Jealousy has never been a turn-on for me, but that's not what this is. This is love. Fierce and strong and overpowering, and I can't get enough of it. It's Axl loving me so much that the thought of anything happening to me tears him apart. I love it because it's exactly how I feel about him.

Footsteps rustle through the forest behind us, cutting through the silence. We all stop moving and turn. None of us say a word. The sound isn't coming from our group, which means it's someone walking through the woods. Through dead leaves and falling limbs.

My hand is still in Axl's when I draw my knife. Thank God I didn't lose it in the river. Unlike my gun. Around me, the others draw their knives as well. Hopefully, it isn't more than a couple zombies.

"You have your gun?" I whisper, not taking my eyes off the darkness in front of me.

"Lost it in the water," Axl says.

Jim nods at my side. "Me too."

Great. Dax isn't holding one either, so I can only assume he lost it. Which means we're down to knives. I hate it when that happens.

Someone steps out of the trees twenty feet or so back, and I tense, but behind me Angus chuckles.

"Rambo," he calls, "thought we'd seen the last of you, but I shoulda known better."

"You're louder than a herd of elephants." Parvarti heads our way, and when she steps into the light, I'm able to get a good look at her. Soaked, just like the rest of us. "Made it easy to find you."

Her gaze moves across us, taking inventory. She has to notice everyone that's missing, but she doesn't mention it. Of course.

"Where'd you come out?" Axl asks.

"A ways back," she says as she passes us. "I got lucky. My leg got caught on a submerged branch. Made it easy to pull myself out. Just wasn't sure where you all ended up."

The rest of us hurry to catch up with her, and even though I'm relieved to know Parvarti is okay, I'm still annoyed by her lack of sympathy. Eventually, something has to break through that tough exterior and make her care about life.

"Sorry to have worried you," I mutter.

Parvarti looks over her shoulder and our eyes meet, but once again she stays silent. Then she turns back to face the front and walks faster. Like she's running from me. I have a good feeling it isn't just me she's running from, though.

We walk through the dark night in silence, each of us lost in our own thoughts and nursing our own wounds. Where Lila and Al ended up is a mystery, and even though I know it's a long shot, I find myself listening intently as we move, hoping to hear a voice or two. Praying we stumble upon them the way we did Parvarti.

Ginny leans against Angus, and the further we walk, the more he seems to be supporting her. Why those two have chosen each other for comfort, I'm not sure, but I do know that disturbing them would be wrong and selfish. Doesn't stop me from wanting to hug her every time I look her way. She and Jon were only trying to move on. To carve a life for themselves out of what was left of this world. I don't understand why God thought that was too much to give them.

If there is a God.

By the time we reach the edge of a town, I'm dragging my feet and shivering from head to toe. Axl hasn't stopped rubbing his hand up and down my arm, and Dax has moved so he's walking on the other side of me. I must look colder than I feel, because Axl doesn't even tell him to get lost.

"Let's find us a house," Axl says, just loud enough that Parvarti and Jim—who are in the lead—can hear him.

Dax detaches himself from my side and jogs to the front of the group so he can lead the way into town. Even though Axl glares, he doesn't mention what just happened, and I'm glad. I'm too tired to rehash the same conversation or reassure him. Right now, all I want to do is strip off these wet clothes and snuggle under a warm blanket with a naked Axl. Preferably in front of a fire.

"House or store?" Dax calls, slightly louder than I like.

I look around, waiting for zombies to come charging, but nothing happens. Thank God. I don't think we have the energy to fight or run from a horde right now.

"Whatever we can find," Axl mutters, moving faster.

He deposits me beside to his brother and Ginny, then jogs to catch up with Jim, Parvarti, and Dax. Joshua drags himself over to stand with us. Even though I'm shivering, I stay close to Angus with my knife drawn. Freezing or not, we can't forget the reason we're on this trip.

"You thinkin' 'bout tradin' up?" Angus asks.

My eyebrows shoot up as I turn to face the man I pretty much consider my brother-in-law at this point. He can't really think I'd leave Axl. Can he? Especially not for that asshole.

"Excuse me?"

"The Rock over there." Angus jerks his head toward the building the others just disappeared into.

"Personally, I wouldn't call that trading up," I say, rolling my eyes. "But since you're asking, no."

"Just checkin'." Angus purses his lips and nods.

"Would you care?"

"Only 'cause it'd break my lil' brother's heart and I ain't really itchin' to kill nobody right now."

"Right now?" Ginny asks, looking up at Angus.

"There've been times when slittin' somebody's throat sounded mighty nice. Especially since all this bullshit started."

Ginny nods like she understands, but Joshua shuffles his feet uncomfortably. Unlike the rest of us, he hasn't had to kill since this started—unless you count zombies—so I'm sure the idea of taking another person's life is still foreign to him. For me, though, I totally get what Angus means.

"Well, you don't need to worry," I say. "I have no intention of ever being with anyone but Axl."

Angus nods, and we go back to waiting in silence.

Up ahead, the other four members of our group come out of one building and move to another. Dax and Parvarti head inside while Axl and Jim stay out front to keep watch. We're too far away to really get a good look at what they're doing, though.

"Let's go see what's going on," I say, heading down the street.

The others follow, and when we get closer, the building comes into view. It's a small church. Nothing too fancy, but it looks secure enough.

We're still six feet away when Dax and Parvarti come back outside.

"Looks good," Dax is saying as we walk up to meet them. "Will be easy to secure since there's only this front exit and one in the back. No dead bodies, and by the smell of things, there never were. Best part: looks like they had a food pantry set up for the needy families of this town."

Angus snorts. "We're the needy bastards now."

We head in as a clump, dragging our feet and shivering. Even Parvarti doesn't look totally devoid of emotion when we step inside and find it several degrees warmer than the chilly night air. I'm not sure what time it is at this point, but it has to be well after midnight. A couple hours of sleep sounds like a dream come true.

But first we have to get some things done.

"Food pantry is over there." Jim points to the right. His eyes settle on me, and he says, "Check and see if they have clothes. I'd be willing to bet they collected that kind of stuff in addition to canned goods."

"I'm on it."

I head toward the food pantry just as Dax says, "We can get a fire going, but first we need to find something to burn and figure out where we're going to do it. Can't risk burning the place down no matter how cold and wet we are."

"If this is anything like the church I grew up in, I'd guess the kitchen will have a large pot," Ginny says through a fog of exhaustion. "We can burn the hymnals in it."

"Not as good as wood, but it's something," Jim says.

His voice fades away, and I can only assume he's headed off to check out the kitchen. Which is fine by me. The sooner they find a pot, the sooner we can use the battery Al left us to get a fire going. I only hope the church has blankets and clothes and things like that as well as food.

"Need help?" Parvarti says from behind me.

I look over my shoulder long enough to see her heading after me, and I nod. Mad or not, I won't turn my nose up at help.

The room this church used as a food pantry isn't the small closet I expected, but there isn't a single window to help give the room light. I step through the darkness with my arms out in front of me until my fingers touch a shelf, then feel around. I'm hoping to find something that feels like it could be clothes, but all my fingers brush against are cans and cardboard boxes that I can only assume hold things like cereal and crackers. Despite the shivering in my limbs, my stomach rumbles.

"Oh!" Parvarti gasps.

I turn, ready to run to her side and help, but before I've had a chance to take even one step, she has a flashlight flipped on. The beam hits me in the eye and I shield my face, but she only shrugs.

"Wouldn't kill you to actually care about something," I mutter as I turn away.

The shelves in front of me are lined with food, just like I thought, and seeing how much is here takes my breath away. We'd be good for a couple months if we got stuck here. That's something at least.

"I care," Parvarti whispers behind me, her voice just as devoid of emotion as it always is.

"Could have fooled the rest of us," I say, moving past the food to inspect the other shelves. Just like Jim thought, they're lined with clothes. There are even a few blankets that are obviously used but not too worse for wear.

"I still feel," Parvarti whispers, making me turn. Her voice sounds unbelievably tiny in the small space, and the sound takes me back to the way she was when we first met. The day we picked her up on Route 66—along with Trey. Back before the world had totally disappeared and the idea of zombies was ridiculous. "That's what makes all this suck so much. No matter how many times I tell myself not to feel, I can't stop it. Every time something bad happens, every time we lose someone or the little bit of hope that's been handed to us is ripped away, it feels like Trey getting killed all over again." She lets out a deep sigh and shakes her head, staring at the ground. "That day I picked the three of you up and saw the bite on Angus, I seriously considered putting a bullet in my head after I finished him off."

Not only is it the most she's said in months, but it's the most emotion she's shown. I really thought everything inside her had died along with Trey, but now I realize that isn't true. She's just not dealing with it. With any of this.

"Is that what you want?" I ask. "For it all to be over."

"Sometimes, yes."

I have the urge to cross the room and hug her, but I don't know the Parvarti standing in front of me, and I'm not sure how this stranger would react. "You're not the only one who wants it all to end. I'm sure we've all had those moments. You aren't alone, Parv."

"Feels like I am."

Axl walks into the room behind us, and Parvarti rips her eyes away from the carpet so she can focus on the shelves. The icy mask slips back onto her face, but this time it doesn't annoy me. It only makes me feel sorry for her. I wouldn't be much better off if I were in her shoes.

Axl stares at Parv for a few seconds before turning to me. "We got us a couple pots and a whole stack of hymnals. You find some stuff?"

"There's a lot in here, actually." I turn back to face the stacks of clothes and start digging.

There will be time to talk to Parvarti about all this. This isn't the last day we have on this Earth. Not if we have a say in it.

CHAPTER THIRTEEN

We manage to find enough clothes for everyone, meaning we're able to strip off our wet stuff so we can let them dry. Ginny and I work together to spread the wet clothes across the church pews while Parvarti and Axl use the supplies Al gave us to get a couple fires going. It's amazingly simple, and within seconds, there are hymnals burning in two pots so large I'm sure they could make enough chili to feed fifty people. Joshua, Jim, and Dax carry canned goods and other food into the sanctuary, while Angus lounges on a pew next to the fire, smoking a cigarette he says he found in the church office.

"Should see if they got any of that communion wine," Angus calls across the sanctuary to where Axl is pulling hymnals from pews.

"Don't know where they'd keep it," his brother says.

I turn to Ginny. "Any ideas?"

I didn't go to church growing up, and it's obvious the brothers didn't either. It's hard to say with the other four, but

Ginny has been open enough about her childhood for me to know she used to have a picture-perfect life. Nice family. Nice house. Church on Sunday mornings and sleepovers with girlfriends on Friday nights. Normal stuff I thought only happened to families who lived inside my TV screen.

"Maybe in the kitchen?" she says. "Not sure."

"Hollywood was too goody-goody to do something like sneak communion wine." Angus shoots her a monkey grin, and even though it's laced with exhaustion and grief, Ginny throws him a weak smile.

"Why do you call her that?" Dax asks as he dumps a handful of cans on the floor. "I get all the other nicknames: Doc, Blondie, Rambo. Obvious. Where's Hollywood come from, though?"

Angus's eyebrows fly up, and he glances Ginny's way. She isn't looking, though. She's helping Axl pull hymnals out of the pews.

"Just a name is all." Angus shrugs as he shoots Dax another grin.

The other man frowns, and it's immediately obvious that he doesn't like being on the outside of things. "Yeah, but—"

"Because I'm Hadley Lucas." Ginny's voice echoes through the room and everyone freezes except her. She just keeps pulling books out of their slots and stacking them in her arms. "I changed my name so I could start over, but there doesn't seem to be much of a point in that now. Does there?"

"Shit," Dax says, looking around the room at the rest of us. "I didn't make the connection. Not even after you all asked about Hadley Lucas that day in Duncan."

Ginny dumps her books in a pile next to the pot, staring down at the flames as they flicker across the pages. Smoke trails up and collects above us in the rafters, eventually making its way to the windows Axl propped open.

"Apparently, I don't deserve a do-over. Maybe none of us do. Maybe this is like the flood. God saw how corrupt the world had become, so he wiped us out, leaving a few of us here so he could have a little fun."

"That's not what you think," Parvarti says, her eyes wide. Almost like Ginny's pessimism is the scariest thing she's had to encounter since all this started. Ironic, considering there are zombies walking the earth.

Ginny turns her gaze toward Parv and shrugs. "I don't know what I think, but I do know that every time things start to look like they're going to end up okay, God decides to take a little piss on our parade."

No one says a word or acknowledges that Ginny is absolutely right. We fight and struggle and work, only to have it pulled away. Maybe this is all some game for God. Like the *Hunger Games,* but instead of President Snow presiding over the event, God and all his angels are watching from their fluffy white clouds, laughing whenever we trip up yet again.

Ginny sniffs once, then turns on her heel, heading out of the room. I know her well enough to know she isn't running off so she can hide how pissed she is. She's teetering on the edge.

"I'll be right back," I say, hurrying out after her.

By the time I get in the hall, she's disappeared.

"Ginny," I whisper.

She doesn't answer, but her sobs echo through the darkness. I follow the sound, going deeper into the dark abyss of the church until she finally comes into view. Curled up in a corner.

I kneel at her side, and she doesn't resist when I wrap my arms around her. Ginny had her cry on the bus, then again by the river while Angus held her, but this is the first chance she's had to grieve away from the threat of the world. Out there, it had to be quick, and she couldn't give herself to it completely. But here, we're relatively safe, and she should take full advantage of that.

"This is my fault," Ginny says between hiccups. "He didn't want to come. He didn't think it was a good idea, but I made him. I was scared and I wanted to be in Atlanta, so I didn't listen to him when he told me it wasn't safe. If I had, he'd be alive."

"You can't think like that," I say. "Jon wouldn't want you to blame yourself."

I hold her tighter, trying to think of a way to take some of her pain away. I did the same thing back in the Monte Carlo after what that man did to her. I didn't come up with an answer then, and I know I won't be able to now either. There's nothing I can do to make this situation okay for Ginny.

She nods, but her sobs don't let up. I don't expect them to. Not for a while at least. So I hold her tighter. Settling in while I wait for her to get it all out. Every shake of her body makes my own throat tighten, and every sniff she lets out goes straight to my chest. Like a bullet. That's what it feels like. I don't understand her pain because I still have Axl, but I can imagine what she's going through.

It takes a while, but eventually her sobs subside and her shoulders relax. Then the sniffles ease, too. When she finally pulls back and wipes her hand across her face, a deep sigh comes out instead of more sobs.

"I'm hungry."

I stand, taking her with me, and do my best not to groan when my back pops.

"Let's get something to eat," I say, pulling her back toward the group.

When we walk back in, the room is totally silent except the occasional crunch of food or crinkle of plastic wrappers. Jim looks up, his eyes following Ginny, and I'm reminded of the conversation I overheard this morning, back in Hope Springs. He promised to keep an eye on her if something were to happen to Jon. That makes me feel better.

No one says anything when Ginny and I sit, and we don't talk, either. Almost like we're afraid to disturb the silence. I dig into a can of pears, not even tasting them or caring that they're grainy and something I would have turned my nose up at before. Across from me, Angus smokes between taking bites of Spam, finishing up one can before moving onto another. Parvarti and Joshua and Jim eat in silence as well, so focused on their food that if I didn't know any better, I'd think they were eating a delicacy. Axl digs into the can of something I can't see while Dax crunches on Doritos. It's odd that he brought them up a few hours ago and here they are. Even more strange that the food pantry had them.

"They had Doritos?" I ask, nodding toward the bag.

Dax smiles through the cheesy goodness. "Found them in the kitchen and couldn't resist. They used to be my favorite. Sunday football with a cold beer and a bag of Doritos was probably one of my favorite things to do."

"Sounds nice," I say, smiling despite the fact that it's Dax I'm talking to and I don't like him and I don't want to be near him.

"What about you?" he asks, lifting an eyebrow.

"Me?"

"What do you miss about the world before?"

I shake my head while I think it over, but all the normal answers don't apply to me. Not having to worry: I don't know what that feels like. Family: didn't have any. Friends: pretty much the same. Job: hated it. What did I do for fun? What did I love? The answer is obvious: nothing. There was nothing about my old life that I really, truly loved. In fact, I have more to care about now than I ever had before. The only thing that kept me going through all those years of pain and struggle was the possibility that it *could* get better, which is the same thing keeping me going now.

That and Axl.

"Hope," I say.

Dax stops chewing mid-crunch, and for once, when his eyes rake over me, it doesn't feel like he's trying to do anything other than *see* me.

Axl scoots closer to my side, and I snuggle into him when he pulls my body to his. Dax starts chewing again, eyes still on me, and even though I've told Axl a million times not to worry, there's something in Dax's look that makes the hair on my scalp prickle uncomfortably.

I push the pears away and shift so my back is to Dax and my face is pressed into Axl's chest. The donated clothes he's wearing smell musty, but it doesn't deter me from closing my eyes.

"You take the first watch," Axl says, his voice echoing through his chest and vibrating against my ears. By the cold tone in his voice, I can only assume he's talking to Dax.

His arms tighten around me, and I allow my body to relax until it feels almost weightless. Sleep creeps its way through me, and I seem to float, rising above the others with Axl at my side and darkness closing in.

I WAKE TO THE UNCOMFORTABLE TINGLE OF A FULL bladder. The room is silent, but the fires still burn in the pots, and when I wiggle out of Axl's arms I find Dax still awake. Staring at me the same way he was when I last looked at him.

"You okay?" he whispers.

"Have to pee," I say, pulling myself to my feet.

Sometime during my nap my foot must have fallen asleep, and when I stand, I'm greeted by the feeling of pins and needles. I lift my foot off the ground and wiggle it to get the blood flowing, holding the pew for support. Dax watches every move I make on the other side of the fires, and something about his expression reminds me of that first night I camped on the side of the road with Axl and Angus. Only instead of me wanting to get to know him more the way I did with Axl, his look sends a shudder through my body.

"I'll be back," I say, tiptoeing my way through my sleeping companions.

I find the church's restroom and squat over the toilet even though there's no water, grateful that the room doesn't reek of urine. Why no one took refuge in this church is a mystery, but one I'm thankful for. There aren't a lot of untouched areas anymore. Not like this.

When I'm done, I head back out into the hall and almost bump into Dax, who is standing right outside the door.

"What are you doing?" I ask, stepping back. Suddenly nervous and wishing Axl would wake up and come looking for me. Even if it would most likely lead to Dax getting his ass kicked.

"Just wanted to make sure you were okay."

"I'm fine," I say, pushing past him. "The church is clear."

Dax grabs my arm before I can get far and spins me around to face him. I try to step away but only end up with my back against the wall and Dax towering over me. His blue eyes study mine, sending another shiver down my spine. This look doesn't remind of the way Axl looked at me when we first met. He looked at me like he could have died happy just listening to me talk. Dax looks like he wants to *own* me.

"You and Axl have been together long?"

"Since this started," I say as my eyes dart past Dax to the room all my friends are sleeping in. I could scream, but I'm not sure if it's necessary. I didn't think Dax was dangerous in *this* way, and I'm still not totally sure. He could just want to talk. Test the waters. See if I'm as committed to Axl as he is to me. "We're happy. I know you're attracted to me, but I'm not going to leave Axl. Not for you or anyone else. Not ever."

Dax frowns, and his eyes hold mine for a few seconds before he says, "Why a redneck like him? I don't get it."

"You wouldn't, so there's no point in trying to explain."

His words prickle at my nerves, but I refuse to lose my cool. It doesn't matter what he thinks of Axl. I'm with the right person, and that is what's important.

"I think I could change your mind," Dax says, his eyes moving to my lips.

"Don't." The warning in my voice is so thick it echoes through the hall.

"You might like it."

"You think you're the first man to ever say that? Trust me, if you have to say those words to a woman, one thing is obvious: she isn't going to like it, and you know it. You're just too self-absorbed to accept it."

Dax moves closer to me, and his chest touches mine, pinning me against the wall. Setting warning bells off in my head. "I *don't* know it, though."

I slip my hand behind me, fingering my knife while I try to decide what to do. Dax licks his lips, making the hair on my scalp prickle. I don't like him, but that isn't the point. We have to get Angus to Atlanta, and we're going to need every able-bodied man or woman we have to make it. Which means, asshole or not, we need Dax.

"Step back," I say coolly, allowing my hand to fall away from my knife and wiggling my toes. Preparing to knee Dax in the crotch. "I said no."

Dax presses his lips together, and I hold my breath while I wait to find out what he's going to do. Finally, after a few seconds, he exhales. "Fine."

Before he's had a chance to take a step, hands close on his shoulders, and he's ripped away. In the blink of an eye, Dax is across the hall, laying on the floor in a heap.

"Thought you was smarter than that," Angus says, glaring down at the bigger man. "When somebody says no, you best listen."

Dax climbs to his feet, dusting his pants off like he's wearing a thousand-dollar suit instead of someone's throwaway sweatpants. "Nothing happened."

"Ain't what it looked like from where I was standin'."

"Come on!" Dax yells, throwing his hands up. "I had to give it a shot. He may be your brother, but you can't tell me you haven't thought the exact same thing. How many women are left in this world? Not enough, and the ones that are left sure as hell don't look like *that*!"

I cross my arms over my chest, torn between the urge to hurl and laugh. Even though Dax is being an ass, he isn't far off. Angus tried to make a move on me once, back in San Francisco. Sure, Axl and I weren't together, but he knew something was going to happen and he tried to get his foot in the door first anyway.

"Forget it," I say, pushing myself off the wall. "Just don't try it again. You hear me, Dax?"

Dax nods even though he doesn't look very happy about it, and I shoot Angus a grateful smile before heading back into the sanctuary.

"Keep an eye on Angus since so you're so worried about everyone's safety," I call over my shoulder.

THE NEXT TIME I WAKE, IT'S BECAUSE EVERYONE ELSE is already moving around. Even Dax, who probably didn't get a whole lot of rest. When I manage to get to my feet, I see why. Someone found a map.

"Where'd you find it?" I ask as I head over to join Dax, Jim, Angus, and Axl.

Dax flinches at the sound of my voice—something I'm sure doesn't escape Axl's notice—but he doesn't look up. "Went down the street to a gas station."

"Thank God," I say, raking my fingers through my blonde hair so I can pull it back. "Do we know where we are yet?"

"Here." Axl points to the map, and I lean closer, making Dax shy away from me even more than he did a few seconds ago. "Not too far from St. Louis. Little more than halfway to Atlanta, which settles the argument I was havin' with Joshua this mornin'."

"What argument is that?" I ask, tracing our route with my gaze. Even on the map it looks daunting, and there are no zombies in this little paper utopia.

"He wanted to head back to Hope Springs and regroup. Thought it was closer, but it ain't. Best thing we can do is push forward. Hopefully, we'll find us a vehicle." Axl looks up, but he isn't focused on me. He's looking at Ginny, who is awake but sprawled out across a pew. "Gonna be rough if we gotta go on foot."

"We'll find something," I say firmly.

Dax lets out a deep breath. "She should stay here."

"What?" Axl and I say at the same time.

Jim shakes his head, which is something he seems to do a lot when Dax talks.

"She's going to slow us down and it's too dangerous," Dax says. "I didn't want her to come to begin with and this is why. She's a liability and a distraction we don't need."

"Out of the question," I say, shaking my head. "You can't leave her here on her own."

"The doctor can stay. Hell, Parvarti can stay for all I care. I'd say you could stay too—" Dax turns to Axl, "—but I have a feeling you wouldn't leave Angus."

"Wouldn't," Axl says.

"Then there's no point in arguing about that. Ginny, though, is something I have to insist on."

"Don't be an ass!" I say, taking a step closer to Dax.

"It's not going to happen," Jim says from behind me, his voice low and firm and way more terrifying than I've ever heard him sound.

"I'm in charge here," Dax replies, puffing his chest out so much that it reminds me of a rooster. "And my priority is getting Angus to Atlanta safely. I said that all along, and that hasn't changed." Dax pauses, looking me over for a second before saying, "In fact, you stay, too. You're as much of a distraction as she is." His eyes are still on me when he jerks his thumb toward Ginny, who is now staring at us. Along with everyone else.

"Fuck you!" I yell, shoving my finger into Dax's chest. "You're not leaving me behind just because I rejected you and you can't handle it. You knew before you played that card that you didn't have a chance in hell, but you decided to go all in anyway. It isn't my fault it backfired."

"What the fuck did I miss?" Axl growls from behind me.

I shake my head, refusing to take my eyes off Dax. "Nothing. That's what you missed. This asshole came on to me, but nothing happened, which is what has his panties in a twist."

"That isn't what this is about and you know it!" Dax says just as Axl grabs his arm and spins him around.

Axl's fist slams into Dax's nose before he's even had a chance to blink, and the big man goes down. I jump back, waiting for Axl to pummel him the way Angus would. But nothing happens. Axl just stands over the other guy with his hands clenched at his sides. Panting. Blood seeps from Dax's nose, but neither one of the men moves.

"I ain't gonna beat the shit outta you this time, but if you ever go near her again, you'll be sorry. Understand?" Dax nods. "Good. This discussion is over. We ain't leavin' anybody behind. We're a family, and family don't run out on each other, and we don't screw each other over, neither. So keep that in mind."

Axl turns and walks out of the room, but everyone else just stares at Dax, who is still sprawled out on the floor.

"You alright?" Joshua asks, heading over to check the big man out.

"Does it look like I'm fucking alright?" Dax growls as he climbs to his feet.

"Don't act like you aren't the asshole here," Jim mutters.

Joshua shoves Dax's hands away from his bloody nose so he can give it a once-over. "Jim's right. You knew what you were doing and you knew what the consequences were going to be. Hope it was worth it."

Dax snorts, which makes him wince, and then he looks at me. "Would have been worth it if she'd said yes."

"You're an ass," I mutter, heading after Axl.

I find him leaning against the wall and a lot less furious than I thought he'd be.

"Anythin' happen?" he asks, not even looking my way.

"No. He put himself out there and I shot him down. I was all ready to kick him in the balls if he didn't back off, but Angus showed up and saved the day."

"He's been a regular hero lately," Axl says, letting out a bitter chuckle. "Still don't seem right."

I'm glad he still has a sense of humor, and I'm glad he isn't going to make a big deal of this thing. Dax got what he deserved, and as far as I'm concerned, it's now over.

"Angus is finding his place in this world," I say, anxious to move onto a different topic. "Better late than never."

"Guess so."

"You know where we're heading?"

Axl finally looks my way, and the little smile on his face is one I haven't seen before. Playful for such a serious moment. "Route 66."

That explains the mood change.

I laugh. "You have to be kidding me."

"Nope. Since it was blocked off for travel, it should be clear. Plus, with all them people tryin' to get places last fall, we stand a better chance of findin' an abandoned car there than any place else. Assumin' we can find gas. And we ain't too far. Just a couple miles, it looks like."

"Well, it's not exactly what I expected, but that doesn't mean it's a bad thing. Route 66 isn't going to be any more dangerous than anywhere else." This time it's my turn to smile. "So I guess it's back to where we started."

"Guess so."

"When do we leave?"

CHAPTER FOURTEEN

"We don't know how long we're going to be on foot. Are you sure you're going to be okay?" I ask, studying Ginny as she shoves her things into her pack.

She shoves one last thing in her pack before zipping it shut. When she looks up, she sighs. "Do I have a choice?"

"I guess not."

"I'm not sure any of us are going to be okay," she says, looking away. "But if you're asking whether or not I can make it, I can."

"Ginny." I put my hand on her arm, and she tenses for just a second before turning back to face me. When her green eyes meet mine, they're shimmering with tears. "I'm so sorry. I—I wanted to do more than just hug you yesterday, but I didn't know what to say. Still don't. Maybe I should keep my mouth shut, I don't know, but I want you to know that I'm here if you want to talk, and that I understand. That I'm sorry and I wish things hadn't happened this way."

"I know," she whispers, her voice crackling with unshed tears and emotion too deep to express with words. "He was so happy about this baby and what the future could mean for us. It just doesn't seem fair."

"I think fair is something we're going to have to get used to doing without." Not that I was ever under any delusion such a thing existed.

"Yeah."

She turns back to her bag, slinging it over her shoulder. It's bulging at the seams, and I have serious doubts about her ability to carry it down the street, let alone across hundreds of miles of possibly hostile terrain.

"Where are we headed?" Ginny asks when she turns back to me.

"Route 66," I say, a laugh forcing its way out despite the pain of a few seconds ago. I still can't believe that's where we're headed.

She gives me a strange look. "What's so funny about that?"

"It's where I met Axl and Angus. Where we picked up Joshua and Parv and Trey. It's weird to think we'll be back on that road after all these months."

"That is weird. You traveled all that way just to end up where you started."

"Story of my life," I say with a snort.

"You girls ready?" Axl yells from across the room.

"Yup!" I call back, my eyes still on Ginny and her overstuffed pack. With it on her back and her belly as round as it is, she looks like she has a couple major deformities.

Together we head to the front door, where the others are already waiting. Parvarti is outside with Angus and Jim, smoking, but the other three men are waiting at the door for us. Dax's nose is swollen and turning purple, and he's standing away from the others with arms crossed, looking more like a solemn child than a fearless leader. Hopefully, he doesn't let his hurt pride get in the way of doing his job. Because Dax is right: getting Angus to Atlanta is still the most important thing in the world.

"Let me know if you get tired of carrying that," I say as Ginny and I join the men.

Axl shoves the door open, and his gray eyes sweep over Ginny, stopping on her pack. He frowns but doesn't say anything. He's probably biding his time. Trying to pick the best thing to say to her at the best time so she'll admit she needs help. She's always been tough, and I'm glad to know that Jon's death didn't destroy her the way Nathan's destroyed Moira, but that doesn't mean she has to struggle alone.

The view on our walk to Route 66 is really no different than anything else we've seen over the last few months. Empty streets dotted with the occasional abandoned car, as well as miles and miles of utter nothingness stretching out in front of us. Trash blows down the street, and the doors to houses and businesses hang open like the people just walked out and left everything behind. The life they had before totally forgotten.

Seeing it all fly by as we barreled down the road, hidden in the safety of our bus, made it possible for me to ignore the utter stillness that has taken over the world. This is more unsettling. The empty streets are too quiet to feel real, even after all these months. There should be some noise. The hum of electricity or the roar of an engine as a plane passes overhead or even the motor of some distant car. Instead, there is nothing but silence, and the burden of it seems so heavy that I find myself wanting to scream after less than an hour of walking.

"Do you really think it's possible to rebuild all this?" Ginny asks out of nowhere.

I shrug and glance toward her, shielding my eyes from the bright morning sun. "We can't restore it to the way things used to be. Not exactly. But making *something* has to be possible. Right?"

"Yeah," she whispers. "I guess you're right. I mean, we started out with nothing. Hundreds of years ago when the first settlers came here. Look at us now. It may take centuries to get somewhere substantial again, but we can do it."

There's little hope in her voice, despite her words.

"We can do it," I say, attempting to sound more positive than I feel. I don't think it works.

Ginny rubs her hand across her belly and lets out a deep sigh, and I expect her to say something. About the baby or Jon or what she hopes life will be like for her child. Instead, she goes back to walking in silence.

We break for a bit when we reach Route 66, giving Joshua time to take Ginny's blood pressure and force some water down her throat. All of us take the opportunity to rest except Axl and Dax, who pace—a good distance from each other. Axl's gaze is focused on the surrounding area, keeping an eye out for zombies or anything else that might be a threat, whereas Dax alternates between staring at Angus and staring at me. His gaze makes it difficult to relax.

When we get ready to head out again, Jim takes Ginny's pack and starts walking before she even has time to protest. He's silent most of the time, but it hasn't escaped my notice that he's keeping a constant watch on his partner's widow. It makes me like him—and trust him—even more than I already did.

By the time we start walking again, the sun is right above us. I've begun to sweat, causing my shirt to stick to my body, and before long, a tingle has started in my exposed skin, slowly morphing into a feeling that's a little too close to burning for my comfort.

"We should try to find some sunscreen next time we pass a gas station or convenience store," I say, rubbing my arms like that will somehow brush the sun's rays off me.

"And hats." Joshua sweeps his dark hair off his forehead, and a drop of sweat falls to his cheek, rolling down to his chin before he's had time to brush it away. Like me, his shirt is drenched in sweat.

"Sun's hot," Dax mutters, pulling his shirt over his head

to reveal a body that's so chiseled it doesn't look real. More like a statue carved from marble that you'd see in an art museum.

Axl snorts but doesn't say a word.

I fall back until I'm standing at Ginny's side. "Take a drink," I say, holding the canteen of water out to her.

She shakes her head and pushes it away. "There isn't much left."

"Doesn't matter. You're thirty-four weeks pregnant. If anyone needs it, you do. Don't make me give you a lecture about how you need to do it for your baby, if not for yourself."

She sighs as she takes the bottle from me but takes a big gulp anyway.

When she hands it back, she says, "Before Jon and I worked things out, I didn't want this baby. It was a curse because I couldn't know for sure who it belonged to, and it was a constant reminder of what had happened. Of that asshole—" She swallows. "But Jon and I made something of this life. Together. Before long, I found myself actually enjoying the idea of having a baby. It was easy to be happy when I thought of Jon and who he was and the kind of father he'd be. But now…I don't know what I'm going to do."

"This baby is Jon's," I say firmly.

"We'll never know that for sure, and I'm terrified that when I look into its eyes, all I'll be able to see is that monster."

She clenches her hands into fists, and suddenly Hadley Lucas is standing next to me. Only she isn't Hadley the movie star. She's the Hadley who walked out of the Monte Carlo, damaged and almost beaten. Angry and bitter. I was sure that woman had died and been buried, but it seems she might have suffered the same fate as all the other poor souls who died from the virus.

I wrap my hand around her fist and give it a gentle squeeze. "No matter what happens, all you need to know is you won't be alone. We'll get through this together."

Ginny just nods.

The sun slips through the sky, getting lower and lower the farther we walk. It's almost touching the horizon by the time a building comes into view. The blue sky surrounding it has morphed to bright orange, bleeding into pink and purple the higher it goes. Soon it will be dark, but even if night wasn't closing in on us, I know we're done for the day. We need rest.

Ginny and I walk at the back of the pack, but the others aren't too far ahead. Parvarti and Jim seem to have taken to walking in the lead. Maybe their mutual appreciation for silence is good for bonding. Dax keeps close to Angus, while Axl tries to keep his distance from our *leader*. Joshua stays toward the middle.

Ginny shields her eyes so she can get a better look at the building in front of us. "What is that?"

"Looks like a diner," Jim throws over his shoulder.

"Might be a good place to stop for the night," Joshua says from only three feet in front of Ginny and me.

"And look for a car," I mutter.

We get closer and I'm able to get a better look at the building, and a strange feeling of nostalgia comes over me. The diner has to be over fifty years old, but by the time the virus hit, it probably wasn't much more than a truck stop. There have to be dozens—or hundreds—of diners that look like this along Route 66, but to me, this one is different than all of them. Special, even. Because I've been here before. Back when I was a different person living in a different world, still hopeful that I'd be able to have a future with my daughter.

This was where I first saw Angus.

"Angus!" I call, laughing as I jog to catch up with him. "Do you recognize this place?"

I'm grinning so much my cheeks hurt, which of course makes Angus look at me like I've sprouted a couple extra heads. Not that I care. There's something about coming back here after all these months that has made me almost giddy.

"Should I?" he asks, spitting before turning back to study the diner.

"I stopped here on my way to California and ordered a cup of coffee. It's where I saw you for the first time. Remember?" I elbow him playfully. "I know you remember the first time you saw me. You looked at me like I was on the menu."

Angus snorts but runs his hand over his head, still looking at the diner. "Oh I remember, but this here looks like a million other shitholes on this strip of highway. You sure this is the right place?"

"I'm sure," I say, turning back to face the diner. "I'd bet my life on it."

"If you say so," he mutters.

We reach the diner a few minutes later, and I wait close to Ginny's side while Dax and Jim go in to check the place out. Joshua leans against the wall while Angus and Parv smoke—a habit that's gotten more and more common as time goes by—and Axl stands with his knife out like a horde is bearing down on us. After less than five minutes, Dax comes back out. Alone.

"Where's Jim?" Ginny asks, glancing past the large man so she can look through the open door.

"Inside." Dax waves for us to go inside. "The place is clear other than a couple bodies in the kitchen. We'll have to drag them out. Can't say it smells that great, but it's pretty much par for the course these days."

"As long as there's a place to sit and put my legs up, I don't care." Ginny pushes past Dax and heads inside, practically running. Her feet must be giving her more trouble than she's letting on.

Parvarti goes next, not saying a word, and I follow behind her, oddly excited to see the inside of the diner again. Even though Angus isn't sure about the place, I'd know it anywhere.

Just like Dax said, the air is stuffy and carries the faint scent of decay. It isn't just bodies, though. The stink of rotten food is just as strong, which makes sense. It is a diner.

The place is dark, and the little bit of light shining through the windows only serves to highlight the dust floating in the air, but it's exactly the way I remember it—minus the mass of terrified people clogging the place. The red-and-gray vinyl booths are cracked and covered in duct tape, and the grease coating the grimy walls is visible even in the dim light. I remember standing in front of the bathroom sink, trying to see myself in the cracked and filmy mirror but also not wanting to see myself. Back then, my reflection always betrayed me. It would smile back, looking pretty and put-together. Young and fresh. But on the inside, I was always searching for something more. Hoping that if I just hung on long enough, things would get better. That I'd end up with a life filled with happily-ever-afters.

I was too naïve to realize those things didn't really exist.

Axl stops next to me and puts his hand on my lower back. "You okay?"

"Yeah. Just thinking about how much has changed since the last time I was here."

My gaze moves over the dark and dusty diner, stopping on the register. The handwritten *Cash Only* sign hanging above it is a reminder of what the world had come to before most of humanity disappeared. Above that, an old tube TV is mounted on the wall, and I can't help smiling.

"Last time I was here, the news was on. There was some story about two guys who had held up a few convenience stores in the St. Louis area." I raise my eyebrows when I turn to face Axl. "You know anything about that?"

He chuckles but shakes his head. "We didn't hurt nobody."

"You told her that shit?" Angus grunts and looks around. "Figures. Never could keep your trap shut. Don't matter now, though. All that money we got was worthless less than two weeks later. Might as well be out of a board game."

"You robbed stores?" Ginny asks from the booth she's sprawled out in—the same one Angus and Axl were sitting in the last time I was here.

"Needed some cash," Angus says with a shrug. "Let's get them bodies out and get a fire started. That kid pack more gum wrappers and batteries?"

"He did," I say, dropping my pack on top of the table so I can dig through it.

"Good. We'll need to boil some water if they don't got none."

"Where's Jim?" I ask, looking around. He came in with Dax but didn't come back out. As far as I can tell, though, he isn't around.

"Kitchen," Dax says as he heads that way. "I'll go see if I can help him." He ducks through the door, muttering about how he's the one who's supposed to be in charge. As if Angus shouldn't waste energy using his brain just because he's immune.

Angus ignores Dax and says, "Rambo, you head on back and see what kinda canned food they got. I'm gonna look for knives. Big ones they used for cuttin' up meat. We're short on weapons, and it don't hurt to be prepared."

He heads after Dax, and Axl is right behind his brother. Parvarti goes too, moving behind them without a word.

"I want to check you over," Joshua tells Ginny when everyone else has disappeared into the kitchen. "It was a long walk today. How are you feeling?"

"Like I walked a hundred miles. My feet are killing me and my ankles feel like they're about to explode." Ginny leans her head against the wall and lets out a deep breath. "I'm exhausted."

"Let's get your shoes off so I can take a look."

Ginny doesn't fight Joshua when he moves to take off her shoes, but she also doesn't help. Her eyelids are so heavy that I doubt she's going to be able to stay awake much longer, and I'm glad. She needs the rest more than any of us.

"Your ankles are swollen," Joshua mutters.

"Not a surprise, is it?" she says without opening her eyes.

"You need to drink more water and you need to stay off your feet the whole time we're here. Hopefully, we can find a car so you don't have to do this again tomorrow."

"That would be nice," Ginny says through a yawn. "But right now, I just want to sleep."

The booth she's lying in is so narrow I doubt she'll be able to sleep without falling off. We need to figure something else out.

I pull on the table, smiling when it moves easily, then drag it out into the aisle.

"What are you doing?" Joshua asks.

"Trying to make something that's a little closer to a bed," I say, turning toward the booth across from Ginny.

Just like the table, it moves with little effort, making it easy for me to push it over until it's right up against the one Ginny is already lying on.

I stand back and smile. "Now she has twice as much room."

"You're my hero," Ginny says, scooting over so she can curl up on the double benches. She rests her head on her crossed arms and closes her eyes, and within seconds I'm pretty sure she's out.

I turn and head toward the kitchen to see what the others are doing, whispering to Joshua, "I'm going to see if Axl needs any help."

"Sure you are." The doctor chuckles.

I stop and spin around to face him. "Was that a joke?"

He shrugs and his grin doesn't fade, and I find my own smile growing. Joshua doesn't joke around much, and after the way he acted on the bus, I sure didn't expect it from him now. Maybe the distance will help him move on.

"Sounds like Angus might be rubbing off on you."

"Lord help us," Joshua says, his shoulders shaking with laughter. "He's been better lately, but he's still Angus."

"I couldn't have said it better," I reply, heading back toward the kitchen.

I find the back door open and Dax and Jim struggling to drag a body out. It used to be a woman, and she's wearing the uniform I remember from my last visit here: orange dress and barely white apron that's covered in stains. The skin clinging to her bones is so gray and decayed that it's hard to believe she was ever a living, breathing person, and there are bites covering almost every inch of her flesh. Her face looks as if it's been gnawed on, whether by a zombie or rats or some other creature, I'm not sure, but there's so little left of her features that whatever it was definitely went away with a full stomach. It's her hair that stands out, though. It's short and jet-black, so dark and fake-looking that no one would ever mistake it for being natural. I remember it from the last time I was here, and seeing it stuck to her decaying and mutilated corpse sends a jolt through me.

"She got me a cup of coffee when I stopped here," I say, shaking my head.

Angus grunts from the other side of the room, where he and Parvarti are busy piling cans of food on the counter. "Yup. Served us, too. I recognized the name on her uniform. Doris."

"Hope she didn't suffer too much," I say.

"Who cares?" Angus practically growls. "Everybody we pass probably died in pain. Why bother sheddin' a tear for her?"

"Because I met her, I guess. I saw how hard she worked and the kind of life she lived. I doubt anyone working in a place like this had it easy."

"Stupid," Angus mutters. "You had a shit life. Who felt sorry for you?"

I'm not surprised Angus doesn't understand, and I'm not interested in arguing with him about it.

"Whatever," I say, heading out the back door.

CHAPTER FIFTEEN

Jim and Dax are heading back toward the building when I step out, and Axl is behind them. They dragged the waitress's body past the dumpster, over to where a second body is already laid out. Even though I should be used to bodies, there's something about seeing the woman lying under the setting sun that makes me sick. I don't know why. There are bodies everywhere these days, and I didn't really know this woman. What's more, the limited interaction I had with her was unpleasant. To put it nicely.

Dax walks by me, barely glancing my way even though he's spent most of the day with his eyes glued to my ass—when he wasn't staring at my tits, that is. Jim, on the other hand, nods as he goes by.

Axl stops by my side. "What's wrong?"

"Nothing," I say, then sigh. "I don't know. Maybe it's this trip or losing more friends or exhaustion. I don't know for sure. I just know that everything makes me want to cry today."

"Not a surprise," Axl says, glancing back toward the waitress. "Every place we look there are dead bodies or a whole lotta nothin'. It's bound to get to you."

"Yeah, I guess."

He pulls me against his chest, and I wrap my arms around him, resting my head on his shoulder. We haven't been really alone since we left Hope Springs, and it's wearing on me.

"I miss our house," I whisper. "And our bed."

His lips brush against my hair. "Don't need a bed."

He has a point.

I turn my face toward his, raising myself up on the tips of my toes until our lips meet. Axl's mouth moves against mine, coaxing my mouth open. His tongue slides over mine as his hands move down my back to my waist. Then up under my shirt, his fingers trailing along my spine. Leaving tingles behind.

Within seconds, our kissing becomes more desperate, and suddenly all the death that has surrounded us since our bus drove onto that bridge slams into me. All I can think about right now is being with Axl. Just in case it's our last chance. In case a horde attacks us while we sleep or we get killed by a group of assholes on the road tomorrow. I want to hold onto this moment and be together.

My hand moves to the button of his jeans, and with one flick of my wrist, I have them undone. Axl groans against my lips when I slip my hand inside. He kisses me harder, his teeth clamping down on my bottom lip.

"What the hell?" Angus calls, startling me so much I let out a little yelp.

"Shit." Axl pulls away and buttons his jeans.

Angus heads our way, shaking his head like he's ashamed of us or can't believe we're making out in the middle of all this. Like he has any room to talk. How many times when we were on the road did I walk up on him and Darla fooling around? Too many.

Of course, given our current circumstances, I can't really

be angry about it.

Angus stops in front of us. "I'd tell you two to get a room, but there's a serious shortage of workin' hotels these days."

"No shit." Axl's hand slides down my arm, and he laces his fingers through mine, but it does little to ease the ache inside me.

"What's going on?" I ask, knowing Angus didn't come out here just to give us shit.

"We found us a truck. It's got a half a tank of gas, and even though it ain't gonna be comfortable, we can fit everybody in if we use the back."

"It's not like there are cops around to pull us over for breaking seatbelt laws," I say.

"Not that it'd stop us, anyway."

Angus turns and heads toward the front, and Axl follows, pulling me with him. Even though I'm glad we have a truck, I'm pissed Angus couldn't wait until later to tell us. We were just getting somewhere.

"It work?" Axl calls.

"Gonna need you to test out them hotwirin' skills of yours to know for sure. It's been sittin' there for a couple months, so who knows."

"What are the odds the battery will still be good?" I ask, trotting to keep up with the brothers, who are walking faster now that they have a purpose.

"Hard to say," Axl replies. "Depends on if it was in good shape to begin with."

We round the corner to find Jim sitting in the driver's seat of a rusted-out, barely white truck that has to be over thirty years old. Dax stands at his side. He turns to face us as we head over, and his eyes go to where my hand rests in Axl's. The frown that had already taken up residence on his face deepens.

So much for the smile that seemed to be tattooed on his face before we left Hope Springs.

I look away from Dax. He doesn't have a claim on me, and I've told him more than once that I'm not available. I gave myself to Axl months before I met this guy. By the time Dax came into the picture, there was no contest. Not for him or anyone else. No matter what else happens, I can never really regret the zombie apocalypse wiping out the population. If it hadn't happened, I wouldn't have this man at my side and my life wouldn't be worth living.

"Your brother says you'll be able to get this thing working," Dax says, crossing his arms. The challenge in his voice is thick.

"I'll see what I can do." Axl doesn't even glance the other man's way.

"If you can get this thing started, I'll kiss your ass," Jim says, sliding out of the driver's seat.

"Not me." Dax waves toward the truck. "Help yourself. I'm going to head inside and get some dinner, then rest up for tomorrow. Angus, you're with me."

"Fuck that," Angus mutters. "I'm gonna get this truck workin' so we don't gotta walk again tomorrow. Hollywood ain't gonna make it much longer like that, and we're wastin' time. We got nearly five hundred miles to cross. You know how long that's gonna take us on foot?"

"A fucking long time," Jim says.

"Doesn't matter." Dax shakes his head and points toward the diner. "You're my responsibility and I'm not letting you out of my sight."

"A month," Axl says from under the dashboard.

Jim turns back to the truck, and Dax's eyes snap toward Axl.

"What did you say?" Dax asks.

"If we keep goin' on foot, it'll take us a month to get to Atlanta. Assumin' we can do twenty miles a day, that is."

"How do you know that?" Dax snaps.

"'Cause I can add," Axl says as he jerks the wires out from under the dashboard, not even looking Dax's way.

"It sounds about right," Jim says, looking back at Dax.

"It is." Axl shakes his head. "We can walk *maybe* two and a half miles an hour, if we're lucky. Assumin' we walk eight hours a day—which is pushin' it—that's between sixteen and twenty miles a day."

"Which means it will take us around thirty-one days to walk five hundred miles," Jim says, backing up Axl's claims.

Dax stares at Axl, not saying a word. The expression on his face tells me he's trying to work it out for himself. Either he's successful or he decides to just take Axl and Jim's word for it, because Dax shakes his head and turns back toward the diner.

"Whatever," he calls. "Get the truck started or not, we're heading out in the morning, and I need some sleep. Angus, come on."

"I ain't a dog!" Angus calls.

"No, you're a pain in the ass who just so happens to be the only hope for the human race, and I don't give a damn if you want to go in or not. You're coming with me so I can keep an eye on you."

"Bastard thinks he's runnin' things," Angus mutters.

"He's a pain in the ass all the way through," Jim says in agreement.

"Just go," Axl calls. "I'll get this goin' and we'll be right behind you."

Angus grunts but follows Dax—like the puppy dog he claims not to be. I have a feeling he doesn't hate the idea of breaking open a can of food while lounging inside the diner.

"Keep a lookout, Blondie!" he says, then pauses to shoot a look at Jim. "Blondies?" Angus purses his lips for a second, then shakes his head before heading off after Dax, who is glaring his way.

"We'll shout if we need your help," Jim says, waving him off even though his back is already turned to us.

"How's it looking?" I ask when the others are gone.

"Ain't bad."

Axl shoves his knife back into its sheath. His torso is blocking the wires from view, so I can't see exactly what he's doing. Not that I know anything about hotwiring a car.

"How did he learn to do this?" Jim asks, trying to get a good look into the truck as well.

"He had a troubled youth," I say with a shrug.

I turn to face Jim, looking him up and down. We haven't spoken much, and I don't really know anything about him other than the fact that Jon trusted the guy with his life, but he's made more than a couple comments about Dax. He apparently doesn't have much respect for the guy either.

"You don't like Dax."

Jim doesn't blink, and his expression doesn't change. Talk about a poker face. "That a question?"

"An observation."

"The end of the world brings out all kind of assholes—" he pauses and looks me over, "—which I'm guessing you know something about."

I nod, and Axl pauses in the middle of stripping wires so he can look our way.

"We've had run-ins with a lot of different people out there," I say.

"I figured." Jim glances back toward the diner. "I don't know everything that went down, but between the things Jon told me and the stuff you and Ginny have said to each other—along with the fact that she's trying to erase her past—I'd guess it was pretty bad. Which means I don't have to tell you to watch your back."

Axl stands, the wires under the dashboard forgotten. "What's he done?"

"Cowardice is the biggest thing I can accuse him of at this point, but I haven't had a good feeling about Dax from the beginning. Jon felt the same way, which is why he asked me to keep an eye on Ginny if anything ever happened to him. I promised him I'd get Ginny to Atlanta, and I don't plan on going back on that. You guys seem like good people, so I just thought I'd pass that information on."

Jim pulls a pack of cigarettes from his pocket, lighting one as the three of us stand in silence. He takes a long drag, tossing his head back when he exhales. Smoke floats into the air, and I watch it drift off, wondering once again what we've gotten ourselves into with this asshole as our leader.

"We'll be okay," Axl says after a second, climbing back into the truck.

Jim nods, and I'm still thinking everything he said through when the truck's engine roars to life a few seconds later. Axl only lets it run for a few seconds before turning it off and scooting out. He wipes his hands on his pants even though they don't look much cleaner than his palms do.

"The thing's got two tanks, but only one is full. That should get us 'round two hundred miles, so we're gonna hafta find more gas if we wanna drive the whole way."

"Every little bit helps," I say, wrapping my arms around him again. "Can you imagine walking for a month?"

"It'd take us longer than that," Axl replies, shaking his head but pulling me closer. "Hadley—"

"Ginny," I correct him, shooting a look Jim's way even though the cat is out of the bag. He doesn't seem to be paying attention to us even though he's only two feet away.

Axl shakes his head. "Can't get used to that."

"Whatever her name is," Jim says. "She isn't going to make it that long." Guess he's paying attention after all.

"How much time do we got 'til she's due to have that baby?" Axl asks.

"Six weeks," I say.

"Shit." He lets out a deep breath. "She shoulda stayed behind."

"You know why she didn't."

"Yup, and we woulda made the same decision, but that don't make it the smart thing to do."

"You not make an intelligent decision?" I say with a smirk. "I don't believe it."

"Yeah, well, when the people you love are in trouble, it clouds your judgment. I ain't no different than anybody else on that point."

Axl kisses me, but it's cut short when Jim clears his throat.

"Think I'll head inside. Give you two a chance to be alone."

Jim heads off, but I don't tell him goodbye. I'm too busy thinking about what would have happened behind the diner if Angus hadn't interrupted us.

"Speaking of being alone," I say. "How do you feel about picking up where we left off? We have a truck and it's getting dark. Seems like the perfect opportunity."

"You know how long it's been since I had sex in a car?" Axl asks, grinning.

"No idea and I don't want to know, either," I say, pushing him back toward the open door of the truck. "All I know is this may be our last chance to be alone for a while, and I want to take advantage of it."

We climb in, and Axl's mouth is on mine before he's even had a chance to shut the door behind us. It's been a long time since I had to fool around in a truck, but it seems natural with Axl. I climb onto his lap, straddling him as he pulls my shirt over my head. His mouth attacks mine, and he has my bra undone in seconds and his hands are on my breasts.

Since we don't have a lot of time, it only takes me a few minutes to slide off his lap. I undo his pants, and my own zipper comes down just a couple seconds after his. Then we're both squirming around in the cab, trying to wrangle ourselves out of our pants. The second they're gone, I'm back on Axl's lap, lowering myself on to him. Closing my eyes as we move together.

Blocking out everything we've been through the last two days is almost impossible, but I manage to make it happen by focusing on Axl and how much I love him. On this moment that exists only for the two of us. That's all we need, anyway. Each other.

When we've finished, I collapse against him. The air in the cab is thick with moisture and the windows are so fogged up no one would be able to see in if they tried, but I'm too comfortable against Axl's chest to even think about moving. Even when my stomach growls.

"We could just sleep here," I say through a yawn.

"I think you'd regret it in the mornin' when you couldn't move your neck."

He has a point.

"Okay, we'll sleep inside, but I want to stay for a little bit longer. Enjoy you without Dax breathing down my neck or Angus making dirty comments. Just pretend we're two teenagers who snuck away in your dad's truck."

He kisses the top of my head. "Alright."

We go back to lying together in silence. Axl runs his hand up and down my back, making me shiver despite the humid air clogging the cab. When my eyes begin to grow heavy, though, I realize it's time to move. The truck isn't the best place to sleep even if we are alone.

"We should get going," I say through a yawn.

"Yeah," Axl says, helping me sit up.

We manage to find our clothes pretty easily, but it takes longer than normal to shimmy my way back into my pants. You'd think by this point I'd be used to getting dressed in tight spaces, but I'm not. My skin is so slick with sweat that my shirt sticks to my skin, making it almost impossible to find the armholes, and even when I manage to get it on, the material gets bunched up around my stomach.

"I could use a shower," I mutter, moving to the edge of the seat so I can untangle my shirt.

"That'll have to wait 'til we get to Atlanta." Axl grabs the handle but glances back at me before pushing the door open. "You ready?"

"Everything is where is should be," I say.

He pulls the handle, and the door swings open, letting a burst of cool air into the cab. Axl slides out as I inhale, filling my lungs once before blowing it out. The second time I inhale, the stink of rot fills my nostrils.

"Axl!" I cry, reaching for him right before a zombie steps into view.

The thing snarls and grabs Axl's arm, pulling him forward just as my fingers close around his other arm.

He slips from my grip and tumbles forward, slamming into the zombie so hard the thing loses its footing. They fall, the zombie first and Axl right after him, his body landing on top of the decaying monster. I'm out of the truck before they've hit the ground, pulling my knife free and screaming for Angus, but I've only made it a step when another zombie appears, moaning and reaching for me. On the ground, Axl and the first zombie struggle, kicking up dirt that fills my lungs with every breath I take. They're blocking the second zombie, making it impossible for him to get to me, but also for me to go to Axl's aid.

"Angus!" I scream again as the truck door slams into me. It hits my knees and pushes me back against the seats, pinning me between the door and the truck.

Axl grunts, but I can't see him from where I'm trapped. I push against the door, but the zombie on the other side seems to think he'll be able to get to me if he puts all of his weight against it. The metal only slams into me harder, hitting my knees over and over again as the zombie tries to get to me.

"Axl!" Angus screams from somewhere in the distance.

Seconds later, Dax's voice breaks through the moans and growls, yelling at Angus to get back inside. I can't see a damn thing, but the sound of feet running across the pavement is unmistakable. Angus's swearing comes next, followed by moans. Axl's grunts are muffled thanks to the door, but he's still moving. Still fighting.

The door slams against me so hard that I swear my kneecaps are going to shatter. I suck in a deep breath, ignoring the rot that fills my lungs, then shove with all the strength left in me. The door swings open, and the zombie blocking my way goes flying back. Axl comes into view. Angus is next to him, trying to pull the dead man away from his brother while Dax simultaneously tries to get Angus to back off. All he's succeeding in doing is making it worse for Axl, though.

"Stop!" I scream.

Without taking the time to think it through, I slam my

foot into Dax's face. My heel makes contact with his already damaged nose, and his grip finally loosens on Angus as blood pours from this nostrils. Less than two seconds after he's free, Angus manages to get the zombie off Axl. He tosses the thing aside, and Parvarti comes out of nowhere. She slams a butcher's knife into the zombie's skull, and just like that, it stops moving. The second one is down as well thanks to Jim, who stands over the body with a knife still clutched in his hand.

"Shit." Angus leans down and hauls Axl to his feet, giving him a once-over before spitting.

"I'm alright," Axl says, dusting the filth off his pants. It doesn't do a lot of good, though. Zombie ooze isn't easy to get rid of.

"You asshole!" I yell when my concern for Axl morphs into rage—all of it aimed at Dax. "What the hell were you doing? You could have gotten us all killed."

Dax sits on the ground, holding his bloody nose. "My job," he says, his voice low and firm.

"Bullshit," I say, taking a step toward him. "You weren't protecting Angus, you were trying to keep him from helping Axl. You think I would start screwing you just because he was bitten? Well dream on!"

Dax climbs to his feet and swipes his hand across his face to wipe away the blood, wincing. "This didn't have anything to do with you."

"I don't believe you," I hiss.

"You can believe what you want. Of course, if you two hadn't been out here screwing instead of inside where it's safe, none of this would have happened." Dax turns and heads for the diner. "Angus!"

"Fuck him," Angus mutters, shaking his head.

"You both okay?" Jim says, also not following Dax.

"We're fine," Axl says, his eyes leveled on the back of Dax's head. "Let's go inside an' get some rest."

CHAPTER SIXTEEN

The sun is still low when we set out. Dax and Angus in the cab—at the insistence of *the boss*—and the rest of us in the bed of the truck. The mood since last night has been dark and distrustful, and I can't stop thinking about the things Jim said and how Dax tried to stop Angus from helping his brother. It was intentional, and I know it. There isn't a doubt in my mind. The only question now is: how much can I actually trust him after what happened?

"How far do you think we can go on the gas we have?" Joshua calls as we barrel down the road.

"Two hundred miles," Axl replies. "Maybe."

"Then what?" Ginny asks, her voice shaking as the tires bump over the uneven pavement.

We got off Route 66 shortly after we set off this morning, but the road here isn't much better than the forgotten highway. A winter of disuse and neglect has left it full of potholes and covered in debris.

"We'll look for more gas," Jim says, answering for Axl. "There has to be some."

"And weapons!" Parvarti calls.

Her red bandana is tied so tightly around her head that not a single hair has escaped, but mine and Ginny's is all over the place. At least hers is short enough that it isn't in her eyes. Mine has whipped me in the eyeball so hard a couple times I'm afraid I may be blind by the end of the day.

Axl nods but stays silent. Talking over the roar of the wind and engine is just too difficult, so I don't blame him.

The sun beats down on us until I'm pretty sure my skin is going to melt off, and not even the rush of the wind helps alleviate the heat. Jim is wearing a leather jacket that helps keep the sun off his body, but Ginny's face is spotted with freckles, and her nose is now bright pink. Joshua has resorted to wrapping an extra shirt around his face and pulling his arms into the T-shirt he's wearing to limit his exposure. It isn't a bad idea. Axl and Parvarti alone seem unconcerned, although Axl's face has taken on a shade slightly darker than the one I'm used to seeing.

Sunscreen is a must at this point.

I sit up, holding onto the side of the truck tightly so I don't lose my balance. The higher vantage point gives me a chance to get a good look at the road in front of us, but at first there's nothing. Just trees and open fields. A wasteland of forgotten landscape that flies past us so fast it's little more than a blur. Then, after only a few seconds, a few signs come into view. Perfect.

"We need to stop!" I call as I lower myself back to a sitting position. "Bathroom break!" Among other things.

Axl bangs on the window separating the cab and the truck bed, but Dax barely looks over his shoulder—and he doesn't slow. Axl bangs again, and Angus twists in his seat so he can pull the window open.

"Gotta stop!" Axl yells.

Angus nods and says something to Dax. It still takes the asshole a couple minutes to slow down.

He must have read my mind, because he pulls into the gas station I spotted in the distance. The parking lot is empty, and the front windows are broken—meaning we probably aren't going to be able to find much in the way of food—but if luck is on our side, there may be some other things lying around.

I'm on my feet the second the truck pulls to a stop, jumping down and heading for the front door with my knife out. My skin has been singed to a rosy pink, and I'm over it. I need to cover up as soon as possible, and I know I'm not the only one.

"Vivian," Axl calls from behind me. Feet thump against the pavement when he jumps out of the truck.

"Cover me," I say instead of slowing.

Broken glass is spread across the pavement, shimmering in the bright sun. It crunches under my shoes as I walk. I keep my ears and eyes—and nose—open, and my knife ready. So far, though, the only noise is from the truck behind me.

"Looks clear," I say as Axl comes to a stop at my side.

I step through the broken front window, and Axl follows me inside. The store is devoid of any food, and even the refrigerators lining the wall have been cleaned out. But there are still random items on the shelves: Chapstick, feminine hygiene products, bottles of laundry detergent, and shampoo. I head toward that aisle, and the second I step down it, I let out a sigh of relief. Sunblock.

"This will help," I say, pulling it off the shelf and holding it up so Axl can see it. "But I want to see if they have any hats. We need to try and keep the sun off our faces."

"Sounds like a plan," he says.

There's none up front, so I move toward the door marked *Employees Only*. Footsteps crunch against the broken glass at our backs as Axl and I head deeper into the store. I glance behind me to where Parvarti and Joshua browse the few things remaining on the shelves. Jim climbs over the counter, probably in search of cigarettes.

"See if they have dip!" Angus calls from outside the store.

The back room is dark and musty and stuffed full of so many boxes I find it hard to maneuver my way through. They've all been ripped open and thrown everywhere, and one glance inside tells me anything useful has been taken. When I inhale, the scent of death clings to the air. With as faint as it is, though, I'd guess whoever's in here has just recently started to rot.

Something rustles, and Axl and I both pause. I hold my breath, straining to hear over the chatter from the other room. It takes a second, but once again something moves.

"This way," Axl whispers, jerking his head to the right.

For a brief second, I consider going for backup but dismiss the idea as Axl moves forward. Something is in here, but it could just be an animal. If it is the undead, it can't be more than one. There isn't enough noise, and the stench isn't bad enough.

Axl keeps his knife up, expertly dodging the boxes so he doesn't make a sound, and I stay as close to him as possible. Even after all these months, my heart still pounds harder than normal at the thought of fighting a zombie. It probably always will.

We reach the back of the room and step around a pile of empty boxes. A dead man comes into view, and three rats so big they could be mistaken for small opossums scurry away from where they'd been nibbling on the poor bastard. His nose has been chewed off, and little bites cover his face and neck, but it doesn't look—or smell—like he's been dead long. A couple days at the most.

"Must've just happened," Axl says, shaking his head.

He kneels next to the man and grabs a backpack off the floor.

"What do you think happened?" I ask, kneeling as well.

Axl shakes out the bag, and a handful of items fall to the ground. A flashlight that doesn't work when I flip it on, a wallet that holds a bunch of useless credit cards, empty plastic bottles, and a box of Band-Aids. That's it.

"Starved," Axl says, opening the box of Band-Aids. "Look how skinny he was."

Axl is probably right. The guy's arms are like toothpicks, and a rip in his shirt reveals ribs almost poking through his skin. He looks like he hasn't eaten in weeks.

"I know it's rough out there," I say, shaking my head, "but we've managed to find food. Why couldn't he?"

"Didn't know where to look. Some people don't got those reasonin' skills."

He has a point.

"Sad," I say, getting up. "He made it this long, but obviously he didn't learn anything about survival."

"Luck always runs out," Axl says.

He stands, and his foot catches on the dead guy's leg, pushing the body aside. It isn't much, but it's enough to reveal the barrel of a gun.

"Shit," I say, dropping back to my knees.

Axl kneels too, but before I pull the gun out of its hiding spot, I instinctively look around. Voices are still audible from the other room, but no one has come our way yet. My hands are shaky when I pull the gun out from underneath the dead man's leg and remove the clip. Three rounds. Not a lot, but better than nothing.

The gun is loaded, and Axl and I are the only ones who know about it. We should keep it that way.

Why I'd even consider hiding a gun doesn't hit me at first, and then Dax's voice booms through the building, and my heart pounds like crazy. My eyes meet Axl's, and he nods before taking the gun from me. He tucks it in his waistband and pulls his shirt over it. Hiding it.

"Best to keep this between us," he says.

He read my mind. "Yeah."

Footsteps come up behind us, and we get to our feet. Dax barrels down on us, shoving boxes out of the way like they've offended him or they're a threat.

When he reaches us, his eyes move to the dead guy. "Find anything?"

"Nothin' useful," Axl says, his voice level. I love how cool he is under pressure.

My heart is pounding so loud it echoes in my ears. "Junk."

Dax nods before turning around. "We need to get moving."

"On our way." Axl gives my shoulder a squeeze as we head after our leader.

WE'VE ONLY BEEN DRIVING FOR A LITTLE OVER TWO hours when the truck sputters a couple times and the engine goes out. The sound of Dax cursing is audible even through the glass separating us. The truck slows and comes to a stop in the middle of the road, and I turn to the front just as Dax slams his hand into the steering wheel.

"Guess we're out of gas," Jim says, getting to his feet.

Axl and I follow his lead, and we stand side by side, scanning the area. There isn't a whole lot around, but we did get a little lucky. An old farmhouse sits far back from the road, down the longest unpaved driveway I've ever seen. It's going to be quite a walk to get to the house, but at least we'll have a place to sleep tonight and we won't be abandoning the truck for good. Hopefully, they have a car or a stockpile of gas—even a couple gallons stored away for a lawn mower would be good right now. It would get us down the road tomorrow and possibly to a bigger supply. If there is any.

Dax throws the driver's door open, still cursing when he hops out.

"We'll stay here for the night," Axl calls as he throws his legs over the side of the truck and jumps to the ground.

I jump down too, then head to the back so I can lower the tailgate. Parv and Jim are down before I've gotten there—already lighting cigarettes—but Joshua stays in the back and helps Ginny scoot across the truck to the tailgate.

"You okay?" I ask, eyeing her closely. She keeps rubbing her stomach, and it's making me nervous.

Ginny nods and allows me to help her out the truck. "I'm fine. Just uncomfortable."

"That's to be expected." Joshua hops down, but when his eyes meet mine, they're full of concern. "Just a short walk, and you can rest. Maybe even in a real bed."

"That would be nice," Ginny says, letting out a sigh of relief.

I head for the driveway, helping Ginny as I go. We need to get her inside so she can rest, and despite what Joshua says, it isn't going to be a short walk. This driveway has to be almost a quarter of a mile long.

We've only taken two steps when Dax calls out from behind us, "We're not staying here."

I stop and turn to meet his gaze, sure I heard him wrong. "Excuse me?"

"You heard me, so don't pretend you didn't. It's early. We still have a few hours of daylight left, meaning we can make it eight, maybe nine more miles. There's no time for sleep."

"Ginny needs to rest," I say. "Plus, they could have gas in the house. Walking away right now would be stupid."

Axl heads my way, not even glancing at Dax. "We're goin' to the house."

He grabs my arm and pulls me forward a little more violently than he probably intended to, but I don't care. It has nothing to do with me, and I'm just as pissed off as he is. Dax is taking it too far this time. What good will it do to get Angus to Atlanta if the rest of us are dead on our feet?

"We need to regroup and check for supplies," Jim says behind us. "And we need see if they have gas so we can keep the truck. It would be dumb to leave it here when for all we know they have gas in the barn."

"Don't be an idiot!" Dax shouts. "They don't have gas. All the gas is gone, and we're just going to have to get used to walking. If she can't handle it, she should have stayed in Colorado."

"A lot of good that does us now," I mutter, not stopping.

I look over my shoulder as Axl and I lead Ginny down the driveway. Joshua is at our backs, and behind him, Parvarti and Jim walk, smoking as they head toward the house. Even Parv shoots Dax a look that is more than a little hostile. Angus is the only one still standing next to the truck, but I don't know why. He can't be on Dax's side.

"You can keep on walkin' if you like," Angus says. "But that ain' what we're doin'. We're goin' down there and we're gonna rest, and we're gonna do what Axl and me decide is best for the group. I'm offerin' up my life here, which is fine with me, but 'til I step through the gates of Atlanta, nobody has a say in what I do with that life but me. Least of all you."

Angus spits, then turns and heads after us, leaving Dax by himself.

I turn back so I can focus on the house in front of us. A part of me wishes Dax would head back to Hope Springs and leave the rest of us alone. We're all committed to getting Angus to Atlanta, but that isn't our only goal. If we all die, there will be no one left to help keep Angus alive, let alone have his back or get him to the CDC. Dax doesn't seem to understand the big picture here: we need to work together.

We're halfway down the drive when Ginny grunts and stops moving. She bends over with her arms wrapped around her stomach, and my own gut clenches.

"What's wrong?" I ask, leaning down so I can see her face. "What happened? Are you okay?"

Axl and Parv and Jim are suddenly surrounding us, the expressions on their faces just as full of concern as my own.

"She in labor?" Angus asks as he jogs up to join us.

"I'm fine." Ginny shakes her head, but the grimace on her face tells a different story. "Cramps. That's all."

"Shit," Joshua says. "We have to get you inside."

We've still got a ways to walk, and the second Ginny's pain lets up, we start moving again, trying to urge her forward as fast as she can wobble. I've had a baby, so I know what's happening without even asking, but I can't stop thinking it through. Thirty-four weeks, that's six weeks early.

Viable, but still premature and small. How small, though? It's tough to tell. Four pounds, possibly a little bigger.

Axl, Jim, and Parvarti jog ahead to check out the house while Angus hangs back. Joshua and I keep Ginny moving, and thankfully no other pains hit her before we make it to the porch.

We wait outside for the others to come back and tell us the place is clear. Ginny sits on the steps, wincing like every move is uncomfortable—after the last couple days we've had, they probably are. Angus hovers over her with his knife out and ready as if something is going to jump out at any second, while Joshua wrings his hands like a worried old lady. In the distance, I can just make out Dax's outline as he heads down the driveway after us.

When Axl finally reappears and confirms that the house is clear, we move inside. It's dark and dusty, but nicer than a lot of the other places we've taken shelter in over the last few months. When you're on the road, you can't be picky. At least this place has beds and couches.

"Upstairs," Joshua says, urging Ginny forward.

We climb, the two of us supporting Ginny as she huffs. I can't help noticing how much more she's wobbling than she did before. Once we make it to the bedroom and I get a good look at her, I know why. Her stomach is visibly lower. The baby has dropped.

"Bed," Joshua says, looking around frantically. "We need gloves and hot water and soap. I need to wash my hands."

He's shaking, and his eyes are so big he looks like a madman. It's been four years since I went through this myself, and even though I can help Ginny out, I can't deliver a baby. Not the way he can. We need him, and we need him calm.

"Joshua," I say quietly. His eyes snap toward me, and I take his hand in mine. "Relax. We don't even know what's going on yet. It could be false labor. Right?"

He nods slowly as he blows out through his mouth. "Yeah. It's early, so it could be false labor."

As if on cue, Ginny lets out a moan. The sound is so strained and full of hurt that it pierces through me, settling in my stomach and weighing me down. This isn't false labor, and we all know it.

"Okay," Joshua says, then inhales slowly. "Right. I'm going to take a look around and see what, if anything, I can find to help out. I want to see if she'd dilated, but there are things I need to do to prepare first. Mainly getting clean. Stay with her. Hold her hand and keep her calm."

"Okay," I whisper, watching my friend's face contort in pain.

Having a baby out here where we have no running water or supplies is going to be rough. This baby already had a slim chance of making it, but add a premature delivery on top of all the other worries, and it seems like impossible odds.

Joshua heads toward the door just as Ginny relaxes.

"You okay?" I ask, patting her hand.

"Yeah." She nods, but I can tell she's putting on a brave face. She looks like she's utterly terrified, and she should be.

"I'll be right back." I give Ginny's hand a squeeze before hopping to my feet, hurrying after Joshua. I catch him just as he's reached the stairs and grab his arm so he turns to face me. "What are the odds of this turning out good? The baby is six weeks early. How big will it be? Will there be complications?"

Joshua's Adam's apple bobs when he swallows. "It's hard to say. At this stage, the baby should be between four and five pounds, but some babies are five pounds at full term, so we have no way of knowing for sure. It could struggle to breathe if the lungs aren't fully developed, but again, that varies. Some babies are born at this age and they're perfectly healthy. Others…"

He doesn't need to say any more. The unspoken words are written all over his face. But the truth is, if this baby dies, we'll have no way of knowing if it was from a premature birth or if the virus caused it.

"Go," I say, dropping Joshua's arm. "I'll sit with Ginny."

GINNY LETS OUT A GROAN AND CLUTCHES THE sheets when another contraction rolls over her.

"You need to breathe," I remind her.

She nods as she exhales, blowing air out through her nose. I wipe her sweaty face with a washcloth, hoping to ease some of her discomfort. The water isn't exactly cold, but it's better than nothing.

"How much longer?" Ginny moans after the contraction has resided.

I look up and meet Joshua's worried gaze. "It's hard to say. You're at six centimeters, so it could be another four hours, or it could be less. With the way you're progressing, I'd say less."

Ginny nods, and a few strands of hair fall across her face. The sun has set, and as far as I know, everyone else is downstairs. Parvarti came up once to check on us but was back out the door the second Ginny started moaning. The men haven't set foot upstairs as far as I know, and I haven't left the room.

"Your contractions are still five minutes or so apart," Joshua says.

"It's a miracle you found a watch that still works." Ginny says, forcing out a smile.

Joshua pats her leg. "There are a lot of miracles going around these days, and I wouldn't be surprised if we had another one here soon."

"Don't hold your breath." Ginny winces and exhales slowly through her nose. She looks exhausted, but oddly peaceful, which doesn't match her words.

"You're going to be okay," I say, taking her hand. "And the baby will, too."

"No one knows that for sure." Her eyes dart toward Joshua before settling back on me. "I wanted to talk to you about something. I know my timing's bad, but since it might be our only chance, I figured I should just go for it."

I pat her hand. "You have plenty of time."

Ginny nods but looks toward Joshua again.

He stands and stretches his arms over his head, letting out a yawn. "I'm going to grab a bite to eat before things get crazy. I think my stomach is trying to eat itself."

"Sounds good," I say.

Ginny's gaze follows him across the room, and I get the impression she's avoiding looking at me. My stomach tenses in anticipation, but I'm not sure what I'm nervous about. I knew she wanted to talk to me about whatever happened with her and Axl, but there's nothing that should concern me. Right?

"What is it?" I say the second Joshua's footsteps have started to fade away.

Ginny's green eyes finally meet mine, and I hold my breath. Still she doesn't talk, so I start counting. Thirty seconds pass, and I'm still waiting.

"Ginny," I say softly.

"I kissed Axl," she finally blurts out.

Every muscle in my body coils into a tight ball, making it impossible to move. I blink, waiting for a punch line or for her to laugh or *something*. But she just stares at me.

"What?" I finally manage to say. There's no way I heard her right.

"It was back when we were at the hot springs. I was so…angry. At Jon and that asshole in Vegas and the whole damn world, if I'm being honest. I was hurting, and I don't really know what happened, but I found myself standing in front of Axl thinking about how lucky you were. Because you found someone who would take care of not only you but anything else that might come along. I was pretty sure I was pregnant and the future seemed so shitty and I was just…mad."

"You said that already." It's all I manage to get out.

"I know. I'm just trying to explain."

Thinking back to that last day before she and Jon disappeared, how angry she was at Axl and how he wouldn't even look at her. Now it makes sense. She kissed him and he told her to get lost, and then she was so embarrassed she couldn't wait to get away. But why didn't Axl tell me? And why the hell would she betray me like that?

"So you were jealous?" I mumble, trying to make sense of it all.

"No. I mean yes, but not like that. I don't know what I was exactly, only that I was miserable and I wanted to feel something else for a change. To feel like I was someone else. But it was stupid and I knew it the second it happened, and every day since then I've regretted it. I've been trying to figure out how to tell you. How to explain. Axl told me he never brought it up, but I knew I couldn't just let it go unsaid forever. Vivian, you're the best friend I've ever had, and I want to make sure I fix this. I want you to know how sorry I am."

She reaches for my hand, but I jerk away and jump to my feet. "You were jealous, so you kissed Axl. To take him away from me?" She shakes her head and opens her mouth, but I don't want to hear her say anything else. There's nothing she could tell me that would make this okay. Not right now. I back away, holding my hand up to stop her from talking. "It doesn't matter. I just—I can't be here right now. This is too messed up."

I turn away, heading for the stairs so fast I'm surprised I don't trip over my own two feet.

"Vivian!" Ginny calls from behind me.

I don't stop. I take the stairs two at a time, hanging onto the banister so I don't fall. Just as I reach the first floor, Joshua rounds the corner. He's in the middle of chewing, so he can't say anything, which is just fine with me. I don't want to talk to him or anyone else right now. My brain is already so full it's on the verge of exploding.

I shove past him, and when I reach the front door, I push it open and stumble outside.

"Hey!" Dax says, jumping off the porch swing as I run by.

I ignore him and run down the steps. Across the driveway. Not stopping until I reach the field lining the property. What it used to be, I'm not sure, but at the moment it's mostly weeds. They prick at my legs through my jeans when I sink down, but I'm gasping for breath and trying to blink back tears, so I don't care. My thoughts are already so jumbled it makes my head ache. I can't worry about a few weeds.

Ginny— No, not Ginny. Hadley Lucas. She's the one who kissed Axl, but somehow I'm supposed to overlook that. I know I should. It's the end of the world and there are so few people left and I care about her more than anyone I knew before this thing started. But she did something I can't even comprehend. I knew she wasn't in a great place before, and Lord knows I can't blame her, but there isn't a single part of me that doesn't hurt when I think about what she did. I can picture it, too. Hadley and Axl talking, and out of nowhere she throws herself at him. The images flash through my mind, her arms wrapping around his neck as she presses her body against his. Her lips moving against his mouth. He even kisses her back for a brief second before he realizes what's happening, and then he pushes her way. Just like every movie I've ever seen. That's how it always happens, isn't it?

No. Not with Axl. I'm more certain of that than I've ever been of anything in my entire life. Just like I know that if Dax had made a move on me, I would have pushed him away. There would have been no hesitation. I don't want him any more than I want this zombie virus.

Footsteps break through my thoughts, and I look up. Axl is headed my way, cutting through the weed-choked field.

When he reaches me, he kneels at my side and takes my hand. "She told you."

"Why didn't you?" I ask, unable to look him in the eye.

"'Cause she was missin' and you was hurtin', and I knew it didn't mean nothin'. You know that too. Hadley was in a bad place, and she wasn't thinkin' straight."

"I know."

"Then you gotta go in there and tell her you forgive her."

He's right, but that doesn't mean it's going to be an easy thing to do. I'm not even sure how to start, to be honest.

"I may know that I need to forgive her, but that doesn't mean I don't feel like she ripped my heart out and stomped on it. I mean, what she did…" I shake my head. "How can I get over that?"

Axl's free hand moves to my chin, and he tilts my face up so I'm looking at him. His gray eyes are soft and warm when he says, "Because nothin' these days is certain, and she could be dead this time tomorrow. Maybe not from the baby, but from somethin' else. If you don't forgive her, you'll never be able to forgive yourself."

He's right. Of course he is. Axl is always right.

"I know."

"Good."

He stands, pulling me to my feet with him, but before he can move toward the house, I throw my arms around him. Hug him like we're saying goodbye or an angry horde is closing in on us and it might be the last moment we have together.

"I love you," I say with my face pressed up against his neck. "Always."

"I love you," he whispers back.

CHAPTER SEVENTEEN

Dax is heading over to meet us when Axl's hand slips into mine, and together we walk through the overgrown field toward him. In the background, the house is lit up thanks to the candles the guys found, but it's a lot further away than I thought it was. When I came outside, it felt like I'd only run a couple steps before dropping to the ground. Now that we're headed back, though, I realize I made it more than halfway down the driveway.

"I hear you found some gas," Dax calls when he's still a few feet away from us.

"It ain't much," Axl says, "but it'll get us thirty miles or so. Hopefully, we can find some more before it's gone."

Dax stops walking when he's about a foot away, and his eyes move back and forth between Axl and me. "Good."

His eyes meet mine, and something in them sends a shiver down my spine. Only I'm not sure what. At my side, Axl tenses like he feels it too, and I find myself glancing toward the house. Wishing for some crazy reason that one of our friends would come outside to check on us. Angus especially. We're so far away, though. Why did I run so far?

Dax is still staring at us silently when I look back.

"Ginny will have the baby in a few hours," I say, "and we'll need to hang out here for a day or so until she recovers. It will give us time to plan."

"You know we can't do that," Dax says coolly.

"Don't really matter what you think," Axl says. "You ain't in charge."

Dax's body visibly tenses. "I am the leader of this mission, and I *will* get Angus to Atlanta."

"He won't agree to it," I say. "You can't force him, and he won't leave us."

"That's true," Dax says slowly, like he's thinking something through.

The wind blows, and the trees in the distance rustle. Somewhere nearby, something chimes, but I'm not sure where it's coming from. I didn't see any wind chimes when we drove up. The breeze washes over my damp skin, and I realize for the first time how sweaty and filthy I feel after being in the back of the truck for most of the day and at Ginny's side for hours after that.

I'm too exhausted to fight with Dax right now.

"This is dumb. I have more important things to do than argue with you," I say, letting out a deep breath.

When I inhale, the stench that comes with it hits me full force.

"Shit," Axl whispers before I have a chance to say anything.

Dax doesn't move, not even when Axl and I draw our knives. I look around, back toward the house and the forest circling the property, but all I can see is black. Black sky and black shadows that move like trees. The black outline of the barn and a few smaller sheds behind the house. The moon is out, but it isn't bright or there isn't enough of it peeking out of the clouds to help light up the area.

"Where?" I whisper, my voice trembling.

Axl shakes his head while Dax remains motionless.

We should run back to the house, but it's still a good distance away and I'd like to know what we're dealing with first. The wind blows again, and this time the stench is stronger, but it also brings with it the sound of moans. They're coming from behind us.

I spin around, my heart stopping when the figures step out of the black night like they've materialized from nothing. Dozens of them moving together, lumbering right toward us. They don't have far to go.

"Run!" Axl hisses, grabbing my hand as he backs away.

I've only taken one step toward the house when Axl's hand is ripped from mine. He goes down, his body slamming into the ground. He groans but doesn't move to get back up. Moans rip through the silent night, and Dax's heavy breathing echoes in my ears, mixing with my pounding heart. All around me, the moans of the dead mix with the wind until I find it difficult to focus.

What the hell is happening?

Dax takes a step toward me, and just like that, everything snaps into place.

He's willing to do whatever it takes to get Angus to Atlanta.

"What are you thinking?" I hiss, wanting to back away from the man in front of me but knowing I have nowhere to go. Not with the zombies behind me.

"You've been holding me up," Dax says calmly, "and you're right. Angus won't leave you behind. At least not while you're alive."

My gaze darts from Dax to Axl's motionless body, then to the horde of zombies who are now only ten feet away from us. I take a step toward Axl, but before I can do a thing, Dax has my arm gripped in his hand. I swing my knife around, but his free hand wraps around my wrist. He twists my arm until a yelp breaks out of me, and the knife falls to the ground. His other hand tightens on my arm and I cry out in pain and the screams only grow louder a second later when he pushes me toward the horde.

"This isn't how I wanted things to go," he says through clenched teeth.

"Get off me!" I scream, causing the zombies at my back wail even more.

"I gave you a chance."

I struggle as Dax pushes me backward, my feet tripping all over each other. He's moving too fast for me even think about trying to fight back. I can barely stay up. The moans get louder, and my heart pounds violently. I risk a look over my shoulder and find the zombies so close that I can see their milky eyes in the moonlight.

"Stop," I beg as tears stream down my cheeks and a feeling of desperation comes over me. "Please."

"It's the only way. We have to keep moving, and your group is dead weight. If I kill you myself, Angus will never trust me. But I can make it look like an accident."

He's crazy. He has to be or he'd know how flawed his plan is.

Which makes him even more terrifying.

"Get off," I scream as something brushes my back, making my heart pound harder. Faster.

There has to be a way out of this.

I shove back against Dax, twisting my body in the process, and somehow I manage to pull myself closer to him while spinning around completely. My arm gets twisted so hard that I swear my bones threaten to snap, but at least it gets me further from the zombies. Not far enough, though. They're still moving, and Dax is still determined to get me to them. He tries to push me back, but I grab hold of him, digging my nails into his sides. He curses and jerks, trying to wiggle out of my grasp so he can move me forward, but I refuse to let go. Finally, probably out of desperation, he releases my arm, but only a second later, he has me around the waist. Then he lifts me, and my fingernails slide across his stomach, scratching him but allowing him to break free of my hold. My feet leave the ground, and I know it's over. Not only is there nowhere for me to grab him, but now I can't run, either. Can't do anything but flail in his arms as he moves forward.

Dax presses his face against mine and his lips move against my ear when he says, "You had your chance."

Then he starts walking toward the advancing dead.

I scream and squeeze my eyes shut, kicking my feet at the waiting zombies, trying to keep them back while bracing myself. Knowing Dax is about to throw me into the growling horde and there's nothing I can do about it. That this is the end and all the fight has been for nothing.

The crack of a gunshot cuts through my screams, and suddenly Dax's arms fall away. I drop to the ground, disoriented and confused. My ears ringing and my limbs tingling, and even though zombies are barreling down on me, I can't figure out how to move.

Hands grab my arms from behind, and I let out a shriek as I twist and pull, trying to get away.

"Vivian!"

Axl's voice cuts through the ringing in my ears, and I turn to find him standing over me. He pulls me to my feet, but I'm having a hard time focusing. My gaze goes from Dax's lifeless body—now surrounded by the dead—to the horde still barreling down on us, then to the gun clutched in Axl's hand. The gun we found just a few hours ago. The gun we hid from Dax.

"Run!" Axl yells.

He moves, pulling me with him, and I finally snap out of it. I put everything into running, forcing my legs to move faster with each step. The dead are right behind us, their moans breaking through the constant ringing in my ears and causing every hair on my scalp to prickle.

Angus, Jim, and Parvarti wave from the porch, probably calling to us to hurry, but I can't hear them through the buzzing in my ears and the moans at my back. A few zombies come around the side of the house just as we reach the porch, and Axl shoves me in front of him. Toward the front door. My feet pound against the stairs and the wood bows under my weight, but Angus has my arm before I'm all the way up and he's pulling me inside.

We stumble into the living room, and I'm still panting when I lean against the wall. Behind me, the door slams shut and people start yelling. Then furniture is being pulled across the room toward the door and everyone is talking at once and there's so much noise that I can barely think, but I do know one thing. The front door isn't the only way in.

I push off the wall and charge toward the back of the house. Behind me, the front door rattles in its frame, and all through the house, footsteps pound against the floor as moans break through the glass and walls that form the wooden box we're now trapped in. I reach the back door and flip the lock just as the knob rattles, and Jim comes running into the kitchen behind me. In the other room, the sound of furniture being pulled across the floor screeches through the air.

"Fridge!" Jim shouts, yanking on the useless appliance.

I move toward the fridge even though my limbs are shaking so badly I'm not sure I'm going to be much help. The massive thing moves away from the wall, and Jim shoves it toward the door, straining with the effort. The cord pulls tight, so I lean over and yank it out of the socket before going back to helping Jim. He gets the fridge across the room and shoves it firmly against the door before turning toward the table. In the blink of an eye, the thing is on its side and Jim is shoving it against the refrigerator.

"Let's check the rest of the place out," he says, heading back to the front of the house.

In the main room, an antique armoire has been moved to block the front door, and Angus and Axl are busy piling other furniture in front of the windows lining the porch. I hurry to help with my heart pounding in my still ringing ears, barely able to catch my breath. The whole time, all I can think about is Ginny and the baby, and how the virus and the premature birth may not matter at all now. Because we're trapped.

Once the windows are blocked, Axl and Angus step back, panting and dripping with sweat.

"What the hell happened out there?" Angus gasps.

"Dax." I still can't figure it out, but it suddenly hits me that Axl was down and I don't even know if he's okay. "Let me see your head," I say, moving to his side.

"Bastard went crazy," Axl says as I check him over. Other than a bump on the back of his skull, he looks okay. It isn't even bleeding. "He must've seen the horde from the porch. Knocked me out, then tried to throw Vivian to the dead."

"Why the hell would he do that?" Parv asks.

"He said we were slowing him down and he knew Angus would never leave us behind," I say.

"Shit," Jim mutters. "I knew the guy was nuts, but I never thought he'd do that."

"Where the hell you'd get a gun?" Angus asks, turning on Axl.

"Last place we stopped." Axl pulls the gun from his waistband. "Found it in the back and figured it'd be best if that asshole didn't know."

"Lucky you found it, then," Angus says.

The others nod, and I suck in a deep breath. My ears are still ringing, but it's gotten better. Now I can actually hear the zombies as they pound on the door.

"Are the other windows okay?" I ask, eyeing the furniture piled in front of the main window.

"Should be too high for the zombies," Jim says, turning to examine the window to our left.

He's right. This house is built over a cellar, so the main floor is at least three feet above the ground. Not too high for a human if they wanted to climb in, but we've never seen a zombie climb anything, and I doubt it would be able to pull itself up, break a window, and get inside.

At least I hope not.

"So we're good?" I ask, looking around.

"Don't think there's nothin' good 'bout this," Angus mutters.

"I should check on Ginny, then," I say, heading for the stairs. There's no reason to point out the absolute truth in Angus's statement.

"Maybe you should go upstairs just in case," Parv says to Angus. "If the zombies manage to break in you could lock yourself in a bedroom."

Angus snorts. "I ain't 'bout to hide."

I hurry up, only making it halfway before Ginny's painful moans bring me back to reality. I'll let the others worry about Angus. I've got other things on my mind, like the fact that Ginny is about to have a baby and we have no idea what to expect.

I shove the door open, and Joshua looks up from where he sits next to Ginny, holding her hand. He looks terrified but also in control. Which is good. Things have gotten even crazier than we could have imagined, and right now we need stay cool.

"Vivian," Ginny gasps, reaching for me with her free hand.

I hurry over, dropping to my knees at the side of the bed. I grasp Ginny's free hand, feeling like the biggest ass in the history of the world—which is saying a lot, since I know Angus.

"I'm here," I say.

"I'm sorry." Ginny's sobs come out so hard she's gasping for breath. "I'm so sorry I hurt you."

"It's fine," I whisper, patting her hand. "I forgive you. It was nothing. I don't care."

I can't think of enough words to reassure her that it's forgotten, so I just continue patting her hand.

"Breathe, Ginny," Joshua says, then shoots me a look. "What happened?"

I swallow while I try to figure out what to say. Freaking Ginny out right now isn't the best plan, but hiding how bad things have gotten seems like a pretty shitty thing to do.

"Dax is dead," I say and take a deep breath. "And we're surrounded."

Ginny's already big eyes get huge, and Joshua exhales. I squeeze the hand between mine while holding the doctor's gaze. His expression tells me everything I need to know. This baby is coming sooner than we expected.

"How long?" I whisper.

"She's nine," Joshua says. "Any time now."

Ginny squeezes my hand, and I turn back to meet her gaze. "What's going on down there? Are we okay?"

"Don't worry about it," I whisper. "Just worry about you and the baby. Nothing else."

Ginny nods, but the fear in her eyes doesn't fade. It has to be horrible to know you're trapped and in such a vulnerable position.

After that, time both drags and seems to move in fast forward. Ginny reaches ten centimeters, and Joshua urges her to push while I hold her hand. What seems like only a second later, something crashes to the floor downstairs. Followed by shouting and a banging I can't identify.

"Ignore it," I say, realizing it's an impossible request but wanting to keep Ginny calm. "Just push."

Ginny nods, her eyes so big they look ready to pop. Another contraction starts, and her fingers tighten around mine.

"Push, Ginny," Joshua says as footsteps pound up the stairs.

Ginny cries out just as Angus rushes into the room. A second later Joshua shouts, "That's it! The head is out. Slow down now. Take a deep breath. Don't push!"

"Son of a bitch," Angus says.

He tries to leave, but Jim materializes out of nowhere and pushes him back. "We need to keep you safe."

Downstairs, there's more commotion, and all I can picture are dozens of zombies pouring into the house while Axl and Parvarti try to hold them off.

"What's happening?" I say, torn between the urge to stay and help Ginny and the desire to know if Axl is okay.

"They broke the window, that's all," Angus says. "This asshole panicked and ran. Left the other two down there to take care of it by themselves." Angus spits, and the glare he shoots Jim could kill a zombie outright.

"I'm not scared, you moron," Jim mutters. He's standing half in the room and half out, staring down the hall. "Axl told me to get you upstairs."

"I can take care of myself," Angus mutters.

"Shut up!" Joshua screams at the men before turning back to Ginny. "Listen to me, I want to you push on the next contraction, nice and slow. Got it?"

Ginny nods, and a mass of sweaty hair falls across her eyes. I brush it back, feeling totally useless but wanting to help.

She pushes, and just like that, all our lives our change. The baby is pink and wet and smaller than I've ever seen. Ginny sobs while Joshua ties a string around the cord. He flips the baby over and pats the little thing's back, but for a couple tense seconds, nothing happens. Then all at once, the littlest cry I've ever heard breaks through the room and cuts the tension in half, totally overshadowing everything else going on. Proving that God hasn't forgotten us completely.

"It's a girl," Joshua says, smiling. "She's tiny, but she looks good."

Ginny sobs and holds out her arms. "Give her to me."

"Just a minute," Joshua says, then turns to me. "Scissors."

I hand him the scissors we sterilized earlier, and he cuts the cord before passing the baby to Ginny. Her face is streaked with tears and sweat, and she looks exhausted, but I've never seen anything as beautiful as the smile that lights up her face when she looks at her daughter.

"Megan," she says, sobbing. "Jon wanted to call her Megan."

Just hearing the name of the poor girl we met back in the Monte Carlo makes me sob as much as Ginny.

"We still need to deliver the placenta," Joshua says.

"Shit," Angus mutters behind me. "Let me outta here."

This time, Jim doesn't stop him.

Joshua does his part, but I can't look away from Ginny and the baby. Her happiness takes my breath away. Like Ginny, I was worried. Not just about the virus, but about how she would feel when the baby was born. If the demons she's been trying to escape would come swooping in, destroying any chance of happiness for her.

The expression on her face tells me that hasn't happened.

When he's finished his part, Joshua stands and stretches until his back pops, then lets out a deep breath. "She looks good. I can't believe it, but she looks perfect. Seems to be breathing okay, and she's nice and pink. She's small—I'd guess not even five pounds—but she's healthy."

He smiles, and I can visibly see it when the tension rolls off his shoulders.

"She's perfect," Ginny whispers, staring at her daughter. "And she looks just like Jon."

CHAPTER EIGHTEEN

The zombies are still banging on both the front and back doors when I tiptoe down the stairs. Axl kneels in front of the barricade they've built, watching it closely like he's afraid it's going to collapse at any second. He turns my way when I make it all the way down the stairs and holds his hand out to me. I take it and move over to kneel at his side.

"She okay?" he whispers.

"Perfect. It's a girl and she's perfect, too."

Axl nods and goes back to staring at the barricade, my hand held in his. "Good."

"What now?" I ask, nodding toward the wall of furniture in front of us.

"Don't know. Maybe they get bored and leave, maybe they don't and we gotta figure out another way."

"Is there another way? We're kind of boxed in here."

"There's gotta be."

We sit in silence, and after a few seconds, my legs start to shake. I give up trying to kneel and settle for sitting on the floor. Axl doesn't move, and he doesn't shift his gaze from the barrier they built. The only thing standing between us and the zombies.

Footsteps walk into the room behind me, and I turn as Parvarti heads our way, a box packed full of food in her hands. "Thought I'd take this upstairs to the bedroom. Just in case we have to barricade ourselves in."

"Shit." I run my hand through my hair and twist it into a knot on the top of my head. "Why does it keep coming to this?"

"Because this is the world now," Parvarti says, then turns and heads for the stairs.

Axl pats my knee like he's waiting for me to say something about Parvarti's attitude, but I don't. It would just be me repeating the same things I've already said a hundred times, and right now I'm too tired to try to work out a problem that has no solution.

The stairs creak as Joshua drags himself down. He smiles when he sees us, but the dark rings circling his eyes make me wonder how he's even standing. He has to be exhausted. Emotionally and physically.

"How is she?" I ask, dragging myself to my feet.

"Sleeping."

"And the baby?"

"Megan is doing great. Nothing like the other babies as far as I can tell."

"So she's immune?" Axl asks a little too loudly. A zombie on the other side of the furniture moans, and the whole barricade shakes.

"Umm…" Joshua eyes the wobbling furniture and takes a step back. "Not sure yet, but it looks like it. From what I was told, the other babies had trouble breathing from the start."

Axl nods, and Joshua takes another step, this time sideways. Like he's trying to inch his way toward the kitchen.

"Ginny's resting, so I thought I'd grab something to eat."

"I should go up and sit with her," I say. "Hold the baby so she can really rest."

Joshua shakes his head. "Angus has her."

He moves closer to the kitchen, keeping his eye on the barrier, which means he doesn't see it when I smile. Of course Angus has the baby. He has a few weaknesses: dip, beer, and kids. An odd combination, but one that makes him almost loveable. Almost.

"I'm going to head up anyway," I say.

Axl grabs my hand as I turn, and I give his a gentle squeeze before dragging myself up the stairs. I peek into the first room but hurry away when Ginny's sleeping form comes into view. She had a long night, and I don't want to disturb her.

I come to the next room and freeze in the doorway. Angus is sitting in the rocking chair with Megan cradled in his arms.

"What are you doing?"

He doesn't look away from the sleeping baby. "Just givin' Hollywood a chance to rest."

"She isn't the only one," I say through a yawn.

My gaze moves across the barely lit room, landing on the bed. It looks so soft and warm that I find my legs wobbling. A little nap would do me good too. It's been a rough couple days, and I'm starting to feel the drain of it all.

"Don't let me stop you," Angus says.

I nod as I cross the room, my eyes not moving away from the bed. The mattress groans in protest when I drop onto it. I kick my shoes off before crawling farther into bed, pulling the covers down as I go. Then I curl into a ball and pull the blankets over me, snuggling into the warmth. My eyelids growing heavy in seconds.

"Wake me if you need anything," I say just before I pull the sheet over my head.

THE BED DIPS, WAKING ME FROM A SLEEP SO DEEP that it almost feels like I'm climbing out of a cave.

"You awake?" Axl whispers as he slips his arm around my waist.

I crack one eye but shut it again when I'm met with darkness. "No." I twist my body to face him, and his nose nuzzles my neck. "Are they still out there?"

"Yeah." His warm breath sweeps across my skin, comforting me despite the ominous feeling his answer brings.

"How long can we make it with the food we have?"

"A couple weeks."

I nod as I scoot closer, trying to suck comfort from his body heat. It doesn't work, not really. Not when I think about staying in this house for weeks, just waiting to see if these bastards will wander away. Especially when deep down I know they won't.

"Get some sleep," Axl whispers.

Again, I find myself nodding. I try to say okay, but what comes out is more of a grunt. Apparently, my throat has tightened so much that it's now impossible for me to form actual words.

At my side, Axl's body slowly relaxes, and I try to do the same. Try to shut my brain off and focus on anything other than the zombies surrounding us, but it's impossible. Every time I close my eyes, I think about all the things that could go wrong. About zombies breaking through the barrier we've created and charging into the house, ripping us to pieces. I think about running out of food or water and about how horrible it would be to slowly die of dehydration. To know the end was near and the solution was so simple, but also so impossible.

No. I won't let that happen. I'll run outside and lead them away before I let us all die. Angus has to get to Atlanta, and almost every person I care about is inside this house. I can't even comprehend just sitting here and doing nothing.

Axl's breathing slows and deepens, and the arm he has draped over me grows heavier, but I'm still wide awake. Sleep is so far away that I don't see the point in staying where I am. Once I'm sure Axl is in such a deep sleep that I couldn't possibly disturb him, I slip out from under his arm and slide out of bed. The floor is cold against my sock-clad feet, sending a shiver through me even though the air in the room is stuffy. We could open the windows, but that would only be inviting the stench of death into the house, so it's better to leave things the way they are.

The hall is just as dark as the bedroom was, but a light flickers at the bottom of the stairs. So faint it can't be more than one tiny candle. I head that way, peeking into Ginny's room as I pass. She's still asleep. Good.

Downstairs, the rest of our group is gathered in the living room, including our newest addition. Just like when I crawled into bed, Megan is asleep on Angus's chest. It's as if she's never been anywhere more comfortable than in his arms. Joshua is sprawled out on the couch, his long legs hanging over the arm and his eyes wide open. Like he finds it impossible to sleep with the dead banging on the wall next to him. Not a surprise.

Parvarti too is awake, but sitting on the floor with her back up against the couch and her knees pulled tightly against her chest. She looks so small and young and vulnerable. Like a child who has lost her parents and finds herself among strangers. Which is basically who she was when we first picked her up on Route 66, but it's been months since I've seen this side of her. For some reason, it gives me hope. Like if she can just come to terms with the emotions trapped inside her, she may be able to get through this after all.

Jim stands away from the others, halfway between the kitchen and the front door like he's trying to keep an eye on both at the same time. Like he's the only reason zombies aren't already inside the house, ripping us apart.

"How is she?" I whisper as I tiptoe across the room.

"Strong." Angus says, grinning.

"And Ginny?" I ask Joshua.

"Tired, but good." He stares at the ceiling with his arms crossed over his chest. "She's in some pain, but that's normal. It's just her uterus trying to shrink back to its normal size."

I nod, remembering the painful cramps from four years ago when I went through it myself. After Emily was born and long gone, off with the people who were supposed to be her hope for a better life. I guess no one can predict a zombie apocalypse.

"Can I hold her?" I ask when I stop in front of Angus.

He nods as he hauls himself to his feet. "Take a seat."

I do, lowering myself into the rocking chair he just vacated. Angus waits until I'm seated to hand me the little bundle, almost like he's afraid I'll drop her if he gives her to me while I'm still standing. I'd be insulted, but this side of Angus is too adorable to wish away.

When Megan is in my arms, all I can do is stare down at her in amazement. She twists her tiny body and makes a little noise that reminds me of a kitten or some other small animal. It's adorable and heartbreaking at the same time. She's a lot smaller than Emily was—a good three pounds—but holding her is like going back in time. I only had my daughter for a couple hours after she was born. Just long enough for it to rip me apart when the social worker came to take her away.

I rock back and forth while the room around me settles into semi-silence. Joshua's eyes close despite the moans from the zombies, and soon his breathing has slowed. Angus sprawls out on the floor, and even Parvarti lays her head back. Jim alone doesn't try to get any rest. He's as alert as ever as he stares at the furniture barrier.

After a bit, Megan stirs. She lets out a little whimper as she turns her head to the side, opening and closing her mouth like she's looking for something. Maybe she's hungry?

I get to my feet, causing Angus to sit up as well. I didn't even know he was awake.

"I'm going to take her up to Ginny," I say. "I think she needs to eat."

Angus nods as I head by.

I reach the stairs just as Axl comes down.

"Woke up alone," he says, his eyes moving to the baby in my arms.

"I couldn't go back to sleep."

"You goin' up?"

"I think she's hungry."

Axl nods and moves to the side so I can squeeze by, his eyes not on me but on Megan. Something about the softness in his expression makes my uterus quiver, and I find myself smiling. Maybe one day, if we can survive this and make it to Atlanta, the baby in my arms will be ours. Axl's and mine. It's a nice thought, even if it does seem far-fetched.

I reach the bedroom and pause long enough to rap my knuckles against the door before pushing it open. "You awake?" I whisper.

The candle on the bedside table is lit, but it doesn't give off a lot of light. Just enough to create dark shadows in every corner and across Ginny's face when she turns my way. She shifts until she's sitting, wincing when she moves too fast, and I have the urge to run over and help, but of course I can't. My hands are a little too full at the moment.

"She ready to eat?" Ginny asks after she's managed to prop herself up.

"I think so. I don't have a lot of experience with babies..." I shrug and lower myself until I'm sitting on the edge of the bed. "How are you feeling?"

"I'm okay. Really worn out, but after everything we've been through, you'd expect that." Ginny shifts again, and her face scrunches up. She rubs her lower abdomen. "Is it supposed to hurt this much? I swear some of these cramps are worse than when I was in labor. And I'm bleeding like crazy."

"It's been a few years," I say, handing over the little bundle. "But I remember the recovery being pretty rough." I'd always assumed my emotional state made the whole thing worse, but maybe not. "It won't last too long."

"Joshua says it's normal for the cramps to be painful and that the bleeding should slow soon."

"It is. I think."

She nods, but her attention is now on her daughter. The baby mews, and Ginny pulls her breast out, but I look away. Hoping to give them privacy. This was a part of motherhood I never got around to. In fact, everything after labor was lost to me, which at this particular moment makes me sadder than I've ever been in my life.

"What was your daughter's name again?" Ginny asks, lifting her green eyes from the baby.

"Emily," I whisper. "Having her was life-altering. It showed me how strong I was and proved that I could make it through even the most painful things. It taught me to strive for something bigger in life. It led me to Axl when this virus hit, which took me across the country and to the shelter. Gave me a new family and a fresh start. Because of Emily, I learned what love really is and that there are people in this world who really care about others. I never had any of that growing up. If I'd stayed where I was, I would have been stuck in that life forever. Until the day I ran out on my dad, I couldn't see a real future for myself. All I saw was me living in the trailer park. Settling for a man who treated me like shit simply because that was all I knew and the only thing that seemed normal."

"You are the strongest person I've ever met," Ginny says.

I turn to face her, realizing for the first time that I'm staring at the wall. Too lost in my own thoughts to know what I was looking at or where I was or even who was sitting next to me. Ginny smiles, but tears shimmer in her eyes, and the sight of them takes my breath away. We've all been through so much that sometimes the weight of it feels like it's going to crush the entire Earth, trapping us in this hell forever.

"You're just as strong," I say, taking her free hand.

"I don't know about that. If Megan had died, I wouldn't be sitting here. I'd already made up my mind, and I don't think anyone or anything could have changed it."

"What?" I ask, shaking my head in disbelief.

"Jon was the only thing keeping me anchored to the ground for so long, and the thought of facing our baby's death alone or going on without him… It just hurt too much. I'm tired of hurting. Tired of hating life and myself and wanting to punch the mirror every time I look in and see Hadley Lucas staring back at me. Because I can change my name and I can tell everyone I'm just Ginny Lewis from Ohio, but it doesn't change the past and it never will." She looks down at the tiny bundle cradled in her arms. "If she'd died, I would be dead, too. I would have made sure of it."

"Ginny, I—" I shake my head again because I don't have a clue what to say, and her words terrify me. Right now Megan seems fine, but all that could change in the blink of an eye, and then Ginny would be gone, too. "Please don't say that."

"It's okay," she says, looking up. "I think I can make it now. I didn't know how it would feel once she was born, but now that she's here, I know it's *right*. She's mine and Jon was her father, and one day when she's old enough, I'll be able to tell her about the man who saved me in every way imaginable. And she'll be proud of where she came from."

"I'm so sorry for all the things you went through," I say, taking her hand again. Squeezing it between mine and wishing more than anything that I could go back and change what happened to her. Of all the things we've gone through, Ginny's pain is my biggest regret.

She rolls her eyes, but she's still smiling when she says, "You and Axl suffer from the same delusion: that you can somehow control everything that happens. You can't and we all know that, and when something goes wrong we don't blame you two."

I laugh and swipe my hand across my face when a tear slides down my cheek. "That doesn't stop me from thinking I could have done more or been more. That I *should* have been able to figure out a way to make things turn out better."

Megan lets out a little gurgle before unlatching from her mother's breast. I watch as Ginny switches sides, the movement looking totally natural even though she's a new mother. Almost like it was meant to be.

"None of that matters now," Ginny says, staring down at her daughter. "Because we are exactly where we are meant to be, and I suddenly have this faith I haven't had in a really long time. I believe we will get out of this house. That these zombies won't get us and that Atlanta is just a few short days away."

I give her hand another squeeze. "We'll make it happen. I don't know how, but we will, because dying here isn't an option."

CHAPTER NINETEEN

"Vivian."

A hand shakes me awake. I open my eyes, and the room is so bright that I have to cover my face with my arm. When I roll over, Axl is hovering over me.

"What?" I mumble, blinking as I try to clear the sleep from my foggy eyes and brain.

"Hadley's got a fever."

I'm sitting up before the words have really sunk in. My blonde hair tumbles across my face, and I push it out of the way so I can focus on Axl's gray eyes.

"What? What's wrong?"

"Don't know. Joshua's with her, but she wanted me to get you."

"Shit," I mutter, sliding out of the bed and hurrying from the room.

Three days we've been stuck here, and with each passing hour, the walls seem to close in on us more and more. We want to move, but between Ginny and the zombies surrounding us, we haven't been able to come up with a plan. Megan, thankfully, has been doing well, and until now, so has Ginny. She even went downstairs for a little bit yesterday. She was tired, but that's normal. At least I thought so.

"Ginny," I gasp when I rush to her side. "What's going on?"

Beads of sweat dot her face, clinging to her brow. The pink of her cheeks is more prominent than ever before, but her arms—wrapped around her sleeping baby—are covered in goose bumps.

"Fever," Joshua says. "And her bleeding has gotten worse, not better. She's passed some clots, which is bad." He swallows, and the pain in his eyes tells me who he believes is at fault for the current situation.

Axl and I aren't the only ones who take way too much blame for the things that are out of our control.

I lower myself to the bed and take Ginny's hand, holding it between mine. "Are you okay?"

"Cramping. Freezing. Nauseated." She shakes her head, but it's slow and labored. "I haven't felt great since Megan was born. Really tired and weak. And the pain has been so bad. When I woke up today it was so much worse, though."

"What is it?" I ask, turning to Joshua.

"I don't know for sure." He lets out a deep sigh. "Possibly a retained placenta, but it could just be an infection. You heard Atlanta. This virus has changed things. Made infections stronger."

Retained placenta. I'm not sure what it is, but it can't be good.

"What's a retained placenta?"

"Sometimes the placenta breaks apart and a piece is left in the uterus. It would explain the excessive bleeding and the clots, but..." He sinks his teeth into his bottom lip and looks away.

"What?" I snap.

Joshua's eyes meet mine, and I can see the answer before he's had a chance to say it. "If that's what it is, there's literally nothing I can do about it. I don't have the ability to do a D&C."

"I'm going to die," Ginny mumbles, but she doesn't sound like this is the first time she's heard it. They must have talked about it before Axl came to get me.

"No," I say, shaking my head. "That can't be it. It has to be an infection or something, which means all we have to do is find some antibiotics."

Joshua raises his eyebrows, and I know what he's thinking: I might as well be asking for a pot of gold.

"Even if that were true, we didn't bring any antibiotics with us, and there are none in the house. We already checked. Plus, with the way things are now, I'm not totally convinced they would work. We need the new stuff the CDC created."

I get to my feet and cross the room while I think. "There has to be a way," I hiss, but I'm not sure if I'm talking to Joshua or myself, or maybe even to God.

"There isn't," Ginny says firmly, drawing my attention her way. Even though tears slide down her cheeks, she holds her head high. "You need to take care of Megan." She pauses and looks down at her sleeping daughter before bringing her tear-filled eyes up to meet mine again. "Understand? You and Axl. You are her parents now."

The full impact of what is about to happen hits me, and that feeling of uselessness comes back. Only it's so much worse than it's ever been before. I've never in my life felt as powerless as I do now.

A pain moves across my chest that I can only imagine is yet another crack in my heart, and just like that, I start to sob. There are so many pieces inside me now, and each one has someone's name permanently etched on it. Emily. Trey. Jess. Winston. Darla. Jon. All of them took a piece of me with them when they died, and now Ginny is going to take even more. How the hell am I supposed to keep going when I feel like my insides are held together with Band-Aids?

I move over to kneel at her side, grabbing her hand

between mine. "Nothing's going to happen to you," I say through the tears.

"Vivian." Ginny's voice is firm. Not even a tremor in it.

I force myself to look up. To meet her gaze and pay attention even though every inch of me hurts. "I'm listening."

"You have to promise you'll be stronger than you've ever been. For Jon. For me. For Megan."

Tears slide down my cheeks in a constant stream, but I don't wipe them away. "I promise. I'll take care of her. Love her and keep her safe. Make sure she grows up protected. And one day when she's older, I'll tell her all about the mother and father who made her and how much they loved each other and how much they loved her."

"Good," Ginny whispers, her bottom lip trembling. "That's all I wanted to hear. Now I can die and know it's going to be okay."

Fresh tears stream down my cheeks, but I don't argue this time. Joshua sits at the foot of the bed, staring at his hands like they're covered in Ginny's blood. He'll blame himself for the rest of his life, but this isn't his fault. This is something that is totally out of his control.

Maybe Ginny should have stayed in Hope Springs. Jon would still be alive, and Megan would have been okay there. If she were there right now, they could do surgery and save her. We could have seen her again one day, after things had settled down. She could have come to Atlanta with her husband and baby.

But that will never happen now, and none of it is Joshua's fault.

"Stay with me until the end," Ginny whispers.

I wipe the tears from my cheeks and nod. "I'm not going anywhere."

I pull myself up and settle at Ginny's side. Right next to the arm cradled around little Megan. The baby is sound asleep, and Ginny's eyes are glued to her peaceful expression. I can't look away from my friend, though. It's like my mind is trying to memorize every line of her face. Every twitch of her cheek or tear that fills her eyes. I want to remember her like she is at this moment. How happy she was at the end despite everything she'd been through.

MY ARM BRUSHES AGAINST GINNY'S. HER SKIN IS SO hot it feels like it's burning me. I run my hand across her damp forehead, and it's like a branding iron against my palm.

"She's hotter," I say, shaking my head.

Joshua nods, and Ginny shivers, her teeth chattering despite the heat radiating off her skin. It's been close to two hours since Axl woke me, and already the rags Joshua has been using to soak up Ginny's blood have been changed twice. I've never seen anything like it. She's weak, and the couple times she's tried to sit up have been unsuccessful. She's fading fast. Faster than I thought she would.

"Take her," Ginny whispers, trying to hold Megan out to me. "My arms are so tired."

I scoop the baby up but keep close to her mother's side. Her eyes never leave her daughter's face.

"At least she lived," Ginny says in a gravelly voice. "That's all I really wanted, anyway."

I swallow back tears as I bounce the sleeping baby. "I'll make sure she's always safe."

Behind me, someone walks into the room, but I don't look away from Ginny until Angus has stopped at my side. Her eyes move away from her daughter just long enough to see who it is.

"Did you come to say goodbye?" she whispers, giving him a weak smile.

He sniffs as he kneels at her side. "Can't let you slip outta here without givin' you some shit."

I move to give Angus more room, and even though I don't go far, Ginny gives me a panicked look.

"I'm right here," I say gently, almost like I'm trying to soothe a frightened child. "I'm not going anywhere."

Ginny nods and looks back at Angus, forcing out a smile that is strained and painful. "I never thanked you," she whispers. "For that day at the Monte Carlo. I couldn't have asked for more compassion. It took me so much by surprise that I didn't know how to react. You're a good man."

Angus swallows but tries to shrug her words off. "You thanked me in your own way. After that, you never treated me like the asshole I am. That meant somethin'."

"Was," Ginny whispers. "You're not an asshole anymore."

Angus nods but looks away. Pressing his lips together like he's trying to trap something inside. After a second, he says, "Don't you worry 'bout your kid. We'll get her to Atlanta. I promise. Gonna miss you, Hollywood. You never take any of my shit."

Ginny pats Angus's hand, but neither one says anything else. After a few seconds, he stands. Before he heads out, Angus pauses just long enough to plant a kiss on Ginny's forehead.

Beneath Ginny, the sheets are now soaked with her blood.

Axl walks into the room, and Joshua covers Ginny like he's trying to hide how much blood there is, but the image will be in my mind forever.

"I'm glad you're here," Ginny whispers, her voice more strained than ever. "I needed to say I'm sorry."

"Nothin' to be sorry 'bout," Axl says.

"She's yours now." Ginny looks toward Megan and me, but she doesn't turn her head. Only her eyes. As if moving more would be too much effort for her. "I know you'll be a good dad. That's why I acted the way I did. Because you're so good."

Axl nods, then shakes his head, clearing his throat before saying, "Not sure what to say."

"Just say goodbye," I whisper through my tears.

"Goodbye." Axl steps forward, and just like Angus, he kisses Ginny on the head. As he pulls back he says, "We'll keep her safe."

Axl slips from the room, and I turn, waiting for Parv or Jim to come in. When no one does, I go back to sitting on the edge of the bed.

Joshua is still at Ginny's feet, totally silent and utterly tortured by what is about to happen.

"Let me hold her," Ginny whispers.

She tries to lift her arms, but she's so weak they don't get far. It doesn't matter. I'm at her side, and I lay Megan next to her mother. Right in the crook of her arm but still on the bed so Ginny doesn't have to exert any effort. She doesn't have the strength at this point, and I know she wouldn't want to risk hurting the little thing.

"Hey," Ginny whispers, smiling when the baby shifts and yawns. "I'm leaving soon, but before I go, I wanted to tell you how much I love you. You were worth it. All the shit—crap—I went through doesn't seem to matter now that you're here. Your daddy loved you too, even if he didn't get to meet you."

The baby lets out a little cry, and Ginny gently bounces her, whispering soothing words until her daughter quiets once again.

Then she lets out big sigh and closes her eyes. "I don't feel like I have the energy to even hold my head up."

Her voice is so quiet I have to lean forward. My gaze moves over her frame, watching the rise and fall of her chest that seems to get shallower with each passing moment. The sheets Joshua laid over her only a few minutes ago are now stained red. There isn't much time left.

"It's okay," I say, rubbing the arm wrapped around her sleeping child. "Just relax."

On the other side of the bed, Joshua shifts until his head is in his hands.

"I'm so sleepy," Ginny says, trying to open her eyes.

"Just go to sleep."

She nods slowly, then lets out another shallow breath. I wait for her to inhale yet again, but nothing happens. Joshua moves his hand from his head to her wrist, and I hold my own breath while I wait. It only takes a second for him to stand.

"She's gone," he says, then turns and walks from the room.

Tears fall from my eyes, and I don't even try to hold them back. Ginny's with Jon now, and even though I know she'd rather be here with her daughter, I can't help thinking that all her suffering is finally over for good. She doesn't have to worry about painful memories trying to rip her apart anymore or a zombie taking a bite out of her. All the struggles of this new world are forgotten now, and there's a part of me, although very small, that's jealous.

Megan stirs, and I force myself to stand. To wipe the tears from my face and pick the sleeping infant up. Soon the heat will fade from her mother's body, and it's my job to keep the baby warm.

CHAPTER TWENTY

Everyone but Joshua and Parvarti are standing in the living room. Angus looks like someone punched him in the balls, and Axl isn't much better off. Jim stands off to the side by himself, but even he looks affected by the loss.

"She's ours now," I tell Axl even though he already knows.

He stares down at the baby like he's seeing her for the first time but doesn't hesitate when I hand her over. In his arms she looks impossibly small and fragile, but he's so gentle that I don't bother telling him to support her head. He knows what to do, and he'll keep her safe.

"Never held a baby before," he says, just staring at her.

"You're doing a great job," I say, looking around. "Where's Parv?"

"Rambo's in the other room," Angus says, nodding toward the small study on the other side of the stairs.

She's the only one—other than Jim—who didn't come up and say goodbye. Now that the hard part is over, I can't stop anger from surging through me. She and Ginny have been through so much, and back when Trey died, we were all there for Parvarti. She should have come to say goodbye. Should have thought about someone other than herself.

"I'll be back," I say, heading toward the study.

I reach the door, just barely cracked, but the sound of sobbing freezes me in my tracks. It can't be Parv. Can it? She's been like a robot for so long, and even though she told me just a few days ago that she still hurts, I didn't totally believe her. Is she crying for Ginny?

The door creaks when I push it open, and Parvarti turns my way. Tears stream down her cheeks, illuminated by the moonlight shining through the single window.

"Parv?" I say, stepping inside.

"I should have told her goodbye." She shakes her head and wipes at the tears. "I thought I could stop myself from hurting if I just avoided it, but I think that just made it worse. When Joshua came downstairs and said she was dead, it felt like he had sliced me in half."

I step further into the room and do something I'm not sure either one of us is going to appreciate. I wrap my arms around her. Parv stiffens and sucks in a deep breath, and even though everything in me says to let her go, I don't.

"We aren't done yet," I say instead, tightening my hold until she finally allows her body to relax into mine. "We have more to do on this earth."

In my arms, Parv feels impossibly small and fragile, and it hits me for the first time in a really long time that she's still just a child. Only a couple years younger than I am, but she was so much less experienced. This zombie apocalypse slammed into her so much harder than it did me because she'd had a nice life and a bright future in front of her. In fact, if we hadn't picked her up that day on Route 66, I doubt she'd still be alive. She and Trey probably would have died. They didn't know how to take care of themselves, and I don't know if they would have been able to figure it out without help.

I pull back but keep my hands on Parv's shoulders. "It's

over for Ginny, but not for us. We're still standing and fighting, and I promise you, we are going to make it. Don't give up on life. Not yet."

Parv sniffs and wipes her nose on her sleeve. "I'm not sure I can keep doing this."

"You can," I say firmly. "You're stronger than you think you are. You just promise me that you're not going to throw in the towel. Don't do what Winston did—"

My voice cracks and Parv nods, and for the first time in months, I see a glimmer of hope in her eyes.

"I promise," she says. "I won't give up just yet."

"Good."

I step back and let out a deep breath. "I'm going to check on the baby. Take your time and pull yourself together. Okay?"

Parv nods, and I give her arm a pat before I walk away.

In the living room, Axl is still holding Megan, the zombies are still banging on the door, and everyone else is standing around like they don't have a clue what to do. But there's a part of me that feels better. More sure of what's coming. Why, I don't know—we're still trapped—but I feel like there's hope somewhere. We just need to find it.

"We got nothin' for a baby," Angus says when I come over to stand at Axl's side.

"We'll have to get formula," Joshua calls from the kitchen, and I turn as he comes out holding a can. "Until then, we can use this. It isn't ideal, but it will tide us over."

"What is it?" I ask, leaving the baby with Axl so I can see what Joshua has.

"Evaporated milk. We mix this with boiled water and a little sugar, and it will get us through a couple days, but we can't do it for long. We're going to have to get out of here and get her some real formula. As well as bottles and diapers and all the other stuff a baby needs."

Jim lets out a little snort. "You make it sound so easy."

"Shut up," Axl mutters, crossing the room to Joshua and

me. "What are we waitin' for? Let's get her somethin' to eat."

The three of us head into the kitchen together even though it will only take one of us to prepare Megan's food. I think Axl and I just want to learn what to do—I know that's why I'm going, at least.

We use our little fire-in-a-can trick to heat water, and then Joshua adds some to the evaporated milk, followed by a teaspoon of sugar. Once that's done, he shows us how to teaspoon-feed the liquid to Megan a little at a time.

"Thank God you knew how to do this," I say, watching the baby lap up the milk.

"I wouldn't thank me too much," Joshua says, shaking his head. "If I had paid better attention, I would have noticed the placenta didn't come out whole and I could have done something about it then. By the time I figure it out, it was too late to do anything. Ginny is dead because of me."

"It isn't your fault," I say firmly. "It was dark in the room, and there was a lot going on. You had too much on your plate. Between the premature birth and the zombies and us worrying that the baby wouldn't make it an hour outside the womb, anything could have gone wrong." I pause and hold his gaze before bringing another spoonful of milk to Megan's lips. "You did the best you could, but you aren't God."

"Yeah," Joshua mumbles. "That's one thing you don't have to remind me of."

Once the baby is fed, we change her diaper, using yet another hand towel from the bathroom. It isn't going to be long before we're out of towels, and then we're going to have to move on to clothes or something.

Or get the hell out of here and find real diapers.

Of course, how to make that happen is something I don't have a clue about. We're surrounded, and it doesn't seem like the zombies are going to give up any time soon.

We get back into the living room and find Parvarti and Angus in the middle of heated discussion.

"What's goin' on?" Axl asks.

Parvarti's eyes are dry when she turns to face us, and her

expression is more determined than I've ever seen it. But for once it isn't devoid of emotion. The pain from Ginny's death is etched in every line of her face.

"I'm going out," she says.

"What?" There's no way I heard her right. "I thought we discussed this! You said you weren't going to give up."

"I'm not. I promise. But we can't stay in here or it won't be long before we're all dead, and they aren't going away. We can't be any quieter than we're already being, and every sound we make causes them to get riled up again. One of us needs to go out and make a run for it. Draw them away so the others can get to the truck. It's the only way."

"You're crazy," Joshua says, shaking his head. "You can't do that. It's the same as committing suicide."

"Do you want to go instead?" she asks pointedly.

Joshua's mouth drops open, but it only takes a second for him to shake his head again "No, I don't."

"Then I'm willing."

Parvarti turns away like she's ready to throw the door open, but I step forward, cradling the baby against my chest. "Wait! We need a plan. We need to discuss this!"

"She's not going at all," Jim says, stepping into the room. "It's a good idea, but there's no way in hell she's going out there while I'm still standing."

"Don't be a sexist ass," Parvarti mutters, her eyes still focused on the door.

"That isn't why. I don't give a fuck what you have between your legs. You all need each other. You're a family, and you've already lost too much. But I'm nobody. Not here and not back in Hope Springs. There's nothing for me, and letting you sacrifice yourself would be the most selfish thing I could ever do." He nods once, then lets out a deep sigh. "Besides, I promised Jon I'd keep Ginny safe. I couldn't do that, but I can make sure their baby has a chance."

"Shit," Angus mutters. "You sure 'bout this?"

Jim ignores him and scans the room. "In Hope Springs we used leather to protect us, but I've been all over this house and they are seriously lacking in motorcycle gear." His eyes stop in the middle of the room, and he grins. "This just might work, though."

He rips the rug up off the floor, pulling it out from under the furniture, causing a small end table to tumble to its side. I step back, trying to get out of the way as he flips the rug over so he can inspect the other side.

Jim smiles. "They'll never be able to get their teeth through this."

"Son of a bitch," Axl says, moving over so he can get a better look. "It's genius. All we gotta do is cut it up and tape it to you. Kinda like armor."

"You're gonna need some kinda mask, too," Angus says, joining his brother and Jim. "But if we do it right, you just might make it through the mob without bein' bit. You could get away."

"I can outrun them," Jim says confidently.

Axl nods once, then drops the rug and heads for the kitchen. "We gotta find something to cut it with and some tape!"

I sit in a rocking chair with the baby while the men and Parvarti run around like crazy, gathering rugs and rolls of tape. Then they get to work cutting the stuff up. They wrap it around Jim's arms and legs, covering it with silver duct tape to keep it in place. They use small strips so he'll still be able to run and move his arms to fight the zombies off. Even though his knees and elbows are exposed, I think he'll be okay. Assuming he can get through the horde, that is.

Angus slaps a pair of thick winter gloves and a couple scarves on the table and steps back, his eyes narrowing on Jim. "Should be good. Them gloves'll keep the bastards from bitin' your fingers off, and if we wrap them two scarves around your neck that oughta be good. We gotta figure out what to do about your face, though."

"We'll do the same thing," Jim says. "Cover my face with some thick material and shove a hat over my head to keep it from falling off. Hell, you can wrap duct tape around my head for all I care. Doubt those bastards could get through that stuff."

"He's got a point," Axl says, picking up the single roll of tape we have left. "This shit's serious."

"Let's do it, then," Jim says, grabbing a scarf.

He wraps it around his face while Parvarti goes back to the closet Angus found the stuff in. When she comes back, she has two more scarves. Axl helps Jim wrap the fabric around his neck and up his face, adding a new one each time one ends. Once all four are secured to his face, Axl goes about the process of covering as much of Jim's head and face with the silver tape.

By the time they're done, the only parts of Jim visible are his eyes. They move my way for a second, stopping on the baby before focusing on Axl again.

"We're going to need a distraction so I can get out the back door."

"You got something in mind?" Axl asks.

"I do."

"Well, spit it out," Angus mutters. "We're runnin' outta time."

Jim hesitates, and when he finally speaks, his eyes are focused on the ground. "Ginny."

My stomach tenses as my grip tightens on the baby. Not a lot, but enough that she whimpers in her sleep. "What did you say?"

"She's gone, okay. Dead. And if we tossed her body out the window, it would distract them and give me a head start." He doesn't look my way, but he doesn't back down either. "She would want us to be safe."

He's right, of course, but the idea of throwing Ginny's body to the zombies makes me physically sick. We can't do that, can we?

I squeeze my eyes shut and shake my head. "You're an asshole."

"Vivian," Angus whispers, forcing me to open my eyes.

He *never* calls me *Vivian*. "What would Hollywood say if she was here?"

"If she was here we wouldn't even be discussing this," I spit at him.

"You know what I mean, and you know she'd tell you to do this."

I exhale slowly and hold the baby more firmly to my chest. Angus is right, of course, but it seems so despicable that I can't really think about it. Didn't people go to jail for defiling a corpse? Is that what this is?

Even more important: would Ginny tell me to get over my shit and let it happen?

Probably.

Doesn't mean I want to be the one who tosses her out the window.

"I don't want any part in this discussion," I say, getting to my feet.

I head for the kitchen. The person in question is upstairs, and I can't make myself go near her, but I need to get out of the living room and away from Jim.

The kitchen isn't much better, though. Not with the zombies still going crazy outside. Of course, now all I can think about when they moan is Ginny's body.

My heart pounds wildly as I pace, cradling Megan in my arms. Each pass seems to take less time than the last one did, and I can't help wondering if the walls have actually started moving. They seem closer. The room smaller and the air thicker, and even though the rational part of my brain tells me I'm imagining things, I can't help wondering if I'm about to be crushed.

Parvarti steps into the room, and I freeze.

"Are they doing it?"

"I thought you didn't want to know." Her voice is less robotic than it was yesterday but still guarded.

"I don't," I say, keeping my eyes focused on the ground. I want to keep my emotions in check, and I'm afraid if I look at Parv I'll start to cry. "But I think I need to."

"You know she isn't there anymore, right?" This time, the pain in her voice is so thick I'm forced to look up.

"I know, but that doesn't mean I have to stop caring."

Parvarti nods once, and then her eyes go to the floor. For the second time today, she looks small and young and lost, and I can't help wondering what's going through her head. She's the one who volunteered to run out and distract the zombie's, after all. I thought our conversation had done its job, but maybe it didn't. Maybe she's decided to give up after all.

"Parv?"

She lifts her head and her brown eyes hold mine, and I'm suddenly catapulted through time. Back to the day we picked her up on Route 66, when she could hardly leave Trey's side.

"I'm tired of caring," she says. "Aren't you tired of doing this every day? We never seem to make any progress, no matter how hard we struggle, and it's *exhausting*. Why do we keep doing this to ourselves?"

The last sentence is so loud it seems to echo through the room, but when the aftershocks have faded away, neither one of us speaks. Megan lets out a little cry, and my eyes move down to her pursed lips. She wiggles in my arms until her arm breaks free of the blanket, and she turns her head. Rooting for something that isn't there. Something that will never be there again. The thought is so sad that it should cement Parvarti's words in my brain, but instead, when I look at Megan, all I can see is hope.

"This," I say, holding the baby out. "This is why we keep going. One of the last things Ginny said before she died was that it had all been worth it. Everything she'd gone through, everything she'd lost. It was all worth it because of Megan. But now Ginny's gone, and it's our responsibility to get Angus to Atlanta and to keep this baby safe."

"And after that? After we get to Atlanta, then what?"

"We find something else to keep us moving, then something else. Good things can still happen. All the people we've met and loved since this thing started are proof of that. I know it hurt to lose Trey, but would it have been better if you'd never met him?"

Parvarti shakes her head. "No. I would never trade my time with Trey."

I cradle Megan to my chest once again, holding her securely while Parvarti and I stare at each other. After a few seconds, a shaky smile turns up her lips.

"I'm going to keep my promise," she says.

"You won't give up?"

"Not as long as I'm still breathing."

CHAPTER TWENTY-ONE

"We need to be ready for anything." Jim glances our way in the middle of his pacing. "Everyone know what their part is?"

"We got it," Angus says, shoving some things into a bag.

"Good." Jim nods once, and his blue eyes move across the room. Across all of us. "I can outrun them. I'll make it through this, and I'll see all of you in Atlanta."

I swallow, unsure of what to say. It seems impossible that Jim would be able to pull this off, but I'm not going to be the one who pisses on his parade. Especially not thirty seconds before he's about to run out the door.

"Vivian."

Parvarti's voice draws my attention away from Jim, and when I turn, she holds a sheet up in front of me. It's been cut into a square, but I don't know what she expects me to do with it.

"What's that for?"

"A sling." She lays it out across the table and begins folding, her eyes focused on the fabric in front of her. "I had a big family. Not a lot of siblings, but cousins and aunts and uncles. Indian families are close, and we spent a lot of time together. We helped each other with everything." She folds the fabric, her brown hands sliding over the creases to smooth them out. "I've taken care of babies since I was young, and a sling is the easiest way to carry them around. It will be safe for Megan and for you. Keep your hands free while you're out there." She turns, holding the now-folded sheet up. "Put Megan against your chest, and I'll help you get this on."

I cradle the tiny baby against me as Parvarti wraps the folded fabric around my body, expertly crossing one side over my right shoulder and the other my left side. She brings the ends of the fabric back around my waist, where she ties them, keeping the sheet tight enough that Megan is tucked inside. Warm and safe against my chest.

"There," Parvarti says when she stands back.

I hesitantly move my hands away, marveling at how secure the baby feels. "It's amazing. Thank you."

"It will keep her safe." Parv smiles.

"Everybody ready?" Jim calls as he heads for the kitchen.

"Ready," I say, letting out a deep breath.

Axl heads for the stairs, shooting me a look on his way by. No one is looking forward to what we have to do, but we all know it's necessary. Even me.

"It will be okay," I say firmly.

"Let's get this done," Angus barks, following Joshua and Axl up the stairs.

Jim is already standing at the back door when I walk into the kitchen, his carpet armor making him look slightly crazy. Behind him, Parv stands with a knife in her hand, and I join her. Ready to take out any zombies that might not be drawn away from the door when Axl and the other two men throw Ginny out the window. I don't want to think about what they're doing, even if I know, deep inside, that it's our only chance of making it out of this alive.

"How will we know when it's time?" I ask, shuffling my feet. Patting Megan's little back to reassure myself that she's okay.

"They're going to toss the body, then watch through the window to see if the zombies go running." Jim's eyes are on the door, so he doesn't see it when I wince. "I'll be able to hear them through the door, too. Once it sounds like the coast is clear, I'll go. If our plan works, none of them should get in. If it doesn't…" His eyes move toward me. "Be quick."

"Got it," I say tightening my grip on my knife.

"Where will you go?" Parv asks.

"I'm going to run like hell, and if all goes well, I'll see you in Atlanta."

Footsteps scratch against the porch on the other side of the door, drawing our attention that way. Jim reaches for the knob but doesn't turn it. There's more scraping and footsteps. Growls and moans break through the barrier separating us from the dead, and the hair on my arms stands up.

"They're on the move," Jim whispers, then glances my way. His eyes are on the baby, though. "Keep her safe."

"I will."

Behind me, someone runs down the stairs.

"They went for it!" Joshua calls.

Without a backward glance, Jim rips the door open and charges into the night. Parv and I rush forward together, but she reaches the door first. She throws her body into it, and the thing swings forward, slamming shut. The second it's closed, I throw the deadbolt. I'm panting and my heart is pounding in my ears, but nothing got in, so *we* should be okay. Jim's fate, however, is less certain.

Parv, Joshua, and I stand in the kitchen, silently listening. Through the door we can hear Jim's voice as it fades into the distance, screaming at the zombies to follow him. It disappears, but we have no way of knowing if it's because he's stopped yelling or because he's too far away for us to hear him now. If he's dead or if he's alive.

There's only one way to know for sure.

"Up!" I say, dashing for the stairs, holding Megan's head with my free hand so she isn't jostled around.

I take the steps two at a time and charge toward the back bedroom when I reach the top. The room is so dark I can't see where I'm going, and I end up slamming my knee against the bed, sending a sharp pain through my kneecap. I make it to the window without any other injuries and press my face against the glass, using my hands to block out the tiny bit of light in the house.

"I can see him!" I say when someone walks into the room behind me.

Outside, Jim runs through the field at the back of the house, already past the barn and heading toward the trees in the distance. Behind him dozens of zombies are hot on his trail. They're like a wave trying to crush him. He's moving fast, though. He could make it.

"I think he'll be able to outrun them," I say turning to face Axl.

"He'll be good." He grabs my arm and pulls me toward the hall. "We gotta go."

I let him lead me out of the room and down the stairs, where the others are already waiting. Angus and Joshua have moved most of the furniture, and Parvarti waits at their side. The outside is startlingly silent after days of zombies moaning and pounding on the door.

"We're gonna hafta be quick," Axl says, stopping with his hand on the knob. "The truck's ready to go, but who knows if they all ran. Stay close and keep your eyes open."

"No problem," Joshua says.

Axl nods once, then rips the door open. Angus and Parv are out first, and Axl shoves me out after them. I cradle the baby's head with one hand, keeping the other wrapped tightly around my knife. Joshua and Axl are right behind me, but as far as I can tell, all the zombies have run after Jim.

We make it to the truck much faster than I thought possible, and Angus hurries to the driver's side while Parv and Joshua climb in back.

Axl rips the passenger door open and shoves me forward. "In!"

I climb inside without arguing even though I'd usually want to stay with Axl. I have Megan to worry about now, and inside the truck is the safest place for her.

Once I'm in, Axl slams the door and heads for the back. Within seconds, the engine roars to life. I'm still cradling Megan to my chest when Angus hits the gas, and as we pull away, I catch sight of a few zombies heading up the drive after us. That's it, though.

"We're on our way!" Angus yells, slamming his hand against the steering wheel.

"Don't celebrate yet," I say, shifting the sling so I can see Megan's face. Her eyes are closed and her expression is peaceful. Too peaceful for this crazy world. "We don't have much gas and absolutely nothing to care for a baby. We're going to need to stop before too long."

"Hopefully, we'll come 'cross a town here soon," Angus says, taking his eyes off the road long enough to glance toward the baby. "She 'kay?"

"Sleeping."

"Good. We'll get her to Atlanta, don't you worry. I told Hollywood that, and I meant it. Axl and me had a shit childhood, but at least we didn't grow up in the middle of this. Gettin' to a town with a wall 'round it is her only shot at a real life."

"I hope I can do it," I say, voicing the concerns that have been nagging at the back of my mind since Ginny died. "I didn't do such a good job with Emily."

"Wasn't your fault. We didn't know what was goin' on back then, and we weren't prepared for the way things went down. We're different people now. Strong and ready for anything."

"You're sure different," I say, smiling despite the doubt still clawing at my insides. "I can't believe how much you've changed."

Angus chuckles. "Don't feel no different, but I suppose you're right."

"Really?" I ask, arching an eyebrow at him. "Even after what happened with Winston, you don't think you're different?"

Angus purses his lips, keeping his eyes focused on the road in front of him. "I think it's the world that's changed, not me. I'm the same asshole I've always been, it's just that I fit into this world a little better than I did the last one."

"I think you're selling yourself short, Angus."

He grins my way. "Ain't that what you're always tellin' my brother?"

I snort. "Yes, and he doesn't listen to me either."

Angus just chuckles.

We drive a few miles before a town finally comes into view, and by then, the sky has gotten lighter. It helps us see, but that isn't always a good thing. Not when the things around you are nothing but death and destruction.

Angus slows as we roll through the center of town, and I instinctively hold Megan tighter. Almost as if it will shield her from what I'm seeing. Houses have been burnt down, and we pass a pile of burnt bodies. I try to convince myself they're just zombies, but when we drive by a naked woman strung up on a fence, I have a tough time believing it. She's been up for a while—weeks at least—but that doesn't stop a shiver from moving down my spine. Just because she's been up there for a while doesn't mean the people who did this aren't still around.

"Maybe we should try to find another place to stop," I say, my eyes on the rotten corpse that used to be a woman.

"We got no idea how far away the next town is."

He's right.

I glance over my shoulder at the others. Axl and Parv are on their knees, scanning the area like they're afraid we'll be attacked at any moment. I can't blame them. Every inch of this town feels hostile.

"This isn't good, Angus."

"Do we got a choice?" he says in a voice that's a lot softer than I expected. His eyes are on Megan.

"No, I guess not."

We reach the end of the block, and a drugstore comes into view. Just like all the other buildings we've passed, it looks as if it's been through a tornado. The windows are busted out, and someone has spray-painted *The Watchers* on the side of the building. I don't know what it means, but it sounds ominous.

Angus nods toward the building. "That right there's gonna have what you need."

"We'll have to be fast," I say, my heart pounding as I study the area. The road looks empty, but looks can be deceiving.

"I say you, Axl, and the doc go on inside and get what you need. Rambo and me'll go for gas," Angus says as he drives up to the drugstore. "Don't wait for us. You drive the truck outside town. A mile out at least. Then you park it someplace outta sight. Rambo and me'll get some gas one way or another, then head your way."

"And if you can't find any?"

"We'll just come your way."

Angus pulls to a stop in front of the pharmacy, and I inhale deeply, trying to steady my nerves. All I can think about is that damn ER in Vegas. What if this is a trap too?

I don't have a chance to think about what will happen, because the second the truck is off, Angus throws the door open and jumps out. I follow, keeping one hand on Megan's head. My eyes are moving so fast, looking between the store and the road and Axl in the back of the truck, that they feel like a ball in a Ping-Pong machine. I have to force myself to move toward the store. We don't have time to goof off.

Behind me, the others jump out of the truck and head our way.

"You two are with Blondie," Angus calls. "Rambo's with me."

"What's the plan?" Axl asks when he's jogged to catch up with me.

"Move fast," I say, heading for the pharmacy door.

Axl steps in front of me before I can go inside. He sticks his head through the busted-out door and lets out a low whistle, causing me to tense all over. Nothing moves.

"Come on," Axl whispers as he ducks inside.

Joshua and I follow him into the store, and together we move as one, stepping over broken glass and other debris. Moving though the dark pharmacy toward the back. The shelves are mostly bare, and what little is left has been scattered all over the floor. Just like outside, someone has spray-painted *The Watchers* across the wall.

"Who the hell are the watchers?" Joshua mutters.

"I don't think we want to hang around to find out," I say, moving faster.

It takes us thirty-seven seconds to find the baby aisle. I know, because I'm counting each breath I exhale, and they're coming out so fast I'm practically gasping. I move down the aisle, making a checklist as I go.

Formula, bottles, diapers, and wipes. Some clothes too if we can manage it. That's it. Those are the essentials.

Axl and Joshua search the darkness with me, and in less than two minutes, we have what we need—they even have a couple cheesy onesies with silly sayings on them that I grab. Axl pulls a cheap Winnie the Pooh diaper bag off the shelf and rips the paper filler out, tossing it to the floor before stuffing our baby supplies into the bag. Joshua scoops up every bag of diapers he can carry and shoves them into a second bag. As an afterthought, I grab a pacifier and toss it on top of the other stuff.

"We're good," I say, patting Megan's little butt as I look around. The store is so quiet we could hear a grain of rice drop. I can't believe it was this easy. "Let's get out of here."

Axl once again leads the way, and behind me Joshua is breathing so fast I'm afraid he's on the verge of a heart attack. Or hyperventilating at the very least.

"Shit," he mutters, making Axl and me turn. "Water. We need water."

He nods toward a couple jugs of water sitting by the register—almost like someone left them for us—and Axl scoops them up before moving on.

"What's the plan?" Axl whispers when we're almost to the door.

"We get in the truck and drive away. Out of town. At least a mile. Angus and Parvarti will catch up."

"Don't you think Angus should have stayed with the truck?" Joshua says.

Shit. I hadn't even thought of that. I'm so used to Angus offering himself up like this, and I was so focused on keeping Megan safe that it didn't occur to me this shouldn't have been the plan. But what would have been the alternative? Parvarti going by herself? Axl going with her? Yes. That's what should have happened. As much as I don't like thinking about it.

"You're right," I say. "We shouldn't have let him go."

"He'll be fine," Axl snaps.

We make it back outside and hurry toward the truck, all three of us squeezing into the cab. Axl sets the jugs of water down, pushing them out of the way so his feet have access to the pedals, then he tosses the diaper bag at Joshua.

"Hang on," Axl says as he slams the door shut.

I hold my breath, not relaxing even when the truck starts. Axl jerks the steering wheel around and does a U-turn, heading out of town. Once again the road is empty, but each building we pass shows signs of the people who live here. More mutilated bodies, and windows knocked out of every house we pass. *The Watchers* spray-painted on a building at least once every block. Whoever these people are, I don't want to bump into them.

We make it out of town, but Axl doesn't slow until we come to a mass of trees on the side of the road. Once we're past them, he pulls into the grass and parks just out of sight. He throws the truck into park, and all three of us climb out, but we stick close together. The town is still visible in the distance, but we're far enough away that I don't feel exposed. Hopefully, Parv and Angus show up soon.

After a few minutes, Megan starts to fuss. It's soft, but it reminds me that we now have the things we need to make her a little more comfortable. I can even get her dressed.

"Help me out here," I say, trying to loosen the knot Parvarti tied around my waist.

Axl unties the knot, and I ease the baby out. Like magic, she instantly starts wailing. Handling her still makes me nervous—she's so tiny—but I gently ease her onto the seat of the truck to get her changed anyway.

"Here," Joshua says from behind me, holding out a few wipes.

I shoot him a grateful smile. "Thanks. Believe it or not, I've actually never done this. Have you?"

"A couple times when I was a student, but I can't really say I'm good at it."

"I guess we'll have to learn."

Megan wiggles and cries louder when I wipe her off, which makes getting the diaper on a challenge. Not only that, but the newborn diapers Joshua took from the pharmacy are huge on her. I have to fold the top over before I can secure it, and even then there's such a big gap I'm sure it will leak. Somehow I manage to get the thing on, and by the time I'm done, Joshua has already made a bottle.

"It's not sterile," he says, holding it out.

"Nothing in this world is anymore."

I scoop Megan up, and when I offer her the bottle, she immediately sucks the plastic nipple into her mouth, silencing her cries.

"See anything yet?" I ask Axl now that Megan is dry and quiet.

"Not yet."

"They'll be here soon," I say. I don't doubt it, either. It's gotten to the point where I can't see Angus being taken out. Especially not by zombies. Almost like his immunity has made him as invincible as he claims to be.

Axl nods and glances toward Megan. "She good?"

"Better now, and so am I. Not having anything to feed her had me worried."

Axl runs his hand over her head, smoothing down the few dark hairs she has. "We're gonna get her some place safe."

"Yes," I say firmly. "We are."

"They're coming!" Joshua calls.

Even though I know he's talking about Parvarti and Angus, my heart starts racing. A side effect of living in a zombie-infested world. I narrow my eyes, trying to find Angus and Parv in the distance, and when they finally come into view, a huge smile breaks out across my face. Angus is jogging across the field with Parvarti at his side, and in his right hand is a gas can.

"What you get?" Axl calls when they're closer.

"Little over a gallon, but that's all. Couldn't hang out there." Angus comes to a stop in front of us, panting.

Axl takes the can from him and heads to the back of the truck, where the gas tank is already open and waiting. It only takes a couple seconds to pour the liquid in, illustrating just how little gas Angus and Parv were able to find. Hopefully, we can find more. And soon.

"Some serious shit went down," Angus says, running his hand over his head. "We didn't see nobody, but after the stuff we did see, I wasn't 'bout to hang 'round."

"How far do we have to go?" Parvarti asks.

"More than a hundred miles." Axl tosses the now-empty can into the bed of the truck and lets out a deep sigh. "What we got here will get us another thirty miles or so, but then we're gonna hafta find us some more gas."

"Which way you thinkin' 'bout headin'?" Angus asks.

"Gotta figure that out," Axl says, ripping the map out of the truck so he can spread it out.

The two men spend a few minutes looking over the map, studying the route we plan on taking to Atlanta, while Megan finishes her bottle. When she's done, Parv shows me how to burp her, and then together we get the little thing back into the sling.

Once she's secure, I say, "We're ready."

"Good," Axl says, holding the passenger door open for me. "Let's get outta here before somebody spots us."

I pause long enough to kiss him before climbing back inside, patting Megan when she whimpers. Her little body squirms against mine, but she settles in when I press my hand against her back. Like she needs the assurance that I'm with her and I'll keep her safe. The heaviness of the burden isn't lost on me. The life of this baby is in my hands now, and I need to make sure we do everything in our power to keep her alive and well.

Axl, Joshua, and Parv climb into the back, and Angus starts the car, looking in the rearview mirror while he waits for them to get settled. When he pulls into the road, he says, "Don't look so worried, Blondie. We're gonna make it."

"I don't know how. If we can only find a gallon of gas here and there, it seems unlikely."

"Ain't you supposed to be the one who's always lookin' on the bright side?" he asks grinning my way.

"Sometimes I can't help wondering if there is a bright side to all this."

I pat Megan's back when she sighs, and Angus's grin grows wider.

"There is," he says. "There is."

I hope he's right.

CHAPTER TWENTY-TWO

This time when we run out of gas, we aren't lucky enough to be close to a farmhouse or even a town. Or anything else, as far as I can tell. Which means it's time to make some hard decisions.

"We're on foot," Axl says, dumping his pack out in the bed of the truck. "Least for a while. We gotta go through all this shit and figure out what we *need* and what can stay behind."

"Why do we have so many damn diapers?" Angus mutters as he sifts through the supplies we got for the baby. Supplies that we might now have to leave behind.

"Because babies can go through seven to ten diapers a day when they're newborn," Joshua says.

"You're shittin' me." Angus shakes his head and grabs two bags of newborn diapers. "Guess we gotta take these, then. If she starts cryin', she'll draw every zombie 'round our way."

"We need the formula too, and enough water to make bottles for her and keep us hydrated." I bounce Megan as I look everything over. There's so much. How can we carry all this and still have enough energy to keep going?

"We may have to pick water up as we go," Joshua says. He shoves a couple packs of diapers in his own bag, along with a can of formula, making the thing almost full to capacity.

"I guess you're right," I mumble.

After we're loaded down with supplies, we start walking. With more than sixty miles to go, we have days of this ahead of us unless we find another car, and I'm just not sure how long we'll be able to keep at it. I think back over Axl's calculations of sixteen miles a day and do the math in my head. Four days, maybe. It could be less if we push ourselves, but I'm not sure we can. Not with as worn out as we already are, and not with a newborn. She may sleep most of the time, but she still needs attention.

It's May in Georgia, which means it's already hot. The sun pounds down on us, totally unrelenting. Megan's little body works as a heater against mine, and it doesn't take long before both my clothes and the sling are soaked in sweat. The baby, too, seems restless, and I know it has to be from the heat. It makes our progress on the first day slow, and by the time we find a house to stop at for the night, I'm so exhausted I'm not sure how I'm going to be able to walk inside, let alone all day tomorrow.

"Parv and me'll check it out," Axl says. "The rest of you wait here."

Joshua lets out a deep sigh and sinks to the ground, while Angus slumps against the side of the house.

"My whole body hurts," I say, stopping at Angus's side.

"Walkin' in the sun is gonna kill us." His face scrunches up and he looks around. "Gotta find us a car."

"Not you," I say firmly. "We can't let you out of our sight again. We were stupid the last time we stopped, and I'm not going to make the same mistake."

"She's right," Joshua says from where he's sitting.

"I'll be fine," Angus mutters.

I shake my head, but before I can argue, Axl sticks his head out the front door and waves us in. "We're clear."

It takes more effort than it should to drag myself inside, and based on the grunts from the men behind me, I'd guess I'm not the only one who's struggling.

There's very little about the house that stands out other than the fluffy, overstuffed couch. I drop onto it, keeping Megan close to my body as I fall, and it's so soft I don't even care that dust puffs up all around us.

"Oh my God, I could stay here for the rest of my life," I say, throwing myself back against the cushions.

"Rest up," Axl says. "Parv and me are gonna take a look 'round town. See if we can find us a car for tomorrow. If we do, we'll be there in no time."

"Car," I say with a snort. "I'd settle for a horse right now."

"Ain't a bad idea," Axl mutters.

I crack one eye to see if he's serious, but it's too dark in the room to tell.

"You serious?" Angus asks for me.

"Doubt we'd find a horse, let alone five. Although it'd be nice." He heads toward the door with Parvarti, calling over his shoulder, "We'll be back in a bit."

We murmur our goodbyes, too tired to do much else, and it isn't until after they've left that I realize I should have hugged Axl or kissed him or told him that I love him. Something. Just in case.

Shit.

I shift so I can take the sling off my body, making Megan squirm.

"How far do you think we walked?" I ask as I change the baby's diaper. A task that's already gotten easier.

"Eight miles." Angus throws himself into the chair across from me. "What you think, doc?"

"Seems like more, but that's only because I'm exhausted. It was probably less." Joshua lets out a deep sigh as he too sinks into a chair. "I'll make her a bottle."

"So we still have over fifty miles."

I scoop Megan up, shaking my head. There was a time when fifty miles was nothing—less than an hour by car if you didn't run into traffic. Now, though, it feels like an insurmountable distance.

"How are we going to manage it?" I ask.

Joshua freezes in the middle of mixing a bottle, and Angus purses his lips. We just sit there in silence while we think it over. All the obstacles out there, all the things that could go wrong. There are too many to count, and all of that with a baby to worry about.

"We'll make it," Angus says firmly.

Joshua nods and goes back to preparing the bottle while I bounce a fussy Megan. Her little face roots against my body, but of course I don't have anything for her.

The doctor finishes making the bottle, and I sit back, holding it for Megan as she sucks the liquid down. When Joshua tells me to burp her, I do, then go back to feeding her, all the while my mind on other things. On Atlanta and how we'll make it in one piece, on Axl and Parv and what they're doing right now. On the zombies in this city and the men who could be lurking in the shadows. On a million other things that could happen.

Megan drifts off to sleep, the bottle still in her mouth. I pull it away and cradle her closer when she squirms. After a second, she settles back down, drifting off again. Angus isn't far behind, and his gentle snores are oddly comforting after all these months together. Right now, the world seems so empty and forgotten that I'll gladly cling to anything recognizable.

My eyelids grow heavy, but I can't let myself sleep. Joshua, too, seems to be staying awake. Waiting for Axl and Parv to come back.

"They've been gone a long time," I whisper, staring at the

door.

"They're looking for a car and gas," Joshua says. "It's going to take some time."

"True."

He yawns, and a second later, I copy him.

"Get some sleep," I say, my own yawn only half over.

"You don't want me to wait up with you?"

"It's fine. No sense in all of us sitting here awake."

Joshua nods, but his eyes are already shut. He doesn't open them, and literally seconds later, he too is breathing heavily. It makes staying awake tough, especially with Megan weighing me down. She may be tiny, but her body is warm and comfortable against mine.

I get to my feet and pace, cradling Megan to my chest as I try not to worry about where Parvarti and Axl are or if they're in trouble. It's an impossible task, of course. These days, you worry about people every time they leave your sight.

The sky outside gets darker, and every few minutes I find myself looking out the front window. Even though the area is pretty clear, I catch sight of the occasional zombie in the distance. None too close to us, but close enough that it makes me even more uneasy over Parvarti and Axl's absence.

More time passes, and I'm so focused on the street in front of the house, counting the zombies as they pass by, that when a knock echoes through the house I nearly jump out of my skin.

Joshua doesn't stir, but Angus is on his feet a second after the sound. He doesn't move, though, and neither do I. We stand in the middle of the living room, staring at each other while we wait for whatever it was to happen again. A few seconds pass, and a soft knock once again echoes through the house. This time, I can tell it's coming from the back door. Angus arches his eyebrows at me as he pulls his knife.

"Axl?" I whisper.

"Guess we'll see," Angus replies as he heads into the kitchen to check it out. "Stay back."

I do as I'm told because I'm holding the baby, but once again I realize as soon as Angus is out of sight that I shouldn't be letting him take risks like this. He's the one we're supposed to be keeping safe.

It's a hard thing to get used to.

"Joshua," I hiss, giving his leg a nudge.

The doctor bolts up just as a third knock echoes through the room. "What?"

"Take the baby or go help Angus or something!" I hiss.

Joshua hurries toward the kitchen, pulling his knife. I'm not sure how much help he's going to be since he isn't totally awake, though.

I hold my breath and tiptoe closer when I hear the doorknob jiggle. Angus opens the door, his knife ready, and I let out a sigh of relief when Parvarti and Axl hurry inside.

"Shut the door," Axl hisses. "The area's crawlin' with the dead."

Angus shuts the door and bolts it as Parvarti and Axl head into the living room. They're panting, and I can tell they probably had a hell of a time getting back, which makes me even more annoyed that I didn't think to kiss him goodbye.

"You okay?" I ask.

Axl nods and gives me a quick kiss, almost like he's reading my mind. "Fine. No gas that we could find, but we got a plan."

"What's that?" Angus asks, jerking the curtains shut so he can turn a flashlight on.

"Found us a bike shop," Axl says, grinning. "There's more than enough for everybody."

"Bike?" Angus purses his lips and narrows his eyes on his brother. "Like a motorcycle?"

"No," Parvarti says. "Bicycles."

Joshua laughs and drops into a chair. "You have to be kidding."

"You know how long it's been since I rode a bike?" Angus shakes his head.

"They say you never forget," I point out.

"That ain't reassurin'." Angus glares my way. "It'll be hell if we run into a horde."

"It would be worse on foot," Parvarti says. "And this way we wouldn't have to worry about breaking down or running out of gas."

Joshua just laughs again.

"You got 'nother idea?" Axl asks. "If you do, now's the time."

"No," Joshua says. "Nothing. I guess this is as good of an idea as any, but it still sounds like a death sentence."

"What doesn't these days?" I ask.

"Fine." Angus sinks into the couch. "Where's the place and what's the plan?"

"That might be the problem." Parvarti looks at Axl, who swipes his hand through his hair.

"Shit," Angus says, shaking his head. "What's standin' in the way?"

Parv holds his gaze. "A hell of a lot of zombies. We're going to need a distraction."

We all sit in silence for a few seconds, each of us absorbing the news. It should be routine by now, only it never feels that way. It always feels like a new obstacle, because we're always in a different place when it happens. With a different set of circumstances.

"How many?" Angus asks.

"Less than the farmhouse." Axl throws himself into a chair.

The rest of us follow his lead. No point in standing when we need to get some rest. Even if we do come up with a plan, we won't go until we've gotten some sleep.

"Don't suppose anybody else wants to lead them off?" Angus asks, looking around.

Parvarti's gaze moves to me, and I shake my head.

"No," she says firmly.

"We'll figure out a way to distract them," Joshua says. "We've done it in the past. What's worked?"

Axl's eyes are focused on the ceiling like he's thinking it through. "Back when we was leavin' the Monte Carlo, we cut one of the bastards open. Used the insides as a kinda camouflage."

"You did what?" Joshua says.

"You heard me," Axl replies, but there's no annoyance in his voice. "Was messy, but it worked."

"We can't do that," I say. "We have Megan now. Zombie guts or not, if she starts crying she will give us away."

Axl purses his lips and nods.

"Good point," Angus mutters. "We gotta find somethin' that'll make an even bigger racket than she can. Somethin' them dead bastards won't be able to ignore."

"We've used car alarms," I say. "Of course, at this point—and in this town—finding a car with an alarm is going to be tough."

"Can't tiptoe 'round the place lookin' for one," Axl says, sitting up. "That's for damn sure."

"Gotta blow something up," Angus mutters. "Did it more than once in Vegas, and it always worked. Could be our only shot."

"Can we burn a house down?" Parv asks.

"That ain't gonna be enough noise. No. We're gonna hafta cause an explosion. It'd get the attention of every damn zombie in this town and keep their attention long 'nough for us to pedal our asses outta here." Angus nods slowly. "Yeah. That's what we gotta do."

"What exactly are we going to blow up?" Joshua asks. "Obviously there's no gas or we'd be able to drive out of here, so gasoline is out."

We all sit in silence for a few seconds. Joshua has a point. We might be able to come up with a little gas, but enough to make a big explosion? Doubtful.

"Can't be the only thing that'll explode. Shit. There's all kinda stuff 'round the house that'll blow up," Axl says, shaking his head. He tears his eyes away from the ceiling and looks my way. "That book Al gave us got anything to say 'bout it?"

"Good point." I turn to Angus. "It's in your pack now."

He digs the book out, and Joshua flips the flashlight back on, passing it to Axl, who is closest to his brother. Angus flips through the book, and we all lean forward. I know we're missing something obvious here, but we're all running on empty. Emotionally and physically drained, hungry and exhausted. There's an obvious solution that we just haven't thought of, and thanks to Al, we may not have to use the little bit of mental energy we have left to figure it out.

"Here we go," Angus says. "Flammable items."

He doesn't say anything as he scans the page, and even though I'm dying to know what it says, I keep my mouth shut and let him read it.

"Shit." Angus shakes his head as he looks up from the book. "We're a bunch of dumbasses, you know that. Aerosol cans. We get 'nough of them and put them in a house, start the thing on fire. They'll explode before long."

Angus is right. We are dumbasses.

Axl gets to his feet. "Good. Let's search the place, see what they got. Anything'll work, right?"

"An aerosol can is pressurized," Joshua says, standing as well. "So in theory, if it gets hot enough, it will explode. There are no guarantees, but I think Angus is right. If we get a lot of them, we're bound to have some kind of explosion. Whether it will be big enough to get the attention of every zombie in town is the part I'm not sure about."

"Don't hurt to try." Angus tosses the book down and stands.

"Unless we burn the whole town down," Parv says as she too gets up. "If the fire spreads but doesn't draw the zombies away, it could trap us here."

Once again, none of us move.

Parv is right, but we're at the point where we may not have another choice. The longer we stay here doing nothing, the more trapped we could become. These things don't just get tired and go away. Something has to draw them away. Noise, maybe even a smell—it's hard to say for sure—but something has to happen to get them to decide to move on.

"We'll deal with that if and when it happens," I say, holding Megan close to my chest as I stand. "For now, let's find some aerosol cans."

We spread out, Angus and Axl heading for the garage while Joshua goes to the kitchen. Parv moves toward the bedrooms, so I take the laundry room. Aerosol cans are less common than they used to be, but that doesn't mean we won't find a few. And, if we're quiet, we might even be able to check out a couple of the other nearby houses. Joshua is right about one thing: if one can explodes it might not be loud enough to attract the zombies, so getting a lot of cans is the key.

I hold Megan close as I dig through the cabinets in the laundry room. It's small and cramped, and there aren't a lot of places to look, but I do manage to find a can of starch. Why someone in this day and age would need starch is beyond me. I never knew anyone outside reruns of *Leave it to Beaver* who used the stuff.

"What've you got?" Angus calls when I come out of the laundry room.

"One. You guys?"

"Found us a couple cans of spray paint." He sets them on the counter, and I head over to put mine next to his. "But that ain't all. We also got us a propane tank."

"Oven cleaner," Parv says from behind me.

I don't look away from Angus. "Will that explode? Don't they take measures to make sure something like that won't happen?"

"Sure, but anything'll explode if you do it right. Just need to apply the right pressure."

"Makes sense."

Axl comes in from the garage, lugging the propane tank, and Parv comes out of the kitchen with her oven cleaner. A couple seconds later, Joshua is back with two cans of hairspray. That's it, though.

"We'd be a helluva lot better off if this was the 80's. Back then they had all kinds of shit in aerosol cans," Angus says, shaking his head.

"We could check out a couple other houses," Parv says. "We're going to have to pass them on our way to starting the fire, anyway. Might as well."

"That's a good point." I bounce Megan as I look back and forth between Axl and Parv. "Have you figured out which house you're going to blow up?"

"Gotta be far away from the bike shop," Axl says. "Don't want them bastards anywhere near us when we're headin' out."

My stomach tightens when I think about Axl going out there without me yet again. I have to hang back now that I have Megan—she's my responsibility—but that doesn't mean I have to like it. And I don't. I don't like sending Axl off to do the hard work while I wait on the sidelines, and I don't like not knowing what's going on out there. Wondering if I'm ever going to see him again is torture.

But I also refuse to repeat the mistakes I made with Emily. Back then, when all this zombie bullshit was brand new, I thought the best way to take care of her was to go out and get things done. Now I know that isn't true. I should have stayed by her side. Made sure she was safe every second of every day. Been there to protect her. That's what I'm going to do with Megan. It's what a mom does.

"When?" I say, turning to face Axl. "We need to get some rest first. It would be stupid to head out when it's dark and we haven't had any sleep."

"We ain't leavin' yet," he says, his eyes holding mine. "We'll rest up and do a little more surveillance in the mornin'. I ain't runnin' out there unprepared."

"Good," I say, but I swallow when my throat constricts. Just the thought of him running anywhere without me makes me sick. "Then let's get some sleep."

"Sounds good," Joshua says, yawning. "Unless somebody has a problem with it, I'm going to take the couch."

"There are two bedrooms," Parv says.

Joshua waves her off. "Take the bed."

"Thanks," Parv says as she turns and heads back toward the bedrooms.

Axl crosses the room to stand at my side. His eyes go from me to Megan, then back up to my face. "She doin' okay?"

"She's perfect as far as I can tell," I say, studying the baby in my arms.

She already feels like mine. It's odd how quickly a bond can form. Part of it is that I know this little baby is the only thing left of Ginny, but I also feel like I've somehow been handed a second chance at motherhood. I screwed up with Emily so many times I probably couldn't count them all, but I won't do it this time. Not after everything Ginny and Jon fought for. Not after they gave their lives for this baby. I'm going to get her to Atlanta and keep her safe. Forever.

"I'm beat, though," I say, looking back up at Axl. "I need some rest."

"Go on and sleep. I'll take first watch," Angus says.

He holds his hands out, and it takes me a second to realize he's waiting for the baby. I hand her over even though she isn't much of a bother and I could probably sleep with her in my arms.

"You call if there's trouble," I say. "Not just for her, but for yourself."

"There ain't gonna be trouble," Angus says, bouncing the little bundle when she stirs. "But don't you worry. I ain't gonna put her at risk."

Axl slings his arm around me, and I give Megan one last look before allowing him to pull me back toward the bedroom.

CHAPTER TWENTY-THREE

The sleep I get doesn't feel like rest. It's more like tossing and turning, waiting for someone to attack or for a baby to start crying. But I must have slept more soundly than I thought, because I'm alone when I wake up.

Outside, the sun is just coming up, so I roll out of bed. My body is stiff from the restless night, but at least I feel a little more refreshed than I did yesterday. Hopefully, everyone else does too.

"You sleep?" I ask when I walk into the living room and find everyone else up.

"We all caught some shut-eye," Angus says from the couch.

Axl sits next to him, feeding Megan. It's the first time he's done it, and something about the image makes everything in me feel warm and tingly. She looks natural in his arms. And perfect. More perfect than I ever could have imagined.

"We got us a plan," Axl says, not looking up from the baby. "Picked a house. Parv and me even found us a couple more cans next door."

"Now all we have do is start a fire," Parv says.

"And make it across a zombie-infested town," Joshua reminds her.

Parv frowns. "And that."

Megan's eyes are closed, and her face is peaceful. Calm. She has no idea that the world outside this house is anything but safe. She doesn't know how it used to be and what's changed, and she doesn't know that we might not make it out of this alive. To her, everything is perfect and clean and pure.

If only it could stay that way.

"It kills me that one day she will see the reality of this world," I say, smoothing down the fuzzy hair on her head. "That things won't stay perfect for her."

"We just gotta keep her safe." Axl takes my hand in his, balancing the baby and the bottle with his other one. "Which means gettin' outta here and to Atlanta."

I nod, unable to speak.

Angus gets to his feet and picks up the book Al gave us, tossing it my way. "We wanna be sure to take this. Just in case."

I catch the book midair and hold it in my hands, pressing it between my palms as I think about Al and Lila. Wondering where they are and if they're alive. If they drowned or died horrible deaths at the hands of zombies. If they're dead, I can only hope it was fast for them.

"I wish I could thank Al for packing this," I say, shoving it in my bag. "Everyone laughed at him, but he knew what he was doing."

"He was a smart kid," Joshua says. "And tough."

"Balls of steel," Angus replies, nodding. It's the same thing he said the day Joshua had to cut Al's arm off.

Parv gets up, not saying anything but nodding as well, and she too gathers her things. I follow her lead, moving through the house and taking anything that might help us along the way and won't be too much of a pain to carry.

"She's ready," Axl says from behind me.

I turn, but he doesn't have the baby, and I look past him to find Joshua changing her diaper. Before I even have a chance to look back, Axl has pulled me into his arms. His hand moves up my back to my head, and his grip tightens on me as he presses his lips to the side of my face. Right next to my ear.

"We're gonna make it. Today. We'll reach Atlanta. All of us. And we'll be safe. We'll have a life and a family, and things are gonna be better."

My eyes fill with tears even though I nod. He's right. I know he is. *We* will make it and life will be better for *us*, but not for all of us. Not for Jon and Ginny, not for Al and Lila. Not for Winston or Jess or Darla or Trey or Jim or any of the other people we lost along the way. Not for Emily, who would be standing next to me right now if I hadn't been so naïve about what this world had turned into. If I had been stronger, things would be different.

"Do you really think we can start over?" I ask. "That we can forget everything we've lost and build a life that means something?"

Axl pulls back so he can look me in the eye, his hands still on my shoulders. "We don't forget. If we did that, we'd have nothin' to keep fightin' for. We remember everybody we lost and we live for them. Every day."

He's right. I would never want to forget our friends or the things we went through together, no matter how much it hurts. They made me who I am right now. Stronger and smarter and braver than I ever thought I could be.

"I love you," I say.

Axl kisses me, pulling me against him so tight that it's hard to breathe. When he finally lets go, I gasp, filling my lungs with air and life and hope for the future.

"PARV AND ME ARE GONNA HEAD TO THE HOUSE ON THE farthest side of town," Axl says. "We'll set up all the cans and the propane tank, then start a fire."

"Then you'll come back?" I look them both over as Parvarti pulls a backpack full of aerosol cans over her shoulders.

"We'll take cover in a house one street over until we know for sure the fire is spreading," she says.

I shake my head. "No. You need to come here, and if there's no explosion you can go back out. If you're close to the fire when the cans explode, the zombies will be all over the place and you'll be stuck."

Axl exhales and looks everyone over. "That what you all think we oughta do?"

"You gotta," Angus says. "Blondie's right. You're there when those cans light up, you might not make it back here alive."

"Or you could draw the whole horde our way," Joshua points out. "They could decide to follow you instead of heading toward the fire."

"Shit." Axl nods once. "Fine. That's what we'll do, but if things get sticky, we'll head to the bike shop. If we don't come back right away, you go there. We'll meet you."

"We don't even know where it is," Joshua says.

"Cut through the houses and go three streets over," Parv says, pointing to the back of the house. "When you get to Main Street, take a right. The bike shop is at the end of the road. You can't miss it."

My heart is pounding like crazy as Parv's words sink it. If we need to use the directions, it will mean she and Axl haven't made it back. That they ran into trouble. Trouble means zombies, which could mean death.

"You'll be at the bike shop, though," I say.

Axl's gray eyes search mine, and I know he can see my worry. "We'll do our best, but you gotta go if we don't show up. Five minutes, that's all the time you got. If we ain't there by then, you get on them bikes and you head out. You get away. Understand?"

I nod even though I don't know why. I don't understand. Not this. Not leaving him behind and never knowing what happened to him.

"But you'll be there." My voice is thick with tears, and it makes me feel pathetic.

"We're gonna do what we gotta." Axl picks the propane tank up off the floor. "Right now, we gotta go. Get this done so we can move."

He heads for the back door with Parv right behind him, and I'm on their heels. In the sling, Megan's body is warm against mine, but it doesn't help ease my pounding heart.

"Be careful," I say when they reach the door.

"Always am." Axl doesn't look back before pulling the door open and heading outside. Parvarti follows him without a word.

I shut the door and lock it, watching them through the window as they disappear around the side of the house. If this doesn't work, we're going to have to come up with another idea. The thought of doing the same thing we did at the farmhouse makes me sick, but I have a strong suspicion that's what Parv would suggest. She's doing better, acting like she cares more, but I think she'd see it as her duty. Axl and I have each other and the baby, and Angus is necessary to the survival of the human race. Joshua is a doctor, which we might need if we run into trouble, and Parv would argue that she's disposable. That it's logical for her to be the one to stay behind.

She'd be right and wrong. I don't think anyone as strong as she is can really be disposable these days. The world needs people like her.

"You gonna stand there the whole time?" Angus asks.

I turn away from the window. Angus is leaning against the wall with his arms crossed, watching me.

"No, but that doesn't mean I don't want to. I just think I should save the energy."

"Then take a load off." Angus jerks his head toward the living room. "Let's sit."

I follow him out to the couch, where Joshua is already sitting. There's nothing for us to do but wait. Our backpacks are ready and waiting by the door so we can grab them on our way out, and Megan is fed and changed so we don't have any last-minute things to take care of. When Parv and Axl get back, all we'll have to do is make a run for it—assuming the zombies take the bait. But it could be a half hour or more before they get here, and even longer before the fire is big enough to make the cans explode. Between now and then, I could go crazy.

"Settle down," Angus says, his voice gentle.

I'm still not used to him having such a soft side.

"I'm fine," I say even though my legs are shaking. "How long do you think it will take us to get to Atlanta? We have forty miles to go?"

"Something like that," Joshua says. "I doubt we'll be able to ride it all in one day. Sitting on a bike that long takes too much out of you."

"So you're saying we're going to have to stop tonight. Again."

Joshua shrugs. "Probably."

"Shit," Angus says before I have the chance.

All I can think about is going through this again tomorrow morning. Being surrounded by zombies, trying to draw them away or risk dying. Again. No matter what we do, it always seems to come down to this.

I hold Megan tighter and lean back, staring at the ceiling. Maybe we're closer than we think. Maybe we'll run into a group from Atlanta when we're still ten miles or more away. Maybe they send groups out just like Hope Springs does. We can hope. Can't we?

The silence drags on as each of us gets lost in our own thoughts. Outside this house, I don't know what Axl and Parv are dealing with or how soon they'll make it back, but in here, the three of us are already on our way to Atlanta. Already fighting zombies we haven't even encountered yet. Already walking through the gates.

Just a little bit longer. That's what I have to keep telling myself. Just a little bit longer and we'll be safe.

A soft boom penetrates the walls of the house, making me jump to my feet. Angus and Joshua are up only a split second after me. We stare at each other for a moment, not moving while we wait. For Parv and Axl to show up or for another explosion. It's hard to say for sure. Maybe both.

Nothing happens, so I move.

"That was an explosion, right?" I ask, heading for the kitchen.

"Sure as hell sounded like it," Angus says from behind me.

I reach the door and pull the curtains aside, but the backyard is empty. Of course. The yard is fenced in, which is why Parv and Axl used this door instead of the front one. Easier to control.

"Can't see a thing." I mutter.

I head back into the front room, passing Joshua and Angus, who are just coming into the kitchen. I don't wait for them to catch on but instead rush to the front window. The curtains are drawn, and I move the fabric aside carefully. I don't want draw any unwanted attention our way. There are few zombies headed down the street, and in the distance, a trail of smoke billows into the air.

"I see smoke," I hiss when footsteps come up behind me. "Why was that the only explosion? And where are Axl and Parv?"

My heart is pounding like wild, and I can't move, expecting them to come into view at any second. They don't, though. There's nothing but zombies trailing down the road.

Another explosion rips through the air, this one louder. It could be more than one can, or maybe the propane tank. Whatever it was, more smoke joins the little bit already billowing into the sky. Still there's no sign of our friends.

"We should go," Joshua said. "Axl told us to go if they weren't back by now."

"They could be trapped!" I say, finally dropping the curtain and turning to face the two men. "What if they're trapped?"

"What if they just can't get back here?" Joshua says. "What if they're at the bike shop already? Waiting for us."

He's right. I know he is, but that doesn't mean the thought of leaving here is easy. If we get to the shop and Axl isn't there, I don't know if I'll have the energy to walk out the front door, let alone pedal a bike to Atlanta.

Angus's eyes meet mine, and in them, I can see the same conflict I'm going through. "We gotta," he says gently. "We got other things to worry 'bout now. We made a commitment to get to Atlanta and to keep that baby alive. We gotta follow through."

"You're right," I whisper even though the words feel like a betrayal. "We need to go."

Joshua nods, and a second later, he's running for the kitchen. I follow, my hands shaking like crazy and my legs not much better. Angus grabs my arm when I'm passing him, helping me to the kitchen like he's afraid I'm going to collapse. I feel like I might, with the way my limbs are trembling and as hard as my heart is pounding.

But I know I can't, so I force myself to move. To pull my arm from Angus's grasp and take the bag Joshua holds out to me. I sling it over my shoulder, careful not to disturb Megan. At my side, the men grab the rest of our gear, and then what feels like a split second later, we're at the door and moving into the yard. We all have knives out, and Angus keeps close to my side while Joshua takes the lead. Something he never does, but right now he knows he has to. Angus has been our priority since we left the walls of Hope Springs, and that hasn't changed.

We're quiet when we open the gate, pausing to look around before stepping out. The coast is clear, or seems to be, at least. There are no zombies in sight, and the air is fresh. We follow the directions Parvarti gave us, heading through the alley between the houses, then across the street. We pause what seems like every two steps, checking around corners or listening to make sure the way is still clear. There's nothing around, though.

"Should be just at the end of this street," Angus says, stopping in the shadow of a couple bushes.

"What do we do if they aren't waiting for us?" I whisper.

Angus looks back, but his gaze only holds mine for a second before he's once again checking the street. "They'll be."

When did Angus become the optimistic one?

I nod and suck in a deep breath.

"Looks clear," Joshua says.

"Yup." Angus tightens his grip on his knife. "We go."

Joshua doesn't hesitate when he steps out from behind the bushes. Angus and I follow, keeping close to the doctor as we move down the street. Businesses line the road, but most of them have been broken into. Glass covers the pavement, crunching under our shoes as we hurry down the street. I keep one hand on Megan's head and the other curled around my knife. My eyes move as quickly as my feet, scanning every corner and alley we pass. Looking into every store, searching for trouble. The place is a ghost town, though. So deserted you'd never know zombies had been stumbling up and down this street only an hour earlier.

"There," Angus hisses, picking up speed.

I do the same even though my calves already ache from days of walking and I know I need to conserve energy. Axl and Parv should be there, and I don't know if I can wait a second longer to find out if they made it.

Just like all the other stores, the front window of the bike shop has been smashed out, making it easy to get inside. Joshua goes first, then Angus, who turns and helps me over the glass even though I don't really need it. The store is pitch black, and bikes line the walls, with five sitting in the middle of the room. Waiting for us. On the floor next to them is a small handheld pump and a couple boxes that look like extra tubes for tires, but other than that, the store is empty.

"They aren't here," I say, leaning against Angus when my knees wobble.

His arm goes around my waist and he eases the pack off my shoulder, but he doesn't say anything.

"We wait," Joshua says firmly.

Even though I'm glad he's not ready to ride off—because I can't leave right now—I know we won't be able to wait long.

"Ten minutes," Angus says even though Axl told us five. "That's all we can do."

He has to be kidding himself if he thinks I'm leaving this store in ten minutes. I can't. I won't make it down the street. "You'll have to leave me."

Angus grabs my chin and forces me to look up, his gray eyes holding mine. "No. You'll go and you'll ride and you won't give up 'til we're in Atlanta. That's what you gotta do. Don't matter how hard it is, that's what's gotta be done, 'cause I ain't gonna stand by while you give up like Winston. You're stronger than that, Blondie, and we both know it."

Damn, I hate it when Angus is right. He is. I can't see myself giving up the way Winston did, and even though it hurts and even though I don't know how I'm going to find enough energy to ride out of here, I know I will. It isn't in me to not try, and no matter how much every pump of my legs is going to hurt, I know I have to go.

"Ten minutes," I say.

Angus nods once, then lets go of my chin. I'm frozen as he and Joshua move about the room, packing away the few supplies we'll need for the ride. Checking the bikes over. Time passes, and even though we don't have a clock, I know when ten minutes has gone by. Even if Angus didn't look like someone just ran off with his wife, I'd know.

"This here'll be your bike," Angus says, pushing the bike my way. "We can't wait."

I nod, feeling slightly numb, and before I even realize it, the handlebars are in my hand. Then, in the blink of an eye,

I'm following Joshua and Angus to the door. We push the bikes outside, and I find myself climbing on, feeling even more numb than before and a little bit like I'm watching myself from above.

The streets are still clear and the sun is brighter than it has any business being, and in the distance, the cloud of smoke has grown darker and bigger. The whole house must be on fire now, and possibly the one next to it. Soon the fire will spread, moving from street to street until this whole town is engulfed in flames. Taking with it every trace that anyone ever lived here. Every house and memory left behind, every zombie and probably even the bodies of Parv and Axl. Then there will be nothing but rubble.

"Let's go," Angus says, his voice firm and authoritative and slightly broken.

He and Joshua start pedaling down the street, and somehow I find that I'm right behind them. My legs moving up and down as my hands squeeze the rubber grips until I'm sure my bones will break from the effort.

CHAPTER TWENTY-FOUR

We make it out of town before the tears start. At first it's just enough to fill my eyes and make the road in front of me fuzzy. I blink the tears back, but seconds later, my vision is cloudy again. This time when I blink, there's no stopping it. A tear slides down my right cheek and another down my left. One after the other after the other they fall. Then I'm gasping as sobs shake my body, and the bike is wobbling underneath me. Inside, I'm being ripped apart. Piece by piece until every inch of me aches and I feel like screaming, only I can't because I can't catch my breath. And I can't stop crying. I don't think I ever will.

"I." Hiccup. "Have to." Hiccup. "Stop."

I stop peddling, and my bike hits the ground as I stumble off it, holding Megan against me while also trying to hold myself together. In the distance, the town is no longer visible, but the smoke still is. It's gotten bigger. Darker. More ominous.

"Vivian." Angus's hands are on my shoulders, turning me around, but I don't want him to. I don't want to look ahead. Not if it means putting Axl behind me.

"No," I say, trying to shove him off. Trying to stop him from comforting me.

"Come here."

Angus, the asshole who hit me the first day we were together, wraps his arms around me. Hugs me. Holds me as I sob into his chest. The little baby between us squirms, a constant reminder of why I need to go on even though all I want to do is drop down in the middle of the street and never get up again.

"This isn't what was supposed to happen," I sob into Angus's chest. "This wasn't the plan. God, I feel like I'm dying. I have to be. Don't I? I can't be in this much pain and still be alive. It's not possible!"

"None of this was supposed to happen," Angus whispers. "But it did, and now we gotta keep on keepin' on."

"How?" I shake my head, rubbing my tear-stained face against his chest. "How is that even possible? How do you do it? Don't you want to give up? When she died, didn't you think it was going to destroy you?"

Angus pulls back, and the tears streaming down his cheeks match my own. So does the pain and loss in his eyes. "We just gotta look ahead. That's it. It hurts and it don't ever go away, but we can do it. We can move on."

I want to call his bullshit, but I can't. He's done it. All these months since Darla died, he's been going on despite the pain. He hasn't given up, and I can't either. If Angus can do it, so can I. It doesn't matter if every second of every day hurts, I will move forward.

"Wait," Joshua says from behind me. "I think…yes. They're coming. They're coming!"

My heart goes crazy, and I spin around, one hand automatically going for my knife while the other goes to Megan. I half expect a horde of dozens of zombies, but that isn't what's heading our way. There are two figures. Just two.

And they're riding bikes.

"They made it," I say, the knife falling from my hand as my heartbeat transforms from a pounding fear to a soaring thump.

I want to run, but I can't, so I settle for stumbling. Down the center of the street, trying to close the distance between Axl and me so he's in my arms sooner. So I can see him and look him over and know he's in one piece. So he can ease the ache moving through me and make me whole again. Because he's the only thing that can do that.

They get closer, and their smiles tell me they're fine before I even get a chance to look them over. When they're still five feet away, Axl stops riding and practically jumps from his bike. Then he's running toward me. When he throws his arms around me, he's careful not to crush Megan, but the baby doesn't keep him from slamming his lips into mine. And just like that I'm crying again, only these tears are here to wash the other ones away.

"I thought you were dead," I say against his lips. "I thought I would never see you again."

"I'm sorry," he says. "I'm so sorry. We got caught and couldn't make it out right away."

"We left." I step back and wipe the tears from my eyes so I can get a better look at him. "I should have waited longer. I shouldn't have given up so fast."

"No," Axl says firmly. "You did the right thing. It's what I told you to do."

I nod even though I don't agree. It feels like I gave up too fast. Ran out on him when I should have waited. Should have known he'd never leave me.

"You scared the shit outta me," Angus says from behind me.

Axl lets me go long enough to give his brother a hug, then does the same for Joshua. Parv too has gotten off her bike, and I go over to hug her. I don't even care if she doesn't like it. I'm just so glad to see them both.

Angus lets out a chuckle. "Now that I had my heart attack for the day, I say we get ridin'. We got a lotta ground to cover before dark."

"Right," Axl says, letting out a deep breath as he turns to face me. "Hand over that bag. I'll carry it."

I slip the bag off my back, handing it to Axl. His eyes hold mine the whole time. The pain of thinking he was gone is still present. I'll never be able to forget how I felt when I thought I'd lost him.

"Let's get a move on," I say, forcing myself to move away from Axl.

At first, pedaling is automatic. My legs move up and down like they have a mind of their own, and I'm able to think about the future and what life will be like in Atlanta when we finally make it. But after just a couple hours, the ache in my thighs and calves makes the movement more difficult, and thinking becomes impossible. Pumping my legs is the only thing I can focus on. Up. Down. Up. Down. Over and over again until it feels like they weigh ten times more than they actually do and the ache in my muscles turns into a burn.

By the time we stop to feed Megan and take a break, my body is weak and shaky. I'm not the only one struggling, either.

"There has to be a car or something around here," I say, pulling to a stop next to Axl. "I don't know how much longer we can go on like this."

Parvarti nods. "As close as we are, we might only need one gallon of gas to get us to Atlanta."

My bike falls, and Axl has to reach out to steady me. It's a good thing, because once I'm on my feet, I realize I'm even more unstable than I thought I was.

"How long have we been riding?" I ask as Axl helps me ease to the ground.

"A couple hours," Joshua says.

"How much farther?" Parv asks this time.

If I wasn't so tired, I'd find the whiny tone in her voice

amusing. After all these months of her robotic attitude, it's shocking to hear her complain. I'm too exhausted to laugh, though.

"I hate to bitch like a woman," Angus says, dropping to the grass at my side. "But I'm with them. Walkin' is easier. Least then my ass ain't sore."

Axl exhales and drops his backpack to the ground. Even though Joshua looks like he's ready to fall over, he unzips the bag and starts digging through it while I untie the sling. Regardless of how tired we all are, Megan needs a new diaper and a bottle. If she starts crying, we could draw hundreds of zombies our way.

I lay Megan in the grass so I can change her, and the baby starts to squirm and whimper. Angus is up in seconds, his knife out and his eyes moving across the area. Everything seems quiet, but we never can predict what might be lurking in the distance.

"We'll go take a look 'round after she's quieted down," Axl says, pulling out his own knife and mimicking his brother's stance.

I make little soothing noises to the baby while I change her diaper, and at my side, Joshua mixes a bottle. Parv produces a pacifier from somewhere, and seconds later, Megan is silently sucking on the thing. It doesn't last long, though. Once she realizes she isn't getting anything from it, she spits it out and starts wailing for real.

"Hurry," Angus hisses.

My hands are shaking now, but I force myself to stay focused on the baby even though it goes against every one of my instincts not to look around for trouble. Megan. I need to take care of Megan so she stops crying. She's hungry, and taking care of that need is the only thing that will keep her quiet.

I secure the tabs on the diaper, then scoop the screaming baby up. Joshua has the nipple in her mouth a second after that, and like magic the crying stops. The tension doesn't ease right away, though. We're all still searching the surrounding trees. Waiting to see if we drew any unwanted attention our way.

After a minute, I finally allow myself to relax. "Nothing's around."

"Yeah." Axl too lets out a sigh of relief. "We gotta get to Atlanta."

"Let's go," Parv says. "We'll take a quick look around. There has to be something."

Axl nods, his eyes on Megan and me as Parv gets to her feet. "We'll be fast."

"And careful," I remind him.

"Always," he says as he and Parv turn to leave.

The two head off, and I do everything in my power to focus on Megan so I don't have to think about how I felt earlier when I thought I'd lost Axl for good. The ache inside me hasn't eased completely, and to be honest it probably never will. It's like it has been tattooed on my insides. A reminder that all of this could come crumbling down in the blink of an eye.

"They'll find something," Angus says. "They gotta."

Joshua just nods.

It's like a repeat of this morning. Joshua, Angus, and me silently waiting for the others to return. None of us pointing out all the things that could go wrong.

After days of total silence, the sound of a car engine is so foreign that I have to fight the urge to run and hide. But it only takes me a second to realize the sound—although startling—is a good thing. It means Axl and Parv found a car. It means that if all goes well, we could be inside the walls of Atlanta within twenty minutes. That's all. Just a short drive and we'll be safe.

Joshua is up first. He leaves the relative safety of the bushes so he can get a better look down the street.

"That them?" Angus calls from next to me.

"Someone is heading this way," Joshua says.

Angus drags himself to his feet. "Better be ready just in case."

I slip Megan back into the sling, tightening the fabric around her body until she feels secure. She's sound asleep and barely moves.

"It's them!" Joshua calls a second after I've secured the knot.

"Thank God," Angus mutters as he shoves his knife back into its sheath. "My ass can't take any more ridin'. I got a newfound respect for them fruits that used to ride 'round in bright colored spandex."

I laugh. "It seems like you have a newfound respect for almost everything."

"Almost." Angus snorts.

A van comes into view, and the sight of it makes me want to jump for joy. It's old and rusty and the engine sounds like it isn't sure it wants to keep moving, but since we only need it to drive twenty miles, I'm sure it's going to be okay. It has to be. After everything else we've gone through, we deserve a break.

Axl pulls to a stop right in front of us, grinning when he throws the door open. "We're gonna make it."

"Shit," Angus says. "We was always gonna make it. Now we're just gonna make it faster."

"What are we waiting for?" I say, heading for the open door of the van. All ready to relax and enjoy the last little bit of road between Atlanta and us. "Let's get the hell out of here."

"We got much gas?" Angus asks as he climbs inside.

"Couple gallons. I expect the gaslight to come on soon, but the manual said this thing can go thirty miles after that. So we're gonna be alright."

Angus nods as he climbs into the back, and I'm right behind him. The interior smells like dirty gym shoes and the seats are covered in stains, but I don't care as long as we don't have to walk or ride a bike.

Joshua joins Angus and me in the back, shutting the door behind him, and Parv climbs into the front. Axl glances back, shooting me a quick smile before he throws the car in gear. Then we're moving, and I'm grinning, barely able to contain my excitement. Before we know it, we'll be in Atlanta, and we won't have to worry so much. Things will be easier. Safer. We'll have a home.

I was pretty sure it was never going to happen for real.

CHAPTER TWENTY-FIVE

Axl slows the van, and I lean forward, trying to get a better look out the front window. In the distance, Atlanta looms. Even from this vantage point, I can tell there was a lot of damage to the city. A few buildings look like they've been cut in half, their tops jagged against the blue sky. In some places, whole blocks seem to be missing.

"What do you think happened?" I ask, studying the uneven skyline that used to be Atlanta.

"The military, hopefully," Joshua says.

"You hear anythin' 'bout this before you left Maryland?" Axl asks.

Joshua shakes his head. "As far as I knew, everyone on the East Coast had pretty much given up by then. Of course, now we know different. They must have made a stand here."

"Must've," Axl mutters.

"Look," Parvarti says, pointing out the window. "You can see the wall."

I shield my eyes from the sun, and the wall comes into view. It's massive, dwarfing a lot of the buildings around it and going on for miles. How they managed to do this I don't know, but it must have been a huge undertaking. I'm even more impressed with what they've accomplished than I was before.

But if that's where we have to go, it's going to be challenging. We may not make it all the way there in the van. If the roads are blocked, there's a good chance we're going to have to get out and walk. Which is scary anywhere, but in a city, it's terrifying.

"We're going to have to make our way through the city," Parv says.

"Yup," Axl says. "Might as well get movin'."

He presses down on the gas, and I hold Megan closer as we move forward. She's been quiet, and even though we're so close, we very well could be reaching the most dangerous part of our journey.

We move deeper into the city, sticking to I-85. It means we're out in the open, but at least nothing will be able to sneak up on us. There are more abandoned cars than I expected, considering travel was supposed to be suspended. A few we pass have doors wide open and bodies behind the wheel or in the backseat, but most are empty. Abandoned. Like the owner died behind the wheel, then wandered off after they came back. The car forgotten like everything else from their previous lives.

We reach a roadblock only a mile later, and reality sinks in, feeling a lot like a piano being dropped on my head. We're going to have to ditch the van. I'm not shocked, but I'm also not happy.

"From here on out, we're gonna be on foot," Axl mutters, throwing the van in park. "Get what you need."

"I'm going to change Megan," I say as I unwrap the sling.

"Do we want to feed her?" Joshua asks from behind me.

I kneel on the floor, and I lay the baby across my seat so changing her will be easier. She squirms when I lay her down, but barely opens her eyes.

"It's only been thirty minutes or so. I don't think she'll eat." I look up Joshua. "Do babies eat when they're not hungry? Adults do, but that's because food is more than nourishment to us. She doesn't have that habit yet. Right?"

Joshua shakes his head. "If she isn't hungry, she won't take a bottle."

"Then I'll just make sure she's dry before we get moving. Just to keep her from fussing." Of course, that doesn't mean she can't decide to dirty her diaper in the middle of the city. She's a baby. She can't exactly hold it the way we can.

It only takes a couple minutes to change Megan and get her back in the sling—I'm getting so good at both that it feels almost automatic at this point. Once she's safely inside, Axl opens his door and hops out. Angus follows his lead, and the rest of us are right behind them. I squint when I step out, the sun bright after the darkness of the van. Thankfully, the roads seem to be clear.

Just past the roadblock in front of us, the buildings are shrouded in shadows, blocking out the sun and making every corner seem like it's concealing something. A few probably are. There's no way the people behind that wall have managed to clean out the whole city. If they had, they wouldn't need the wall.

"We stick close together," Axl says, pulling a knife.

He steps past the roadblock with Parv at his side, and I hurry to catch up. Joshua and Angus take up the rear, but just like Axl told them to, they stick close. The world around us is quiet but not completely devoid of noise. The wind blows, and trash tumbles down the empty road. What sounds like a flag flaps in the breeze not too far away, and in the distance, the quiet hum of engines can be heard. Probably behind the wall.

"How much further do we have to go?" I ask, looking around as we move. Keeping Megan close to my body and myself close to Axl. A couple guns would be good right about now.

"Looks like we'll reach the wall if we go this way," Axl says, turning right and heading down a street that's littered with debris.

Angus turns his head so he can spit, then says, "We just gotta get to the wall."

"And find the way in," Joshua points out. "That wall has to have a fifteen-mile radius. At least. It could take us hours to find the gate."

Just thinking about hours of walking through this city makes my legs ache, but even more than that, I'm worried about Megan. If she starts crying, we're going to be in trouble, and stopping to feed her in the middle of the city isn't going to be easy.

"Just a little farther," Axl says, and I do my best to believe him.

Each street we turn down seems as empty and destroyed as the last, but it also brings us closer to the city wall. We can make it if we just keep moving. I know we can.

Megan stirs, and a second later, I hear the telltale signs of her filling her diaper. Then she lets out a little newborn whimper. It isn't loud, but it still makes all of us look around as we wait for zombies to come charging. Angus swears, and even though he's frustrated and exhausted and angry, I know he isn't mad at the baby. If there's one thing I've learned about Angus over the last several months, it's that he isn't as heartless as he likes to make himself out to be.

"Shit," I mutter, patting her back to keep her quiet. "Literally."

"We can make it," Joshua says. "It isn't a good idea to stop. She'll be fine for a few minutes longer."

I don't bother reminding him that he's the one who said it could take hours to find the gate.

I bounce Megan faster, hoping to keep her calm.

Angus stands up straighter and narrows his eyes like he can look through walls. "This way," he says, pointing to a road that veers to the left. "That'll take us right to the wall."

We move as a group. Out of the alley and down the

empty street. I walk practically on the tips of my toes, being careful where I step so I don't make any noise. Cradling Megan's head as I go, hoping to keep her quiet and comforted. Praying she doesn't wake up and start screaming. She can sleep through a dirty diaper. I know she can.

Axl is on my right with Joshua on the other side, but Angus and Parvarti take the lead. We don't see a single moving thing as we make our way down the street, and the city is so quiet it feels like we're watching a movie and someone has pushed the mute button. The world has no business being this silent.

The walls of Atlanta get closer with each step we take. We pause at a corner, and Angus searches the area before we start moving again. Then we're jogging down the street, heading toward the wall. Every step we take makes my heart pound a million beats faster than before, and soon I find it hard to breathe, but I can't stop. We have to get there.

We've been running for close to ten minutes when we turn a corner and come face to face with dozens of zombies. I skid to a halt, backpedaling and praying the mass of dead doesn't notice us. Around me, the rest of my group does the same, but we don't make it far before the first zombie catches sight of us and heads our way. Others follow, one after the other after the other until they're all running. Their feet pounding against the hard pavement like a stampede of elephants behind us. Their moans and growls rising up and filling the air with a song so eerie it makes my skin crawl.

"This way!" Axl calls, pulling me with him as he heads down another street.

Joshua and Parvarti run in front of us as Axl pulls me forward, and Angus takes up the rear, putting himself between the dead and us. We move like we have wings on our shoes. So fast it makes my head spin and causes little Megan to stir. She cries into my chest, and I hold her closer, trying to keep her head from bobbing around. Angus swears every two seconds and Axl won't let me go and in front of me Joshua looks frantic, while Parvarti seems to be having trouble keeping up. But the bodies behind us keep coming. Running and running and running until I don't know how they can keep going.

In front of me, Parvarti trips, and I watch in horror as she slams into the pavement.

"Parv!" I scream, trying to slow.

Axl doesn't ease his grip on my arm, though. If anything he pulls harder. "Run, run, run!"

I stumble over my own feet as I try to decide if I should keep moving or stop. In front of us, Joshua has slowed, but he hasn't gone back to help Parv, who is struggling to get to her feet, and even though it makes me sick, I know Axl is right. We have to keep moving.

We pass Parv just as she stands, and I glance back as Angus throws his arm around her. They move after us, but Parv is limping, and the right knee of her jeans is torn and bloody. Still, she's up and on her way. She's going to be all right. We're all going to be all right.

We keep going, and before long, my lungs feel like they're going to explode and my calves ache from running. Little Megan continues to wail no matter how tight I hold her. Then, behind us, Angus lets out a shriek of pain, and Axl is finally forced to slow. Axl and Joshua run back while I stay where I am, feeling utterly useless as Angus fights off two of the dead, putting himself between Parvarti and danger. Even though I want to run to their aid, I can't. I have Megan, and I can't put her at risk like that.

Axl slams his knife into the head of one creature while Joshua and Parv help Angus fight to keep the other zombies back. Somehow, they manage to break free of the zombies, taking them out one at a time until all the creatures around them are down. But more are coming. And fast.

"Go, go, go!" Axl screams, pulling Angus with him as he starts moving again.

Joshua and Parv are two steps in front of the brothers when I turn and start running.

We've only made it three more blocks before Angus yells,

"Turn!"

I do as I'm told, and when I round the corner, the walls of Atlanta loom in front of us. They're still a good thirty feet away, and so high it makes my head spin, but ready and waiting. All we have to do is get there. I rush forward, my gaze moving over the wall in search of people. Soldiers keeping watch or someone else who can help us escape the horde still charging after us, but as far as I can tell, there's no one around. And we still have no idea which way the gate is.

I take a gamble and turn right at a street that runs parallel with the wall. The pounding feet behind me echo through my head, but I keep my eyes straight ahead. Telling myself the others are on their way and okay and all we have to do is make it a little bit longer, and then we'll be safe. We have to be.

I feel like I've been running for years when my toe hits something, and I stumble forward. My legs wobble like all the strength has drained from them, and I feel myself falling forward. I let out a scream and turn my body to the side as my arms wrap around Megan. It seems to take forever to hit the ground, and when my shoulder finally slams into the pavement, I know I'm in trouble. White-hot pain shoots through me as a scream rips its way from my mouth, and Megan starts wailing even louder than before.

"Vivian!" Axl screams, stopping at my feet.

I try to stand, but the pain in my shoulder makes everything fade and go black. Megan cries, and I force myself to focus on the present, but it's so far away and faded that I can't pull myself out of the fog.

The next thing I register are the screams of Angus and an explosion of gunshots. I blink and force my eyes open, finding Axl in front of me, fighting the zombies back with Parv and Joshua at his side. Angus is trying to put himself in front of his brother at every turn, while somewhere behind me, gunshots rain into the horde.

Footsteps pound against the ground, and someone pulls me up, making my shoulder throb more than ever.

Tears pour from my eyes, and I can't seem to stop them, so I blink and try to focus on my friends. The men who came to our rescue have rushed in and are fighting the dead back. Parv and Joshua are running toward me, perfectly okay, and behind them, Axl supports Angus, who is covered in blood and bites.

The man who pried me from the ground pulls me away from the others, and I find myself fighting him. "Relax," he says with a grunt. "We're getting you to safety. All of you."

"Okay," I say, allowing him to lead me away. "Okay."

He drags me to a truck, and then he's pushing me up. I climb, careful to keep one arm tucked around the baby. It's my injured arm, and I'm not sure it's of much use to me right now, anyway. Every move I make causes my shoulder to throb more than before.

Joshua and Parv climb into the truck behind me, and we're pushed to the back, where we collapse on the floor. More men climb in, then Axl and Angus. Then even more men. Before they've even found a seat, the tires below us squeal against the pavement, and the entire truck lurches forward. Axl stays by his brother's side as the truck shoots through the city, and even though every bump of the tires makes my shoulder hurt like hell, I couldn't be more relived to be safely in the back of this truck.

We're alive. We made it.

A radio crackles, and a man at the rear of the truck lifts a walkie-talkie to his mouth. "This is Michaels. Over."

"You find them? Over."

"Affirmative. Over."

"Are they infected? Over."

The man's eyes move to Angus. There are three bites visible, but with the way he's slumped against the wall, there have to be more. His tan shirt is so spotted with red that it looks like he was in the middle of a paintball fight.

"We'll have to check them all over, but one of them is for sure. Over."

The radio crackles again. "You know what to do. Over."

The soldier puts the walkie down, and when his hand comes back up, he's holding a pair of handcuffs.

"No need for those," Angus says as the man shuffles forward.

"We have protocol. Sorry, but you need to be monitored and put in isolation."

Angus spits, then heaves himself off the side of the truck so he can pull the neck of his shirt aside, revealing the first bite. It's healed, but the scar is so obviously teeth marks that it couldn't be mistaken for anything else.

"No need for all that. This ain't the first time I been bit, and it ain't gonna kill me." He releases the neck of his shirt and shoots the soldier a weak grin. "Name's Angus James, and I'm you're only hope."

CHAPTER TWENTY-SIX

We can't see much from the back of the truck as we pull into Atlanta, but once we're inside, we are able to get a glimpse of the massive gate they've constructed. As well as the men standing armed and ready to stop any zombies that might get through. None do, and the second our truck is all the way inside, the soldiers hurry to close the gate.

The truck moves deeper into the walled city, bumping over the street. From where I'm sitting, I have to strain to get a glimpse of the city. Sharpshooters sit on top of nearby buildings, poised and ready just in case, and armed guards are everywhere. Every person we pass is loaded down with weapons, too. Which makes sense and means whoever is in charge of this place is smart.

Megan continues to cry no matter how much I try to soothe her, so I'm eventually forced to untie the sling. My shoulder screams when Parv helps me free Megan, but I ignore the pain and cradle the baby in my arms so I can look her over. There doesn't seem to be any permanent damage, but she hasn't stopped crying.

"She okay?" Axl asks. He's still at Angus's side, who doesn't look all that great at the moment, but his eyes are on me and the baby—our baby.

"I think so. It will probably take a few minutes for her to calm down after the shock of what just happened. When we get to the CDC, I can change her. She'll be okay," I say with more confidence than I feel.

Joshua scoots closer to the back of the truck as it barrels down the street, trying to get a good look. Even though Megan is still crying and my shoulder has started to throb and I'm concerned about Angus, I can't help trying to see the city as well. The farther we go, the more amazed I am at how much they've done here. People walk up and down the streets like everything is normal. The sidewalks and streets are clean and clear of bodies and debris and abandoned cars. It seems like it's even cleaner than it was before all this, because there isn't even a single piece of trash on the sidewalks.

"You guys really got this place cleaned up," I say to the solider at my side.

He nods. "It took a lot of hard work, but we pulled it off by working together."

"You did an amazing job."

When we pull to a stop, the soldiers all pile out. Joshua and Parv move forward, and I follow, trying to disturb both Megan and my shoulder as little as possible. It isn't easy, and even though one of the soldiers offers to take the baby, I refuse.

I manage to make it down, and Axl climbs after me. But when Angus gets out, he stumbles. A couple of the bites are deep, and the blood pouring from them has completely saturated his shirt. He's also looking a few shades whiter than he was just a little bit ago.

"You okay, brother?" Axl asks, pulling Angus's arm around his shoulders.

"Ain't nothin'." Angus tries to put on a brave face, but it's overshadowed by the wince of pain.

Joshua rushes to Angus's side, grabbing his wrist so he can check his pulse. After a second, he turns his gaze on the nearest solider. "We need to get him inside now!"

"Let's move!" a soldier barks as he heads toward the CDC. He's only taken one step when he lifts the walkie to his mouth. "We need a doctor to meet us in the lobby! Over."

Parv, who is more than a little beat up after falling to the ground, takes her place on Angus's other side. He grunts, saying something about Rambo, but it isn't loud enough for me to hear. Joshua trots along on Parv's other side as we hurry toward the CDC.

Between the baby and my shoulder, I can't really do much to help, so I hurry along after them, trying to ignore the pounding of my heart. Megan continues to cry, and I cradle her against my chest, her diaper bag slung over my good shoulder. She's okay. She's going to be okay. I promised Ginny I'd take care of her.

"The baby is okay?" the soldier at my side asks.

"She's fine," I say. "At least I think so."

The soldier moves faster, and when he gets to the front door, he rips it open and starts yelling. People rush toward us, and there's so much chaos that I don't know where to look. Men and women in white coats come running from the back, carrying medical equipment. Angus collapses, and Axl falls at his side as the doctors surround them. Joshua is spouting off medical information and everyone is yelling at once, but I can't make out a single word. In the middle of it all, Megan starts crying harder.

I find a set of chairs off to the side and gingerly sit down, trying not to move my arm a whole lot as I look Megan over a little better. Parv extracts herself from the crowd surrounding Angus and comes over to join me. Megan squirms as she screams, and together Parv and I inspect every last inch of her, but there isn't a mark on her perfect little body. The full diaper is the only real concern.

"How early was she?" A woman kneels at Parv's side, pulling out a stethoscope that's three times smaller than average.

"She was six weeks early."

The woman—who I can only assume is a doctor—puts the stethoscope to Megan's chest, listening for a few seconds before moving it. I have no idea how she can hear a thing in the middle of all this chaos.

"She was born out there?"

"Yes. Our friend is a doctor," I say, nodding toward the crowd surrounding Angus. "He delivered her."

The CDC doctor nods and listens a little more, then looks up. "I'm going to take her back and check her over. Make sure everything is good. I can only assume this is a post-apocalypse baby?"

"It is," I say.

"It's still a miracle she's alive. We've managed to keep a few babies alive thanks to some new antibiotics, but it's been rough. After several days of being in the open, I'd say this one is in the clear, but we'll check her over anyway."

I start to stand with the doctor but wince when pain pulses through my shoulder.

She shakes her head as she takes the baby from me, holding Megan close to her chest. "She is yours. We won't take her from you, but I want to get her checked out, and you need help as well."

"I can go with her," Parv says.

"You both need to be looked over." The doctor says firmly. "We typically do this at the gate, but we were in too much of a hurry to get your friend inside. We don't let anyone in unless they've been checked over for bites." The doctor waves to someone, who runs over. "This is Patty, she'll take care of you. Okay?"

"I don't want to be away from Megan for long," I say, feeling torn.

I understand what the doctor is saying: they need to be sure we aren't infected. Not only does it make sense, but I agree with them. They have to be careful. Still, I don't see why I can't go with Megan to get checked over.

"I'll bring her back as soon as I'm sure she's good," the doctor assures me. "I promise."

"Okay," I say, giving her permission to take my baby even though it hurts more than my shoulder.

Parv meets my gaze as the doctor heads off, but neither one of us speaks. I'm not sure if I did the right thing or not, but the sinking feeling in my chest says I may have just let Ginny down.

My eyes are focused on the doctor as she walks away, and I don't even glance Patty's way when she grabs my injured arm. She moves it, and pain shoots through my shoulder and I cry out, jerking my arm away, but even then, I only look away from Megan for a second.

"Let me check you over," Patty says. "What happened?"

"She fell," Parv replies for me.

The doctor carrying Megan disappears, and I realize too late that I didn't get her name. I feel slightly dazed when my gaze moves from the now-closed door to the people surrounding Angus. Just like that, my stomach drops to the ground. There are so many doctors around him. It's not that bad. Is it?

"Is our friend going to be okay?" I ask, finally focusing on the woman in front of me. She looks impossibly young. She can't be a doctor.

"He's too important to let die. They're going to help him," she says. "But he's lost a lot of blood, and there are other things we have to worry about. Something about this virus has made regular infections more powerful. They set in faster. Stronger. He's been bitten a lot."

I glance toward Angus, suddenly worried about the number of bites he endured. He's going to be okay, though. The CDC has new antibiotics. They've saved babies. They can save Angus, too.

Patty cuts my shirt away and examines my shoulder, saying something about needing to get a cold compress to reduce the swelling. I'm barely listening, and when Axl and Joshua are pushed through the crowd, Parv gets up without a word and crosses the room to them. I stay where I am, trapped by the non-doctor looking me over.

Parv and Joshua and Axl talk, looking back and forth between the people surrounding Angus and me. I squirm, and the non-doctor at my side asks me to hold still. Even though it hurts me worse than the throbbing in my shoulder, I obey. The sooner she can get me patched up, the sooner I can find out what's happening with Angus.

Finally, my friends head my way.

"What's going on?" I ask when they stop in front of me.

"Heart stopped." Axl swipes his hand through his hair. "Damn. This ain't supposed to be what happens. Angus is stronger than this."

"They won't let him die," Joshua says. "He's too important to the human race."

Parv nods, and Axl looks back toward his brother. The woman at my side says something about a dislocated shoulder and hurries away. Where, I don't know. I'm too lost in my thoughts about Angus and Megan and what's happening here to listen to her words.

I stand, and Axl slips his arm around me. Even though my shoulder throbs, I lean into him. Resting my head on his shoulder. Joshua and Parv say nothing, and the four of us just stand there, staring at the doctors still working on Angus.

"He's stable," someone shouts. "Let's get him back to the lab. And be sure we keep him that way!"

Suddenly Angus is on a stretcher, and he's being rushed away. Axl moves, pulling me with him, and the others follow. We've only made it a few steps when a couple soldiers rush forward, blocking our way. Even though Axl swears, he doesn't argue or fight or try to move past. They're armed and we aren't.

"We need you to come with us," one of the men says.

"Where are you taking us?" I ask, trying to see over his shoulder so I can see what they do with Angus.

"Quarantine."

My eyes snap back to the solider.

"Excuse me?" Joshua says.

"We don't know if you've been infected. Standard procedure."

"Fuck that," Axl says. "We ain't got no bites or scratches, and she needs a doctor!"

"Can't you just look us over?" Joshua asks.

"We will once you've been taken to quarantine. You'll receive medical attention and food, clean clothes. Everything you need. We just need to be sure."

Parv shakes her head, and Joshua shoves his hand through his dark hair. At my side, Axl stiffens when a couple more soldiers head our way. He looks at me, and I shrug.

"There's nothing we can do," Parv says. "We don't have a choice."

The men at our backs nudge us forward, and we don't fight them. There's no point.

"What about my brother?" Axl asks as the soldiers corral us through the lobby.

"And my baby?" I pipe in.

"We'll let you know what happens, but for now we don't know anything yet." The soldier stops in front of a door and holds it open, motioning for us to enter. "That's the doctor's department anyway. My orders are to get you folks to quarantine."

"They have a point," Joshua says. "I know it sounds harsh, but this virus is so unpredictable."

The soldier waiting for us to walk through the door frowns when Axl hesitates. I give his hand a squeeze, and even though he sighs, he walks through. The rest of us follow, staying close together as the armed guards take us down a sterile hallway with white walls and floors. We stop in front of a closed door, and the soldier in the lead punches a number into a keypad. The door clicks open.

The soldier opens it and jerks his head toward Parv and me. "The women go here."

"You can't separate us!" I say.

I take a step back, but before I can do anything else, Parv is shoved inside, and I'm ripped away from Axl. The soldier who has me pushes me forward while two others restrain Axl. I stumble into the room, and pain moves across my shoulder, causing a scream that is half-pain, half-frustration to rip its way out of me.

I'm cradling my throbbing shoulder when the door slams behind me.

"Shit," I mutter, sinking to the floor.

Tears sting at my eyes, and I blink them away, trying to get ahold of myself. This doesn't mean anything. Not really. They're just playing it safe. Being careful. Things could still be okay.

"What do you think?" Parv asks, drawing my attention her way.

"I don't know what to think right now," I say, studying the room.

It's small and totally white. Two twin beds and two nightstands. A table with two chairs around it. Off to the side through an open door, a tiny bathroom is visible. Towels and what appear to be a couple pairs of blue scrubs are stacked on a shelf. Presumably so we can put on clean clothes.

"This is weird," Parv says, shaking her head.

"And wrong." I hoist myself up, nursing my injured arm, and move to the door. Even though I know it's going to be locked, I try the knob. It does nothing, of course, so I slam my hand against the metal a few times. "Hey! I want to talk to someone! Open the door!"

"Vivian," Parv whispers.

I turn, and when my eyes meet Parv's, I almost burst into tears. "This isn't how I thought this would turn out."

"They'll come back in a little bit," she says. "This is just a precaution."

I don't know if I believe it, but I nod and let out a deep breath, trying to blow all the air out of my lungs. Trying to hold it together.

"Let's get cleaned up," Parv says, turning toward the bathroom.

It's the only thing we can do right now, but there's something about it that seems so wrong.

"Okay," I say even though I don't really care how dirty I am right now.

We just need to hang on for a little bit, and then everything will be okay.

CHAPTER TWENTY-SEVEN

After we're clean and dressed, we wait. My shoulder throbs too much to allow me put a shirt on, so I sit next to Parv with my head and one arm through the holes. The scrub top covers only half of my upper body, but it's better than nothing.

"What do you think they did with Angus?" I ask, staring at the door.

"They're patching him up," Parv says. "He was bitten a lot. You know what Joshua said about bites and infection. If what that woman said is true, he's really put himself at risk."

She has a point: the human mouth is filthy. Angus could get an infection, and after all his injuries, he may need blood. They have all the resources here, and it won't be long before he's back on his feet. Then they'll see that we aren't infected and they'll let us out. That's when they'll give Megan back to me. They just want to be sure I don't turn and kill her. So few babies have made it.

My mind spins in circles while Parv and I sit in silence, doing nothing but staring at the door. I think about Axl and Joshua, about Megan and if she's okay. About Angus, wondering if we made it in time. I find myself wondering what happened to Jim after he fled the farmhouse and thinking about Al and Lila. Then there are the people we left on the bridge, and Anne and Sophia back in Hope Springs. Brady, who couldn't bring himself to leave his wife's side. So much has happened. So many people gone. Thinking about it makes my head spin so much that by the time the door opens, I feel dizzy.

Parv stands, but I can't move. Not even when a woman wearing a white coat and carrying a clipboard walks in, smiling. The skin at the corners of her eyes crinkles, but she doesn't look old. Just tired. Her hair is shockingly blonde and neat. Two soldiers walk in behind her.

"Please," she says, motioning toward the beds. "Sit down so we can talk."

"Where are our friends?" Parv asks, not moving.

"My baby?" I whisper.

The woman smiles as she once again motions toward the beds. "Please."

Parv sits at my side, and the woman smiles again as moves across the room. She takes a seat across from us on the other bed, placing the clipboard on her lap. Still smiling. The expression makes me squirm. It looks like it was painted on her face.

"I'm Dr. Helton," she says after a couple beats. "We're working on your friend at the moment, and we expect him to make a full recovery. In the meantime, we wanted to be sure you had the medical attention you needed. It seems you were hurt?" Her eyes move to me.

"Yes," I say, motioning to my shoulder with my good arm. "I fell as we were running away."

"We'll get that looked at. We'd also like to take some blood and administer some antibiotics just to be on the safe side." She takes a deep breath before saying, "We're going to need you to strip so we can check for bites or scratches."

Parv shakes her head. "That seems unnecessary. We're already being observed, can't you just wait to see if we exhibit any symptoms?"

"Normally, yes, but we've had to change our protocol. Since finding out that people can in fact be immune to this disease, we've decided we need to check for infection sights and *then* wait for symptoms. You may have been scratched and not even realize it, which means you could be immune and you'd never know. You'd simply think you hadn't been infected." She gives us a sympathetic smile. "I can promise you that it will be very professional. I'm a doctor, after all."

She may be a doctor, but the soldiers standing behind her are not. I glance their way, but they have their eyes straight ahead. Even with their guns, they aren't very threatening. It's a precaution, and I know it. Plus, we don't really have a choice. They have us in a room. They have guns. If we refuse, they could just force us. It's better to cooperate.

"Fine," I say, getting to my feet.

It takes a moment to pull the shirt over my head thanks to my injury, but once I do, I drop it to the floor. My pants follow, leaving me totally naked. They didn't bother providing clean underwear.

The doctor stands and narrows her eyes on my body, frowning for a second before looking up at my face. "Please turn."

I obey, lifting my good arm so she can look me over, and the hair on my scalp prickles under her intense gaze and a shudder rips through me. This isn't the first time I've had to strip, and even though I try not to let the memories of Vegas in, they come back anyway. Within seconds, every inch of my body is covered in goose bumps.

My arms and legs are covered in bruises, but there are no cuts or open wounds, which should make the doctor happy—or maybe unhappy, if she's hoping to find more people who are immune.

"Very good," she says after a couple seconds. "You can redress."

I bend and pick up my pants, struggling to put them back on with only one arm. Parv helps, and when they're in place, we do the same with my shirt, once again leaving my bad arm out. The doctor is busy scribbling on her clipboard.

"Your name?" she asks, not looking up.

"Vivian Thomas."

"Age?"

"Twenty—" I shake my head. "Twenty-one. I had a birthday at some point."

The doctor nods. "Very good. And you're the mother of the baby?" Her eyes move up to meet mine.

She knows I'm not Megan's mother. I remember how round and squishy my belly was after I had Emily. Megan is so young, and there's no way my body would look like this so soon after her birth. I could lie, but they'd know if they drew our blood.

"I'm not," I say, "But her mother died shortly after she was born, and she asked me to take care of Megan. She was my closest friend."

The doctor nods again. "I appreciate the honesty. It's important in times like these because it lets us know who we can trust. Even a small lie looks bad when things are already precarious."

"I understand," I whisper.

The doctor turns her gaze to Parvarti. "Now you."

MY SHOULDER IS STILL THROBBING, BUT AT LEAST IT'S back in its socket. Thinking about how they had to put it back causes me to break out in a sweat. At least it was quick. Now I've been ordered to rest and keep ice on it—something I never thought I'd see again—while we wait for someone to come draw our blood. We're still clueless about what's going on with the others, although I can only assume Joshua and Axl have met the same fate that we have.

"Three days seems excessive," Parv says. "I think twenty-four hours would be enough to let them know we haven't been infected."

"They're being cautious," I say even though I agree with her.

Parv nods twice while she gnaws on her bottom lip, and when her eyes turn my way, the worry in them is so visible it takes my breath away. "Do you think we have any reason to worry?"

"Honestly," I say, letting out a deep breath, "I have no clue. I hope not, but we both know anything is possible in this world."

Parv nods again, and we go back to sitting in silence. Eventually, someone comes in to draw blood and administer a shot of antibiotics, once again giving us little to no information about our friends.

Dinner is brought to us. We sleep. Breakfast comes the next morning, waking me from dreams of zombies chasing us and a baby crying. Parv and I talk little and sleep a lot, and soon day two in quarantine is gone. We never see the doctor again, and every person who comes in is different from the last one, making me wonder exactly how many people they have living in Atlanta. Definitely more than the hundred in Hope Springs, which is mind-blowing to me. I can't believe this much of the population has survived, but I guess Joshua's theory about the East Coast could be true: maybe the survivors fared better because so many of the initial victims of this virus were cremated before they had a chance to come back.

Sometime after lunch on day three, the door opens unexpectedly. I sit up too fast, expecting to see another person in uniform, and when Axl steps in, I almost burst into tears.

"Axl!"

I scramble to my feet, pushing aside the slight ache in my shoulder when I throw myself into his arms. I haven't been away from him for this long since my time at the Monte Carlo, and the emptiness that had started to settle in my stomach suddenly fills as his arms wrap around me. We kiss, ignoring Parv and Joshua, who steps in right behind Axl.

"You okay?" he whispers against my lips.

"I am," I say, nodding. "I'm okay. Did they let you out?"

"They're letting us all out," Joshua says. "None of us are infected."

A couple disinterested soldiers lean against the wall in the hallway, but no doctors. I still haven't seen the woman who came and stripped me, or the one who took Megan.

"What about Angus and Megan?" I ask, looking back and forth between Axl and Joshua.

"Don't know yet," Axl says. "We're gonna find out, though."

He glances toward the soldiers, who push themselves off the wall.

"When you're ready," one says, sweeping his arm to the left.

"We're ready," Axl snaps.

The men lead us back the way we came, but instead of taking us to the lobby, they turn down another hall even longer than the one we just left. It ends at a door with a glass window, and through it is a tiny room, no bigger than a closet, and a second door. On the other side of that room is Angus. Lying on the table. He doesn't seem to be conscious, and he's hooked up to more tubes and monitors than I can wrap my brain around. The sheet over him is pulled up to his waist, and his chest is bare, revealing bandages covering his many bite marks. A couple doctors wearing masks stand at his side, but I have no idea what they're doing. One tube, attached to Angus's left arm, is bright red, but it's hard to tell if they're giving him blood or taking it away.

"What's goin' on?" Axl grunts, reaching for the door.

Even though I'm sure it's locked and there's a second door separating us from Angus, the solider steps in front of Axl. "Dr. Helton will be out to speak with you in a moment."

Axl frowns but steps back, his eyes focused on his brother.

After a couple minutes, one of the doctors looks up. I recognize her from the day she came and asked us to strip, and right away my suspicions are back on the surface. I don't know what's going on, but I do know something here isn't right.

Dr. Helton says something to the man at her side before heading our way. She steps into the little room and seals the door behind her. A fan roars to life when she pushes a button, and we all wait while she removes her mask, gown, and gloves. When the fan kicks off, she pushes a couple buttons, and the door in front of us pops open, filling the air with a whooshing sound that reminds me of a seal breaking.

The doctor steps out. "I'm glad you're all okay."

"My brother," Axl growls.

"We treated his injuries, but his heart stopped," she says, turning to face the door. "We managed to get it started, but I'm afraid it was too late." She rips her eyes off Angus and turns her gaze on Axl, and the expression in her eyes is so unemotional that it makes my blood turn to ice. "I'm afraid he's brain dead."

I move closer to Axl's side, wondering if he understands what that means. He doesn't blink, but maybe he's just in shock.

After a few seconds Axl says, "He's dead?"

"We're keeping him alive. I know it sounds callous, but we need him. Or his blood, anyway. Thanks to your brother's sacrifice, we are on our way to creating a working vaccine. It will change our lives. Give us hope for a future. Ensure that babies live after they're born."

"What about my baby?" I say.

The doctor's eyes move to me, and she nods. "She's safe and well, and now that you're out of quarantine you'll be reunited. We had to be sure you weren't a danger to her, and we wanted to draw some blood. Compare it to Mr. James's and see if there were any similarities between the two. She will also be a big help in our fight to rebuild humanity."

"I wanna see my brother," Axl says.

I expect the doctor to refuse, but she moves toward the door. "Of course. You have a right to say goodbye."

She punches in a code, and the door once again pops open. Axl steps forward but stops and grabs my arm.

"Come with me." He doesn't look my way.

"You don't want to be alone?" He shakes his head, and I give his hand a squeeze. "Okay," I whisper.

Axl and I follow the doctor into the small room, and the door shuts behind us. We don't say a word as we pull on gowns and masks and gloves. Then the fan starts running, and I feel like I'm holding my breath while I wait for the second door to open. When it finally does, Axl steps through with his hand still in mine, but the doctor stays.

"Dr. Wilson," says the woman behind us, making the other man look up. "Can we give these people some privacy, please?"

The other doctor nods and heads her way, and then they step into the small room behind us, leaving Axl and me alone with his brother.

"I don't know what to say," Axl whispers, not moving. His eyes focused on his brother.

I take a step toward the bed, pulling him with me. "Just say goodbye."

Now that we're in the room, I can fully appreciate exactly how many machines there are. Angus has been intubated, and his eyes are taped shut. Multiple IVs run from both arms, and monitors are taped to his chest, head, and neck. The beeps coming from the machines are constant and loud in the small space, making it feel like the room is half the size.

"Do you want me to go first?" I ask when Axl doesn't say anything.

He nods, and I release his hand so I can close the small gap between Angus and me. Seeing him like this, hooked up to tubes and unable to talk or throw insults or spit… It sends a lump to my throat that threatens to choke me. I swallow, forcing it down, then take Angus's hand in mine, being careful not to disturb the monitor clipped to his index finger.

"You always did have to be such an ass, Angus," I say, shaking my head when tears fill my eyes. It makes me smile because I know that if he could hear me, he would agree. "We're going to miss you. When we first met, there wasn't a part of me that ever thought I'd be able say that, but it's true. We've all been through a lot and changed a lot. Including you, regardless of what you think. Despite everything, you've become like a brother to me." A sob makes me gasp for breath, and I force out a smile to try and ease the pain. "An annoying asshole of a brother, but one I loved anyway."

The last few words are drowned out by sobs. Axl steps forward to stand at my side, resting his hand on my lower back. I think the contact is as much for him as it is for me, but it helps ease some of my pain anyway.

"I wanna thank you," Axl says, focusing on his brother's face. "You took care of me when we was kids, then after Mom died. You showed me how to be strong. I'm here 'cause of you. 'Cause you wouldn't let me be weak or give up or feel sorry for myself. Sometimes, I hated you for bein' such a hard ass, but it made me respect you, too." He lets out a deep breath and closes his eyes. "I don't know what I'm gonna do without him."

I wait for Axl to say more, and when he doesn't, I wrap my arms around him. He pulls me so close I find it difficult to take a deep breath, but I let him because I know he needs the support right now. Angus was his whole world for so long, and even though Axl's learned how to stand on his own two feet, he's probably going to feel like a part of him is missing without his brother.

The door opens behind us, and Dr. Helton steps in. "If you're done, we can take you to the baby now."

I nod, and so does Axl even though he doesn't let me go. After a second, the doctor clears her throat.

I pull out of his arms so I can look him in the eye. "Angus did the most courageous thing he ever could have done, and you should be proud of him for it."

Axl swipes his hand across his eyes. "He's never done nothin' half-assed in his life."

I doubt that's true, but I don't argue with Axl.

I slip my hand into his and take a step toward the door, but Axl doesn't move. Instead, he puts his free hand on Angus's shoulder and says, "I'm gonna miss you like crazy. I love you."

Then he lets me pull him toward the door.

CHAPTER TWENTY-EIGHT

The doctor leads us through the winding halls of the CDC, each one as sterile and nondescript as the last, and by the time we stop walking, I feel so turned around I'm sure I'd never be able to find my way out. The door she opens leads into a lab where several other people in white coats are busily working. Staring into microscopes and typing away at computers, probably working to save the world.

On the other side of the room in an old, white bassinet is Megan.

"Megan!" I say, rushing toward her.

A few people look up and smile, but most ignore us as I scoop the sleeping infant into my arms. In the three days that we've been separated, she seems to have grown, but she looks healthy and stronger than she did so I can't complain.

"We don't have a nursery," Dr. Helton says with a shrug. "So we kept her in the lab with us while we worked. Someone is always on duty, so she was constantly looked after."

"Thanks for keeping her safe." I can't take my eyes off the baby. She's wearing a tiny sleeper that's covered in purple flowers, and her face is peaceful. Happy, almost.

"Of course." The doctor picks up a box and offers it to Axl. It's full of diapers and wipes and formula—everything we'd need for an infant. "We have more supplies and clothes. I'm not sure if the apartment you were assigned is outfitted with a crib, so you may have to look into that. We have a warehouse full of supplies, so getting the things you need shouldn't be a problem."

I tear my eyes away from Megan and focus on the doctor. "Apartment?"

"Yes."

Dr. Helton turns toward the door without further explanation, and the rest of us hurry after her. I meet Axl's gaze as we head back through the halls of the CDC, and the sudden knowledge that we have an apartment and are finally starting our lives over is so exciting that a shiver runs through me. Axl and I will have a room and a bed, and we'll be safe. It's almost too good to be true.

"We make sure everyone has housing when they get here, and you'll be assigned jobs," Dr. Helton says over her shoulder. "We're working on a credit system for luxury items, but food is rationed equally. You'll find that we've done a good job of trying to emulate our old way of life while adapting to our limitations. The hope is that we'll be able to create a vaccine soon, and once that happens, we'll be able to work on taking out the zombie population without fear of infection."

"Couldn't that take years, though?" Joshua asks.

The doctor glances at him briefly before saying, "What is your medical background, if you don't mind me asking?"

"I was a second-year resident working in the ER at the time of the outbreak."

She nods once. "You'll be perfect for the clinic, then. We need doctors with experience in emergent care."

Joshua frowns, and none of us miss the fact that she

hasn't answered his question.

The next door we step through leads out into the lobby, and I'm shocked to discover that it's a lot later in the day than I thought it was. The sky is pink from the setting sun.

"I appreciate your cooperation," Dr. Helton says, staying by the door. "If we need you for anything else, we will let you know."

"What about my brother?" Axl asks. "You just gonna leave him like that forever?"

The doctor frowns. "No. Not forever. We'll let you know when we're able to turn off life support. Now, if you excuse me, I have work to do. They've told me someone will be here to show you to your new apartments."

Just like that, she's back through the door. It shuts behind her with a click that echoes through the empty lobby, and the four of us are left alone. I can't help feeling like a chapter of our lives has come to an end with the closing of that door.

"Vivian! Axl! You guys!"

A voice I never thought I'd hear again echoes through the lobby, and a girlish giggle follows. We all spin around as Al comes charging toward us, waving his stump of an arm, while his other hand pulls Lila with him. The smile on his face is so big it's like seeing the sun after days trapped in a cave.

"You made it!" Al says, racing toward us. "We heard rumors and asked around, but getting an answer wasn't easy. Especially considering we're the new people." The teens come to a stop in front of us, and Al only hesitates a second before throwing his arms around Axl. "Man! We thought you guys had drowned for sure!"

"I can't believe this," I say when Lila hugs me.

She smiles and hugs Parv, who actually returns the gesture.

Al hugs Joshua while running his mouth a mile a minute. "We made it out of the river but couldn't find anyone else, so we started walking. All I could think about was getting here. I knew we'd never be able to find you out there, but I thought that if we made it to Atlanta there was a chance. But we got here and no one had heard from you, and the more time that went by, the more I started to wonder if you ever made it out of the river."

"When did you get here?" Parv asks when she's able to get a word in.

"Five days ago," Lila says.

"Five days?" Joshua shakes his head. "How did you manage to get here so quickly?"

"Motorcycle." Al shrugs. "I'd never ridden one, so it took some getting used to, but once I got the hang of it we made it in record time."

"It was a moped," Lila says with a grin, but it fades after a second, and her eyes move to the baby. "What happened?"

"There were complications," I whisper. "Ginny lived long enough to see her, and to ask Axl and me to take care of her. Her name is Megan."

"I can't believe she's gone," Lila says, shaking her head as her eyes fill with tears.

"Dax? Jim?" Al asks. "Angus?"

"Dax died. Almost took all of us with him, too. We don't know about Jim yet," Joshua replies. "Who knows, maybe he'll walk through the gates in a day or two as well. We got trapped, and he led the horde away so we could get out."

"What about Angus?" Lila asks.

Axl's grip tightens on the box. "Got bit one too many times."

"We got him here, though," Joshua says. "That's the important part. He wanted to save the world, and he will. I'm sure of it."

Lila nods and Al lets out a sigh, and for a few seconds, we let the sadness surround us.

"We should get you to your apartment before it gets dark," Al says, moving on to happier topics. "They've cleaned out the city, but for the time being, there's still a curfew. They just want to make sure the streets and buildings are totally safe before they allow people to wander around at all hours of the night."

"Getting to an apartment sounds amazing," I say.

Al and Lila lead us out of the CDC and down the street, pointing out buildings as we pass them, telling us what they're being used for now. Apparently, most are in the process of being turned into living quarters, with bathrooms being added as more and more people find their way to the city.

"They expect the population to reach two thousand by the end of the year," Al says. "You won't believe how many people there are or how many communities they've made contact with. Apparently, the one in Hope Springs isn't alone. People are trying to rebuild all over the country."

"But Joshua was right," Lila says. "The East Coast did fare better."

The walk to the apartment takes ten minutes or so, and when Al pushes his way through the front door, he smiles. "We're on the same floor. They only gave you two apartments, so I hope Parvarti and Joshua don't mind sharing."

Parv shrugs. "I don't think any of us have a right to be picky at this point."

"Very true," Joshua mutters.

Al and Lila stop at the elevator, and when he pushes the button, I have to laugh. "I never thought I'd use an elevator again."

"They have all the electricity on now, and that's one thing that isn't rationed." Al steps into the elevator when it opens. "At least not yet. They're working on a little bit at a time, starting with food."

"They have a pretty good system," Lila says, following Al inside.

The rest of us move after them, and even though I've spent the last several days sleeping, I can't help feeling like I'm dragging myself into the elevator. Maybe it's just that I'm on emotional overload. We've been given a lot of information in a very short amount of time.

"You two are living together?" I ask. In normal times, they'd both still be in high school, living with their parents. But there's nothing normal about this city, or what's outside the walls.

"If anyone asks, we're both nineteen," Al says with a wink. "We didn't know if it would matter, but we figured it wouldn't hurt to stretch the truth just a tad."

"Smart," I say with a nod.

The elevator stops on the sixth floor, and we step out. We follow the teens down the hall. Axl walks beside me, and it hits me that he's barely spoken. I wish I knew what he was thinking or feeling, but I don't.

"This is us," Al says when he passes apartment 613.

He stops two doors down and pulls a key out of his pocket, handing it to Joshua. "Yours."

"Thanks," Joshua says, moving to unlock the door.

Parv follows but stops at my side and turns to face me. Her gaze moves down to Megan and she smiles. "I'm glad," she says, looking back up at me. "I'm glad I hung on."

"So am I," I say, returning her smile. Feeling like she's back from the dead. It's nice, finding people instead of losing them for a change.

Parv nods, then turns toward the apartment, where Joshua stands holding the door open. On her way past, Parvarti pats Axl on the arm. He nods, and so does the doctor, and our two friends slip inside, shutting the door behind them.

Al walks across the hall to the other door, unlocking it for us since both our arms are full. He holds it open without a word, and Axl goes inside, also not saying a word.

I stop next to Al and smile. "Thank you." I look back and forth between the two teens. "I can't tell you how glad I am to see you. It makes being here so much better."

"Do you think Axl will be okay?" Al asks.

"Yes. It's just going to take some time. I think he's in shock right now, but he knows this is what Angus wanted. If he hadn't wanted to risk his life, he would have said no back when we first learned about Atlanta."

"He wouldn't have done that," Al says. "Angus wasn't like that."

It's funny how much your perception of a person can change over time.

"I know," I say.

Al holds the key out to me, and I slip it into my pocket as I give the teens a smile. Then I follow Axl inside our new home, shutting the door behind me. Pausing a moment to take a couple deep breaths, trying to sort through all the pain and joy and disappointment and triumphs of the last several days.

The apartment is small but neat. I pass the kitchen and head into the living room, where Axl sits on the couch. Whatever personal effects were here before the virus hit have been removed, leaving nothing but the essentials. I'm glad. I don't think I'd want to see the smiling faces of people who have probably been dead for months.

I sit on the couch at Axl's side, and Megan shifts in her sleep, but she doesn't wake. Axl's gaze moves toward her, then up to my face, and when his eyes meet mine, I'm relieved at the peaceful expression in them.

"You're okay," I say, not bothering to make it a question.

"We're here and you're safe, and we got Megan back." Axl nods. "I'm alright."

"I know how much you're going to miss Angus."

Axl nods as he slips his arm around my shoulder. "Life ain't gonna be the same without him, but it ain't gonna be bad. Not as long as I got you. And now we can start over for real."

"It seems almost too good to be true," I whisper.

Axl kisses the side of my head, leaving his lips pressed against my hair as he whispers. "But it ain't."

EPILOGUE

Five Weeks Later

The sun is so bright that it nearly blinds me when I step out. I shield my eyes, and at my side, Axl does the same. I'm hardly focused on him, though, because I'm too busy adjusting the sling so the fabric is covering Megan's face better.

"It's getting hot," I say, my eyes still focused on the sleeping baby.

"Yup. Pretty soon we're gonna be more glad than ever that we got electricity. Imagine livin' here with no AC."

"I don't think I can be any more thankful for electricity than I already am," Lila says, coming out of the building behind us. "A shower is something I'll never take for granted again."

"I'm with you on that." Al grins down at the girl as he slips his arm around her shoulders. "Especially when you're with me."

Lila gives him a scowl that barely conceals her smile as she elbows him playfully. Al, of course, just grins.

"Can't you two ever be serious?" Axl asks, shakin' his head.

"Just because you two have gotten old and boring doesn't mean we have to," Lila says, but she smiles my way. "I don't plan on growing up just yet."

"Good," I say returning her smile. "Stay young. Take advantage of this place as long as you can."

Lila's smile wavers at the unspoken meaning behind my words. This could be temporary. It's there, always following us, even if none of us have acknowledged it out loud yet. As safe as this place seems, we all know it might not last. They haven't created a vaccine yet, and it could still be months or years before they do. Until then, we're in hiding. Doing everything we can to pretend life is normal even though just outside the walls of this city, zombies wander the earth. Even if I'm able to occasionally forget it during the day, the reality never escapes me for long. It comes back in terrifyingly vivid detail at night when I go to sleep.

"We'll never take this for granted," Lila says, leaning into Al.

Axl nods and slips his arm around my waist, and together we start walking. The day is bright and the roads clear of the dead, and people walk up and down the street like life is normal. It doesn't feel that way, but I'm hoping that eventually it does.

"What time is this thing supposed to start?" Lila asks after a few minutes of silence.

"Ten," I say.

"Am I the only one who thinks it's crazy to have a schedule again?" Al asks. "All these months with no watches, and now I have to keep track of where I'm supposed to be and when. How do we even know they have the correct time? And what's the deal with dedicating a building? It seems stupid."

"I think they just want to be able to make things feel real

again." Lila shrugs, but the little smile that curls up her lips tells me she likes the idea.

"That's part of it," I say. "But I also think they are trying to bring us together."

"Still stupid," Al mutters.

At my side, Axl lets out a little chuckle. We had the exact conversation the night he came home from work and told me they were done and that they were going to have a dedication.

The former office building comes into view, and so does the crowd in front of it. Hundreds of people, which I still can't believe. More come in every day, and with them, the need for housing grows. We can't expand the wall any more than we have, and until the zombies are wiped out, it's too dangerous to live anywhere else. So we have to renovate what we have.

"Axl! Vivian!" Joshua calls, waving. He pushes away from the crowd and jogs over to join us, shaking his head. "I can't believe they called me out of work for this. I have patients."

"It's a big day," I say, not looking at him but instead focusing on Megan. She's asleep, but I can't stop looking at her. If I had the energy, I'd stay up all night long just so I could watch her sleep.

"It's silly," Joshua says.

"Parv here?" Lila asks. "I feel like I barely see her anymore."

"There." Joshua points up, and we all turn.

Twenty feet or more above us, Parv sits. She has her bow on her lap and her eyes on the gate like she's waiting for it to burst open and for zombies to come pouring in. It has to be a boring job, but she doesn't seem to mind. Peaceful is what she called it.

"Ugh. I'm glad I'm not good with the bow," Lila says. "I'd hate being up there all day long."

Al and Joshua nod, but Axl's eyes are on Parv still.

"Hey," I say, elbowing him. "What about you? Do you

wish they'd assigned you to patrol or made you a guard?"

Axl shakes his head, and when he rips his eyes away from Parv, he smiles down at me. "I'm good with construction. It's what I did before, and it'll make a difference. Make this city into something real. Plus, I think I was out there long enough. Now, all I wanna do is be with you and Megan. Keep you safe."

"We are safe," I say, leaning into him.

He nods. "We are."

The hum of a speaker cuts through the surrounding conversation, and a hush falls over the crowd. Somewhere, too far away for us to see it, someone steps up to a mic and clears their throat.

"Thank you everyone for being here!" A feminine voice echoes through the air. "Look around you. At the people next to you, at the wall around us, at the building at my back. These are all things that most of us never thought we'd see again. Community. That's what today is about. It's about building something that will last. About starting over, and about moving forward. That's why we've asked you all to be here today, so you could witness what is a big step forward for us. We've taken an office building and renovated it, making room for more people…."

The woman in front of the crowd keeps talking, but I can't hear her. I'm too focused on the people around me. On Parv, who sits above us, ready to defend this city if necessary. On Joshua, a man we ran into by chance who works every day in the hospital now, putting his medical knowledge to use so we can start over. Al and Lila, who started out so very different but have now come together in a way I never imagined possible. Then there's Axl and Megan, my family and my reason for life. All the people who are most important to me in this world are here, but it isn't just them I'm thinking about. It's all the loved ones we've left behind.

"I miss them," I whisper, just loud enough for Axl to hear me. "Jon and Ginny and Winston and Darla and Trey. Angus. They should be here too."

Axl's arm tightens around my waist, and he pulls me against him. He presses his lips against the top of my head and says, "They're here."

He's right. They may not be here physically, but there isn't an inch of myself that hasn't been changed by the people I met on this journey. They've all helped change me into the person I am today, and I'll always be in their debt for that.

Acknowledgements

A very special thanks to everyone who has read and loved this series. While the number of enquiries I received regarding the release date of book five was at times stressful, it's also a great feeling to know that so many people enjoy my books! Keep sending me emails and telling me how much you love this series, it never gets old.

Thanks, as always, to my best friend Erin Rose. I love being able to shoot you a text with any medical questions I have. Thanks also to Jen Naumann for taking the time to beta read and Laura Johnsen who took time out of her life to read and search for typos.

A huge thank you goes to Robert Kirkman and Norman Reedus (AKA Daryl Dixon), as well as everyone working on *The Walking Dead*. Without the popularity and success of the show, my sales wouldn't be where they are now.

And last, but not least, a special shout out to my family. My husband Jeremy and our four kids, who are always patient even when I'm stressed about deadlines and rushing to get everything done. I love you all so much.

About the Author

Kate L. Mary is an award-winning author of New Adult and Young Adult fiction, ranging from Post-apocalyptic tales of the undead, to Speculative Fiction and Contemporary Romance. Her Young Adult book, *When We Were Human*, was a 2015 Children's Moonbeam Book Awards Silver Medal winner for Young Adult Fantasy/Sci-Fi Fiction, and a 2016 Readers' Favorite Gold Medal winner for Young Adult Science Fiction. Don't miss out on the *Broken World* series, an Amazon bestseller and fan favorite.

For more information about Kate, check out her website: www.KateLMary.com

CPSIA information can be obtained
at www.ICGtesting.com
Printed in the USA
FSHW010639261118
54036FS

9 781519 417152